HYPERCANE

"Okay, Professor, what exactly is a hypercane? Is it something like a hurricane?"

"Yes . . . yes, Mr. President. The way a .44 Magnum is like a slingshot."

President Davis scowled. "How much property damage and loss of life can we expect?"

"The output of the most severe plausible scenario suggested that . . . that—"

"In general terms," Davis said, "how bad will it be?"

"Ap-apocalyptic, Mr. President. Along the same lines as global thermonuclear war, or one of the solar system's biggest asteroids striking the earth. . . . Stop thinking *storm* and start thinking *ice age*."

ZERO HOUR

Benjamin E. Miller

AN ONYX BOOK

ONYX
Published by New American Library, a division of
Penguin Putnam Inc., 375 Hudson Street,
New York, New York 10014, U.S.A.
Penguin Books Ltd, 80 Strand,
London WC2R 0RL, England
Penguin Books Australia Ltd, 250 Camberwell Road,
Camberwell, Victoria 3124, Australia
Penguin Books Canada Ltd, 10 Alcorn Avenue,
Toronto, Ontario, Canada M4V 3B2
Penguin Books (N.Z.) Ltd, 182–190 Wairau Road,
Auckland 10, New Zealand

Penguin Books Ltd, Registered Offices:
Harmondsworth, Middlesex, England

First published by Onyx, an imprint of New American Library,
a division of Penguin Putnam Inc.

First Printing, January 2003
10   9   8   7   6   5   4   3   2

PUBLISHER'S NOTE
This is a work of fiction. Names, characters, places, and incidents either are the
product of the author's imagination or are used fictitiously, and any resemblance to
actual persons, living or dead, business establishments, events, or locales is entirely
coincidental.

For Jamie

ACKNOWLEDGMENTS

My greatest gratitude goes out to my parents, who have given me unwavering support, in every way, from the beginning. This book is as much their achievement as mine. I'm also grateful to Jamie Haldeman, who believed in this project through the hardest of times. The scientific basis of this story is a discovery made by Professor Kerry Emanuel and the other researchers who developed the hypercane theory. My thanks to them, and to the many librarians who helped me get the facts straight. My most difficult questions were answered by the experts at http://www1.askme.com/. Last but not least, I am indebted to my agent, Ethan Ellenberg, and my editor, Ron Martirano. Without their keen criticism, original ideas, attention to detail, and patience, this book would not have been half as suspenseful, intriguing, fast-paced, and believable.

NOTE TO THE READER

This story is based on the extrapolation of existing technology and global trends into the very near future. Although the characters and events are fictitious, the hypercane theory is entirely real. Its origin is described in "Hypercanes: A Possible Link in Global Extinction Scenarios" by K. A. Emanuel, K. Speer, R. Rotunno, R. Srivastava, and M. Molina, *Journal of Geophysical Research,* volume 100, number D7, pages 13,755–13,765 (1995).

So far, hypercanes have been observed only in computer simulations, but the chain of events depicted here represents a scientifically plausible scenario that one could develop in the real world. We can only hope that the birth of such a dramatic and terrifying phenomenon will never actually take place.

CHAPTER 1

Steam

Tuesday, August 8

Most of the twenty-four steam-well platforms at Amery Geothermal Station were coated with sparkling frost on the last night of their existence. Their monthly deicing had just begun.

Nothing moved on the precisely level plain of glacial ice surrounding the station, but the sky was alive. Wispy red and green tendrils of the aurora australis writhed across the Milky Way. Dense stars outlined a jagged black horizon on all sides but the east, where the continental ice cap descended to the moonlit expanse of winter pack ice on the Ross Sea. The waning half-moon hung low in the west between high nunataks—sharp granite crags protruding through the mile-deep ice. In the mountain passes, where steep glaciers crumbled into the Warner Basin from the high interior plateau, pale moonlight silhouetted a band of clouds sailing northward behind the Transantarctic Mountains at a hundred knots.

Marshall Dunn stood and turned to squint at the doorway when the overhead fluorescents came on. The harsh, oscillating light had replaced the spectral panorama outside his window with his own weary reflection—a half-bald dome above white stubble on a black face that sagged from thirty consecutive hours of work and worry. Marshall was Amery Station's foreman, leader of the crew that kept the world's most southerly power plant running at six thousand megawatts.

The man who had interrupted Marshall's dark coffee break in the canteen of Platform One shuffled into the room and unzipped his parka. He was Silong Lim, Amery Station's chief engineer. Tall and thin, Marshall was a former college basketball player, and all he could see of the diminutive engineer was the top of his yellow hood.

When Dr. Lim threw the hood back, Marshall was surprised that the engineer's expression was even more grim than usual. "Well?" Marshall said.

"The steam is still getting hotter." Lim's Chinese accent slightly muddled his words. "In fact, its temperature is increasing even faster than before. If this keeps up, it will exceed four hundred sixty degrees."

Marshall leaned forward, gripping the back of a chair with his long fingers. "Are you sure? When?"

"Based on the readings I've pulled off of Platform Twenty-four over the last eighteen hours . . . I'd say we'll hit the red zone by five thirty tomorrow morning."

"Oh God." Marshall put down his mug of black coffee and sagged against the table, returning Lim's stare of fatigue. He glanced at his wristwatch. The local time was 3:51 P.M.

If the geothermal steam reached 460 degrees Celsius, the alloy gaskets between the wells and the turbine houses would melt, and the joints would blow out. That would cause a catastrophic pressure drop, tripping automatic safety valves that would shut off the steam flow.

Marshall knew it could also cause extensive structural damage and loss of life, depending on where the blowouts occurred.

"It just doesn't make sense!" Marshall said, turning back to the window and punching his palm. "Is the pressure still dropping?"

Lim replied with his usual sleepy stare. "Yes."

The pressure of the superheated steam in the bedrock fractures beneath Amery Station had unexpectedly declined over the six months since the station had become operational. The dropping pressure had caused a steady decrease in power output, but it was hardly a crisis. It would never threaten the safety of Marshall's crew or trip an emergency shutdown.

This sudden increase in steam temperature was another matter.

"Temperature should go down when pressure goes down, and vice versa," Marshall said. "That's just thermodynamics. When you heat water in a pressure cooker—"

"Wrong analogy," Lim said, tugging at his perpetually chapped lips. "Gay-Lussac's law does not apply to the void space in the bedrock because percolation of groundwater makes the volume variable."

Marshall nodded. Lim was right, of course.

Silong Lim was Marshall's best-kept secret, a wizard with his laptop, calculator, and CAD drawings. It never ceased to amaze Marshall that Lim had actually memorized all the numbers in the CRC steam tables for easy reference.

"Of course, there's always a chance that the steam will stop getting hotter," Lim continued, still tugging at his weathered lips. "At higher temperatures, more heat should escape into the lake as the steam rises through the well pipes."

Amery Station was the world's only significant industrial structure built on a floating sheet of glacial ice. Each platform's well pipe extended down through forty yards of ice, then nearly a mile of geothermally melted water, before entering bedrock.

Lim looked up at Marshall as if pleading for confirmation of his optimism.

Marshall frowned back. Lim was the expert. If he couldn't say for sure when the temperature increase was going to stop, Marshall certainly couldn't.

Managing the engineers and rig workers was a quirky challenge that usually gave Marshall more satisfaction than stress, but he hated having to take responsibility for decisions like the one they faced now. He picked up his mug with a weary sigh.

"We have to shut down," Marshall said.

Amery Station was the primary source of electrical power for the new industrial operations across Antarctica. The continent's three ore smelters were its biggest customers, but recent development included dozens of exploration and research camps, in addition to oil wells and mines. The station also served twelve hundred personnel at the base camp of ICARE—the International Coalition for Antarctic Resource Extraction—sixty miles south along the coast of the ice-blanketed Ross Sea.

One day off-line would cost millions of dollars and throw the entire continent into chaos, Marshall thought as he and Lim strode down a dimly lit metal corridor and up three clanking steps into Amery Station's main control room.

The dead penguin chick was just a tiny gray smudge on the vast white glacier when Angie first saw it in the moonlight. She pointed with one of her ski poles as Dr. Lois Burnham slid to a halt beside her.

"Look. Another one." Angie's voice was muffled by her rime-encrusted balaclava.

"It wasn't there this morning," Lois said. "Its parents must have left it behind in the rookery. It must have tried to follow them."

Dr. Burnham was a wildlife biologist. Angela Reed was her field assistant. The two women were alone in the Antarctic night, skiing across a barren wilderness of ice and snow amongst towering granite nunataks. Both were bundled in so many quilted layers that a close relative could not have identified them at ten paces. After a day of following tracks, scribbling notes, and photographing clues, they were almost back to their research camp at the edge of the Warner Basin, adjacent to the last remaining rookery of *Aptenodytes forsteri,* the emperor penguin.

The emperor population had been endangered but stable for several years; then it began to precipitously decline, for no apparent reason. The goal of Lois Burnham's research was to explain the rapid decimation of the Warner Basin rookery, in hopes that human intervention could save the world's largest penguin from extinction. Scientists from other nations had also studied the emperors during the austral summer—when there was sunlight and the continent was not isolated by hundreds of miles of sea ice—but Lois was the only scholar with the resources, guts, and concern to stay with the emperors through their unique winter breeding season.

So far, Lois and Angie's arduous investigation had turned up nothing but questions. In particular, they had discovered that the penguins were mysteriously straying into the confusing range of windswept nunataks known as the Ellis Mountains. The duo had spent many days like this one—following webbed footprints, guano, and dead chicks—but the trails always led them to crevasses that their skis could not traverse or were scoured away before their eyes by the brutal wind. Since they had found no excess carcasses in the rookery, they assumed that the penguins were dying on these inexplicable excursions or while feeding in the Southern Ocean, but the cause of death remained unknown.

"Hey, maybe the chick's still alive!" Angie shouted.

She dug in her poles and propelled herself through the powdery snow. The smooth ice field sloped gently downhill. She accelerated swiftly. When she reached the crumpled mound of gray feathers, she twisted left and halted with an expert skidded turn, spraying up a curtain of crystalline powder that made a sparkling moonbow and blew away in the ever-present wind. After two months of tracking penguins through the mountains, skiing had become as natural to Angie as walking.

The chick was frozen. Angie was weighing it on the portable scale by the time Lois caught up.

"It's a male," Angie said. "About three weeks old." She wrote down the carcass's weight and location in her big orange field notebook, using a pencil. Lois had taught her to always use a pen when recording scientific observations, to prevent anyone—including herself—from changing the notes when reading them later. That was just one of the rules that had to be bent in Antarctica, where ink tended to freeze solid.

"Why?" Lois muttered, squatting on her skis beside Angie. "Why are they doing this?"

Angie knew the question was not for her. Dr. Burnham had a habit of talking to herself, probably from years of isolation at remote research camps. Angie always listened, though. After sharing a cramped shelter with her through sixty days of darkness, Lois Burnham was still her idol. At thirty-four, Dr. Burnham was an associate professor of wildlife ecology at Harvard University. At almost nineteen, Angie was already a college dropout and the veteran of a decade-long war with situational depression.

"We have to find out where the emperors are going eventually," Angie said.

Lois sighed, ejecting fog through her balaclava. "Not at this rate. The fall semester starts in three weeks."

Angie frowned. She did not want to think about that. Her first attempt at college had failed because she was so afraid to be away from her father. She had now enrolled again after a one-year respite, this time closer to home in northern Virginia. She dreaded the gut-wrenching stress of moving into another dormitory. I wonder what planet my next roommate will come from, she thought. Or will that remain a mystery like last time?

At least she would be able to cope with homesickness better after her experience in Antarctica. Her first few days on the world's highest, driest, and coldest continent had been pure hell for both her and Lois. Being separated from her father had kept Angie miserable by day and awake by night. But she didn't mind the harsh physical rigors of the field camp, and Lois's patience and understanding had quickly made her feel emotionally secure away from home for the first time in ten years.

The main reason Angie dreaded leaving Antarctica had nothing to do with college. It was knowing how much she would miss this deadly and beautiful wilderness, and the penguins, and most of all, Lois.

"What's the matter, hon? Getting cold?" Lois leaned close and peered at Angie's gaunt cheeks through her misty wind goggles, checking for frost nip.

"I'm okay," Angie said. "I just wish we could stay at the rookery longer."

"Me too," Lois said. "The emperors are probably

doomed unless we can figure out what's killing them before we leave."

"It will be bad for your career, too, right?"

Lois nodded, hanging her head. "Worse than bad. But personal tragedies don't compare with the extinction of a species."

Angie switched off her headlamp to conserve its batteries; they could see well enough to ski by moonlight. After donning her heavy pack, she paused to listen.

"Hey, what's that noise?"

"What noise?" Lois whispered.

"A low rumble. Can't you hear it?"

Lois abruptly lifted her head and twisted in a circle, suspiciously gazing up at the sharp nunataks looming on all sides. She grabbed the binoculars dangling from her pack's chest strap and aimed them at the sparse patches of sheltered snow that glowed like climbing ghosts on the steep slopes exposed to the moon. Angie knew she was searching for the telltale cloud of snow dust from an avalanche.

"I hear it now," Lois said. "Can you tell where it's coming from?"

"No. It's too low." Angie began skiing up the gentle slope toward the pass they had been heading for. It was the last hurdle before their descent to camp. She realized the emperor chick had died at the very bottom of the shallow bowl formed by this convergence of mountain glaciers born on the surrounding peaks, as if he had managed to waddle down one side but the cold had overtaken him before he could begin to climb up the other.

The rumble increased as Angie huffed up the slope. She worked her tired legs harder, feeling a flutter of panic. "Lois, I think it's coming from the other side. It may be falling on the rookery!"

Angie sprinted all out toward the glacial pass.

*   *   *

Amery Station's main control room was hexagonal, its outer half protruding from the building at the base of Platform One to provide a full 180 degrees of visibility toward the rest of the station. The three outer walls were lined with low sloping countertop consoles, which were densely packed with switches and monitors like the cockpit of an airplane. Above the semicircle of consoles was a continuous bank of tall windows.

The control room always made Marshall Dunn feel like he was on the bridge of a spaceship. It never let him forget that he was poised over a deadly void in the jutting nose of an incredibly large, incredibly complex, incredibly expensive structure.

Marshall sat and entered his password, then clicked on a tiny icon that read SOS. A window appeared with bright green letters on a black background: EMERGENCY SHUTDOWN PROCEDURES MAIN MENU. He clicked on WELL-HEAD STEAM VALVE MANUAL OVERRIDE. From that point on, he would be in a region of the software he had never seen before. I'm too tired for this, he thought. I'm going to screw something up and have to call the system designer. That had happened before, and as Marshall recalled, it wasn't just humiliating—it was also memorably expensive.

Marshall rubbed his weary face, stubble raking his big weathered palms. He and Lim had been awake for almost two days. He looked up at the chief engineer, who was swaying with fatigue as he gazed out the window at Platform Two, his wrinkled and frost-nipped face lit from below by the dim green glow of the monitor. "Let's try to get some sleep, Lim. There's nothing we can do until we know for certain that this is for real. Besides, if the temperature increase does continue, we'll have to be able to think straight."

"And act fast," Lim said, shaking his head. "We should stay alert."

Marshall thought about that. This was a personnel management decision, and therefore his responsibility. "No sedatives," he said. "Just a nap. We still have thirteen hours before your deadline hits."

"I could be wrong. The steam could hit four hundred sixty sooner."

"I'll send an all-hands e-mail," Marshall said. "If the steam goes over four hundred ten during the night, we'll have the operator at the hottest platform hit the general alarm."

Lim nodded and trudged out of the control room.

Marshall exited the shutdown menu and sent his priority e-mail to all the well platforms, knowing that the customized software would set off an alarm to alert the platform operators of its arrival.

After returning his console to standby mode and switching off the overhead lights, he lingered for a moment, gazing through the wall of continuous wraparound windows. Most of the other platforms were hidden in darkness, but he could see the red aircraft warning beacons on the twenty-story towers that crowned the platforms, anchoring their five-meter-diameter well pipes in place. The two rows of blinking red beacons converged toward the distant silhouette of a rugged mountain range like runway lights in the sky.

Marshall noticed that the darkness outside was unusually quiet. Most of the time, murderous katabatic winds howled through the steel-frame platforms, vibrating them like idling engines. The polar ice cap constantly chilled the lowest layer of the atmosphere, making it denser. The resulting blanket of supercold air then poured off the continent and out to sea, accelerating all the way, blasting everything in its path. Inside Platform

One, Marshall sometimes had to turn his radio volume all the way up just to hear over the wind. But tonight the air was still, and he could actually make out the deep rhythmic hum of the station's twin steam turbines.

Please don't let the steam get any hotter, Marshall prayed as he staggered downstairs to his cabin.

Five minutes after going to bed, Silong Lim got up and began pacing, too scared to sleep.

CHAPTER 2

Eruption

"Hey, slow down!" Lois shouted. The biologist admired her young assistant's concern for the emperors, but she thought Angie's immaturity made her a little impulsive and reckless at times. "Angie, you're going to fall and break a leg," she pleaded, trying to catch up. "The rookery is not in an avalanche path."

Angie did not seem to hear her.

"Crazy girl is too much like me," Lois muttered.

The biologist's legs burned and trembled with exhaustion. She was muscular and fit but had been on skis for ten hours. Angie was still climbing toward the glacial pass with a full-throttle herringbone stride, kicking deep grooves into the snowy slope above Lois. It wasn't the first time the skinny teen had proven to her mentor that her frail frame was stronger than it looked.

The thought of Angie getting hurt filled Lois with anxiety. They had nearly proven that two lone women could safely winter over at an isolated research camp in Antarctica, an unprecedented feat that many of her peers would have considered impossible. But there was no sense in pushing their luck. Lois had solemnly promised

Angie's father that she would do everything in her power to return his daughter with a better outlook on life and no permanent injuries.

"It's not an avalanche," Lois shouted. She knew that much just ten seconds after the rumble began. This noise was confined to the extreme bass end of the audible spectrum, whereas an avalanche would have hit some higher notes. The rumble was also gradually growing louder. The roar from an avalanche would have already peaked and subsided.

It sounds more like an earthquake, Lois thought.

Angie stopped in the middle of the pass. Lois caught up and stood beside her, gazing out over the Warner Basin.

This was Lois's fourth winter in Antarctica, yet she still found the alien landscape surrounding the rookery breathtakingly beautiful. Even in the deepest night on Earth, the moon and stars and shimmering red aurora gave enough light for her to see through forty miles of clean air to the rugged mountains on the other side of the basin. The floating ice sheet stretched out below her like the floor of the universe, a perfectly flat plain reflecting different shades of white in rippling waves. Lois knew that the waves of albedo variation were due to dunes and valleys only an inch or two thick where the eternal wind had collected old snow in some areas and scoured the ice bare in others.

The only source of artificial light was Amery Station, which rose like a space port from the center of the ice sheet. The distant station's massive structures twinkled with red and white lights that cast a diffuse glow far out on the surrounding ice.

Lois glanced up at the southern constellations. She could read the stars like an analog clock. "I wonder why the station is all lit up," she shouted over the wind in the pass. "The lights are usually off at this time of night."

Gazing through her binoculars, she located the bright station lights and studied the twin rows of gigantic steam-well platforms. Most of the platforms were coated with sparkling crystalline hoarfrost deposited by the geothermal steam vented from the turbine houses. Incandescent lightbulbs festooned the red catwalks around the square white sheet-steel buildings at the bases of the platforms and the white framework towers sprouting from the buildings' roofs. Each bare bulb made a green squiggle on her retinas as her view field danced around.

"I don't see any activity," Lois said. "Or anything unusual except for the lights being on."

The mysterious rumble still filled the air between the brooding serrated ranges enclosing the Warner Basin.

"We should note the time," Lois said. "The geologists will want to know when the sound started, and we're probably the only people hearing it." She still thought it sounded like an earthquake, but earthquakes never went on this long. "When we get to the shelter, you can call ICARE and ask if they know what's going on."

Lois had taught Angie how to use the camp radio and now allowed her to conduct all their communications. In addition to letting Angie practice her new skills, this suited Lois's personality. Contact with civilization was her least favorite part of fieldwork. She had spent most of her life studying, not socializing. A week ago Angie had jokingly described her as "more of a penguin person than a people person." The phrase had stuck in Lois's mind because it was so apt.

Angie dutifully took out her big orange notebook, checked her watch, and scribbled the time, 4:33 P.M. "Do you think they can hear it at Amery Station?" she asked.

"Not over the turbines," Lois said. "But it's getting louder. If it keeps up, they'll hear it eventually."

Marshall Dunn woke to the emergency siren and a dim yellow light blinking in the ceiling. When his eyes finally focused on the digital wall clock, he saw that it was only 6:41 P.M. Still half asleep, he stepped out of his tiny windowless cabin in his red wool flannel long johns.

Silong Lim was jogging down the corridor toward him. In six months at the new power station, Marshall had never seen Lim break his slow, shuffling stride.

"Did the steam hit four ten?"

"No," Lim wheezed, out of breath. "I couldn't sleep, so I went back to the control room to monitor the readings. The temperature increase was slowing, but I noticed minor pressure fluctuations across the board."

"Why didn't you wake me?"

"It looked like it was going to stabilize." Lim was now tugging the sleeve of Marshall's pajamas, leading him up the clanking metal stairs. The shrill siren was deafening in the stairwell, but Lim yelled over it. "Then, pressure fell straight to zero in Unit Twenty-four. So I hit the general alarm and came for you."

They emerged from the stairwell and stepped across the hall into the control room. Two other men and one woman were already there. The woman was Elizabeth Crane, the night-shift operator of Platform One. She sat at her control terminal. The two rig workers stood on either side of her, awaiting instructions.

Marshall joined them in three long strides, leaning on the back of Elizabeth's chair and gazing at the monitor over her head. The screen displayed a time plot of the steam pressure in Platform One. It had been dropping precipitously for the last fifteen minutes.

Marshall reached over her shoulder and flipped a switch that killed the general alarm. "What's happening, Liz? Lim said Unit Twenty-four completely lost pressure."

His own words echoed in his head—a complete pressure loss was impossible, and the station was not designed for it.

Lim bounced on the balls of his feet. "I know what! It must be a volcanic eruption!"

"How do you figure that?" Marshall asked.

"There has to be steam pressure in the bedrock." Lim pointed to the floor. "But the pressure in the pipe at Unit Twenty-four dropped from eighty atmospheres to one, instantaneously. No transition, no wobble in the data, nothing. The gauges just went flat. It was like a safety valve had tripped shut."

For an instant, Marshall wondered whether the automatic shutoff valve inside Platform Twenty-four had in fact been tripped. That thought brought on a microsecond of panic: *Oh God, there's been a blowout!* A familiar daymare flashed through his mind—rig workers cooked alive by an explosion of steam, their charred bodies rapidly freezing solid on the polar ice beside a ruptured pipe. Then he remembered that the pressure gauges were upstream of the emergency shutoff valves.

"So why does it have to be an eruption?" Marshall wanted to put this theory to rest. He could feel Lim's panic spreading to the other members of his crew.

Lim's Chinese accent blended his quick words together. "It is simple. The only way pressure could drop to one atmosphere in the pipe is if the well screen is completely plugged up, and the only way that could happen is if magma has intruded the well."

Marshall felt a bulb of fear sprout in his abdomen. He

stared at Lim incredulously, as if waiting for the notoriously humorless engineer to admit that it was just a joke.

Lim said, "Besides, you can hear it!" He vigorously pointed downward with one hand, holding his other forefinger across his lips.

No one made a sound, and for the first time they could all hear and feel the dull rumble steadily churning below their feet. They remained quiet for a moment, looking at each other and listening for any change in the sound.

The phone rang.

It was Harold Adams, the operator of Platform Twenty-four. "I'm calling from my portable phone," Adams gasped. Marshall put him on the control room speakers so they could all hear. "I'm outside, on my way to Unit Twenty-three."

This they could believe—they could hear the unmistakable sound of an overweight man in mukluks rapidly shuffling through the dry Antarctic snow.

Adams was so out of breath he could barely talk. "Something . . . something has happened . . . to the well pipe in Unit Twenty-four. It must have flooded or imploded down in the lake . . . tearing the platform apart. The struts on Level Two tore loose, and the whole steam manifold fell down to Level One. It ruptured all the outlets. I called as soon as—"

"Was anyone hurt?" Marshall asked.

"No, I don't think so."

"You don't *think* so?"

"Everyone's off the platform, Mr. Dunn. No steam blew out. The pressure was *gone*. There was just a little puff when the ducts tore loose. I sent everybody else to Unit Twenty-two, but I'm going to Twenty-three. The pressure's still okay in Twenty-two, but Charlie says it's dropping in Twenty-three like it did in my unit. I'm going to see if there's anything we can do to brace the struts under Twenty-three's manifold in case . . . Wait a minute."

The personnel in the control room simultaneously heard a loud crash over Adams's staticky phone and felt a series of sharp thumps transmitted through the rigid structure around them.

Marshall stared at the speakerphone. What's happening to my station? he wondered.

He glanced up when Elizabeth switched her console from one large window displaying the declining pressure on Platform One to a bank of twenty-four small graphs, each showing the pressure trend on a different platform. All of them were rapidly dropping, and the three nearest Platform Twenty-four had abruptly fallen to zero within the last minute.

"Oh Jesus!" Adams yelled over the growing clatter in the background, which now included piercing metallic screeches and clanks. "Mr. Dunn, the whole platform's going down! The well pipe must be pulling everything down the well hole with it. A big chunk of ice is sticking up, and . . . *oh God!*"

Adams's voice was gone, but they could still hear the thumps and squeals of Platform Twenty-four being ripped apart and dragged down through the floating ice sheet. Then all sound from the phone system stopped, except for smooth static. A flashing red light on Elizabeth's console told them the signal had been lost.

The sounds and sensations of destruction resonating through the skeleton of Platform One continued to increase.

Marshall gripped the back of Elizabeth's chair again, his long fingers digging into the upholstery. "Call Charlie in Unit Twenty-three."

She hastily punched in the number, then tried again when her fingertip got ahead of her and misdialed.

The phone rang several times.

"See if you can raise Twenty-two. Maybe everyone left Twenty-three to go help Adams and his crew. At least he said they all got off before—"

The power went out, throwing the control room into complete darkness except for the feeble glow of the red aurora in the sky outside. A second later, the overhead fluorescents flickered and came back on as emergency generators kicked in.

Looking out the windows, Elizabeth said, "The lights on the other platforms are still off."

"The external lights are not on the backup grid," Marshall said. "They draw too much power. Now try calling—"

Marshall was interrupted by a loud "Look, there!" from Silong Lim, who was pointing out a window. The ice was illuminated where he was pointing by the crimson glow from four radiant heaters spaced evenly around Platform Two, beaming hundreds of kilowatts of infrared energy up at the tower to deice it.

Marshall flicked off the overhead lights. They all leaned over the control counter and pressed close to the glass to look out. On the snow-powdered ice sheet between platforms Two and Three, a man was running as fast as he could, leaving a weaving trail of footprints that disappeared behind him into the darkness. He was coming toward them at first, but as they watched he veered to the left.

"He's heading for the tractor garage," Elizabeth whispered. Then she whirled and exited the control room in a low sprint. The two rig workers stared up at Marshall for a fraction of a second, then followed Elizabeth, edging to be first through the door.

Marshall picked up the phone, intending to call the platforms one by one and tell his workers to get out. The winter skeleton crew of Amery Station included forty-eight people.

The line was dead.

Platform One was visibly shaking around them. They had to yell to be heard over the rumble and clatter. The word MALFUNCTION was flashing on the monitor that displayed the platform's pressure trend. A computer voice repeatedly blared over speakers in the ceiling: *Warning, multiple steam leaks detected on Platform One.* From the corner of his eye, Marshall saw one of the wheeled console chairs dance across the steel floor, spinning counter-clockwise.

"That wasn't Adams, was it?" Lim asked as they watched the running man disappear into the shadows.

"No. I think that was Vejay from Unit Five."

"Unit *Five?*"

Marshall nodded.

They stood in silence, faces pressed to the glass. Even with the external vibrations, Marshall could feel his heart contracting like a door being slammed. He stared at Platform Two, trying to memorize every detail. No matter how often he had gazed out at the towering monoliths, Marshall had always felt a mix of pride and trepidation at being responsible for such awesome monuments to the cleverness and daring of human engineers.

That feeling was stronger now than ever, although the pride component had vanished.

Like all the other platforms, the square white building at the base of Platform Two was elevated thirty feet above the ice, supported by four arching framework legs sprouting from its corners. Unlike soil or rock, ice would deform over time if exposed to excessive pressure, slowly allowing heavy objects to sink into it. To prevent this, the legs distributed the structure's weight on feet that were circular grids thirty feet in diameter and two hundred feet apart. The framework legs and circular feet reminded Marshall of the Apollo Moon lander, and he knew that the similarity in form arose from identical functions—NASA scientists had given the lander big feet because they feared it might sink into the thick lunar dust.

Above Platform Two's central building—four stories of windowless white sheet steel—the framework tower climbed into the night sky, tapering to a sharp spire above the top of the fat white well pipe at its center. The framework structure was similar to the Eiffel Tower, except it was white instead of black.

The well platform's spiderlike legs were not its only unique engineering attribute. The floating ice sheet gradually bobbed up and down a few yards with seasonal changes in the water level of the subglacial lake. Since the huge steam pipe rising through the platform's tower was anchored in the lake bed but the platform holding the pipe in place rested on the bobbing ice, the platform was designed to move up and down relative to the pipe. This was accomplished by four greased gears mounted on the top end of the pipe. Each gear was twelve feet in diameter and weighed thirteen tons. The gear teeth meshed with slots in vertical beams on the framework tower enclosing the pipe. The twelve chrome steam ducts radiating from the pipe and drooping to the ice outside the tower were flexible enough to accommodate the station's short vertical excursions by bending.

Although the other external lights were out, the red aircraft warning beacons atop the platform towers still blinked in the sky. The radiant heaters deicing Platform Two were also still on—they drew so much power that the engineers ran them on a direct circuit from one of the turbines rather than the station's main power grid. With their glowing coils surrounded by parabolic infrared reflectors, the four heaters looked like satellite dishes aimed upward with bonfires raging in them. The white framework legs and the red catwalks around the central building of Platform Two gleamed smoothly in the heaters' crimson glow, dripping meltwater and casting long stark shadows up over the tower and the well pipe and ducts carrying the steam to the distant turbine houses. The framework struts of the upper tower were still cloaked with irregular patches of crystalline rime, but the polished chrome steam ducts shimmered with reflections of the aurora above and the heater coils below, always kept clear of ice by the hot steam coursing through them.

A gigantic steel mosquito, Marshall thought, proboscis and all.

Then Lim broke his concentration by taking a slow step backward, pointing out the window with a straight arm. Lim's finger trembled in all directions, partly from the shaking of the floor.

Marshall watched in petrified fascination as the aircraft warning beacons atop the towers began to move. He focused on the far end of the twin rows of blinking red lights converging toward the distant nunataks. The farthest beacon in the left row was already missing, and the one across from it was descending straight downward. It sank faster as he watched, then winked out. By that time three other beacons were also sinking. The platforms were collapsing in pairs, starting at the far end of the station and moving toward Platform One.

Motion drew Marshall's eye to the foreground as Platform Two bowed toward Platform Three. Somehow, despite no upward movement of the floating ice sheet, the central well pipe of Platform Two had abruptly descended to the bottom of its vertical range of motion, and the gear assembly at its top was pulling downward on the surrounding tower.

Vibrations began dislodging the rime on Platform Two's bending tower struts. The ice fell in long slender chunks that broke up in midair, raining debris onto the ice sheet and the squat building at the base of the tower. Across the two hundred yards between platforms, the debris appeared to be falling in slow motion. One long rod of ice made it to the ground intact, impaling one of the radiant heaters like a javelin. The heater fell backward in a vivid shower of sparks. Its glowing red coil winked out in the frigid air.

One of the car-sized gears atop Platform Two's well pipe broke off and tumbled down the tower. It crashed into the edge of the base building's roof, tearing a deep gash in the sheet metal, then plunged six more stories to the ice. The thirteen-ton gear bounced once, leaving a crater, then slowly rolled away, wobbling, into the darkness.

The other three gears hung on, and the sinking well pipe continued to pull Platform Two downward. For a moment the pipe's descent was halted by the chrome steam ducts radiating from it. The flexible ducts had bent as far as they could, forming high arches like upthrust elbows around the tower. Then the ducts tore loose, and the pipe fell faster than ever, compacting the tower's steel framework downward, bending and breaking one section of girders after another.

The weakest leg of Platform Two warped and buckled. The base building's walls collapsed inward. The platform's legs were sheared off as the gears atop the well pipe disappeared below the building's roof and dragged most of the platform's internal frame down through the raggedly enlarged wellhole.

"Run," Marshall said.

CHAPTER 3

Evacuation

Marshall and Lim bounded down the stairs and along a dark hallway without pausing to turn on the light, then down more clanking metal stairs until they caught up with Elizabeth Crane and the two rig workers sprinting along the corridor by the pipe storage shed on the ground level. Unlike the other twenty-three platforms, the base building of Platform One extended down to the ice.

"The tractors?" Marshall gasped.

Elizabeth shook her head.

Two snow tractors were permanently assigned to each platform, but their actual locations depended on the needs of the station's roving personnel. Elizabeth had evidently found Platform One's small garage empty. That meant the five evacuees would have to exit on foot and hoof it across the ice to the station's repair garage, where several backup tractors were kept.

Still running, Marshall heard the echoes of a familiar yet unexpected sound from the locker room at the other end of the corridor. It was Lance Mulrone, singing in the shower. As Marshall dashed into the locker room and up to the stall with steam pouring out, Lance let loose an Indian war whoop. The skinny rig worker was splashing in a circle with one hand over his mouth when Marshall pulled back the curtain.

Lance Mulrone was Amery Station's resident dope fiend. He had wandered the Earth in search of a place where he could remain employed while snacking on amphetamines like peanuts, finally finding his home on a desolate ice sheet where the days and nights lasted six months and no one could go to sleep or wake up without chemical help. Here all employees suffered perpetual lethargy and disorientation after a few weeks. At least Lance's bouts of lethargy were punctuated by his speed trips, during which he could do the work of three sober but groggy rig workers—six, if you counted the effect he had on the others' morale when he'd had one or two little black pills and could suddenly remember every dirty joke he'd ever heard.

It was evident from Lance's war dance that he was presently as wired as ever. Good, Marshall thought. Maybe it will help him run.

Lance jumped and landed hard against the back of the shower stall when Marshall yanked the curtain aside. Then he drew back his fist and yelled, "You just clear out of here, asshole! I wasn't hurting nobody."

Marshall put a finger to his own lips and reached with the other hand to turn off the shower. The roar from outside enveloped them. Lance looked puzzled but still angry. Then he looked down. The platform's vibration was making the skin on his thin body jiggle, sending drops of water flying from the tip of every hair. The stall's drain was partially clogged, and water had pooled on the floor. The water around Lance's bony ankles was a dancing jumble of wavelets and drops that spontaneously leaped from the surface.

When Lance looked up, his wired face was a mask of fear and confusion.

"What the hell is going on?"

"The platforms are sinking through the ice. We've got to get out of here."

Lance blinked for a second, again watching the waves dancing across his feet. Then he bolted for the door without stopping to grab his towel.

"Let's go!" Marshall yelled, resuming his dash toward the exit.

Lance started to turn the other way, toward the stairs up to his cabin. Marshall grabbed his slippery upper arm and dragged him along.

Lance's eyes got wide as they neared the external door. In a quavering, high-pitched voice, he yelled, "No way, man! I can't go outside like this."

Marshall released his grip. Lance was right—he would freeze to death in minutes, and frostbite would disfigure him in even less time. The others were not dressed properly either, but at least they had shoes on— they could make it to the garage. The difference between being underdressed and being wet and naked was the difference between life and death across a few hundred yards of the coldest place on Earth.

Lance resumed his dash back toward his cabin. Then he tried to stop, and his wet feet slipped on the smooth metal floor. He fell on his back, then sprang up into a crouch, staring down the long corridor in front of him.

The corridor was bending. The far end was tilting downward. A door popped off its hinges and flew across the hall, crashing into the opposite wall. Then the ceiling collapsed in a tangle of wires and torn ductwork, first near the far end, then in sections, one after another, moving up the corridor toward Lance. He scrambled to his feet, turned around, and screamed, "Go go go!" waving both arms in front of him as he ran.

Marshall reached the exit door before Lance and saw that Elizabeth, Lim, and the rig workers had stopped just inside.

The doorstep was ten feet above the ice.

They stared down as the door continued to rise, until they heard Lance's hysterical scream behind them: "Look out!"

Marshall flattened against the wall just in time, and Lance zoomed past him at full throttle. "No!" Marshall yelled, but it was too late. Lance launched from the doorstep, kicking at the air and rotating his arms.

His scream stopped when he hit the ice.

Marshall crept to the doorway and looked down. He did not like heights. That was part of the thrill he always felt just walking into the window-wrapped control room on the platform's fifth level. But Lance was one of his men, however wired on dope, and he was sprawled face-down on the polar ice, naked, not moving.

The doorstep was at least twelve feet high now, Marshall thought, licking his lips. And it was only getting higher. Shaking, he sat down on the precipice, his long legs dangling over. Then he pushed off.

When he landed, a weak ligament in his left knee parted with an audible snap. The joint had been injury-prone since college, when he had severely sprained it on the basketball court. Marshall had been a star before that, both a consistent high scorer and a charismatic crowd pleaser. In one agonizing instant, that injury had redirected his life, shutting the door on a promising NBA career. It had left him with no choice but to make the most of his mental abilities, which he had done.

Marshall rolled over on the searing-cold surface, groaning and gripping his bent knee. This time a blown-out knee might end more than his aspirations, he realized. It might end his life.

The heaters around Platform Two were gone, so Marshall could only see by starlight and the slowly receding glow from the open doorway above him. As he looked up, three of the four other evacuees jumped in single file. One of the two rig workers remained behind. He lay down on the floor of the collapsing corridor, looking over the rising doorstep with both arms outstretched toward the others on the ice below.

Elizabeth Crane cupped her hands around her mouth to yell. "Jump, you idiot!"

The other rig worker shouted, "Move, Ricardo! Before it's too late, man."

Ricardo did not move.

The near end of the long building began to rise faster. When the floor reached a forty-five-degree angle, Ricardo lost his grip on the doorstep and disappeared. Then the entire structure shuddered, and the prefabricated outer wall containing the doorway detached itself and fell edge-first toward the terrified evacuees.

Elizabeth, Dr. Lim, and the remaining rig worker dived out of the way in three different directions. Marshall squeezed his eyes shut and rolled on top of Lance Mulrone's still-motionless body to protect him from the falling wall. He felt wind and a rain of ice chips as the thousand-pound slab of sheet steel landed on its edge a few inches from his feet and slowly fell over onto the ice away from them.

Marshall tried to stand but lost his balance and fell backward. It wasn't his injured knee that tripped him—the sprain was not as bad as he'd thought at first. So why couldn't he stay on his feet? Had he hit his head when he jumped? Then he saw Lim staggering, swaying from side to side. The others were also holding on to each other and doing the same dance.

Looking around, Marshall realized they were on a slab of ice that had broken loose from the rest of the sheet. One end was being forced downward by a groaning leg of Platform One while the other end tilted up against the starry sky.

"Forget Lance—he's dead," Elizabeth yelled. She bent over, coughing from the cold, then turned and began climbing toward the upraised end of the ice slab, away from the sinking well platform. When she reached the edge, she stooped on her hands and knees to look down. At that moment, the leg of Platform One that was depressing the other end of the slab tore loose, and they all felt a brief sensation of weightlessness as the slab fell back toward a horizontal position.

Elizabeth's piercing scream carried over the grinding of the ice and the metallic screech that tore from Platform One as it shed its other legs. Driven by momentum, the edge where she was perched continued its downward swing past the stationary ice surrounding the slab, slamming her head and shoulders against the far side of the rift. She was hurled backward. She skidded to a halt on her back, motionless. Even in the dim starlight, Marshall could see that her neck was twisted at an impossible angle.

No one spoke as the slab continued to bob up and down, grinding to a halt against the enclosing ice sheet. They watched the tip of the tower from the former Platform One as it descended out of view with a faint gleam of starlight on twisted metal and a muted hiss of steel shearing against dry ice.

Lim stooped beside Lance, probing the side of his throat. "He's gone."

"We have to carry him anyway," Marshall said, flinching with pain as he tested his knee. "No one is dead until he's warm and dead." That maxim was well known by emergency medics in the world's colder climates. Hypothermia often slowed a victim's breathing and pulse enough to mimic death long before recovery became impossible.

Marshall hobbled around to Lance's head and motioned the silently shivering rig worker to take his feet.

Lim sank to his knees beside Lance's head, ejecting a plume of foggy breath. "Wait! He's frozen fast to the ice. You'll rip his skin off." Lim knelt like a praying Moslem and twisted to look at Lance's half-exposed face without contacting his own bare head to the ice. "His left eye is open, and it's touching the ice."

"In another minute, we're *all* going to freeze," Marshall said.

Lim nodded, grasping one of Lance's arms.

Marshall counted down from three, and they heaved Lance upward. The motion was accompanied by a nauseating sound of tearing flesh. Marshall made the mistake of looking down at the depression where Lance's face had been. There, fused to the ice, was what had once been Lance's left eyeball, trailing the bloody tendrils of the optic nerve.

Almost instantly, the glistening wet organ became a dull lump, frozen solid.

CHAPTER 4

Reed

Colonel Tom Reed of the United States Air Force sweltered in a chair that was too padded. He was wearing an uncomfortably warm office uniform with a nooselike tie. Other than that, this was turning out to be anything but a typical workday.

He was alone at the head of a briefing table in a videoconference room a quarter mile down the hallway from his office at the Pentagon. The other end of the satellite link was at the base camp of ICARE on the western shore of the Ross Sea in Antarctica.

A crisis was at hand, so this was no time for Reed's attention to wander. He was usually "focused like a laser," as his daughter had once put it. That professional focus had allowed him to become the chief officer at the Strategic Resource Development Center (SRDC). The SRDC was the newest and smallest branch of the United States Strategic Command (USSTRATCOM), which was headquartered at Offutt Air Force Base in Nebraska. For several years Reed had commanded a large staff responsible for aiding treaty negotiations with other countries on energy-related issues as well as protecting vital infrastructure assets like the Amery Station power plant.

But this morning his mind was torn between the crisis of the day and the only subject outside his work that preoccupied him: his teenage daughter, Angela. Angie was Reed's only child, his only family, in fact, and he loved her infinitely. Nevertheless, he was often frustrated by her habit of calling him at work, sometimes interrupting important meetings just to chat.

When Angie was nine years old, her mother was killed in a head-on collision. Since then, Tom Reed could not refuse a call from his daughter, no matter how much it embarrassed him. Angie discovered soon after the wreck that she was an environmentalist, more specifically a wildlife conservationist, so most of her calls were to inform him of some present or predicted environmental disaster she had just read about, usually in some godforsaken patch of scrub jungle on the other side of the planet. Her counselor explained that it was natural for a girl who had just lost her mother to transfer her anguish onto some cause that she might actually be able to help, but Reed began to worry as the years went by and Angie's environmental fervor only grew, especially since she seemed to know that she was just as helpless to prevent species extinctions as she was to bring back her mother.

This morning, Reed actually longed—desperately—to see his secretary slip into the videoconference room with the sympathetic look in her eyes that meant his daughter was on the phone. As of Angie's last e-mail from the satellite uplink at Professor Lois Burnham's tiny research camp, his baby was somewhere on the Warner Basin ice sheet in Antarctica, not far from the Amery Station power plant, and Reed had just learned of the plant's destruction during the night by a volcanic erup-

tion that was still spewing lava into the basin's subglacial lake.

"Eleven of my rig workers died in the collapse," said
the haggard image of Marshall Dunn looming over the
table. He and Tom Reed had been friends since they
briefly served together in the army, many years before a
word from Reed had won Marshall his position as the
foreman at Amery Station.

Reed gazed up at the screen with dark eyes that were
sleepy, sad, and patient, despite the emergency. He was a
very large man, not thin but so lean that the thick muscles on both sides of his neck stood out like pillars. His
taut face was contoured over the muscles of his jaws. He
was a Caucasian of mostly Italian descent, despite his
English name. Dark skin and thick eyebrows framed his
sad eyes. But the most unique feature of Reed's face was
his mouth. His full lips curled up on the left and down
on the right so that he always looked solemn on one side
and vaguely amused on the other.

"How many were injured?" Reed asked.

Marshall grimly shook his head. "No one who was seriously hurt made it through the cold."

He looks shell-shocked, Reed thought—too tired to
breathe, yet still wired on adrenaline from the battle. It
was nine o'clock on Wednesday morning, Eastern Standard Time, but for ICARE it was eight hours earlier.
Reed realized that Marshall could not have been at the
ICARE base more than an hour or two, hardly long
enough to bandage a few scrapes, much less assimilate
the devastation.

"What I don't get is how an eruption of lava at the
bottom of the lake could cause the surface platforms to
collapse," Reed said. "Are you certain the eruption has
not penetrated the floating ice sheet?"

"There is no visible sign of the eruption at the surface,

Tom. We only know it's still going because we can hear the rumble. We already called in a geothermal energy consultant to help us figure out what happened to the station. He was doing fieldwork between the Bahia Blanca and Pedro Luro geothermal fields near Buenos Aires. He'll get here in about . . . seven hours."

"Good. Maybe he'll have it all figured out by the time I arrive." As commander of the SRDC, Reed had dealt with many crises beyond the borders of the United States, but Amery Station's collapse was the first situation so complex that he had decided to command the disaster response in person. At least he *thought* that was the reason for his decision—he was not a hundred percent certain that it had not been influenced by his need to verify with his own eyes that Angie was safe. After losing sleep for two months, imagining her shivering on the verge of hypothermia, he was primed to panic at the thought of molten lava raining down on her camp.

"It sounds like this eruption is the tame kind," Reed said. "Like the vents that pour out lava in Hawaii and Iceland. But I've heard that one volcano can have different kinds of eruptions. Do you think this one could turn rogue and explode like Krakatoa or Mount St. Helens?"

Marshall shrugged. "I'll ask the consultant."

"Ask him now, if you can. And call me on the plane if his answer is yes." Reed leaned forward, holding his muscular hands stationary to cover the patches of sweat they were leaving on the table's shiny black veneer. "I need to ask for another favor, Marshall. There's a little research camp on the side of the Warner Basin opposite ICARE. Just two women out there—one of them is my daughter. They've been spying on a bunch of penguins all through the winter. I want you to get them out of the basin until we know what this infernal volcano is going to do. I could send an army unit, but your men know the road between ICARE and the basin. I'll e-mail you the camp's GPS coordinates."

One of Reed's greatest triumphs, as he saw it, had been convincing Congress to approve an expensive upgrade to the Global Positioning System, including satellites in higher orbits that could accurately locate receivers over most of Antarctica.

Marshall yelled sideways, relaying the request to someone Reed could not see, then faced the camera again. "We're on it, Tom."

"Thank you," Reed said, closing his eyes for a moment. "Those women are committed to their penguin project, by the way. Tell your men not to be surprised if they meet some . . . resistance. But evacuation of that camp is not optional."

The transport jet's trajectory took it onto the dark side of the Earth somewhere over the Bellingshausen Sea, just south of the Antarctic Circle at sixty-six degrees, thirty-three minutes south latitude, halfway between Tierra del Fuego and the ICARE base on the western shore of the Ross Sea. In Buenos Aires Reed had switched from the plane he had taken out of Washington to a jet equipped with skis for landing on the Ross Ice Shelf.

He did not notice the glorious setting sun—he was too absorbed in an on-line negotiation with his counterparts, the military ICARE administrators from the other participating nations. The purpose of this Internet III conference via satellite phone was to hash out a fair division of responsibility for providing emergency power supplies across Antarctica. An interim agreement was finally settled until the next day, and Reed signed his name on the laptop screen with an electronic stylus. He closed the computer and slid it under his seat, and only then did he notice the sharp, twinkling stars shining through his porthole.

Reed decided to dissipate some nervous energy. He started with a hundred push-ups in the narrow aisle of the passenger cabin, ignoring the furtive stares from the small staff he had brought with him and the forty military police troops who would help maintain order in the outposts with no electricity. Resting after his first set, he squatted in the swaying aisle and stared out at the stars with a boyish grin.

He wondered what Antarctica would be like. Just imagine, he thought, a whole continent so remote that the names of all who have died there are known and recorded.

Reed was accustomed to traveling overseas, but his trips never lasted more than a week and their purpose was invariably administrative. London, Moscow, Geneva, Brussels, the Hague—this was his first trip in a decade to somewhere interesting, a place where his stay might not be confined to a hotel room. Youthful anticipation had been growing inside him all day. Even dread of the hard work and pitfalls ahead could not dampen his excitement.

The allure of prolonged travel to exotic places was one of the reasons Tom Reed had chosen a military life. His craving for adventure had taken root from the stories of swashbuckling heroism he had started reading at an early age. Even now, fat political thrillers and novels of globe-trotting adventure were his primary diversion, outside the gym.

He had excelled in school but was so eager for physical action—any kind of action, even boot camp—that he enlisted in the army the day after his high school graduation. Only a brief bout of heat prostration during a mandatory 6:00 A.M. run had prevented him from finishing Jump School at Fort Benning and becoming a paratrooper. Since he'd missed his goal of joining the nation's quick response force at the Eighty-second Airborne Division—and because his CO insisted he was wasting his excellent academic record as an enlisted soldier—he left the army and enrolled in the Air Force Academy.

His classmates all wanted to be fighter pilots or astronauts, but Reed was still more interested in the tactics and gritty action of ground war, so he became a pilot of the Fairchild Republic A-10 Thunderbolt II, better known as the Warthog. Warthogs were old, clunky, and slow, but they were incredibly durable under heavy antiaircraft fire and fundamentally well suited for taking out enemy forces just over the front lines of a land army. They were essentially flying tanks, with heavy armor and ordnance, and they eventually proved their worth against Saddam Hussein's main battle tanks in Desert Storm. Tom Reed graduated just in time—he got to fly several sorties over Iraq, racking up twenty-one tank kills and 216 bullet holes in the engines and airframes of his Hogs.

After his wife's death, Reed diverted his career away from the exciting track of a field commander and toward the more lucrative offices at the Pentagon, eventually achieving a position that essentially turned him from soldier to diplomat, so he was not likely to ever see combat again. He made sure Angie understood that he had chosen this path for her sake, not his own, and reassured her that he would never again place his life at greater risk than duty required.

Now the live ember of wanderlust Reed could feel smoldering inside made him realize he had never truly rejected his dreams of adventure, he had only compromised them for a higher purpose. It was not at all surprising that he could not sit still on a jet flying halfway around the world to the most remote and hostile land on Earth.

Marshall Dunn called from the ICARE base. Reed went to the private videophone booth at the front of the passenger cabin and cranked up the volume so he could hear Marshall's deep drawl over the humming jet engines. "What's wrong?" he said when he saw Marshall's expression.

"I didn't send a tractor to evacuate Angie and Dr. Burnham like I should have, Tom."

"They're still at the research camp?"

"No, they left in Dr. Burnham's decrepit old machine. She insisted on driving it. That's why we didn't send someone."

"So they're on their way to the ICARE base?"

"Not anymore," Marshall said. "They broke down in the middle of the ice sheet."

Reed stared at the screen. "In the middle . . . *close to Amery Station?*"

"Just as they were passing it. Tom, I'm sorry. We sent a mechanic as soon as they called us on the radio."

Reed forced himself not to scowl. "It's not your fault. It was Dr. Burnham's decision. Do they have enough fuel to idle for heat?"

"She didn't say."

"Call me again when the mechanic gets to them," Reed said.

He signed off and returned to his seat, feeling a spring of partial panic in his stride. What if ordering Lois and Angie to evacuate was a big mistake? Back at their research camp, they had at least been several miles from the demolished power plant, which he presumed was directly above the ongoing eruption on the lake bed. He wondered how he would handle it if anything happened to them now.

Reed's quick decision to evacuate Lois and Angie might have dire ramifications even if they made it safely to the ICARE base. He knew what it felt like to have the funding pulled when he had almost completed a challenging project that he deeply cared about. His evacuation order had done something similar to Dr. Burnham. Only time would tell if it had damaged her new friendship with Angie, which was apparently the best thing that had ever happened to his daughter.

After dropping out of college, Angie had read in *National Geographic* about the exploits of one Lois Burnham, Ph.D., Antarctic wildlife researcher extraordinaire from Harvard University. She then called Reed at work—during a meeting—to say, astonishingly, "Dad, I want to go to Harvard!"

Angie had barely graduated from high school, so she didn't stand a chance of being accepted by an Ivy League school. But a brief stroke of genius led Reed to investigate a branch of the ICARE operations that he had never paid much attention to before, the environmental research budget. It took him less than ten seconds to find Lois Burnham's name on the list of grant recipients.

His first idea was to bribe Dr. Burnham to help Angie get into Harvard. He knew from the way his daughter synthesized and reported what she had read in her piles of books and journals about environmental issues that her academic ability exceeded her mood-hindered performance in school.

By the time he told her his plan, she had changed her mind.

"What do you want to do, then?" he asked, and found out her new passion was at least twice as outrageous.

He flatly refused at first, but she wouldn't let go of it.

Angie would simply die if she could not become Lois Burnham's research assistant in Antarctica. After a month-long power struggle that finally convinced Reed his daughter was too stubborn to freeze to death, he conducted a discreet background check on Lois Burnham that went so deep he could have obtained top secret clearance for her.

Dr. Burnham was thirty-four, Caucasian, childless, and in perfect health; she had never been married. Her credit was spotless but completely unused. She belonged to several book clubs, and over the last five years she had joined a commercial gym and begun purchasing health and beauty products over the Internet. Ninety percent of the paper produced by the security check was her academic record, which was both prolific and excellent.

In other words, she was a typical academic, one of the most reliable types of professionals. Reed saw no reason to doubt that she was trustworthy, so he called the young professor with the good news that her research grant was about to double—on one small condition. His intention had been to make a dream come true for his only child, but what if this minor misuse of his power had instead doomed her to an untimely and frightful death?

Until he landed, there was nothing he could do but wait. Hoping to escape from such morbid thoughts, he opened his briefcase and pulled out a ream of smudgy photocopies bound with a rubber band. These were estimates of replacement costs for the largest equipment at Amery Station. One of his first challenges in Antarctica would be to evaluate how much of the station could be salvaged, whether it could be rebuilt, and how long that would take.

For the foreseeable future, the entire continent would be running on gasoline backup generators. A massive coal seam—the world's largest—was being mapped in the Transantarctic Mountains, but the power plant that would use the coal was still under construction and could not be finished in less than a year. Meanwhile, the mines and smelters and exploration camps that relied on power lines strung across the ice cap from Amery Station were slowly running out of backup fuel. They had allowed their reserves to dwindle since Amery Station had come on-line, burning the fuel intended for emergency generators in thousands of small stoves for supplemental heat.

The dark Antarctic winter was almost over, but the continent was still surrounded by a broad skirt of sea ice. Reed would have to find an icebreaker to deliver gasoline. Ordinary unleaded gas was the current fuel of choice in Antarctica, for generators, vehicles, even heating and cooking. Although gasoline was currently more expensive and dangerous than diesel or omnipurpose JP-8 fuel oil, its higher volatility allowed it to ignite more reliably at ultralow temperatures.

Reed knew that the U.S. Coast Guard's *Polar Star* was in the Southern Hemisphere this season, and that she could plow through sea ice over twenty feet thick. First-year sea ice seldom grew thicker than six feet, so he was confident that the icebreaker could cut through the shipping lane to ICARE's icebound docks, even now when the ice was at its thickest. The question was whether she could do it in time; he had learned from a brief call to her home port in Seattle that the "break-in" from the edge of the ice pack north of Cape Adare could take up to a month. If rationing and conservation could not stretch ICARE's fuel reserves that long—and he suspected they could not—he would have three choices: import fuel by air at exorbitant cost, send tank tractors out on the fragile sea ice to meet the *Polar Star* and haul the fuel back, or evacuate the continent.

Marshall called again. "Tom, I have some bad news."

Reed grabbed the wall of the videophone booth.

"The mechanic we sent to fix Dr. Burnham's tractor has disappeared," Marshall said.

"What do you mean? Have you heard from Angie and Dr. Burnham?"

"I just spoke to them on the radio. They're fine, but the mechanic never got there."

"Maybe he broke down too," Reed said, breathing hard as he recovered from his fright.

"No, he would have called. We can't raise him on the radio, and neither can Dr. Burnham, but she and I can hear each other perfectly. That's how we know he isn't just having a problem with radio reception, since he should be somewhere in between us."

"His radio could have died."

"Maybe," Marshall said. "But he's had more than enough time to get there. The radios in our snow tractors have backup batteries, so there's no way a single malfunction could have killed his radio and disabled his vehicle."

"Good Lord," Reed said. "So that's what you meant by 'disappeared.'"

"And it's not likely that he just got lost," Marshall added. "He knew their exact GPS coordinates and had a handheld receiver in addition to the one in his tractor."

Reed signed off and went to the cockpit. "How fast are we going?" he asked the pilot.

"Six hundred knots, sir."

"Is that the maximum cruise speed for this jet?"

"Yes, sir."

"What's the maximum maneuver speed?"

"Six-fifty."

"Throttle up to six-forty, and don't slow down unless an engine overheats."

"Sir, the fuel . . ."

"Watch how fast it's burning. Throttle back in time to land with at least two." By that, Reed meant two thousand pounds of jet fuel.

"What's going on?" the copilot said.

"I wish I knew," Reed replied. "All I can say until we get there and investigate is that the danger in the Warner Basin apparently didn't end with the power plant's collapse."

CHAPTER 5

Antarctica

The small air force transport jet finally began its descent, and the external floodlights of the ICARE base crawled out of the darkness in front of the right wing. All of the buildings were windowless rectangles of red corrugated sheet steel with black steel roofs held down against the sweeping katabatic winds by guylines. Snow drifts were piled against the inland sides of the monolithic one-story structures. Reed could also make out a long glass greenhouse, an array of satellite dishes, three cylindrical fuel tanks, and a gravel pile the size of a large house. The ground between buildings—a pale blend of dirt, rocks, and ice—was crisscrossed by ruts from bulldozer tracks.

ICARE was a joint venture between governments and private enterprise. In the American quadrant, about half of the funding, materials, and staff had been supplied by the military under Reed's command. Without the mining, petroleum, and engineering companies, the military could never have mustered the expertise to develop the vast but nearly inaccessible resources of the last untamed continent. On the other hand, the corporations would never have considered developing Antarctica without being subsidized by the army's infrastructure projects, the air force transport flights, and the navy shipping. Subtle shifts in military activities could make or break individual corporate profits in the highly artificial Antarctic economy, and that clearly made Tom Reed the most powerful man on the continent. Looking down with pride and trepidation at the rapidly approaching floodlit monoliths that were the barracks, garages, hangars, and tank farms of the ICARE base camp, he realized the irony of such power, considering he'd never even seen the continent until now.

They flew low over the base, getting oriented, then banked back to the north and descended toward the airstrip on the Ross Ice Shelf, beneath the rocky bluff where the ICARE base stood. The permanent floating ice shelf made an ideal site for an unpaved runway. Its surface was perfectly flat and firm, and its thickness ranged from over three thousand feet where it was fed by glaciers from the continental ice cap to seven or eight hundred feet where it met the sea as a tall, vertical cliff.

The plane taxied into a hangar so its passengers would be protected from the brutal wind as they disembarked. Reed waited at the door, first in line. Marshall shook his hand when he stepped off, then drew him aside.

"Tom, we're ready to drive into the Warner Basin right now. I already told Major Dawson and Max Bloom that you had changed your mind and wanted to see Amery Station as soon as you got here."

Major Dawson was the senior officer permanently stationed in Antarctica. Maximillian Bloom was the chief executive of the American corporate conglomerate at ICARE. Reed had planned to meet with them and some representatives from the foreign quadrants before his first trip to investigate the remains of Amery Station.

"Did I guess right?" Marshall asked.

"You guessed right," Reed said. "And thanks for the cover that I'm in a hurry to see the station. Let's go."

Reed and Marshall marched to two large vehicles idling by the hangar's door. Reed guessed that the temperature was about ten below zero, Fahrenheit. The high, oscillating fluorescents gave his foggy breath a greenish tint. The floor was white glacial ice. It felt as hard as concrete beneath his boots.

"Did you send the helicopter to look for the missing mechanic?" Reed knew that ICARE kept only one search and rescue helicopter on the continent during the winter, when all Antarctic operations were cut back to the bare essentials.

"Right after I called you," Marshall said. "So far, they haven't found a trace."

The two snow tractors were the same model. One was flamingo pink; the other was frog green with a broad canary-yellow stripe running around the middle. Reed presumed the bright colors were to make the heavy vehicles more visible in the perpetual winter darkness, or during a blizzard. They had wide wheel bases and a low stance like a HUMV, and their bodies reminded him of an armored personnel carrier—flat plates of thick sheet steel fastened to the frame with hexagonal rivets. The windshields were narrow slits. The windows were palm sized. All the glass looked to be at least an inch thick. Each tractor had eight fat balloon tires, four in front and four in the rear. The tires were at least four feet in diameter and two feet wide. Sharp cleats protruded several inches from their treads.

"Can I drive?" Reed asked. Under other circumstances he would have wanted to try driving one of the exotic vehicles for the fun of it. Now he just wanted to set the pace.

"Are you sure you want to?" Marshall said.

"Yes. Why?"

"The weather is at condition two," said Silong Lim, who had stepped out of the green tractor to shake Reed's hand.

"Condition two?"

"Antarctic weather is reported according to three conditions," Marshall explained. "Condition three is fair, which means the wind won't necessarily knock you down and it takes a while for your limbs to freeze solid. But it's *miserable* outside in condition two."

"Condition two has sustained winds above fifty-five miles per hour," Lim added. "Also visibility less than a quarter mile and a windchill below negative seventy-five Fahrenheit. *Miserable.* Condition one has winds faster than sixty-three miles per hour, a windchill worse than a hundred below, and visibility less than a hundred feet."

"What's it like to go out in condition one?" Reed asked.

Marshall and Lim looked at each other. "Nobody goes outside in condition one," Lim said. "Ever."

"Okay, let's get going," Reed said. "If I can't handle it, I'll let someone else drive." He had opened the left front door of the green tractor, which had a vertical latch like the lever on a walk-in freezer. He presumed its purpose was the same—to form an airtight seal around the door. After starting to get in, he pulled his head back out. "Where's the wheel?"

"Other side," Marshall said, getting into the back. "These buggies are built by New Zealand Motors, which is actually a Cadillac plant in Auckland."

Reed grimaced as he jogged around to the right side. It was too bad he would not get to enjoy his first drive across Antarctica in the ultimate SUV.

An attendant raised the hangar door. Reed eased the tractor into low gear and pressed the stiff accelerator pedal. The ten-liter gasoline engine roared, and the heavy machine slowly rolled out into the Antarctic night. The endless white ice shelf was almost blinding beneath the four halogen headlights. Marshall told him which way to go.

Once he was up to top speed—forty miles per hour—Reed broke the tense silence inside the tractor's dark cabin. "Exactly how cold does Antarctica get?"

"Here on the coast it is not so bad," said Dr. Lim. "Usually above minus thirty, even now at the coldest part of winter."

Reed scanned the barren ice, which was totally devoid of color and landmarks. "It's like the dark side of the Moon! Is there any life here at all?"

"Not much," said the man sitting in the front passenger seat. "Emperor penguins are the only warm-blooded animals that stay on the continent during the winter. The native plants are no higher than your boot soles—just a few lichens, mosses, algae, and molds. On the inland ice cap, there's only some bacteria . . . and humans, of course."

Reed glanced at his passenger as the man spoke with a deep voice and a mild Greek accent. His face was clearly visible by the headlight beams reflecting from the ice. Marshall had introduced him as Dr. Pavros Corcoros, the geology professor from MIT who moonlighted as a geothermal energy consultant. Corcoros was as big as Reed, with big hands, an ample paunch, a large nose, and a thick curly salt-and-pepper beard.

"The coldest temperature ever recorded on Earth is minus one hundred twenty-nine," Corcoros added. "That was at Vostok Station in the interior. You piss in air that cold, it's just little frozen beads by the time it lands in the snow. Or so I've heard. Personally, I wouldn't pull mine out when it's that cold. Only a crazy Russian would—"

"Marshall, how long will it take us to get there?" Reed asked.

"We should pull into the station sometime before noon."

Reed glanced at his luminous wristwatch and cursed under his breath. The local time was only five a.m. on Thursday.

"That's assuming whatever happened to the mechanic does not happen to us," Silong Lim added.

A few hours after the tractors had climbed onto the continent, total darkness gave way to predawn gloom so slowly that Reed hardly noticed. By the time the winding road entered the vast level emptiness of the Warner Basin, the clear sky was pale lavender blue with twilight. Reed's body reacted by continuously anticipating sunrise within a few minutes. When the sky reached its maximum brightness for the day and stopped getting lighter, he got a creepy feeling that time was standing still.

"Hey, Marshall, do you think we're within radio range yet?"

"Could be," Marshall said. "Give it a try."

Corcoros woke with a lurch and a snort in response to Reed's booming voice. The overweight professor had been snoring for the last two hours. Marshall and Lim had also stopped talking. Reed knew that he must be running out of energy too, but he had never slackened his grip on the wheel or lifted his throttle foot off the floor except when necessary to safely navigate a curve.

He tried several times to raise Lois and Angie on the radio. There was no response, not even static. Marshall then called the ICARE base, which came in as clear as a local FM station. They told him the rescue helicopter had given up looking for the lost mechanic. "Did they spot Dr. Burnham's tractor?" he asked.

Reed heaved a sigh of relief when the voice on the radio said, "Yes."

After signing off with ICARE, Marshall said, "Maybe their batteries went dead, Tom. They've been out there a long time now."

Reed drove at top speed, following the trail of triangular magenta marker flags across the ice sheet. The flags flapped vigorously in the wind on the exposed glacial ocean, their carbon composite poles bending so far that some flag tips were smacking the ice. The wind also shook the tractor. Reed had to keep the helm twisted a quarter turn to the left just to continue going straight.

"I don't see the station," he said.

"Because it is no longer there," Lim said with a forlorn sigh.

"No," Marshall said. "Not all of the platforms collapsed. We're just too far away."

The whole Warner Basin was visible—the empty expanse of the floating ice sheet, the jagged gray nunataks surrounding it on three sides, the steep glaciers tumbling into the basin from the high ice cap beyond the mountains, their white surfaces streaked with rock debris and crenellated with thin black crevasses. Reed could even see foglike plumes of spindrift launched by the wind into the lavender-blue sky from the cornices atop the highest ridges. He found it hard to believe that any part of the floating ice sheet could be so far away that something the size of a power plant would be invisible.

Then again, he knew the human eye judged distance by perspective, which could easily be deceived by expanses of flat ground. He'd seen the optical illusion created by Death Valley, where hundreds of pioneers had set out on the low desert plain thinking the mountains on the far side were only a few miles away, then perished in the dry heat halfway across.

"How high are those peaks?" he asked, pointing ahead.

"Those are the Ellis Mountains," Marshall said. "The highest nunatak is Shackleton Peak, around thirteen thousand feet."

Reed whistled. *Real* mountains. Their lower slopes were obviously buried beneath the ice, leaving only the summits exposed.

"Dr. Lim, will there still be enough light for your camera by the time we get there?" Corcoros asked. Lim had said he wanted to document the wreckage with photographs. That would allow them to pore over the details back at the ICARE base.

Lim checked his wristwatch and frowned. "We should go faster."

"Can't," Reed said. "When will it get dark?"

"Long time," Lim said. "This is civil twilight, the sun less than six degrees below the horizon. It will last until about four p.m. Then we will have nautical twilight—the sun between six and twelve degrees down—until around six. Then there will be another two hours of astronomical twilight, with the sun still above minus eighteen degrees . . . but that is just dark to me."

"When will the sun actually start rising?" Reed asked. "I thought the winter was almost over."

Lim said, "Marshall?"

Marshall pressed a button on his wristwatch and said, "Three days, two hours, and forty-nine minutes, God willing."

Lim chuckled. "I knew Marshall could tell you. He hates the winter down here."

"I suspect I'll hate the summer too," Marshall said.

CHAPTER 6

Breakdown

"Dr. Corcoros," Reed said, "did you figure out exactly what happened to Amery Station?"

Corcoros nodded and cleared his throat. "This basin is a giant volcanic caldera, a bowl-shaped depression forty miles wide and two miles deep. It was formed by subsidence of the ground after some prehistoric eruption blew out a zillion tons of magma. Those mountains that ring the basin are holding back the polar ice cap. All those alpine glaciers you can see spilling down from the passes—those are actually fed by the ice cap."

"What about that way?" Reed asked, nodding to the right. On that side he could see no mountains—the ice sheet stretched on until it met the sky.

"The Ross Sea is over there," Corcoros said. "The open part. Actually, it's covered by thin sea ice this time of year, but the edge of the permanent ice shelf is way behind us—we've been traveling north. We're at a pretty high elevation here in the basin, so the ice over there gradually descends to sea level as one broad glacier."

Reed nodded the other way, to the left. "Why haven't

those glaciers filled up the basin to the same level as the rest of the ice cap?"

"Because they melt," Corcoros said. "The old volcano is not extinct. It's just dormant—*was* dormant. The magma chamber is still shallow enough to keep most of the water in the basin in liquid form. The floating ice sheet is maintained at a constant thickness by cooling from the atmosphere, so as more ice pours into the basin, it ends up melting and raising the lake level. When the water gets high enough to overflow the subglacial caldera, it seeps beneath the ice into the Ross Sea."

"You mean the lake is held back by a continuous ridge around the edge of the caldera?"

"Precisely," Corcoros said. "It's a natural dam. Some-where to our right, or maybe under us—I'm not sure—the seaward side of the caldera sticks up into the ice sheet, above the level of the water in the lake. It just isn't high enough to rise above the ice where you can see it, like the nunataks on the other sides do. The lake level varies a little, but it can only get as high as the lowest point along the seaward ridge before water spills over beneath the ice."

"Okay," Reed said. "I still don't see how an eruption on the lake bed destroyed the station."

Marshall took over the explanation. "Amery Station was unique, Tom. No one had ever tried to tap the super-heated steam immediately overlying a magma chamber. We first pumped water in at superhigh pressure to frac-ture the hot bedrock. That provided permeability so steam could move toward the well screens. When we began operating the station, water from the lake was supposed to percolate down through the fractures and vaporize to replace the steam we were extracting."

"But that didn't work?"

In his rearview mirror, Reed saw Marshall grimace as

if he had just swallowed a spoonful of coffee grounds. "The lake water couldn't infiltrate fast enough," Marshall continued, "because the layer of fine glacial clay on the lake bed was as tight as a plastic landfill liner. The lab tests they did on sediment cores before the station's construction must have overestimated its vertical hydraulic conductivity. Big time."

Reed's collar suddenly felt hot with vicarious embarrassment. He knew that somewhere at least one geologist or engineer was looking for a new career.

"They should have measured the permeability of the intact sediment instead of taking cores," Lim added. "But in situ testing would have cost more, and Max Bloom would not approve the budget for it."

"Removing too much steam allowed magma to rise through the bedrock fractures and pour into the well screens," Corcoros said. "That blocked the steam flow and caused the pressure inside the well pipes to drop below the hydrostatic pressure in the lake water around them. The pipes flooded and lost their buoyancy, which was what had supported their weight."

"And the mile-long pipes were too heavy for the surface platforms to hold up," Reed said.

"Precisely," Corcoros confirmed.

"I wonder if this is the world's first man-made volcanic eruption," Reed said.

Corcoros grinned, shaking a finger in the air. "You know, that's exactly what I said!"

Marshall shrugged, obviously too weary to care.

"This juxtaposition of fire and ice is not as unusual as you might think," Corcoros said. "There are lots of places where volcanoes erupt beneath glaciers and ice caps. One reason is that really high volcanoes form their own alpine glaciers above the snow line. You'll see them in the Andes, in Alaska, on the Kamchatka Peninsula, even the Cascade Range from Washington to California. Iceland is a volcanic island lying directly on a rift between tectonic plates. The Icelanders have a special word, *jökulhlaup,* for the floods that occur when meltwater produced by volcanoes suddenly breaks loose from beneath a glacier. The Grímsvötn caldera in Iceland is a system similar to the Warner Basin. It's in the middle of the Vatnajökull ice sheet, the largest glacier in Europe. There are volcanoes of all types right here in Antarctica, although only five of them are considered to be active—six, now. The stratovolcano, Mount Erebus, is part of the same geothermal system as the Warner Basin. On the other side of the continent at Deception Island, there's a—"

"—calling the tractors. This is Angela Reed, calling the tractors. Come in if you're out there."

Reed leaped at the familiar sound of his daughter's voice. He cranked the radio volume to the max and yelled into the handset. "Angie! It's me! Are you all right?"

She let loose a triumphant squeal. "We're fine, Dad. Cold, bored out of our minds, but fine. We had emergency rations. Where are you?"

"Less than twenty minutes from your GPS coords."

"All right!" Angie yelled. Then her voice sobered. "Uh, Dad, Lois wants to talk to you."

"Colonel, there was absolutely *no* reason for you to evacuate our research camp." Even over the tinny radio, Lois Burnham's voice was like a salvo of sharp icicles. She went on to explain how her camp was twenty miles from Amery Station and had its own generator. Reed listened, but his mind was preoccupied with savoring the relief that was washing over him like the calm after a storm. Drowsiness hit him for the first time since he had left the Pentagon. It was eleven a.m. on Thursday,

ICARE time—seven p.m. back home—so he had been wired on worry for thirty-four straight hours since the first videocall from Marshall.

As Dr. Burnham's tirade wound down, Corcoros winked at Reed and whispered, "Uh-oh, are you sure you want to rescue *her*?"

Not funny, Reed thought, but he laughed anyway, because he was so relieved that the tractor his daughter was in had not vanished like the mechanic's.

He had no problem finding the little orange two-person snow tractor. He spotted it more than a mile away. He could also see Amery Station off to the left. It was not as close to the disabled tractor as he had feared.

"Are we leaving now or staying until our tractor is fixed?" Angie asked on the radio. He had told her that one of the men in the pink tractor was a mechanic.

"Staying," Reed said. "Sorry, Pumpkin, but I have to spend a few hours at Amery Station anyway. If your tractor isn't running by then, we'll leave and come back for it later."

"Won't it still be dangerous at the station?" she asked.

"Probably," he said.

When he slowly halted the green tractor, Angie was waiting outside in full polar garb, leaning into the brutal wind. She threw her arms around his chest the instant he stepped out. Thoughts of the power shortage, the calamity at Amery Station, the dangers they might still face getting out of the basin—all his worries faded in his daughter's embrace.

"Thanks for coming to get us, Dad."

"He came a long way," Marshall said, patting Reed's back.

They had never been apart for so long. He held her bony shoulders at arm's length and looked at her, then embraced her again. She would turn nineteen in three days but was as thin as ever and still a little stooped in a way that made her look closer to twenty-nine. Her posture had always unnerved his military sensibilities. And she still had those puffy blue sacks under her dark brown eyes from chronic lack of sleep. But he saw something in her face that he had not seen in years, something distinctly positive.

While the mechanic got to work in the bitter cold, the others all dived back into Reed's vehicle, shivering.

"Colonel, the emperors are in trouble," Lois said. "At least let me return to the rookery alone. Angie can go back to the ICARE base with you."

"No, I can't!" Angie shouted.

Great, Reed thought. Two against one. "Look, Dr. Burnham, I'm sorry your tractor broke down. I know you've had a rough day."

"Day and a half," Lois corrected.

"But once we get you back to the base, you can't return to the Warner Basin until we understand what other effects this eruption may have."

"Dad, that's ridiculous! Nobody understands the Earth. It's mysterious. And the erupting fissure is under the ice cap. Good grief."

"I'm a civilian," Lois said. "You can't stop me."

"Guess again. At my request, the commander in chief proclaimed martial law for all of the American operations in Antarctica, as of noon yesterday. You must have missed the announcement."

Lois stared. "Doesn't that violate the Antarctic Treaty?"

"Probably," Reed said. "But the proclamation will remain in effect until I can get a shipment of fuel down here and distribute it to the outposts. Some of them are completely without heat or power. There is no civilian police force, just private security, and I've seen things turn ugly in a heartbeat in situations like this. If that happens, someone will have to keep the peace."

"Dad, does that mean you get to order *everybody* around?"

Reed nodded. "Basically." He tapped his daughter's nose. "And that includes you."

He looked closely at Lois Burnham for the first time. Her long blond hair was frizzy and dull and her lips were cracked and desiccated from long-term exposure to the cold dry wind. But despite her weather-worn appearance, he thought her face was pretty—blue-green eyes, even white teeth, muscular cheeks with deep dimples, fair skin with scattered freckles. She was not beautiful in a movie-star way—her eyes were bloodshot and her chin had a few scars. She was also in desperate need of a haircut; her fine bangs hung over her eyes.

"Dr. Burnham, do you really think a flock of birds is important enough to risk human lives for?"

Lois gasped and sputtered but finally found words. "Colonel, *it's the last flock.* We're not talking about the value of a human life versus the value of a penguin life. We're talking about a human life—one of seven *billion*—versus their *whole species*!"

"That's right, Dad."

Lois turned away and looked out a window. Reed saw her wipe a tear from her weathered cheek. Mercy, he thought. He almost found himself looking forward to the stuffy boardroom full of overweight men waiting for him back at camp. The negotiators from ICARE's foreign quadrants would be ruthless and tricky in their efforts to make his country shoulder the entire financial burden of replacing Amery Station, which had been the United States' primary contribution to Antarctic development, but at least they wouldn't be so emotional.

Before leaving, Reed asked why they had broken down at this location, which was not on a marked trail. "I was driving above the subglacial ridge across the mouth of the basin," Lois explained. "Just in case the ice had thinned over the lake." She showed him a map that convinced him they were above the narrow strip of dry land between the Warner Basin lake and the Ross Sea.

Since he could think of no apparent danger over the subglacial ridge, Reed decided to take both of the ICARE tractors into Amery Station but leave Angie and Lois in their disabled vehicle, along with the busy mechanic. If anything happened to one of the tractors at the station, he reasoned, they would need the other tractor to make a hasty retreat or call for help.

CHAPTER 7

Return to Amery Station

Reed slowed the green-and-yellow tractor to a crawl as he drove in among the quiet wreckage of Amery Station. A solemn hush fell over his passengers, as if they feared that ghosts might overhear them. The subglacial eruption was now audible over the engine, even inside the insulated cabin. It was the deepest rumble he had ever heard, as if the vibrations were transmitted directly through the tractor's huge tires and into his skull from his seat.

The low buildings at the perimeter seemed unharmed. That was good news—everything in them could be recovered, even the construction steel. But looking up from the buildings, he saw two ruined wellhead derricks looming in the distant twilight. The white framework towers were leaning against each other, seemingly on the verge of falling, like the Leaning Tower of Pisa. Several struts were torn and bent downward on both platforms. Reed doubted that anything at all could be salvaged from the devastated monuments, at least not safely. Swallowing hard, he glanced back at Marshall and Lim, who were staring out through their tiny windows with expressions of awe and grief.

Dr. Corcoros wore a wicked grin. "When you screw with mother nature, sometimes she screws you back double."

"How thick did you say this ice is?" Reed asked.

"Forty yards," Marshall said. "Don't worry. It might as well be solid ground."

Reed recalled that the disaster had been caused by the well pipes losing their buoyancy, not by thin ice cracking. That made him feel better about driving the five-ton tractor beside a hole so large that a structure the size of a skyscraper had been compressed and dragged down through it. Nevertheless, he gave the hole a wide berth, afraid a sudden wind change could blow the tractor into it. Also, deep grooves—some deep enough to wreck the tractor—radiated across the ice from the hole. Reed surmised that the jagged trenches had been gouged out by pieces of steel protruding from the missing platform as it was compacted inward.

"We should check the turbines," Lim said. "They are the most valuable parts."

Reed followed their directions to one of the long low turbine houses. Marshall got out, opened a garage door, and motioned both tractors to drive inside. As he rolled through the door and the lavender-blue sky disappeared, Reed shot a last suspicious glance at the two leaning steam-well towers that soared nearly to the zenith beside the turbine house.

Corcoros commandeered the pink vehicle and drove it back out to take some photos and scientific measurements.

Marshall closed the garage door to shut out the wind. The sprocket chain of a counterweight on the heavy door made a loud ratcheting sound that echoed through the dark cavernous enclosure. He then took a large black garbage bag from a supply locker at the rear of the tractor and handed it to Reed as he stepped out. "ECW gear."

Reed upended the garbage bag over the driver's seat and a pile of multicolored clothing fell out. "ECW?"

"Extreme cold weather," Marshall explained. "It's as chilly in here as it is outside. When the air is this cold and dry, it will eventually freeze you to death no matter how much you wear, because you still end up heating and humidifying the air you breathe."

Reed had on no outer layers except the gray-and-white camouflage battle dress uniform he had worn during his flight. The cotton-poly fabric was heavy, designed for polar operations, but nothing compared to the mound of insulation Marshall had given him. "It can't be lower than absolute zero," he grumbled as he donned the quilted parka, snow pants, and large white bunny boots, but he had to admit that the air inside the turbine house was harsh on his lungs and most likely the coldest he had ever breathed.

Once he was encased like an astronaut, Reed curiously examined the dull blue-green domes of the turbine housing, which stretched away as far as the tractor's headlights could penetrate the indoor darkness. The housing was a series of long metal cylinders lying on their sides, half submerged in the ice floor. Some segments in the cylinder train were larger than others. All of them dwarfed the bulky vehicle.

Lim gently spread his gloved palm on the first cylinder and mumbled something in Chinese, his eyes closed.

"What's he saying?" Reed whispered to Marshall.

"Probably a prayer of thanks that we didn't lose the turbines. Their blades are made of a tough titanium alloy that costs a fortune to machine, and they're plated with a thick layer of gold to protect them from corrosive gases in the geothermal steam."

*   *   *

Pavros Corcoros drove through the wreckage of the brand-new, state-of-the-art, custom-built power plant, gawking at the sheer scale of the destruction and marveling at the folly of overambitious politicians and engineers. Finally he found what he was looking for, one of the empty well holes. His plan was to take the lake's temperature. Just like a doctor with a feverish infant, he thought as he stepped out into the brutal wind.

He knew the eruption was bound to have heated the lake water to some extent, probably less than one degree Celsius. By measuring the temperature rise and estimating the lake's volume, and correcting for losses due to melting of the floating ice, he could calculate the total quantity of heat the eruption had spewed out, and thus the amount of lava.

He tethered himself to the tractor's door with a long orange climbing rope. Marshall and Lim had taught him that anyone venturing out on the ice sheet alone should tie on to something heavy, in case he fell and the wind sent him sliding. Corcoros could just imagine his rotund frame spinning out of control across the vast smooth plain, maybe all the way to the Ross Sea. In addition to the tether, he wore crampons on his boots, steel frames sporting ten triangular spikes that protruded down from the soles to grip the ice like claws.

As he retrieved the mile-long reel of thin wire he would use to lower an electronic thermometer into the lake, he noticed something odd about the well hole. Its chipped, notched, and beveled lips seemed to glisten in the diffuse predawn twilight, as if the ice were wet. That couldn't be, Corcoros thought. The air temperature was no more than minus twenty Fahrenheit—over fifty degrees below freezing.

He staggered toward the dark, thirty-foot-wide pit, leaning backward to balance the heavy cylinder of thermometer wire atop his round belly. Breathing hard with exertion, he caught an unexpected whiff of a foul odor, like rotten eggs.

The smooth glistening of the ice around the hole did not disappear as he got closer. It was certainly no mirage. A few feet from the pit, he found himself stepping onto the ice that looked wet. He leaned over, balancing precariously between the weight of the wire drum and the force of the frigid wind slamming against his backside. Holding the drum under one arm, he reached out with the other and rubbed his gloved fingers across the glistening ice.

"Oh my God," Corcoros whispered.

Reed took a clipboard from Marshall and helped his team inventory the equipment stored in wire mesh cages along the walls of the turbine house. They had been working for only a few minutes when a loud groan echoed through the enclosure. It was like a heavy old door creaking, Reed thought, except amplified and slowed to a lower frequency.

The groan was followed by eerie silence, except for the now-familiar rumble of the eruption spewing lava into the lake far below them. Reed looked around. All of the men had stopped working. They were listening, he realized.

"What *was* that?" he whispered, beaming his flashlight up at Marshall's chin. The black foreman's stubbly face looked grimly concerned. He just pressed a long forefinger to his lips.

The groan came again, this time accompanied by a series of sharp pops.

Reed felt a tremor in the floor.

"In the tractor!" Marshall yelled. "Move!"

*   *   *

The ice beneath Dr. Corcoros jerked to the left, and he fell to the right. When he landed he dropped the heavy cylinder of wire, and it rolled into the well hole. Watching it accelerate, he realized that the ice here was sloping downward in that direction.

And that the ice really was wet.

And that the wind was blowing toward the hole.

Corcoros panicked. If he had not, he would have simply grabbed hold of the segment of his orange rope tether extending between the tractor and the coil of slack by his feet. But instead he scrabbled at the wet ice with both hands and both feet, frantically trying to stand up. All he could think about was getting a grip with his crampons again. Then it wouldn't matter how slippery the surface below was.

Meanwhile, the ice was still shaking, making it impossible for him to balance.

By the time he realized his mistake, it was too late. He had slid too far to reach the slack coils. He abandoned his attempts to stand up and grabbed the end of the rope tied around his waist, then began hysterically jerking the rope through his hands, trying to get rid of the slack and get a grip on the rope close enough to the tractor to arrest his skid.

At the moment the rope finally lifted from the ice, taut between his hands and the tractor door, his heavy legs fell into the hole and he lost his shifting grip.

Marshall ran to the garage door in the side of the turbine house and yanked it up. Reed jumped into the driver's seat of the green tractor. The groaning noise coming from the ice got louder. Marshall lunged into a backseat along with Lim and the three rig workers as Reed began backing up.

The noises from the ice had increased in pitch and

volume to become a squeaking, popping, grinding stridulation.

They sped out into the twilight, accelerating in reverse. "Turn around!" Marshall shouted.

Reed twisted the helm and hit the brake. The tractor skidded sideways. He shifted to first gear as it whipped around. Fighting to straighten the tractor's fishtail wobble, he heard a loud screech of bare metal on metal. At first he thought his sliding Y-turn had damaged the tractor, maybe warped an axle or a universal joint.

Then he realized the sound was coming from outside. "What's going on?" he shouted, peering out and wishing his windshield were not so narrow.

"The ice is cracking," Lim said. "The last two platforms must be— Oh Jesus!"

Reed hit the brake and glanced back. Lim was staring out his tiny window, his breath fogging the glass, cursing continuously in Chinese. Marshall leaned across the engineer's lap to look out another window on the same side. Following their example, Reed leaned to look out the front passenger window.

The two white framework well towers were swaying back and forth against the dim stars and the dark blue sky, like skyscrapers in an earthquake. They were also *twisting,* Reed realized, as if trying to twine around each other. Then one of the bent spars entangling the leaning towers broke loose, and he realized that the towers were actually pulling apart from each other.

"What are you doing?" Lim shouted. Reed had nearly stopped the tractor. "Go! Now! Fast!"

"Go, Tom," Marshall added.

Reed tore his gaze from the dancing towers and hit the accelerator. All eight tires spun for a moment, whining and pelting the wheel wells with ice chips. Then the tractor accelerated forward, pressing the passengers back in their seats.

Reed glanced in his side-view mirror just in time to see one of the massive towers topple like a felled sequoia. The sheer scale made the spidery monument seem to descend in slow motion. It finally slammed down across the middle of the turbine house. Many of the tower's framework struts broke apart on impact. Aluminum roof panels from the demolished turbine house whipped through the air. Reed also saw a flicker of something gold spinning away in an arc. The noise was incredible, a prolonged roaring crash that vibrated the whole tractor.

"No!" Lim moaned.

"Where's the other tower?" Reed asked. The ice was still groaning and popping all around them.

"I can't see it," Marshall said.

"You want me to turn?"

"No. You'll spin out at this speed."

Reed continued accelerating toward the other end of the station, returning the way they had come. Buildings and dark, empty well holes whizzed past on both sides. In his mirror, he saw the tangled remains of the fallen tower sliding backward, dragging pieces of the turbine house with it.

"I see the other tower!" Marshall shouted. "It's falling, too."

"Which way?"

"*This* way!" Lim yelled.

Reed saw a fuzzy shadow of framework struts stretching across the ice behind his speeding tractor, coming closer. The shadow briefly overtook them, pulling ahead by a few yards, then pulled back. The tower crashed down behind them, shaking the ice. Huge shards of red glass were flung forward past them, overhead and on both sides. Reed surmised that they were pieces of the tower's aircraft warning beacon as chunks of flying debris crashed into the tractor.

"Faster," Marshall yelled.

We're already going too fast, Reed thought. If he lost control, they could easily skid across the ice and plow into one of the surrounding buildings. Or plunge into a well hole. "Why?" he shouted. "Both towers are already down."

"Because something else is coming!" Lim shrieked.

CHAPTER 8

Icequake

At first Corcoros thought he had landed on a ledge inside the well hole. The impact was that solid. It knocked out all of his breath. Then every pain receptor in his skin fired at once, burning out circuits in his brain with the ultimate physical agony. With his ability to perceive pain saturated, it could not have hurt any worse if he had fallen into a blast furnace full of molten slag.

Yet the pain somehow increased when he opened his mouth to scream and liquid fire poured down his throat. The boiling water gurgled its way into his ear canals, filling his head with the last sound he would ever hear. In the moments before his optic nerves melted, he saw the water churning all around him as bursting bubbles released tendrils of condensed steam that danced upward above him like souls of the dead departing for heaven.

Even though he was in agony, with his senses severed, his mind still functioned partially—well enough to realize he was being boiled alive. He flailed around for his tether. His skin could sense no texture, nor could it feel the coldness of the ice wall. But his arm detected pressure when it hit the hanging rope.

He pulled off his gloves to improve his grip.

He grabbed hold and began to climb, in complete darkness and silence. He had coughed out the fire, and now he could breathe, but just barely, and he could feel his breath catching in his throat, dragging and rattling. Despite his flabby bulk, his arms were strong enough to pull his own weight up the rope, as long as he kept his crampon-clad feet walking up the vertical wall of ice in front of him.

He was completely out of the water—he was sure of that, because the pain all over his body had been replaced by total numbness—when he felt his grip slipping. At first he thought his fingers were sliding down the rope. Then he realized that the flesh on his palms was adhering to the rope perfectly, perhaps freezing fast in the subzero air, but the boiled skin of his hands was slipping away from the bones.

Although Corcoros could hear nothing, he could feel himself screaming as he fell back into the boiling cauldron.

Reed shifted his gaze back and forth between his side-view mirrors. He noticed that the first tower to fall had completely disappeared, but he could see no movement behind the tractor. Then the terrible sound of splitting ice abruptly grew louder, and he saw a crack zigzagging across the ice sheet from behind them, heading straight for the tractor. Before he could begin to turn, the crack shot forward between the wheels and continued on in front of them, propagating along the rutted road at hundreds of miles per hour.

The ice sheet was shuddering, bouncing Reed's tractor around as if he were driving along a fault in the middle of an earthquake. At first he had feared that the ice would pull apart and dump them into the subglacial lake, but the two sides of the crack remained flush against each other. The only reason he could see the crack at all was its vertical offset—the right side was gradually climbing higher than the left side, with an earsplitting symphony of squeaks.

"Oh no, oh no, oh no!" Lim chanted as the tractor tilted up on the right and down on the left.

"Hang on!" Reed shouted. "I'll try to turn left and get us off this—"

"No!" Marshall yelled. "Look." His long arm pointed past Reed's shoulder to the line of empty well holes on their left. The black pits were easily large enough to swallow the tractor if Reed lost control when his right wheels bounced down from the scarp.

"Hey, there's the other tractor," Reed said. "Where's Corcoros?"

The fault's vertical offset was still increasing. When the green tractor was tilted at a forty-five-degree angle, it began wobbling with the temptation to roll onto its left side. Reed began losing control of the wheel and decided to turn left despite Marshall's warning. At least he would have a chance to maintain control if he could keep the machine upright.

As the right wheels were about to drop from the sharp edge of the scarp, the painful squeaking abruptly ceased. Reed held his breath and stopped turning left. The tractor was not tilting any farther. Fighting for control, he eased to the right until the right tires were firmly back in place on the higher ice slab.

The icequake was over.

The fault's offset declined as they drove along it, gently lowering the tractor's right side until the crack disappeared behind them.

Marshall exhaled a sigh of relief. "Ease up, Tom. I think we're in the clear."

Reed whipped the tractor into a controlled skidding about-face, sweating cascades inside his ECW suit. "Not until we get Corcoros and get the hell out of here."

Reed saw the orange climbing rope as he approached the pink tractor. He traced it with his eyes, across the ice from the open driver's door to the well hole. The rope was straight but not taut, which meant that Corcoros was not using it to rappel on the wall of the pit. "He's in trouble," Reed said.

He let the tractor skid to a halt, then ran to the well hole. When he saw that the ice around the rim was wet, he knew that he could not safely get close enough to see Corcoros. He grabbed the rope and began reeling in slack. At first the rope was stiff with ice, which meant it had been in the water. Then suddenly the rope was limp and wet.

And steaming.

Reed tried to pull up the weight at the end of the rope but could not get enough purchase on the ice without crampons. Then Marshall and Lim arrived, wearing their spikes, and Reed helped out by bracing his feet against theirs. Within a few seconds, they had dragged the sopping, steaming remains of Pavros Corcoros from the boiling subglacial lake.

Reed had seen grizzly pictures of victims from all kinds of weapons, from napalm to nuclear blasts, but he had never seen anything like this. The man was bloated, pulpy, and covered with a reptilian pattern of patches that were grotesquely pale, almost bone white. Between the patches his skin was bright pink. His eyes were swollen shut, and his nose was bleeding. Most of his beard had fallen out, leaving clumps of long strands here and there.

The body twitched.

"He's breathing!" Marshall yelled. "We have to help him."

They tried to pick Corcoros up, but he twisted and lurched in their grasp, falling back onto the ice. Before they could try again, he rolled onto all fours and rose up on his knees, moving his head back and forth as if he were trying to see through the lobes of swollen flesh enclosing his eyes. His breath was a rasping gurgle. His burned, wet body was shivering wildly. He reached out, blindly groping for human contact.

Marshall stepped forward and clasped one of the grotesquely bloated hands. Corcoros grunted like a deaf-mute, then squealed like a pig. His jaws flexed, his Adam's apple bobbed up and down, and pale pink froth bubbled from his lips.

"He's trying to say something!" Reed gasped.

Corcoros snatched Marshall's pants leg with his free hand, then transferred the hand Marshall was holding to the tall foreman's belt. He continued climbing until he could reach up and grab Marshall's shirt. Marshall glanced at Reed, his eyes full of horror and confusion.

Corcoros ran one hideously swollen and gnarled hand back and forth over Marshall's chest until it came to rest on a ballpoint pen in his shirt pocket. Corcoros grabbed the pen and let go of Marshall, falling back to the ice at his feet.

He began to scratch at the ice with the pen.

"He's writing something!" Reed said.

"Lim, go get a blanket," Marshall said.

Lim ran to the tractors.

Reed and Marshall stooped over the hideously injured geologist and watched him write. Corcoros was shivering uncontrollably, and as his strength waned, his writing became more and more illegible. Reed and Marshall argued over each letter as they tried to decipher the dying man's last message.

Marshall gave up and tried to drag Corcoros toward the tractors. The blind and disfigured professor fought him off with a phlegmy snarl and a punch that barely missed his groin. The writing continued until what appeared to be twelve huge letters were scratched in the ice:

CAVVVOTHAIRF

Then Corcoros's increasingly difficult breaths became whistling, shrieking spasms and he collapsed on his back, his swollen face turning purplish.

Reed helped Marshall drag the gasping burn victim toward the pink tractor. "Get him out of here. Head straight for the base. I'll detour to the stranded tractor."

"His message must be important," Lim said. "Do you know what it means?"

"No idea," Reed said. "Maybe we read it wrong."

Reed held the accelerator pedal on the floor as he sped between the sheet-steel buildings at the station's outskirts. He watched the dashboard tachometer and shifted up whenever the needle neared the redline at five thousand revolutions per minute. The ten-liter engine roared like a launching rocket, and the deep tire treads hummed on the smooth ice.

He called ahead and found out the mechanic—Steve something—had not yet fixed Lois's old snow tractor. Reed told him to pack up.

"I wish I didn't have to just abandon it here," Lois said when he arrived. "This little machine and I have been through a lot together."

"Trust me, lady, you ain't losing nothing," Steve said

once they were under way in the green tractor. The mechanic was a small, frail man—at least by Reed's standards—about Angie's height and with a similar build. Reed got the impression that he was not more than thirty-five, despite his wrinkled, gaunt, acne-pocked complexion and the big saggy circles around his eyes. He looks like some kind of long-term junkie, Reed thought. Especially his haunted eyes. Maybe he had just lived and worked in Antarctica too long.

Reed saw Lois's hurt expression and whispered to her. "I'll try to get enough added to your budget for you to buy a new one." That made her smile, a little.

They continued driving above the subglacial ridge, following Lois's navigation. Reed considered going slower for safety but decided their best bet was to vacate the basin as soon as possible. It was 2:45 P.M., and the civil twilight seemed almost gone. He kept a lookout for crevasses on the left—where the ice sheet descended to the Ross Sea—or for faults and steam over the subglacial lake to the right, but he saw neither.

Reed told them about the bizarre message Corcoros had scrawled and asked if they had any idea what it could mean. Lois and Angie were obviously too weary from their ordeal in the stranded tractor to do their best sleuthing, but they grew quiet, apparently pondering the riddle.

"If I thought I was dying," Steve said, "I'd just write those three special words to my wife. If I had a wife."

"Maybe it was some kind of medical alert," Reed said. "Or something to do with his will. Or confession of a crime. Could be just about any—"

A loud alarm began beeping from a speaker in the ceiling. Reed frantically scanned the dashboard for an indication of what was wrong.

Angie lunged forward from the backseat, pointing to a

blinking red LED on the most remote corner of the control panel. "It's the crevasse detector!" she shouted.

Reed said, "The *what*?"

"Did you turn on the detector?" Lois asked.

"I didn't know there *was* such a thing," Reed said. "It must have already been on when I started driving." He looked at the crevasse detector's control panel. As he watched, the dark window of its digital display came to life with glowing red characters: RANGE 180 METERS.

"Uh-oh," Angie said.

Reed said, "Lois, are you sure we're still over the subglacial ridge?"

"Absolutely." She flipped a switch that killed the alarm.

"And you're positive that the ice over the ridge has no crevasses?" She had assured him of this when they briefly discussed what route to take back to ICARE.

"None whatsoever. The detector must be malfunctioning, or picking up something other than a crevasse."

"Like what?"

Lois shrugged. "Who knows?"

"I've heard these things are surprisingly reliable," Steve said.

The digital characters blinked and changed to RANGE 140 METERS. Reed had started braking when the alarm went off. Now he pressed on the brake pedal as hard as he could without skidding—he knew the stopping distance would be even greater if the wheels locked up. "Are you sure it's not a false alarm? How does it work?"

"It's like a radar," Steve said. "It looks for the boundary between air and ice. But we don't work on them— they come in a complete assembly when we replace one—so I couldn't tell you if it's on the fritz."

The detector's display switched to RANGE 100 METERS.

"Dad, you'd better stop."

"I *am* stopping!"

RANGE 80 METERS.

"Don't slam on the brakes," Lois warned. "You'll skid."

RANGE 70 METERS.

Reed slammed on the brakes. There was no use trying to avoid a skid—he could see that the tractor was not going to stop in the next seventy meters, no matter what he did.

RANGE 60 METERS.

"There's nothing out there!" Reed yelled. The tractor's skidding deceleration was leaning him forward against his seat harness, giving him as good a view as possible through the narrow windshield in the fading twilight.

RANGE 40 METERS.

They held their breath and watched the detector count down. It paused a little longer before each ten-meter update.

RANGE 20 METERS.

"You're right," Lois said. "There's no snow here to hide a crevasse, and I don't see so much as a pothole that could be within twenty meters."

"Me neither," Angie said.

RANGE 10 METERS. The glowing red characters began to blink. Reed clenched his teeth but kept his eyes open.

The detector went blank.

A second later, the tractor finally stopped.

No one spoke. They listened for any unusual sounds over the idling engine and the wind humming around the tractor body. They looked out at the lavender-blue dusk. The icy waste appeared unbroken, placid, eternal.

"Malfunction," Lois pronounced. "Maybe the variable topography of the subglacial ridge threw it off, or just a slight dip in—"

She was interrupted by an eerie groan that seemed to come from directly beneath the tractor. Reed recognized the sound—it was similar to the first noise he had heard before the icequake at Amery Station. And like that other, louder groan, it was followed by an accelerating sequence of staccato pops.

Reed shifted to first and floored it.

All eight of the tires spun against the ice, pummeling the metal wheel wells with ice chips dug up by the treads.

Come on! Catch hold!

Reed was caught off guard by the unexpected sensation of free fall. He got the briefest perceptible glimpse of the ice crumbling all around the tractor; then the blue gloom of the Warner Basin was replaced by a rough, angular, vertical surface of fractured glacial ice that appeared to zoom upward past the tractor's hood, illuminated by the headlights. Of course he knew from the fact that he was floating weightless against his seat belts that the tractor was actually plummeting downward into some kind of trap hidden within the ice sheet.

Reed looked back at his screaming daughter with only one thought: If this crash gets you, Pumpkin, I hope it gets me too.

CHAPTER 9

White Water

"Just tell me one thing," Marshall said as he drove the pink tractor at top speed toward the ICARE base. "How in the world can water be boiling when it's in constant contact with ice?"

Lim was looking over his shoulder at Dr. Corcoros, who was prostrate in the backseat, groaning, wheezing, and feebly squirming a little as he slipped in and out of consciousness. They had radioed the base and asked if the rescue helicopter could meet them, but the chopper was already on its way to a vehicle accident three hundred miles in the opposite direction. The amount of traffic on the ice cap and Antarctica's dangerous primitive roads had more than quadrupled since the power outage, as backup fuel was redistributed and refugees fled from outposts with no source of heat at all.

"The water heated by lava must be rising swiftly below the station in a smooth column," Lim replied, "not mixing much with the cold water around it until it hits the ice and spreads out."

"So most of the lake is still cold?" Marshall asked.

"I would think," Lim said. "Otherwise, we would see

clouds forming over the basin from steam escaping through cracks in the floating ice."

"But the water was boiling even at the surface in that well hole, *surrounded by ice,*" Marshall protested. "That seems almost . . . supernatural."

"No," Lim said. "Under one atmosphere of pressure, the boiling point of water is a hundred degrees Celsius, two twelve Fahrenheit. But where it quenches the lava at the bottom of the lake, the water starts out much hotter than that. The boiling point increases more than two degrees Celsius per meter of depth because of the increased pressure, so the hot water could cool at that rate as it rises and still boil when it reaches the surface."

"So the water is rising in the middle of the lake and going back down at the edges after it cools?" Marshall said. "I wonder how fast it's melting the floating ice."

"Hard to say," Lim mused. "I would guess maybe a meter or two per hour. But it probably is melting faster in some places than others. Spots where the ice was already a little thinner will collect steam and the hottest water, and that will make them melt faster than the rest."

"Do you think that's what caused the vertical fault that almost flipped our tractor?" Marshall asked.

"Yes," Lim said. "The ice is melting fastest directly above the eruption. As the thinnest ice loses support from below, it's held up only by the surrounding layer. Eventually, rings of vertical faults will form, allowing the thinner ice to drop downward until it's floating again."

"The lake can't just keep soaking up heat forever," Marshall said. "What if all the water starts to boil before the ice is gone? Or is that impossible?"

"It's impossible for every *drop* of the lake to reach the boiling point with ice still on it," Lim said. "There will always be a layer of cool meltwater adjacent to the ice.

But if the eruption continues I would not be surprised if most of the lake is boiling hot before the ice melts away. In a sense, the ice may actually be insulating the lake from the atmosphere, preventing the deep water from cooling by mixing and evaporation."

"So what happens when the ice is all gone and the water is free to mix and turn over at the surface?"

"Steam," Lim replied. "A lot of steam will shoot up into the air."

The impact was not as painful as Reed had expected. His forehead smacked the steering wheel. Then his head flopped back against his seat, but not hard enough to sprain his neck. He knew what had cushioned the tractor's fall when water splashed across the narrow rectangular windshield.

"Angie?" he croaked, fumbling for his harness buckle. He turned around on his knees.

She was staring at him, wide-eyed. Her lips were pale and trembling. Her voice was gone, but she mouthed the words, "I'm okay, Dad."

They heard a moan and looked at Lois. She was crumpled on the floor in front of the front passenger seat, holding both hands to the left side of her head. Reed sprang from his seat, noticing a bloody splotch of fine blond hair on the intact window above her. Kneeling at her side, he tried to pry one of her hands away. "What happened?"

"What does it look like?" Lois snapped. He could hear the pain in her voice. Blood oozed between her fingers, and tears leaked from her closed eyelids.

Angie unbuckled her harness and slid into the seat above Lois. "Let me see." Lois removed her bloody hands from the injury. Angie sucked in her breath when she leaned forward and pulled the matted hair back above her mentor's left ear. "I'll get the kit," she said as she walked back along the central aisle, stooping beneath the tractor's low roof.

Reed dug a clean tissue from his pocket and handed it to Lois. Instead of pressing it to the wound, she blew her nose. "I'm sorry," she said.

Reed watched bright red blood seep through her fine hair. At least it wasn't a real gusher, and he could see no obvious indentation in her skull. He placed a hand lightly on her trembling shoulder. "This is no time to worry about manners."

Reed looked back at the mechanic, who sat stooped over with his face in his hands. "Steve? You all right?"

"Yeah, as long as I don't have to get out and walk."

"Your legs got hurt?"

"No, my pants got wet. I'd freeze out there."

Reed looked out the windshield. So far, his attention had been on his passengers because the tractor was no longer falling; nor was water gushing in, at least not where he could see it. Feeling the cabin sway and seeing the white waves sloshing against the hood, he realized the tractor was floating. It's a good thing these vehicles are built airtight to keep out the cold, he thought.

The weight of the engine held the front end down, tilting the cabin floor at about fifteen degrees. The engine had died, but all four headlights were still burning underwater. Their beams struck the white ice of the stream bed and reflected an eerie, diffuse glow up into the air around the tractor.

The vehicle was floating down a swift subglacial river. About half of the roughly round tunnel appeared to be filled with the surging flood. The arching roof was smooth, glistening, dripping meltwater. Reed knew that the water and the ice should have been white or blue, but for some reason everything he saw looked slightly pinkish.

"The lake must be overflowing," Lois groaned.

Angie returned, lugging a white plastic suitcase with a fat red cross on each side. She opened the first-aid kit on the seat beside Lois, glanced at the contents, and said, "Oh my."

Reed peered over her shoulder. Every cubic inch inside the case was precisely filled with some gadget or container. Two large compartments were labeled FROST-BITE and HYPOTHERMIA. He picked up a small bottle of pills. A finely printed leaflet was attached to the bottle with a rubber band. The front page of the leaflet read AL-TITUDE SICKNESS. He tossed the bottle on the seat and dug down past the sunburn ointment, blister pads, and eyedrops for snow blindness. "Where the heck is the bump-on-the-head stuff?"

They finally found some disinfectant, gauze, tape, and five-hundred-milligram ibuprofen tablets. As they prepared the bandages, Lois said, "Jeez, Tom, you're hurt worse than me!"

"What?" He wondered if she was delusional.

"Your face is all bloody," she said. "And your collar."

Reed swiped at his face and chin, then looked at his bloody sleeve. Apparently his head had hit the steering wheel harder than he'd thought. He reached up and felt the ragged, tender edges of a long gash between his eyes. Now that his adrenaline was not surging so strongly, he was also beginning to feel the stinging pain.

At least the laceration explained why everything looked pink—blood in his eyes. "It's just a scratch," he said. "Shouldn't need more than five or six stitches. Scalp wounds always bleed a lot—yours will too."

Lois finally tried to crawl back up into her seat. Her legs trembled. Reed reached out his hand, and she took

it, allowing him to give her a boost. Her hand was cold
and trembling, but he didn't want to let go of it.

"It's getting hotter," Angie said.

"Humid too," Steve said.

Lois pressed her palm against the windshield, leaving
a bloody print. "The water must be warm, like the water
Dr. Corcoros fell in."

"Doesn't look like it's boiling," Reed said.

"It couldn't be boiling," Lois said. "It's surrounded by
ice and there's no heat source here. But it could still be
plenty hot. It must be coming from the lake, and flowing
at this speed it wouldn't cool much by the time it got
here."

"Where do you think we're going?" Steve asked.

"To the ocean," Lois said, her voice quavering with
pain. "But we'll probably never get there. The farther we
go from the lake, the cooler the water will be. This tube
will get smaller because the water is not melting the ice
as fast. Eventually the ceiling will close in and we'll be
completely submerged."

Reed looked at Angie. He did not need Lois to tell
him what would happen to the tractor after that.

Both headlights on the left side of the floating snow
tractor winked out at once. "Flashlights!" Reed shouted.

He and Angie found eight battery-powered headlamps
in the tractor's locker of emergency supplies. Before
they could distribute them, the other two headlights went
out, plunging the cabin into total darkness. "Oh man, I
hate the dark," Steve said. "That's the worst thing about
Antarctica. I mean I don't just hate it. I really, *really*—"

Reed snapped on one of the headlamps and handed it
to the mechanic. "Oh, whew, thanks," Steve said.

The tractor lurched sideways and a squeaking noise
filled the cabin. Reed and Angie were thrown to the
right. They grabbed an overhead bar of the exposed

heavy-duty roll cage. The squeaking and lurching continued.

"I guess we've hit the ceiling," Angie said, looking up.

Reed gave Lois a headlamp, then held his own up to the windshield so the beam would shine out. The water had risen almost to the top of the glass. "You were right," he said to Lois. "The roof is closing in, squeezing us down into the water."

"Once the air is completely gone, pressure will start to increase," Lois said. "This vehicle floats, but it's not a submarine. Water will squeeze in through the door gaskets, or pressure will build up until the windshield implodes and it hits us all at once."

Steve moaned, shining his headlamp into the clear water outside his submerged window.

They waited in silence. Reed held Angie's hand. Lois held her bandaged head. The squeaking noise and Steve's moans of fright continued.

Then the squeaking stopped. So did the sound of waves lapping against the tractor's body. Steve stopped moaning and held his breath. Reed could hear his own drumming pulse in the silent cabin.

"Here it comes!" Angie yelled as a fountain of water gushed upward from the base of the driver's door. It was joined by other pressurized streams squirting toward the middle of the door from the top and both sides.

"Get up on the seats, away from the doors," Lois said. "We may get out of this yet, but only if we stay dry. Anyone who's wet will freeze to death in minutes if we have to get out and walk."

They squatted on the seats, puncturing the lime-green vinyl with their crampons, which they had already donned in case they got a chance to climb out. The water was several inches deep before it started to gush in around the passenger door. Then the flood crept toward the seats twice as fast. Reed felt pressure in his ears and yawned to relieve it. As the cabin flooded with water, its air was being compressed.

"Well, I guess it was nice meeting you all," Steve said.

Angie reached across the aisle and held his trembling hand.

The fountains kept squirting in faster until there was nowhere the doomed tractor's occupants could go to escape the ricochets of lukewarm spray.

CHAPTER 10

Maelstrom

There were no paramedics or orderlies to admit Dr. Corcoros to the ICARE infirmary. Marshall and Lim had to carry the huge man in from the pink tractor by themselves. Even with the help of other rig workers, Corcoros slipped from their grasp twice. Partially liquefied fat slithered around beneath his bloated skin, making him nearly as difficult to grip as a spilled raw egg.

The infirmary was a nexus of pure chaos, surrounded by bedlam in the closest rooms and corridors, then skirted by mere confusion and impatience in the outlying areas of the ICARE base. Refugees from outposts with no power had swelled the patient admission rate to ten times what the infirmary was designed to handle. Marshall and Lim had to wade through a rank and noisy gridlock of human misery with Corcoros's inert bulk before they could even get the attention of a triage nurse, who helped them skip line without fisticuffs.

The partially cooked geologist was still alive, barely, when he was finally given a space to lie on the floor while the doctor intubated him with a pure oxygen ventilator and started an antibiotic IV. Fortunately, the ICU equipment needed to sustain his remaining thread of life was not in high demand—the vast majority of the patients awaiting treatment had only minor injuries from accidents following the loss of power and the unfamiliar activities that ensued.

The sweaty, stubbly, exhausted doctor took a break to count off the top complaints on his fingers for Marshall. "The most common problem is first- and second-degree burns, from handling gasoline stoves. Then we've had a lot of minor frostbite. No excuse for that—these guys just get careless when something like this happens. War mentality. There have been quite a few vehicle accidents and violent altercations, even a rise in food poisoning from lack of proper cooking facilities. Let's see— assorted bruises, breaks, and scrapes from blundering around in the dark. Now we're starting to see the first pneumonias from long-term cold exposure. Those will get a lot worse if we don't get more fuel soon or get these people out of here. And I don't need to tell you what a tragedy it would be if a candle or stove tipped over and started a fire in this hellhole."

One of the primary rationales for building Amery Station had been public safety. In the extremely dry air and constant high winds of Antarctica, structural fires were a more deadly threat than anywhere else in the world. Providing abundant electricity was one way to discourage cooking, heating, and lighting with open flames or combustible liquids.

Marshall showed the doctor a rumpled piece of paper on which he had written twelve capital letters: CAVVVOTHAIRF. "Do you know what this means? Corcoros wrote it after he was burned. Whatever it is, he thought it was urgent."

"Is it complete?" the doctor asked.

"I don't think so. He was still writing when he collapsed."

"Some kind of combination or security code, maybe. It can't be a word. No word has three *V*s in succession. Maybe it's some kind of phone number."

Marshall shook his head. "He would have just written the numbers. Believe me, he was trying to communicate, not throw us a riddle. I'm sure the letters are not meant to stand for something else, and they aren't scrambled. This *says* something, in English."

A haggard nurse tugged the doctor away.

Marshall and Lim headed for ICARE's radio room to call Colonel Reed, whom they did not expect to arrive at the base for another half hour. Perhaps he, or one of his passengers, had figured out what the strange cipher meant.

"Hey, I think I see a light outside!" Angie yelled.

The water in the tractor cabin was now lapping against the seat cushions. Spray was flying everywhere from the fountains gushing in around the doors, filling the cabin with splatters and hisses.

"Turn off your lights for a second," Lois said.

"No way," the mechanic whined.

Angie squeezed his hand. "Come on, Steve. Just a second."

With a groan, he flicked off his headlamp after the others. Before he flicked it back on a half second later, they clearly saw a dim spot of bluish light bobbing outside the tractor. "There!" Angie pointed. "It must be the end of the tunnel."

A few seconds later the submerged tractor began rotating back and forth, then spinning all the way around counterclockwise. "Hang on!" Reed yelled.

"I hope it doesn't roll upside down!" Angie said.

The tractor spun faster, causing the two feet of standing water to climb up the walls from centrifugal force until the outer ends of the bench seats were submerged.

Dim blue light suddenly surrounded the tractor. At the same time, it stopped spinning and bobbed upward. Water poured off the windshield, and they could see whitecapped waves all around them. "We're out of the tunnel!" Angie yelled.

"And in a canyon," Reed said, leaning over the flooded aisle to look up through the windshield.

The twilight was almost gone. The brightest stars were visible above the deep and narrow canyon. The steep walls were rough and angular, a patchwork of cleavage planes that met at various angles. "This is still part of the tunnel," Lois said. "The roof has just fallen in here."

"I guess we know now what probably happened to the first mechanic's tractor," Reed said. "He must have fallen through the ice somewhere back there like we did."

After several sharp bends and a reach of steep rapids that sloshed the water in the tractor and bounced its occupants around, the floating vehicle emerged from the canyon and came to rest on its tires. Reed opened his door long enough to drain the cabin, then climbed on the seats and poked his head out through the emergency hatch in the roof. The blue twilight was now so feeble that the half-moon had taken over as the brightest source of light, casting a broad halo in the thin ice clouds hurtling past it. The Milky Way arched overhead. The moisture on Reed's mucous membranes temporarily froze with each breath he inhaled.

At first he was facing upstream toward the mouth of the canyon. The narrow rift was flanked on both sides by steep piles of rubble, broken ice chunks ranging from the size of a snowball to that of a dump truck. The rubble slopes reached all the way up to the canyon rim, at least a hundred feet above the flat bench where the tractor sat in the middle of the stream delta.

The closest dry ice chunks were at least twenty feet away on both sides.

The canyon was disgorging a churning torrent of clear water that spread out and slowed on the delta, lazily undulating across the smooth ice and lapping around the tractor's tires. He could hear the stream's gurgles echoing from the canyon. He could also hear a deep throbbing roar that couldn't possibly be coming from the small stream, so he turned to look behind him, in the direction the stream was flowing.

What he saw made the source of the thundering roar obvious. It also quickened his breath and weakened his knees.

Reed grabbed the edges of the tractor's roof hatch, afraid his feet would slip from the seat backs as he gazed in terror at the vista opposite the mouth of the ice canyon. About a hundred feet downstream of the tractor, the flat delta ended at a sharp, straight precipice. The broad stream thinned to a smooth sheet in the last fifteen feet as the water accelerated and spilled over the edge. Turbulent swirls of ice mist billowed upward from the crashing waterfall below, catching the rays from the rising moon to form a broad arch of prismatic colors like a rainbow. The moonbow disappeared and reappeared as clouds of frozen spray wafted across it. Reed wondered how deep the chasm was, then realized it didn't matter. From the churning mist and the waterfall's thundering roar, the drop was obviously long enough that the tractor would be smashed like a run-over soda can if it lost its grip on the wet ice and plunged to the bottom.

Refocusing beyond the moonbow, Reed saw a sheer

ice wall towering above him on the far side of the chasm, at least six hundred feet away. At the bottom, the distant wall faded into the gloom before his view was truncated by the waterfall's lip. Higher up, the flat vertical surface was a deep cobalt blue, shaded from the rising moon by his side of the chasm. Above the shaded area, the vast glacial wall reflected stark white moonlight, shining almost as brightly as the moon itself, as if the Earth were also orbited by a pale band of ice.

There was a deep but narrow notch in the upper edge of the shadow on the distant ice wall. Reed realized it was the projection of the canyon mouth behind him. Within the notch, he could see the vague shadows of the falling water and billowing mist, moving like dancing phantoms. There was also an infinitesimal bump at the base of the notch—the shadow of the snow tractor.

He slowly lowered himself back into the cabin, careful not to dislodge the tractor by shaking it. Lois and Angie were looking at him expectantly. "What?" Angie said.

"Better see for yourselves, but I suggest you don't rock the tractor."

He eased himself into the driver's seat and tried the ignition key. Even the starter wouldn't turn over. He tried the radio. No response but static.

He heard Angie's voice from above the hatch. "Okay, this definitely sucks."

As she climbed down, Steve said, "No, don't tell me. I don't even want to know." He was slumped against the wet wall with a dejected expression.

Lois was looking out a window at the undulating waves that reflected tiny images of the half-moon all around the tractor. "Tom, it's getting deeper."

Reed started putting on his crampons.

"What are you doing?" Lois asked. "We can't wade to

the bank. Even if crampons will work underwater, it's deep enough now to get in our boots."

"Go take a look at what's going to happen when it gets deep enough for these big fat tires to float the tractor again."

Lois went back to look out the hatch.

Reed glared across the green hood at the rising water. There has to be a way to get to those infernal piles of rubble without getting wet, he thought.

"Maybe we could somehow use the winch," Steve said, without much enthusiasm.

The winch!

Lois was gingerly climbing down from the hatch when Reed reached it. Her dimply cheeks were streaked with frozen tears that melted within a second or two inside the cabin. She sat down beside Angie and hugged her. Reed saw that blood had soaked through her thick bandage.

Steve remained slumped with the same morose expression. "I guess God is still pissed about that weekend in Tijuana."

Reed gently climbed up through the hatch.

"Dad! Where are you going?"

"I'm going to get us out of here."

CHAPTER 11

Tightrope

Angie found a hacksaw in the tractor's tool locker. Reed used it to cut off the winch cable. He tied the severed end to one of the roll bars under the tractor's roof, then stood on the hood and hurled the cable's heavy hook into a hole in the rubble slope on the right side of the canyon's mouth. A hard tug on the cable confirmed that the hook was lodged securely.

Lois and Angie both shrieked in protest when he returned to the cabin and began deliberately shaking the tractor by swinging back and forth from one of the tubular crossbars of its exposed heavy-duty roll cage. Finally the tractor slipped until the cable pulled taut. "The slack would have dipped us in the water," he explained.

Lois stared along the straight cable, which rose at least twelve feet over a distance of about forty. Her tear-streaked face drooped in dismay. "Tom, Angie and I are not strong enough for that climb."

"What? Oh, I didn't expect you to swing up the cable by yourselves! I'll have to make two trips. Who's first?"

Lois looked down at the swift current that was jostling the tractor as it flowed around the bulging tires. In a few

minutes it would obviously be deep enough to float the
machine again. Her jaw trembled. "Take Angie."

Steve slowly sat back down. He had briefly stood to
watch Reed's throw, then looked along the cable as Lois
had. Reed glanced at the frail and weather-worn young
man and saw a tear slide down his left cheek.

Angie saw it too. "What's wrong?" she asked.

Steve shrugged. "I'm not strong enough to climb that
cable, either."

"So?" Reed said. "I'll make three trips."

Steve jumped up, eyes wide. "Really?"

"You thought I wouldn't?"

The gaunt mechanic shrugged again. "I believe in
evolution. You know, survival of the fittest. Besides, I
didn't really expect to survive this hellhole when I came
down here."

They had climbed onto the roof. Reed gripped the
cable with both hands and swung beneath it, crossing his
knees over the cable with his head aimed upslope.
"Climb on, Pumpkin."

Angie squatted on the roof by his feet. "How, Dad?"

"Facing me so you can get a good grip."

His elbows popped as Angie shifted her weight onto
him. Her light 110 pounds was well within the strength
limits of his gripping and pulling muscles, but he wasn't
sure about his endurance. He tilted his head back to look
up the cable, upside down, feeling the blood pressure increase in his face. "Hang on," he said. "We'll have to do
this fast."

Angie clinched her arms and legs around his torso. He
could hear her fast and fearful breathing beside his right
ear. He began to climb, dragging them hand over hand.
All he could do with his legs was help support their
weight. He looked down past Angie's frail shoulders and

saw Lois and Steve sitting by the cable, staring at the moonlit water.

Lois smiled and waved, then shouted, "Hurry up!" as if she were joking.

Halfway up the cable, Reed's swift climbing rhythm established a resonance that made him and Angie sway back and forth in increasingly wide arcs. Angie whimpered as the swaying began to tilt them up sideways, giving Reed alternating glimpses of the half-moon above and the dark water below, first on the right, then on the left, then right, then left. . . .

"I don't feel good," Angie moaned, her mouth an inch from his ear.

He kept going, ignoring the terrifying pendulation, afraid to slow down because he didn't know how much longer he could hang on. Then the cable swung so hard that he nearly lost his grip, and he finally paused to let the oscillation die down. He could feel his pulse pounding in his temples. Sweat had pooled on his eyelids.

A few seconds after he resumed climbing, his knuckles slammed against ice. "Can you get off?"

Angie swung around until she was draped over his torso crosswise. Her sharp elbows dug into his abdomen. She reached toward the slope with one foot.

"Hurry," he pleaded.

Then she was off him, and he dropped onto the narrow ledge he'd seen from the tractor. "Damn," he groaned, stretching his arms out above his head. His biceps were knotted in pain, and a strained muscle between his spine and left shoulder blade was twitching. He wiped sweat and blood from his brow. His surging pulse had started the split in his forehead bleeding into his eyes again.

"Tom, please hurry!" Lois shouted over the roar of the waterfall, with no feigned humor this time. The water was now up to the yellow stripe around the boxy frog-green tractor, causing the machine to yaw back and forth as the current swept around it. Its fat tires were still touching the streambed, but the cable was obviously all that prevented it from sliding over the falls.

Reed stood on the narrow ledge and began kicking at a car-sized ice block with his right crampon's toe points. Angie raised her arms to shield her face from the flying chips. Finally he broke loose a hefty chunk and picked it up.

"What are you going to—?"

Before Angie could finish, he had swung beneath the cable, holding the ice chunk with both hands so that it pressed down on the cable, bearing his weight. The cable cut into the chunk by pressure melting, forming a rut that held the chunk in place.

He kicked off and silently zipped down toward the tractor, holding his legs up to clear the water. "Look out!" he shouted. Lois and Steve scrambled back just in time as his sharp crampons clanged against the tractor's roof. He grabbed the cable with his gloves and discarded the ice chunk, which the cable had sliced nearly all the way through.

"Hurry," he said. This time his arms would be starting out tired. Also, Lois and Angie were about the same height, but with her athletic musculature, Lois was at least thirty pounds heavier.

Lois climbed on and wrapped her limbs around him. Her strong thighs squeezed his hips between them. He could feel her breasts pressing against his chest muscles. Her smooth right cheek was hot against his, her breaths deep and frantic.

Reed's body responded strongly to the close contact with Lois, not as it would have under safe circumstances but with a burst of raw energy. He whisked her up the cable and deposited her on the ledge beside Angie before she could begin to doubt him.

"Dad!" Angie yelled.

He whipped around toward the urgent cry. Angie was sitting on the ledge across the cable from him, her legs dangling fifteen feet above the rushing deluge. The ice block behind her was scooting and tilting outward. Reed knew why the block was moving—it was obviously the one the cable hook had snagged, and now the current's drag on the tractor was pulling it forward, shoving his daughter off her narrow perch.

Reed reached across the cable as Angie fell. He managed to grab her parka hood with one hand. Her dangling weight started to pull him off the ledge, but he hung on to the cable with his other arm. For a moment Angie screamed, twisted, and kicked in midair, staring at the torrent below her. Then she realized her motion was making it harder for him and held still except for involuntary trembling. Her parka pulled up beneath her armpits, and he feared she would slip out of it. "Hold your arms down!" he shouted.

The cable began jerking up and down, and Reed glanced along it. Steve was swinging beneath the cable, trying to imitate Reed's climbing technique but barely managing to hang on.

Reed dragged Angie over the cable, which was now shaking violently as Steve's lack of control fed its vibrations. Angie shrieked as it raked against her chest. Lois leaned forward, grasping Angie by the collar, and together they hoisted her back onto the ledge.

When the cable hook pulled free with a sharp squeak Reed had no time to react. The floating tractor resumed sliding toward the precipice. As the hook raced to catch up with the secured end of the cable, it snagged Reed's parka behind his left arm.

Together, both he and Lois were yanked off the ledge.
"Dad! No!"

Angie's scream was the last thing he heard before his head plunged beneath the surface of the flood.

Lois and Reed clung together as the lukewarm current swept them toward the thundering waterfall, both trying frantically to pull the cable hook loose from Reed's parka. She glanced up in time to see the huge green tractor tilt up sideways, exposing its gray underbody for a moment before it silently slipped beneath the lip of the falls.

She also saw Steve. He was floating upright, still hanging on to the cable, staring upstream at her with an expression of incredulous dismay. "Let go!" she tried to yell, but before she could get the words out the cable pulled taut and yanked him over the edge.

The cable began dragging Reed through the water with bone-breaking force, accelerating as the tractor fell free. Lois instinctively held on with all her strength, gasping and choking as the lukewarm water surged against her face.

They were almost to the falls when the force of drag from the water finally tore Reed's parka and the hook let go. At least they would not be pulled to their deaths by the plummeting tractor, Lois thought, but that reprieve would only delay the inevitable. The current was too strong to swim against, and they were too far from either bank for any hope of catching one of the dry ice chunks.

"I promised Angie a million times that I would never do this to her," Reed said.

"So did I," Lois said.

The stream grew shallower and faster. The thunder from the falls became an earsplitting torment, drowning out their screams as they were both swept over the edge.

CHAPTER 12

Moulin

Twenty-one snow tractors of assorted psychedelic colors sped through the polar night, preceded by their headlight beams and followed by the pale red glow of their taillights on the floating ice sheet of the Warner Basin. The moon was momentarily hidden behind distant nunataks, but reflections of the nascent green aurora australis shimmered on the tractors' windshields. They were in a side-by-side formation, spaced a hundred yards apart so the passengers could scan a broad swath of ice for anything out of the ordinary.

Marshall Dunn was leading the search for the missing tractors, Reed's and the first mechanic's. ICARE's rescue helicopter was on its way from another ambulance run and would join the search soon.

When Marshall had decided it was time to round up a search party, he had made an announcement on the public-address system of the ICARE base. He described Reed and the four civilians who were still missing, then outlined the known dangers in the Warner Basin. He begged any volunteers to meet in the garage. By the time he and Lim had repeated the announcement twice and walked to the garage, wondering if anyone else would show up, he found every able-bodied man and woman in the ICARE base mustered around a fleet of idling snow tractors.

So far, all they had found was Lois Burnham's abandoned vehicle and a deep canyon where warm water overflowing from the lake had undercut the ice. The obvious conclusion was that the missing tractors had fallen into the canyon and been swept away by the flood surging along its bottom, but Marshall and Lim discounted this theory and kept up the search simply because the canyon was easy to see from many times the stopping length of a snow tractor—it was inconceivable that anyone could have accidentally driven into it.

The passengers pressed their faces to the frigid glass portals inside the lead tractor, hoping to glimpse either the missing parties or whatever was making the horrendous noise outside. The tractor was speeding at full throttle, its knobby tires creating painful vibrations in the cabin, yet they could barely hear the roaring engine and humming tires over the earth-shaking din from the direction of Amery Station.

The quality of the noise was as terrifying as its intensity. "It sounds like a billion injured rig workers screaming in agony," Marshall shouted.

Silong Lim shook his head. "More like a leak in a huge steam manifold."

"What do you guys really think it is?" Max Bloom yelled over the whistling, rumbling screech.

Marshall glanced at Max. Of all the volunteers in the garage, Mr. Bloom had surprised him the most. Rumor in the ICARE ranks had it that the CEO had never actually set foot outdoors in Antarctica. The prematurely balding executive looked carsick. His pasty round face wobbled at the end of his long skinny neck, and his sparse blond mustache twitched whenever the tractor hit a bump.

"It must be steam escaping through the empty well holes," Lim said. "The lake is much hotter than it was earlier today."

"Geysers," Marshall added, gesturing with his broad hands as if they were blobs of spewing water.

Max swallowed, his large Adam's apple bobbing up and down. Then he licked his scraggly mustache and wiped it with his fingers, staring at Marshall with frank terror in his watery blue eyes. "Are you s-sure dr-driving on the ice is safe?"

"I'm sure it's *not*," Marshall said.

Angie stumbled across the flat ice toward Lois's disabled snow tractor, sparing her headlamp batteries because she could see well enough by moonlight. She could not see the tractor—it was too far away—but she knew how to find it. She and Lois had been navigating by driving along a straight line between Shackleton Peak—the highest nunatak near the rookery—and an unnamed peak on the opposite side of the basin.

Climbing the rubble slope to the rim of the canyon had already exhausted her, and now she had to fight the wind for every step. Her boots were weighted down by heavy hinged crampons made of chromium-molybdenum steel. They felt like buckets of concrete. At least the last two months of polar mountaineering had built up her stamina, otherwise she would already have been frozen.

Despite the wind whipping at her parka hood, Angie could hear the drone of the eruption, which had been audible across the Warner Basin since the night of Amery Station's collapse. The deep bass rumble seemed to have grown louder. It had also been joined by a powerful whistling hiss.

After a while she could no longer feel her hands or feet. Her face also went numb. She had been regularly palpating her cheeks, checking for the telltale stiffness that indicated frostbite, but later she could not even tell where her fingers were, much less discern the texture of her face through her mittens.

She tried to run a little, knowing it would get her warm, but her legs were stiff and difficult to control. She couldn't tell whether they were too cold or just dead with fatigue. She settled for walking as fast as she could, breathing hard from exertion but not sweating a drop. When she began to shiver—the first stage of hypothermia—she knew her body's core temperature had begun to collapse.

The shivering made her movements even harder to coordinate, yet she lurched onward, determined to reach a radio and call for someone to rescue her father and Lois. If I don't make it, I'll die trying, he thought.

Tears filled her wind-stung eyes again and again, freezing into heavy blobs of ice on her lashes. She swatted the frozen tears away with her right mitten, a crude motion that sometimes scraped her raw corneas.

After stumbling on for a while, she saw a long arc of headlights way off to her left and guessed correctly that they were searchers from ICARE. The fleet of snow tractors was heading in the opposite direction from her, back toward the base.

Giving up, she thought.

She tried to jump and settled for hysterically waving her arms. She also screamed until the cold made her cough uncontrollably. The searchers sped on, too far away to see her.

A few minutes later she finally spotted Lois's little orange tractor and hurried toward it as fast as she could, half jogging and half walking with a stumbling, irregular gait.

She opened the door, sat behind the wheel, and simultaneously turned the ignition key and the radio knob.

Nothing happened.

Both the engine battery and the radio's backup battery were dead, their life sucked out by a day and a half of use after the engine had quit, followed by a night of Antarctica's deep-space cold.

Lois wanted to scream as she fell, but the huge pair of arms squeezing her chest would not even let her take a breath. Wetness and weightlessness were all she could feel until her back collided with a hard surface. She realized the surface had to be nearly vertical—after falling so far, she would surely have been smashed to a pulp if she had landed on a flat slab of ice, especially with the bulk of Tom Reed on top of her.

They were still moving fast. Through the behind of her wet snow pants, she could feel tiny irregularities in the otherwise smooth ice whizzing by. The surface seemed to have a concave curvature; she felt a crushing pressure that could only be centrifugal force squeezing her and Reed against it.

The cold surface pressing against her back abruptly disappeared. A split second later, she felt it rubbing her knuckles, which were behind Reed. She had not felt the sensation of rolling over, yet somehow the slanting wall they were sliding down had switched to the opposite side of them.

A weird reverberating echo drew her attention to her ears. It reminded her of a childhood experience, peering into the mouth of a culvert with muddy floodwater rushing through it. How her mother had scolded her! Listening, she realized that the roar of the waterfall had mysteriously subsided to a subaudible vibration.

Throughout their fall, gusts of cold air and splashes of warm water alternately struck her face.

She forced her eyes open. What she saw was so amazing that she momentarily forgot they were about to die. She and Reed were hurtling downward like human bullets through a completely enclosed tube. It's like a ride at a water park, she thought. Except longer, faster, and *way* scarier. The tube obviously ran close to the glacier's surface, because moonlight was diffusing through the translucent ice, filling the strange burrow with a dim azure glow.

Lois had heard of such tubes but had never seen one. Glaciologists called them *moulins*. They were formed when meltwater seeped down through a narrow crack and enlarged it by melting. She and Reed had obviously been diverted into this moulin, along with a small fraction of the stream flow, after slipping over the waterfall.

The moulin was roughly six feet wide and nearly vertical, although it twisted back and forth, sometimes spiraling like a corkscrew. Twice now it had almost leveled out to form a horizontal tunnel. Lois prayed it would never turn and travel upward. Such a crook in the tube would hold standing water like the trap in a sink drain. At their present velocity, the trapped water would surely drown them, if it didn't crush them on impact.

Lois could see different strata of the ancient glacier whizzing past. Some were more opaque than others, some a deeper or lighter blue. The visual effect of plummeting through the layers so swiftly was like a strobe light in a disco—the blue moonlight winked rapidly on and off, providing brief still-frame glimpses of the objects around her. Falling blobs of water took on shapes like three-dimensional Rorschach tests, sometimes ap pearing suspended in midair as they fell at the same velocity as she and Reed. She also saw snapshots of Reed's face, which was contorted out of shape with terror, wind, and g forces from the turns.

"Look out!" Reed yelled.

In the next blue flash, she saw that he was looking down past their feet. The following flash showed her what he had seen, a fork in the tube. The dividing wall rushed up at them with shocking speed.

Lois felt the impact in her shoulder blades when Reed launched from one wall of the moulin, slamming her against the opposite side. His maneuver positioned them so that they would zoom down into one of the two forks rather than smashing up against the divider, but his feet caught against the divider and spun them upside down.

They craned their necks back as they shot downward headfirst, watching the approaching curves for another fork, and Lois realized the walls had begun to constrict. "Hey, it's getting tighter!"

"Let me get ahead of you!" Reed yelled. He pushed off from her shoulders, and she saw his boots slide past her face.

It made sense to Lois that they could pass through a narrower aperture one at a time, but why had he decided to go in front? She was smaller, only half his width through the shoulders. Then she realized that he had been considering their size difference after all. If the moulin became too narrow for him to pass through, his downward momentum would carry him on into the shrinking passage until he was compacted like a cork in a bottle. Even if his cracked ribs didn't impale his heart, he would quickly suffocate. But his body would eventually grind to a halt, also stopping Lois behind him, probably at a point where she would still have room to breathe.

She looked "up." Beyond a chain of tumbling water blobs, all she could see of Reed was his gleaming crampon spikes sticking back toward her like a shark's teeth. *Don't slow down now, Tom!*

The moulin leveled out again, becoming almost horizontal. *Oh no, we're going to hit a trap!*

Suddenly they were falling free in air that felt as cold as outer space. Lois had to close her wet eyes to avoid corneal frostbite. She saw a dim light through her eyelids that seemed to whirl around her. She felt herself chaotically tumbling and spinning, wet hair whipping her face and stinging her closed eyes. The reverberating culvert echoes of splashing water were gone. She had time to wonder where they would land, whether it would be a slab of glacial ice as hard and lethal as concrete, or if another miracle like the moulin would stay their execution for a few more minutes of torture.

CHAPTER 13

Cascades and Crevasses

Angie stayed inside the orange tractor until she could feel her extremities again. She knew she could safely survive in the tractor for days, even without heat—certainly long enough to await rescue. But as soon as she felt able, she climbed back out into the frigid darkness and marched on toward Lois's camp shelter, where she hoped the radio still worked.

She could not remember how far they had driven before breaking down, but a quick visual estimation told her the shelter was about one or two miles away, somewhere beneath the black band of jagged nunataks silhouetted by the moon. She didn't know one of the bright stars from another, but she knew the Ellis Mountains so well that she could navigate to the camp just by the serrated zigzag of the horizon.

Her hands and feet were numb again by the time she reached the little red sheet-steel shack, and each breath stung like a stab wound. She had dragged the polar air deep into her lungs thousands of times during the strenuous trek, searing them with a touch of internal frost nip. Coughing like a consumptive, she leaned on the lee wall of the shelter and pried her left eye open. The lashes had finally frozen together about an hour ago. Breath ice also clung to her bangs like hair beads.

As she rounded the corner to the shack's front, she glanced toward the rookery and froze for a moment. The five or six huddles she could see from camp had dwindled to less than half their former size. The emperors had been disappearing for months, but now they had suddenly left the rookery in a mass exodus.

What could it mean?

She had no idea and no time to think about it.

She reached for the door, but her hands were too numb to manipulate its heavy-duty latch. She tried to poke her stiff mitten-covered fingers into the space behind the handle so she could pull it outward. Then she pulled off the mitten in frustration and thrust her naked hand behind the latch. She could not bend her fingers, so she tugged on the handle with her wrist.

The door opened, but she could not let go of the latch handle. Her bare inner wrist had frozen fast to the metal surface. She leaned and twisted herself loose, feeling the pain of torn flesh penetrate the partial numbness of her forearm.

She staggered inside, glancing without much interest at the swatch of fresh blood on her wrist. After pulling the chain to turn on the autolighting gasoline heat stove and the battery-powered overhead lamp, she slammed the door shut on the cold and wind and the rumble-hiss from the eruption.

She intended to sit on one of the two wooden chairs, but her legs gave out in the middle of the room and she landed on the floor, knocking the chair over on its back. "Can't quit now," she groaned, thrusting her elbows onto the front legs of the overturned chair. Her hands were still too numb to grip, her legs too weak to stand, but somehow she had to get to the radio on the desk. Once she was on her knees, she leaned her arms on the edge of the desk and pulled herself up far enough to sit on the chair's front cross brace. She looked at the black radio, trying to focus her windburned eyes on all its knobs and dials.

The shelter was already beginning to warm, and the brief rest was reviving her stamina. With a feeble lurch, she pitched forward and landed with her chest on the flat desktop. Now the radio was within reach. She pecked clumsily at the controls, then leaned on the fat orange TALK button with the heels of both hands. "This is Angela Reed, calling ICARE base! Come in, ICARE!" Her voice was so hoarse, she wondered if anyone would understand her.

"This is ICARE base," the radio squawked back. "We've been trying to contact your party, Miss Reed. Is everything okay?"

"No!" Angie blurted. "The tractor fell through. My father and Dr. Burnham are in the water. You have to send a rescue. Over."

"Please repeat," the operator said. "Did you say they are *immersed in water*?"

"Affirmative. Oceans of it."

"How long have they been there?"

"I don't know. Hours."

"State your location," the operator said. "The helicopter will be on its way immediately."

"I'm at the emperor research camp, *but I'm okay*. My dad and Dr. Burnham are the ones in trouble." She tried to describe where she had last seen them.

"I just spoke to the helicopter's crew," the operator said. "They're already in the Warner Basin, assisting the ground search. They're going to pick you up first, then look for the bodies on the way back."

Angie stood up and slammed her numb hands down on the TALK button. "They're not dead, you stupid son of a bitch. *Why won't you listen to me?*"

There was no reply.

In spite of her exhaustion, Angie's heart raced like an engine with a slipping clutch. She paced to the door and back, amazed by how much strength her legs had regained after sitting for two minutes. She held the back of her bloody wrist against her trembling lips. "They're coming *here,*" she muttered to herself. "The stupid creeps are coming *here.* They're not even going to look for them!"

Suddenly she realized what the rescuers must be assuming. She ran to the radio and leaned on the TALK button. "The water they fell in is warm! It was heated by the eruption. And there's no use sending your helicopter here, because *I won't be here.* Copy that? I'm leaving now, and I won't get on your helicopter anywhere except beside that stream."

She grabbed a spare headlamp, an ice ax, a full canteen, and a bag of climbing gear, then replaced her mittens and dashed from the shelter.

The moulin had disgorged Reed and Lois into a flooded segment of a glacial crevasse. After ditching their heavy crampons, they had floated for several hours, awaiting rescue or death.

Smooth vertical walls of sapphire-blue ice towered over the pool on all sides, stretching up at least a hundred feet. The walls were wet almost halfway up, glistening in the moonlight and reflecting the wavy pool like mirrors. The pool was shaped like an elongated eye. It was perhaps two hundred feet long but only forty feet wide at the middle and tapered at each end to a narrow corner. The water had no perceptible current, but it was slowly exiting the pool at one end, spilling over a narrow waterfall with clouds of moonlit mist billowing beyond the U-shaped surface of the pouring water.

Nestled between the pinching walls at the other end of the pool was a surreally tall and thin cascade falling from a point just below the top of the crevasse. Halfway down, the plummeting strand of water was exploding into mist. The mist swirled out from the tight corner in turbulent eddies, like a column of dense smoke turned upside down. The highest feathers of mist were freezing as they blew away from the cascade, forming a moon-sparkling snow that drifted down onto the pool throughout its length, disappearing into the thousands of tiny reflections of the half-moon that danced on the waves.

The crevasse was filled with echoes from waves lapping the walls and the *hiss-splash-tumble* of the upstream cascade.

The water in the crevasse pool was much cooler than the water in the subglacial river had been. It didn't feel cold, but they knew it would slowly suck away their body heat once they ran out of energy. Since water conducted heat away from the human body twenty-five times faster than air at the same temperature, an immersed human could eventually freeze to death in water that was almost ninety degrees Fahrenheit.

There was nothing they could do but watch the stars gradually rotate across the swath of black sky above the crevasse, and talk. After describing her frustration with the mystery of the rookery's dwindling population, Lois launched into a conservationist polemic that was eerily familiar to Reed. She pointed out how other forms of environmental destruction might someday be reversed if the human race ever got a handle on its runaway growth—but extinction was *forever.* "Mankind may colonize the stars someday, but we will never again lay eyes on a dodo or a mastodon," she said. "According to the latest estimates, several tens of species are disappearing each day from overharvesting, pollution, deforestation . . . the global mass extinction due to modern human development is the swiftest in the history of the Earth. Without meaning to—without most people even being aware of it—we are irreversibly driving the planet to genetic bankruptcy."

It was uncanny to Reed how she and Angie had listed exactly the same global problems, in the same order, and proposed the same solutions. He had never known another adult who shared his daughter's anxieties, so he had always attributed them to teen angst or misplaced grief. Now he knew better. He felt a chest ache of shame that grew worse with each word as he realized how he had underestimated Angie, and how he would probably never get a chance to tell her he was sorry.

Angie peered down over the steep rubble slope at the mouth of the ice canyon. The treacherous mountain of loose debris had been daunting enough before, when the moon was shining on it and she was climbing upward, and her legs were not dead with fatigue and numb with cold.

Now the perilous descent looked impossible. The rugged slope was shaded from the moon by the opposite bank, and her headlamp only illuminated a few ice chunks at the top. Beyond those, she could barely discern the sharp, angular silhouettes of more chunks and the undulating starlit water far below them.

She had no idea how she had found the stamina to trek all the way back to the canyon, especially carrying a load of climbing gear. It had taken twice as long as the hike from the canyon to the shelter. The fronts of her hips burned with overuse, as if nails had been driven into her pelvis.

The rescue helicopter had flown past her once, low in the distance, shining a searchlight beam down at the ice.

Several times she had ground to a halt, certain she could go no farther, yet she had found the will to move on before she could freeze. While staggering back and forth, dizzy with cold and fatigue, she had caught the crampon spikes of her right foot on her left pants leg and fallen on her face. Now the blood from her cut chin had frozen in her balaclava.

Angie had never considered giving up. She knew her father and Lois had probably drowned or frozen to death hours ago, that their lifeless bodies had probably been washed out to sea by now. But she still clung to the hope that they had somehow grabbed hold of the stream bank above the falls and had miraculously survived the cold.

It was a good thing I brought the rope, she thought. She was too weak to climb down over the rubble without it. She tied it around a truck-sized ice boulder and began her descent.

When she reached the ledge where they had been sitting when the cable hook had pulled loose, she swept her headlamp beam downstream along the edge of the surging torrent. Then she scanned the whole bank of rubble.

They were not there.

There's nothing more I can do, she realized.

Fresh tears welled up in her eyes, and her exhausted legs began to tremble. Her throat burned and constricted, and she felt sick to her stomach. Without her father and Lois, Angie would be totally alone in a world where no one wanted her. Perhaps her body could survive that, for a while, but she knew her mind would not. She sank to her knees, dizzy, and leaned against the ice wall, weeping with lurching childlike sobs, mashing her thick mittens against her ears to block out the cruel thunder from the waterfall.

She remained on all fours, watching her tears splash onto the moonlit ice and freeze solid, until she realized how cold she felt. Sweat had soaked her thermal underwear during the harrowing climb down the rubble, and now she was shivering in the damp shroud. She knew she should get going before she got too cold to move. But she was so darn tired! She had never imagined that someone could feel this exhausted and still remain conscious.

She just wanted to rest for a few minutes.

In addition to being cold and tired, she was hungry and thirsty. She had drained her canteen hours ago. Now she was thirstier than she had ever been in her life. She could refill her canteen from the stream, but that would require more climbing. Instead she just sat cross-legged on the ledge and watched the mesmerizing undulations of the starlit water. She hunched over with her numb hands buried in the pockets of her parka, rocking forward and back a little. Her tears splashed onto the black Kevlar knee patches of her yellow snow pants, ejecting tiny droplets that crystallized in midair and sparkled in her headlamp beam.

Her shivering grew worse.

Just a few minutes of rest, she thought. She'd already had several shivering spells on this terrible night and had gotten over them. Shivering was just the body's natural way of keeping warm.

A far corner of Angie's mind was still thinking. It screamed for her to remember that shivering only worked below a certain rate of heat loss, and then only if the body had reserves of fuel and stamina. But the thinking part of her brain was no match for the part that was feeling her grief and pain and fatigue.

A while later—she had lost track of time—the shivering stopped. There, see? I'm . . . warm . . . again. The thought was sluggish, barely cast into language.

She really felt much better. The grief was still there—it always would be—but she no longer felt pain from the cold and injuries. In fact, a peaceful relaxation had come over her, making her feel like saving herself might actually be worth the effort.

She tried to get up.

Her legs would not move.

They're just stiff, she thought. Or maybe they had gone to sleep while she was sitting on them.

Intending to help herself up with her arms, she tried to withdraw her hands from the parka.

Her arms wouldn't move either.

Angie felt a wave of panic, but it was a slow, torpid wave. Like the rest of her body, her adrenal glands were too exhausted for more than a perfunctory response, even to the prospect of imminent death by hypothermia.

For a moment her sluggish heartbeat accelerated and she could twitch her thighs; then the brief burst of energy was gone.

She wondered if someone would find her in this position, sitting up on the ice ledge with this horrible expression of grief and fear literally frozen on her face. Or would she eventually pitch forward, bouncing down into the water and over the falls?

The feelings of peace, warmth, and numbness grew stronger. She closed her eyes and concentrated on breathing, which suddenly seemed difficult, as if a tight elastic band were squeezing her chest.

She heard the modemlike squawk of an adult emperor penguin and opened her eyes. She could see nothing beyond her knees except indistinct ghostlike forms all around her. The fuzzy shapes were obviously ice chunks illuminated by her headlamp. Listening, she realized she could no longer hear the thundering waterfall. All she heard was a dull buzz, like a dial tone.

Angie knew that the penguin squawk had been an auditory hallucination—there were no penguins nearby. She also knew why her eyes and ears would no longer work properly. A line came to mind from a polar safety brochure Lois had made her read several times: *Judgment and alertness will steadily deteriorate, until reversible blindness and deafness set in at eighty-six degrees, followed by coma and death at seventy-eight.*

She tried to start rocking again, hoping the motion would generate enough heat to get her legs moving.

It was no use. The only thing she could still move was her neck, and its range of motion decreased with every nod. The dial tone in her ears had become a roar. Her eyes were wide open, and she could see nothing but terrifying blackness.

Angie was just dimly aware of the impact that should have been painful when her abdominal muscles finally went slack and she pitched over backward on the ledge. The back of her head bounced once against the hard ice, and she ceased to move.

CHAPTER 14

Hypothermia

As most of the Warner Basin's subglacial lake reached the boiling point, thermal expansion of the water column ceased and escape of steam through holes and cracks in the floating ice began to lower the lake level. This change abruptly cut off the source of the warm flood that was spilling from the lake. As the upstream cascade replenishing the pool where Reed and Lois were trapped dwindled to a trickle, the pool grew colder and began to leak away through cracks in the floor.

Lois watched the wavy moonlit surface gradually creep down the wet sapphire walls like bathwater draining from a tub. "Looks like we won't have to float much longer."

"Great!" Reed said, treading water.

"Actually, this is bad, Tom. If the water gets too shallow—"

"—we won't be able to stay submerged, and we'll freeze to death," Reed said, thumping his bruised right temple.

They held each other for warmth as the water cooled and drained, their hopes diminishing as the hours passed by with no sign of a search party. "When the water's gone," Lois said, "it's going to be quick but painful."

"Better dunk," Reed said. "Your bandage is growing frost again." They had been dipping their heads every minute or so to prevent the subzero air from frostbiting their wet faces.

They began talking about their lives to avoid thinking about losing them. He asked what she had meant by "So did I" when they were going over the falls and he told her he had promised Angie a million times that he would never leave her alone.

"It took her about two weeks to get used to being away from you down here," Lois said. "We both had it kind of rough."

"So you just up and promised that you would always look out for her if something ever happened to me?"

"Exactly," Lois said.

"Always and forever?"

"Yes."

"Just to calm her down?"

Lois glared at him. "No! Because I meant it."

"Wow," Reed said. "I mean, thank you."

The aurora australis was fully developed. Three wavy vertical ribbons of light graded from greenish white at the bottom to crimson at the top, where they divided into several streaks disappearing toward the zenith. The hundred-mile streams of glowing ions cast clear reflections in the pool and glistened on the crevasse walls like Christmas lights. The three ribbons appeared to be tilted together at the top, and the one in the center was smaller than the other two. A family of ghosts dancing among the stars, Reed thought. What a beautiful place to die.

The rescue helicopter passed over twice, perpendicular to the crevasse, once in each direction. The crisp thumping of its rotor echoed through the crevasse long before and after the huge dark airframe zoomed overhead. The searchlight stabbed down into the crevasse like a flash from an alien camera, briefly illuminating the walls with blue light reflected from the clear pool's bottom. The second time, they floated on their backs and waved their arms, to no avail.

"There has to be some way to signal them," Lois said.

"Build a fire?" Reed suggested.

"Ha. Funny."

"We're already wearing bright red parkas. It's just too dark, this crevasse is too deep, and we're too small."

At this point, Reed just hoped that Angie had made it up the rubble slope and back to Lois's tractor or camp, and that she would eventually get out of Antarctica and find some way to make a worthwhile life for herself.

A CH-53E Super Stallion hovered near the bottom of the glacial chasm that had swallowed Reed's snow tractor. The helicopter's fat fuselage was fire-engine red and over seventy feet long. Its rotor—composed of seven black titanium-ribbed blades—spun just twenty feet from a Niagara-like cascade. Prop wash parted the tumbling water and whipped swirling eddies of spray around the enormous aircraft, which was currently the world's fastest and most powerful production helicopter, with a top speed of nearly two hundred miles per hour and an external sling load capacity of eighteen tons.

The clear plunge pool at the base of the falls was illuminated by the helicopter's powerful searchlights. In the middle of the pool lay the frog-green snow tractor, upside down and completely submerged. Although the ice, the floodlight beam, and the frothing water were all white, reflections from the helicopter tinted the walls and the rushing cascade with reddish gleams, while the tractor's body cast greenish hues on the bottom of the plunge pool.

Lieutenant Nathaniel Simmons, pilot of the helicopter, spoke into his radio. "We located the colonel's tractor, Mr. Dunn. It doesn't look good."

The radio crackled and transmitted Marshall's deep drawl. "So they went into the canyon after all. Describe the situation, Nate."

"Three wheels are missing, and it looks like the passenger cabin is completely crushed in and flooded. That's about all I can make out through this white water."

"Can you see any bodies?"

"Negative," Nate reported.

"Any sign of the mechanic's tractor?"

"Negative. Maybe it was washed on downstream— this flood is something else. Do you want us to give up and fly back to the canyon to look for the girl again?"

"Yes, go," Marshall said.

Nate hit the throttle, and the bright red seventeen-ton aircraft ascended straight upward in front of the steaming white wall of plummeting water.

When the Super Stallion climbed above the lip of the cascade, its engines and rotors became louder in the crew's ears than the deluge crashing into the chasm below. The huge aircraft tilted and wobbled as Nate fought the turbulent updraft that strangely accompanied the falling water.

"Look!" the copilot shouted, lowering his binoculars to point.

Nate peered along the jumble of broken ice that formed the right bank of the stream delta atop the waterfall. He saw a faint yellow glow behind one of the blocks.

"It's a headlamp," he said, hitting the throttle.

He swung the Super Stallion up over the delta and carefully lowered it between the steep banks of loose rubble. Now he could clearly see the source of the dim light that was shining up at the stars with less than one-thousandth the luminosity of the helicopter's powerful searchlights. It was indeed a headlamp, still fastened around the frost-covered hood of a human figure lying prone on a narrow ledge. When Nate aimed one of the searchlights at the motionless figure, he could see that it was a woman.

"Let's get her in!" he shouted.

The two paramedics seated behind the pilots were already unbuckling their seat harnesses.

The copilot looked through his binoculars. "If she isn't dead, she must be close."

They lost view of the victim as Nate edged the Super Stallion over her so the paramedics could drop onto the ledge from the cable winch in the ceiling of the cargo bay. He stopped when the spinning rotor approached perilously close to the ice rubble. The Super Stallion's long tail still protruded over the chasm, buffeted by the turbulent updraft so that the whole aircraft pitched and yawed a few degrees.

Nate called Marshall Dunn on the radio. "We found Angela Reed, Mr. Dunn."

"What's her status?"

"We'll know in a minute."

"Take her straight to the infirmary if she's alive. I'll round up all the searching tractors and get them back to the base before something happens to one of them, too. Over."

Even when they began to shiver, Reed and Lois held each other tightly and avoided any movement that was not necessary to remain afloat, knowing that their survival time would be cut in half if they allowed cold water to swirl through their clothing. Their conversation grew more intimate and intense, relieved of the inhibitions that come from expecting tomorrow and spurred on by the warming effect of telling secrets. It's like flying a Warthog, Reed thought—thrilling enough to jerk a sweat. He figured it might give them an extra half hour.

Before getting to know her, Reed had found Lois physically attractive but not particularly charming. Now he was growing convinced that his first impression had been wrong, that her apparent irritability and emotionalism had been temporary results of a long hard day. He also learned several basic facts that quickly multiplied his personal interest in her.

To begin with, Lois was obviously intelligent and educated. That meant the world to Reed. Angie's mother had been a doctor. After her, he could not bear the thought of daily conversations with someone who didn't know much of anything interesting to talk about. He would rather have fought daily with a partner about real issues than chat pleasantly about some TV show. This preference, more than anything, had cut short his few attempts at dating over the last decade. He considered himself a desirable man. He was not wealthy, but he certainly had status. He also had a hirsute but stunningly developed physique, a rare asset for a desk worker in his forties. But at his age, women who were both bright and still available were simply hard to find.

Too bad we found each other too late, he thought.

Shivering all over, Lois hugged him with her head tucked in the crook of his muscular neck and her breasts mashed against his chest. Somehow her crown of sopping gauze had stayed on during the ride through the moulin. He could see diluted blood trickling down her neck and diffusing into the water. A glaze of ice had formed over her wet hair like a tight helmet. He laid his cold cheek against hers and whispered in her ear. "Lois, if we should manage to make it out of this, I would definitely want to take you out."

"Yeah," she said, her teeth chattering. "I thought you'd never ask. I'd love a personalized tour of Washington if you really—"

Reed gently laid a wrinkled forefinger across her bluish lips. The noise from the waterfalls had decreased as the flow dwindled, allowing him to detect another sound—a barely audible but steady thumping.

"The helicopter?" she whispered.

He nodded, peering up at the aurora. "It must be hovering somewhere nearby."

Lois flinched, then shook his shoulders. "Tom! Quick! I know a way to make them see us this time, if it's not too late."

Angie moaned and arched her back, taking a deep rasping breath. Color flooded her bluish face. Tears streamed down her temples into her ears, and she grimaced in pain.

"I'll go make a report while the water's warming," said the senior paramedic to his partner. "Turn off the electric blanket when she hits ninety-eight, but leave all of her clothes on if they're dry."

He walked to the Super Stallion's cockpit. "She'll probably be okay," he said before Nate could ask. They called the tractor convoy. "Angela Reed is alive, Mr. Dunn. She had the appearance of severe hypothermia, but her temperature was moderate, not cold enough for brain damage. Frankly, I'm surprised she was unconscious. I think she mostly passed out from exhaustion. She also has some frostbite, though, at least second degree."

"Get her to the infirmary," Marshall said. "All the tractors are together and headed home now. Good work, guys. Over."

The paramedic returned to the bay to help stabilize Angie for the rough flight back to ICARE through a katabatic crosswind.

Marshall called again. "One more thing, guys. . . . I knew Tom Reed for a long time. He was a good man and a good father. His advice got me out of trouble more than once at the station. I would appreciate it if you all would just treat his daughter as . . . as nicely as you can. She may live, but believe me, she lost everything tonight."

CHAPTER 15

Frostbite

As sensation returned to her extremities, Angie began to hurt in places she had never known existed. She kept expecting the pain to subside. She still felt paralyzed, knowing she could move but not wanting to because it would hurt so much.

Her heels in particular ached as if the bones had been shattered. They probably *are* broken, she realized—laced with microfractures from jogging in warm but unsupportive glacier boots.

She emitted a weak croak. One of the paramedics listened closer while she repeated it.

"Did you find my dad?"

He glanced up at his partner, who was looking down at his feet, arms crossed.

Angie knew what that meant. "Aspirin," she gasped, forcing her knees to bend.

The younger paramedic held out two ibuprofen tablets and a cup of water.

She looked suspiciously at the pills. "This kind won't put me to sleep, will it?"

He assured her it wouldn't, and she swallowed the medicine. "Why does it hurt so much?"

"Your body resorted to anaerobic metabolism when your breathing rate declined and vasoconstriction caused poor circulation to your limbs. Lactic acid accumulated in your tissues. If you had lain there much longer—"

"*Iiiyeee!*" Angie screamed in agony and jerked her right hand out of the bucket of water it had been soaking in. She stared at the trembling appendage, eyes wide in horror. The fingers were pink, swollen, and covered with white blisters.

Why were they boiling my hand?

She was in too much pain to vocalize the thought. All she could do was groan. But the young paramedic understood her reproachful stare.

"The water's not that hot." He plunged in his own hand. "See? Only a hundred four degrees Fahrenheit. We have to thaw your frostbite. I know it hurts, but rapid rewarming in hot water is the best treatment as long as there's no chance of refreezing."

Tears streamed down Angie's cheeks. She clutched the injured hand to her chest and rocked it like a baby, sobbing from the physical torment.

"We still have to do the other one," the paramedic said, hesitantly. "And your feet."

Angie rolled over and arched herself into a kneeling position, balanced on her elbows and one knee, with the other leg stretched out because it didn't want to bend. She rested in that position for a moment, still clutching the thawed hand, bent over with her left temple on the cold metal floor.

"The blisters and pain are actually a good sign," said the young paramedic, as if he was unsure what else to do. "If the frostbite were deep, your hand would be blue and purple and numb. You're lucky you were wearing good mittens."

Finally she could talk. "Are we on a helicopter? Where are we going?"

The senior paramedic spoke up. "Don't worry, Miss Reed. You'll be safe in the infirmary in just a few minutes. We're still hovering where we found you, but we'll head back to ICARE as soon as we can get you strapped in."

Angie managed to stand, with help, although her heels thundered with pain and vertigo made her wonder which of the chopper's constant sways and spins were real.

Motion sickness overtook her so abruptly that she retched before she could turn away from the paramedic. Nothing came up but the pain pills and a little water. "Airsick," she wheezed.

"You want some Dramamine?"

She shook her head, stifling another retch. Tears ran from her eyes. "I know for sure . . . that stuff . . . will knock me out."

"Why don't you want to sleep on the way back?" said the young paramedic.

She glared up at him, teeth clenched, still bent over in case she threw up. "Because I'm not *going* back! I have to look for my dad. If you won't search with this helicopter, I want you to put me back down."

The paramedics exchanged dumbfounded glances.

Angie staggered up to the cockpit.

"We already tried that," Nate replied when Angie asked him to fly downstream inside the broad chasm where Reed and Lois had gone over the waterfall. "And we don't have enough fuel to do it again."

"It won't take long!" Angie pleaded.

Nate glanced back toward the paramedics. "I have orders."

"From whom?"

"From the Amery Station foreman, Marshall Dunn."

"Marshall is not your commander, Lieutenant." Angie tried to imitate her father's famous command voice, hoping it would give her statement some impact despite her pitiful condition. She knew the pilot's rank was second lieutenant from the smooth one-inch-by-three-eighths-inch gold bar on his shirt collar.

"Mr. Dunn was supervising the search," Nate explained. Angie could see the pilot's tanned jaws working in frustration beneath his reflective helmet visor.

"Call him again," Angie said. "You must have misunderstood him. I know Marshall. He would never tell you to give up as long as we have plenty of fuel." She tapped the analog gauge with her throbbing forefinger. She actually had no idea whether they had enough fuel to keep searching, but the needle wasn't quite on empty.

"Mr. Dunn clearly instructed us to call off the search!" Nate snapped. "Either they climbed out on the bank or they went over the falls. Either way, he knows as well as I do that their odds of survival are zero. If we'd gotten here a half hour later, you would have been an E901 yourself."

E901 was the code used on death certificates to designate accidental deaths resulting from "excessive cold."

Angie closed her eyes and grabbed the back of the copilot's chair to steady herself. A terrifying wave of dizziness had nearly made her fall. She realized she was still so weak that the slightest overexertion might cause her to faint.

Seeing her stumble, Nate started to reach out to her, then quickly returned his hand to the Super Stallion's shuddering controls. "Hey, guys!" he shouted to the paramedics. Then he swore at himself, biting his lip, and said, "Look, kid, I'm sorry I—"

"Just . . . please . . . call him," Angie moaned. The copilot and the paramedics were guiding her into a seat.

"I can probably squeeze another ten minutes out of the tanks," Nate said, operating the radio. He reported their status to the tractor convoy and said, "Please advise."

Angie heard Marshall's deep drawl over the cockpit speakers. "Nate, our tractors couldn't get near the chasm where you found the colonel's tractor—it's down where the ice sheet is riddled with crevasses because it's descending to the ocean. But you can do whatever Angie asks as long as you have enough fuel to get home and no other emergency calls come in. Got it?"

Nate surprised Angie with a relieved smile beneath his helmet visor. "Buckle up," he said. "Here we go."

Max Bloom had been in a much better mood since the search party had headed home across the floating ice sheet, this time in single file with the lightest tractor on point in case they encountered thin ice. Max had come along on this dangerous and pointless expedition because he knew it was just a matter of time until the national news media discovered the events in the Warner Basin and spun them into high drama. When that happened, his physical participation in the search for the missing persons would give him an excuse to occupy the spotlight. It would work wonders for his résumé, maybe even land him a new job that paid as well as his executive position at ICARE but was located in a place with warm air, fresh food, and pretty girls. Or at least ugly girls—even that would be a big step up.

Max sat on the bench seat in front of Marshall and Lim. He had left his safety harness off so he could turn around and talk to them. "That wasn't so bad after all," he said. "Waste of resources, though. I told you we wouldn't find anybody."

"It was not a waste," Marshall said. "If we hadn't seen the canyon, we wouldn't have known where to tell the chopper crew to look for Angela."

Max wondered why Dr. Lim's eyes were closed. The engineer was quietly muttering something, ignoring the other passengers. Maybe he's saying a prayer, Max thought. Then he heard a few syllables of Lim's chant: ". . . H, I, J, K . . ."

Why the hell is he saying his ABC's?

Lim's eyes abruptly opened wide. "Else!" he shouted.

"What?" Max said. He could never understand Lim's accent, especially with the background noise of the speeding tractor.

Lim turned to Marshall. "A capital L could be mistaken for a V if it's crooked. Maybe they were L's instead of V's."

Marshall jerked out a tattered piece of paper and read, "C-A-L-L-L-O-T-H-A-I-R-F."

Max was bewildered. "What are you guys talking about?"

"The message Dr. Corcoros wrote when we pulled him out of the boiling lake. We still haven't figured it out."

"Maybe it's just nonsense," Max said. "He was out of his mind with pain, right?"

"No," Marshall said.

"More than one word," Lim said. "First word is 'Call.' But what does the rest mean?"

Marshall read the letters again. "Lothair is a man's name. French, I think. I remember seeing it just recent—"

"Where?" Lim asked, grabbing the paper.

Marshall gripped his bald forehead and frowned. "I don't know."

"Must be a relative," Max said. "Who else would he

want you to call? Oh, Christ, I'll bet it's his attorney. If he lives, he'll probably sue ICARE for—"

The red brake lights of the tractor ahead came on. The driver of Max's vehicle yelled, "Stop!" and stood up on his brake pedal. The radio briefly squawked with several shrill voices that spoke too rapidly to be understandable.

Max turned toward the windshield in time to see the gap swiftly closing between his tractor and the one in front. As the rear hatch of the other tractor raced toward him, he threw his arms over his face and let loose a piercing, nasal scream.

After a one-second skid, Max's tractor plowed into the other tractor's rear end. Max was hurled from his seat. He struck the dashboard and slammed down on the floor with a grunt.

After skidding together for another second, the tractors came to a halt. Max sat up, wiped his chin, and looked at his hand in wide-eyed terror. "Oh my God, I'm bleeding!"

Marshall unbuckled his harness and stooped over Max. "You got a split lip."

A blast of background static and more shrill voices came over the radio, including the driver of the lead tractor. His words were garbled by poor radio reception and panic. "Mr. Dunn! Mr. Dunn! You'd better come take a look at what's in front of us."

When Angie was strapped in, the Super Stallion tilted upward and slid back and to the right until it was over the center of the giant glacial chasm. Then it tilted forward and swooped down between the walls, heading downstream, leaving the thundering cascade behind.

Nate could not fly very fast. He had to fight the peculiar updraft rising from the white water at the bottom of the great chasm, and even in perfectly still air he would

have needed time to safely bank the ninety-nine-foot helicopter around the occasional sharp bends.

"Wait!" Angie yelled. She was looking out a left side
window, back toward the receding waterfall. "Go back!"

For a brief fraction of a second, one of the searchlights had illuminated a slender crack in the chasm wall
behind the plunging water. The crack ran almost vertically halfway up the wall and then cut horizontally until
it ended a few hundred yards downstream. Angie got the
impression that the crack was deep and nearly parallel to
the chasm, separating a thin vertical slab that should
have fallen long ago from the main body of the wall.

Some of the water from the cascade her father and
Lois had gone over was spilling into the crack.

Nate pulled the Super Stallion up to an altitude where
the chasm was wide enough for them to turn safely.
Then he banked tightly around and started to descend
again, heading back upstream.

"No, wait!" Angie said. "Go back again."

Nate pulled up and hovered. "We'll wait here while
you make up your mind."

"Go back! Go back!"

"Which way?"

"Downstream."

When the chopper had pulled up to turn around, Angie
had seen that the crack extended farther than she'd
thought. It was just so narrow that only intermittent gaps
were visible in the feeble starlight.

She cupped her hands around her eyes and pressed
them against the cold window to block out the multicolored lights from the dark cockpit's instrument panels.
Following the trend of the crack, she traced it up to the
lip of the chasm, then across the ice sheet. As she had
suspected, it headed almost parallel to the chasm, in the
downstream direction, until the two features rejoined on

the far side of a leftward bend in the chasm. Angie realized that the portion of the waterfall being swallowed by the crack must be draining along it and returning to the main chasm at the other end.

Sure enough, as the Super Stallion flew around the leftward bend in the chasm, she could see ahead and to the left a small waterfall tumbling down in a billowing plume from the bottom of a vertical crack in the upper two-thirds of the chasm wall.

Angie pointed. "They're in there!" she shouted, confidently.

"You're kidding," Nate said. "How?"

She tried to explain.

"I guess that's conceivable," he said. "But they probably just got washed through that crack and dumped back into this Grand Canyon we've been following."

"Fly in there."

Nate gaped at her. "Our rotor is wider than that crack!"

"Fly along above it then."

"Roger," Nate responded. The Super Stallion ascended, pressing its passengers down into their seats.

"Slowly," Angie added. "And aim the lights straight down."

As they approached the mouth of the narrow fissure in the chasm wall, the radio crackled and they heard Marshall Dunn over the cockpit speakers. "ICARE convoy calling Rescue One. Are you there, Nate?" The voice was sharp and nervous, not at all like Marshall's usual deep drawl.

"We're still here, and we still haven't found anybody," Nate said.

"You have to come to the tractor convoy now, as fast as you can," Marshall shouted. "We're in big trouble. Angie, I'm sorry, sweetheart. Over and out."

CHAPTER 16

Geysers

Angie stared numbly at the Super Stallion's radio. Her face buzzed and tingled as she tried to take a breath. The bright green and orange lights on the instrument panels grew dim and fuzzy. She started to unbuckle her seat belt and get up, but she was too weak—the ordeal was finally catching up with her.

After Marshall's urgent SOS, Nate quietly adjusted the controls and the giant helicopter's nose pointed downward as it accelerated at full throttle, mashing its passengers into their seats. Zooming along less than a hundred yards above the narrow fissure, he reached up and flicked off the searchlights.

One of the paramedics yelled for him to stop.

Nate let off the throttle, causing a moment of weightlessness. "What is it?"

"I don't know. Something weird."

"No time for sightseeing." Nate hit the gas again.

"Something floating in a long pool. It looked like—"

Angie was on the paramedic's lap, pushing him back from the window so she could look out. "Turn the lights back on!" she yelled. "Lights! Now!"

The chopper swung around and descended, its powerful twin searchlights stabbing down into the fissure.

They were hovering over a deep oblong pool with a narrow waterfall at each end, one pouring in and one pouring out. The Super Stallion's searchlights penetrated the crystal-clear water and diffused throughout it, making the pool glow with secondary light that illuminated the vertical walls of sapphire glacial ice and the cloud of spray at the base of the thready upstream cascade. As the chopper gently rotated back and forth a few degrees, a vivid rainbow encircling the mist at the base of the waterfall winked on and off.

"God, that's beautiful," Angie said. She was so dizzy that the thin cascade appeared to be falling sideways.

"All right, I'm out of here," Nate said. "We have an emergency to deal with, guys."

"What's all that stuff in the water?" the paramedic asked. "It looks like snow floating on the surface. That can't be, can it?"

Angie looked closer, pushing her nose out of the way against the frigid glass. Her eyes still wouldn't focus quite properly, but she saw what the paramedic was talking about. A white substance was floating all over the pool's surface, scattered in random strings and clumps.

The copilot said, "Maybe it's just foam, you know, churned up from the waterfall."

Nate shook his head. "I wish I could see. It can't be foam. This is probably the cleanest water on Earth, and you have to have some crud dissolved in the water before it will foam."

The copilot was scanning the surface of the pool with his binoculars, squeaking the upper edge of the rubber rims against the window. He abruptly stopped. "You are *not* going to believe this."

Angie snatched the binoculars. "*Where?*"

The copilot guided the binoculars with his hand until Angie shrieked. She could see her father and Lois in the water, floating on their backs to maximize their visible area. Reed was waving up at her.

Angie tried to adjust the binoculars for her eyes with one trembling hand, jabbing the eyepieces hard against her skull. She didn't make a sound as Nate asked, "What?" and the copilot said, "They're down there . . . *alive*!"

Nate looked up at the ceiling and released an enormous sigh, then tugged on the tail of Angie's parka. "You going to breathe, kid?"

"Ha!" Angie said, just one loud bark of triumph. She still didn't move.

"We have to hurry," Nate reminded them.

The paramedics were already harnessed up, repeating the routine they had used when they rescued Angie. They opened the floor hatch, letting in a blast of frigid air and the deafening *whump-whump* of the hovering rotor. Angie ran to the hatch when she heard it open.

The paramedic controlling the winch frantically motioned her to step back from the open hatch. She did, then lay down and crawled across the floor to peer over the edge at the expanse of blue water churning in the prop wash. The height and whirling motion made her reel with vertigo, and she scrambled back against the wall.

The suspended trio ascended through the floor. Lois was resting her head on Reed's chest, her eyelids drooping with exhaustion, but Reed was beaming at Angie. He raised his arm, wincing with the effort, and gave her a weak salute. She saluted back, her vision fading in and out.

The pilot's voice came over the cabin speakers. "Everybody hang on. We have to take off."

The paramedic who had stayed in the chopper closed the hatch and helped unhook the others as the Super Stallion surged upward. Reed handed Lois to the paramedic and piled onto the floor beside Angie. Lois's eyes fluttered open, and she looked around the cabin with a droopy stare, her bandaged head wobbling.

The strain suddenly caught up to Angie, and tears dripped from her chin. She stared at her father, sobbing in little choking gasps. "You're really alive," she moaned.

He saw her looking at the bits of white fuzz on his pile of wet clothing. "Down," he said. "Seven hundred and fifty weight goose down. Worth almost its weight in gold, literally. Lois and I tore up both of our parkas and pulled the down out of their baffles. The stuff disperses on water like motor oil."

She slowly sighed and closed her eyes, then opened them just briefly with a feeble grin. "I really need a bath," she said, and her head slumped forward on her chest.

"I'm never going to take a bath again," Reed muttered. He waved one of the paramedics over and nodded toward his daughter. "Hey, she's not hurt, is she?"

The pilot's amplified voice interrupted. "We're about to ascend above the level of the Warner Basin ice sheet. We will be exposed to regional winds. There may be minor turbulence."

The paramedic helped Reed pick Angie up and get her safely into a seat. "Your daughter suffered at least first-degree frostbite, sir."

The giant helicopter abruptly rolled to port at what seemed to Reed like a ninety-degree tilt. At the same time, the aircraft lunged in the direction opposite the roll so that everyone and everything on board that wasn't bolted down slammed into the ceiling. Reed heard shouts and a warning buzzer in the cockpit as he got his breath back from the blow. Fortunately, he had hit the roof with the broad part of his back.

He grabbed hold of a seat to prevent another fall as the chopper spun around clockwise and swung back and forth like a pendulum. Finally the pilots seemed to get the shuddering behemoth under control. "Report!" Reed ordered. "What happened?"

"Heavy wind, sir . . . caught us off guard. I've flown through here a hundred times and never felt wind like this."

"Can you fly through it?"

"I think so, sir. It appears steady. It just slammed us when we entered it from the calm air below the ice cap's local elevation."

"Gordy, help!" The voice of the young paramedic who had been looking after Lois was charged with panic.

The driver pulled Marshall's tractor up beside the one in front of it so Marshall and Lim could look ahead of the convoy without getting out. What they saw shocked all of the passengers into stunned silence, except for Max Bloom, who repeatedly cursed in a soft whisper and groaned when he touched his split lip.

A hundred feet in front of the lead tractor, steam was shooting upward from a round hole in the ice about thirty feet wide. A few feet above the ice, the invisible steam condensed into white fog that shone brilliantly in the convoy's headlight beams. The fog was blasting into the dark sky like an ash cloud from an exploding volcano or the smoke from a launching rocket turned upside down. The opaque cloud column pooched and puckered as the violent updraft gave birth to turbulent eddies and then reabsorbed them within milliseconds. The lumpy, writhing surface gave Marshall a creepy feeling, as if a horde of angry creatures were trapped inside the column, trying to get out.

The noise from the geyser was as terrifying as its appearance. At such close range, the whistling, pounding screech had more texture and detail than the roar of the distant, larger geysers at Amery Station.

"Come on! Let's get out of here!" Max yelled.

"We have to wait for the helicopter," Marshall shouted. He pointed to another cloud column erupting from the ice to the right and behind the first one. So far, he had counted five of the screaming genies surging into the sky within the periphery of the convoy's many headlights. Way to the left, he could barely make out a sixth geyser that was so large he could not discern its width or even its curvature. It was just a wriggling, pulsating wall of charcoal-gray cloud. "The ice is melting through all around us," he explained. "We need an eye in the sky to guide us between the thin spots."

Gordy, the older paramedic beside Reed, lunged back into the Super Stallion's cargo bay/infirmary. Reed followed him.

Lois was sprawled on her back, her limbs askew. Her eyes were open and her mouth was slightly ajar, but she was not moving. Her normally fair complexion had become pasty and sallow, the color of homemade ice cream. A puddle of dark blood was growing on the gray steel floor around the back of her head. Tiny standing waves generated by the chopper's vibration radiated across the surface of the viscous fluid.

The young paramedic hovered over her, his nostrils flaring and his eyes full of fear.

"No!" Reed bellowed. He grabbed the young man's shirt below the collar. When his viselike grip tightened on the fabric, it tore loose at both shoulder seams. *"What did you do?"*

The young paramedic made no attempt to pull free. He began hyperventilating, his gaze locked on Reed's distinctive rank insignia, a silver eagle with open wings. "Sir, I'm sorry, sir. I was strapping her into a litter when we almost crashed. She hit the ceiling with her head, right in the same place where she was already hurt."

Reed let go of the shirt, plucked a pen light from the paramedic's chest pocket, and shined it into Lois's right eye. The pupil contracted in response, slowly. He tested the other eye and it did the same. After removing the light, he compared her pupils. They appeared to be the same size. Reed knew that pupils of different sizes were a grim sign in a person who had been knocked unconscious. They indicated massive brain hemorrhaging and were often followed by death within minutes.

"Excuse me, sir," Gordy said.

Reed fell aside, leaning against the wall. Then he reached out and closed Lois's eyes.

Through all the danger and pain and exertion and fear, he had been okay until that moment, but as he gently pressed her eyelids shut a sensation of ultimate misery tore through him like a grenade going off in his stomach. A monstrous hybrid of grief, remorse, and dread that had lain buried since his wife was killed suddenly lurched from the grave, reanimated by the sheer injustice of it all. He and Lois had not been given a chance to even begin exploring the joy and relief they might have someday brought each other.

Convulsed by torment, Reed pulled his knees up and clasped his hands around the back of his neck, flexing his arms so that his lacerated forehead was squeezed against his thigh until he saw bright flashes of pain. He knew from experience that one kind of pain could block

out another. A man just had to choose the pain he pre-
ferred.

The paramedics lifted Lois onto a bunk. While they
were strapping her down, Reed staggered to the cockpit
as if he were under water. He wished he could take a pill
to clear his head of fatigue and emotions. "Go!" he
barked. "Get us back to base as fast as you can."

Nate was still fighting the controls. "I'll try, sir. We
still have to help the tractors, and this wind . . . it's way
beyond normal for this location."

Reed grabbed a safety bar as the Super Stallion
pitched forward and accelerated, swaying from side to
side. He worked his way from one handhold to another
until he was kneeling beside the copilot where he could
reach the radio. "This is Colonel Reed calling the tractor
convoy. Over."

Marshall's deep drawl replied. "Tom! It's good to hear
your voice. You sound pretty beat up, though." Reed
could hear a screeching hiss in the background that did
not sound like static.

"I am. What's the weather like out there?"

"Funny you should ask. We have overcast skies, thin
ice, and mile-high geysers erupting on all sides."

"Wind?" Reed asked.

"Gale force," Marshall said. "The usual."

"We're getting thrashed," Reed shouted. "The pilot
says it's not the usual at all. Call the ICARE weather station and ask them to find a meteorologist who knows
what effects a volcano or a flood of hot water might
have on—"

"That's it!" Marshall yelled.

"What?"

"Tom, do you remember the message Dr. Corcoros
wrote?"

"No, and I lost my note."

"C-A-L-L-L-O-T-H-A-I-R-F," Marshall yelled. "Lim thinks the V's were actually L's. If he's right, it says 'Call Lothair F.' I think I know who Corcoros meant. We found him on a list of technical experts from all over the world. The name below his was Lothair Ferrand—or Forehand, something like that—consulting meteorologist."

"Corcoros is a geologist, not a meteorologist," Reed said. "Why would he know this other guy?"

Silong Lim's accent came over the radio. "Colonel, the list was a printout from a database. I wanted to find a consultant from a place with a good reputation, so I sorted the entries by location."

"Corcoros and Lothair are probably neighbors," Marshall added. "But that still doesn't explain why Corcoros thought it was so important for—"

"Maybe Lothair will know," Reed said. "Give him a call while you're waiting for us."

Professor Lothair Ferrand had been watching his wall clock while the men in Antarctica droned on about the boiling subglacial lake in the Warner Basin. The Friday-evening class Ferrand was supposed to teach in the first-floor lecture hall was scheduled for seven, so he was already five minutes late. He would be even later by the time he rode the Green Building's sluggish elevators down from his office on the sixteenth floor.

Designed in 1964 by I. M. Pei, the Cecil and Ida Green Building—better known as Building 54—was one of the tallest structures on or around the long riverfront campus of the Massachusetts Institute of Technology. At twenty stories, it added a singular appearance to the Cambridge skyline with its pale, Spartan, cast-concrete architecture and the bright white plastic sphere enclosing scientific instruments on its roof. The slender building was impractical in some ways, despite its magnificent views of Cambridge on one side, Boston and the Charles River estuary on the other. Its closed HVAC system tended to make it hot on the sunny side and cold across the hall. And the elevators took forever. Even the first floor was really at a third-floor height above an open archway in the middle of the building. Building 54 was entirely occupied by the Department of Earth, Atmospheric, and Planetary Sciences, better known on campus as Course 12 or EAPS.

Ferrand paced back and forth in front of the elevators at the end of the hall, his short but energetic legs swishing against each other. He was a small man with hazel eyes and coarse blond hair that stuck straight up. He had spent a lot of time outdoors, and his face was craggy, with a deep ruddy tan that made him look perpetually sunburned.

Since he was late for class, and lecturing always made him nervous, he had not paid very close attention to what Mr. Dunn and Dr. Lim had told him on the phone. Sometimes Ferrand wished he had never published that one paper that had garnered so much attention from the excitement-starved science columnists. He had lost count of the paranoid nitwits who had called or e-mailed him, asking if the squall brewing up outside might be the end of the world. He had to admit, though, that this call was by far the most interesting one he had ever received. And the callers probably were who they said they were—Ferrand had seen the news of Amery Station's collapse on TV.

While waiting for an elevator, he finally began to seriously ponder the dynamic natural system Marshall Dunn and Silong Lim had just described. One thing they were right about: When the melting ice sheet finally peeled back and exposed hundreds of square miles of boiling water to the frigid polar air, the sudden release of pent-up heat to the atmosphere would be phenomenal.

Astounding.

Unprecedented.

CHAPTER 17

The Winds of Hell

Professor Ferrand pushed the DOWN button again, frantically. When the elevator arrived, he stepped in and reflexively selected the button for Lindgren Library, which occupied the Green Building's second floor. He often went to the department library when he had to concentrate on a tough problem and his office, which was on the sunny side of the building, was too hot.

Ferrand had forgotten about the lecture for which he was now ten minutes late.

He strode into the library, past the tiny circulation desk, and turned left to the nearest window. There he laid his lecture notes on a study desk by one of the huge windows and stood looking down from the sharp Boston skyline and the sunset-bronzed Charles River to the *Big Sail,* a forty-foot, thirty-three-ton black iron sculpture by Alexander Calder that reminded Ferrand of ship sails twisted at impossible angles by some unearthly gale. The sweeping iron plates of the *Big Sail* blurred in Ferrand's vision as his eyes lost focus, their share of his cerebrum temporarily diverted to help with mental calculations.

Ferrand's academic specialty was computer modeling of tropical cyclones with sustained winds exceeding seventy-four miles per hour. In North America and the Caribbean, these largest and most destructive of all storms were called hurricanes. In Asia they were called typhoons. Hurricanes and typhoons were generated only within thirty degrees of the equator, where broad expanses of ocean could become warmer than seventy-nine degrees Fahrenheit.

The roaming herds of thunderstorms that plagued warm seas did not always coalesce into hurricanes, however. The trigger that actually precipitated hurricane formation was still unknown—it was the secret that Ferrand and his students had been stalking for years in his computer lab and on the Lockheed WC-130 he flew through mature hurricanes to collect data. If this mystery could be solved, forecasters could start predicting hurricanes before they actually began.

The processes controlling hurricanes once they got started were much better understood—so well, in fact, that the sophisticated numerical models running on supercomputers and high-end workstations in Ferrand's lab could synthesize essentially every nuance of hurricane behavior from basic equations of thermodynamics and fluid mechanics. All hurricanes were driven by the evaporation of seawater, which transferred heat to the air, making it expand and rise. Whether simulated or real, a juvenile cyclone would grow in size and intensity until friction in the churning air and water counterbalanced the buoyancy force of the central updraft. Then the convection cycle would rage on for up to a month, with winds up to two hundred miles per hour and waves as high as ninety feet.

No matter how long they lasted, though, real hurricanes never exceeded a certain maximum intensity.

Professor Ferrand had published calculations early in his career showing that larger storms were actually impossible on Earth. Sea surface temperature determined a storm's power, and the sun could only make the oceans so hot.

No one had bothered to consider the hypothetical behavior of the atmosphere above an impossibly hot ocean until late one night early in Ferrand's career, when one of his graduate students reported bizarre output from a routine hurricane simulation. The simulated storm had winds that approached the speed of sound at 760 miles per hour and reached well into the stratosphere, the atmospheric layer between ten and thirty-five miles above sea level. Ferrand and his student knew that the fastest winds on Earth, found in rare F-5 tornadoes, barely approached 300 miles per hour. They also knew that real storms on Earth were confined to the troposphere, the atmosphere's bottom ten miles.

The student assured Ferrand that the input file he had prepared was correct—both of them knew that input should always be checked first when a trusted program apparently failed. Ferrand then spent a week looking for an insidious flaw in his hurricane simulator's calculations or in the theory behind them.

Finally the student saw a typographical error and confessed to Ferrand.

At first, Ferrand was just relieved that the problem was not in his simulator, which was the synthesis of his life's work. Later, when he saw the student's error and realized its implications, he was ecstatic. The input error was an initial ocean temperature of 140 degrees Fahrenheit, much hotter than the maximum temperature of a real ocean heated only by the sun.

Ferrand dubbed the mind-boggling theoretical storm a hypercane.

But would a real hypercane be generated if an ocean *could* somehow reach 140 degrees? Ferrand conducted some numerical experiments, which predicted that the fury of a cyclone would abruptly escalate from a normal hurricane to a hypercane if the water became hotter than 120 degrees, provided the water was open to the atmosphere across an area at least thirty miles in diameter. The Earth had been much warmer early in its history, before multicellular life. Hypercanes could have been common back then.

He also searched the libraries for any exotic natural phenomena that could potentially heat a large body of water to 120 degrees. He found several, but the most plausible scenario was the local heating of an ocean by a celestial impact. An asteroid. That led Ferrand to hypothesize that hypercanes might have played a vital role in the global disaster that struck 66.4 million years ago, wiping out three-quarters of the species on Earth, including the dinosaurs and all other animals with an adult weight over fifty-five pounds.

Most scientists still believed that cataclysm's ultimate cause was the giant meteor impact that had left a now-buried 170-kilometer crater on the Yucatan coast near Chicxulub, Mexico. That explosive impact supposedly ejected enough particulate material to darken the atmosphere and block out the sun, inhibiting photosynthesis and plunging the entire globe into a brief but intense ice age. Mild versions of this shading and cooling effect had actually been observed by scientists when explosive volcanic eruptions like that of Mount Pinatubo in 1991 threw out thousands of tons of ash and sulfuric acid droplets.

There was just one problem with the meteor-impact theory—based on the crater size, models of the impact indicated that it should not have released enough airborne debris to cause an ice age. So what could have lifted the rock pulverized by the impact into the atmosphere?

Aside from an improbably intense volcanic eruption or a meteor impact even greater than the one at the end of the Cretaceous Period, only two known phenomena were capable of darkening the whole stratosphere. One of these phenomena was a global nuclear war, in which soot from burning cities would almost completely block out the sun, chilling most of the Earth below freezing. Such a cataclysm was known as nuclear winter, and it was almost certainly a realistic possibility, broadly accepted by the scientific community. Yet mankind's awareness of nuclear winter was derived entirely from theoretical simulations conducted at research universities.

The only other phenomenon powerful enough to bring on an instant ice age was also known only from computer simulations. *It was a hypercane.*

Although the winds and sea swell in a hypercane would be locally devastating, far worse than a comparatively trivial category-five hurricane, the potential of a single hypercane that lasted several weeks to cause an ice age also made it a global threat. The key to this ominous possibility was the storm's height. By reaching miles into the stratosphere, which normal weather could not penetrate, a hypercane could deposit a huge payload of airborne particles where later rains could not scavenge them. Although a hypercane would spew up debris at only one point on the globe, the stratospheric jet streams would swiftly spread it into a worldwide cloak, like venom diffusing through a victim's body from the bite of a viper.

In his quest for plausible situations that could generate a real hypercane in the modern world, Ferrand consid-

ered volcanic heat sources. Geothermal hot spots certainly contained enough heat to boil oceans, but he dis-
missed this scenario because the Earth couldn't release
its heat *fast* enough. Any body of water large enough to
generate its own weather would cool so efficiently by
evaporation that even the most rapid eruptions would
heat it only a few degrees, not enough to reach the
threshold temperature for a hypercane.

Until now, it had never occurred to Ferrand that a
large water body overlying a geothermal heat source
might somehow be insulated from evaporation until the
water was hot enough to drive a hypercane. It was especially nonintuitive that floating *ice* could prevent a lake
from cooling. But the data from the Warner Basin would
allow no other interpretation.

As Ferrand stood by the window in Lindgren Library,
lost in thought, the awesome and terrifying chain of
events that he had started unconsciously predicting while
on the phone with Marshall and Lim finally linked together in his mind. All large cyclonic storms, including
real hurricanes as well as theoretical hypercanes, were
driven by the same thermodynamic instability—the difference in heat content between warm water and cool,
dry air. The intensity of the storm just depended on the
magnitude of this difference. So what kind of storm
would come when a cauldron of boiling water forty
miles wide was suddenly exposed to the coldest and driest air on the planet?

Professor Ferrand bounded down the windowless
concrete stairwell of Building 54, wondering how
many steps he could safely take at a time. Better leave
it at three, he thought, going sideways. Breaking a leg
now would be the most irresponsible thing he had ever
done.

The hard concrete stairs were giving him shin splints

by the time he reached the basement and flung open the heavy door. He turned right and raced down a gently descending underground corridor between locked specimen cabinets on his right and clanking white insulated steam pipes on his left. The concrete tunnel was hot and smelled vaguely of sulfur, as always. After waiting for a wide gray automatic door to open, he dashed through and skidded several feet, nearly falling. He had forgotten about the puddle on the gray tile floor beneath the notoriously leaky pipe valve known as 66A.

Ferrand regained his balance, turned right again, and almost collided with a cart full of test tubes and partially dismantled oscilloscopes. Soon he was flying through the red doors with big round windows that told him he was now under the Ralph Landau Building, better known as Building 66.

Building 66 was several floors high, and although just up to the ankles of his own department building, it was also a distinctive structure because of its triangular shape. The steepest vertex of the triangle greeted pedestrians crossing the street from the subway stop like the prow of a battleship, a gigantic concrete wedge rising straight from the sidewalk, appearing razor sharp from a distance. Ferrand's destination was 66-080, a tiny basement room under the very tip of this corner. Like several other oddly shaped and positioned rooms across the MIT campus, 66-080 was an Athena cluster, filled with high-end computer workstations linked together via the campus-wide network.

Ferrand peered through the cluster's windows. Four of the workstations were occupied, but the other eighteen were free. Good—his students could work together and usurp CPU time from other machines all across Athena. He punched in the security code and flung open the door. One of his graduate students, John Mason, was already logged in and opening their modeling software. Ferrand had called John from the library, finding him, as expected, in the tiny room full of microcubicles where the grad students lived.

"What's going on?" John asked as Ferrand dashed up behind him.

"Get Holly and Chang down here," Ferrand said. "I have to tie up these computers so other students won't come in and take them."

John called his fellow grad students, relaying to them what Ferrand had told him so far. "Get your butts down here, and bring your WeatherMod notes." When he turned around, Ferrand was feverishly taping OUT OF ORDER signs on all the monitors. The four undergrads already in the cluster were looking around nervously, wondering what was happening. None of them asked, of course, each afraid he was the only one who didn't already know.

Ferrand's first goal was to build a computer model of the undisturbed atmosphere above the Warner Basin, as it had existed before the eruption. If the model worked—if its output matched reality—they could use it to conduct numerical experiments, changing certain input parameters to find out how the real atmosphere might behave differently under different conditions. In particular, they could enter a boiling temperature for the lake and remove its cap of floating ice to see what effect the release of heat to the atmosphere would have.

But first they had to develop a model that truly behaved like the real system, and the hardest part of that was calibration—finding a unique set of input parameters and boundary conditions that were scientifically plausible and yielded realistic output.

"Why aren't we using the computers back in the lab?" Holly asked when she and Chang arrived.

Ferrand spoke quickly, not looking up from his terminal, his stubby fingers tap-dancing on the keyboard. "To cover all plausible scenarios, we'll need hundreds of simulations. A 3-D transient model with this many cells will take hours to run, so we'll have to do them all simultaneously—there's probably no point in even starting this unless we can finish by tomorrow morning."

"What are we starting?" Holly asked.

"You'll see," Ferrand said with the mischievous grin he gave his students whenever they asked what would be on his final exam.

John was pointing to the computers as he counted. "We can't do hundreds of parallel simulations on just twenty-two workstations."

Ferrand absently waved a hand. "Of course not. We'll use these machines as remote terminals to log on to others across Athena. We can write batch files to launch all the runs at once."

"That's against the rules," Holly said.

"It'll bog down the whole MIT network," John said.

Chang whistled and grinned.

"The rules don't apply to what we're doing tonight," Ferrand said, wiping sweat. The Building 66 Athena cluster had been insufferably stuffy since the physical plant people had finally responded to the complaints that it was always too cold. "I have an old account at HCC," he added. "We'll take over *their* whole campus network if we need to."

HCC stood for Harvard Community College, which was how some insiders at MIT facetiously referred to the rival Ivy League university that was just two stops farther out on the Boston subway's Red Line.

"Let's get started," Ferrand said. "I want you to help

me build an atmospheric model faster than you ever thought possible. Just pretend the fate of the world depends on it. All you need to know is that there's a weird volcanic caldera called the Warner Basin buried in the Antarctic ice cap. . . ."

CHAPTER 18

Midnight·Modeling

It took Professor Ferrand and his students less than two hours to build a computer model of the atmosphere over the Warner Basin, a job that any of them would have normally expended at least a day on. At nine p.m., they gathered around Ferrand's monitor and watched as he superimposed an image with hundreds of tiny black arrows representing simulated wind speed and direction over an image of the Warner Basin scanned from a paper map. The map was pink and green and slightly unfocused. Next he imported another file with the same basemap and similar arrows, except these arrows were red instead of black and represented real wind velocity data from anemometers around Amery Station. Using his mouse, Ferrand grabbed the imported image and moved it across his screen until the two basemaps were aligned. As he did so, the red arrows moved atop the black ones, covering them almost precisely. After twenty-one previous tries, this was the first time the real and simulated winds had matched.

"We have a calibration!" Ferrand announced.

They began the sensitivity analysis, varying one parameter in each input file so the hundreds of simultaneous simulations would give them a library of information about how the real system might respond under different conditions. Each student was assigned a different parameter to examine. John varied the temperature of the lake water, Holly tested the speed at which the hole in the ice grew, and Chang handled variations in the lake's thermal convection rate.

On the fourth floor of the student union at the other end of campus, several undergraduates were furiously pounding away at an Introduction to Psychology term paper in the largest of the Athena clusters. They began swearing when their cursors simultaneously froze. Then they regained control of their text editors, but their keyboard input remained perceptibly slow to appear on the screen. The more sophisticated users called up a summary of CPU resource allocation and could see that thirty, fifty, or even seventy percent of their computers' power had been usurped by a job sent from somewhere else in Athena, a job ominously named ENDWORLD.BAT.

Michael R. Kincer—head of the EAPS department— sat up in bed, blinking and scratching his thin goatee. The phone was ringing downstairs. It had rung three times a few seconds before, and he had heard his own voice mumbling from the answering machine. Now the caller was ringing again, unsatisfied with leaving a message.

"What time is it?" his wife muttered.

Dr. Kincer grabbed his eyeglasses and looked at the clock. "Ten till midnight."

He stiffly staggered across the bedroom and down the dark stairs, patting down his thinning black hair. Dr.

Kincer covered the length of his spacious home with a few long strides. He was a very tall and lanky man, a regular Abe Lincoln, except with a sharp goatee instead of a full beard.

The caller was trying a third time now. It must be an emergency, Kincer thought. Both of his daughters were at a tough college—by ordinary standards—and one had just been dumped by her boyfriend. And his mother in Orlando had been battling a pancreatic infection. . . .

He snatched up the receiver. "Hello?"

"Mike, you have to contact that air force colonel in Antarctica and tell him to get everyone away from the Warner Basin as fast and as far as possible."

"Lothair? What the . . . ? Are you still on campus?"

"Yes," said Professor Ferrand. "I also want you to call FEMA for me. Ask them if—"

"Who's Fema?"

"The Federal Emergency Management Agency. Ask them what kinds of disaster planning they've done for the Antarctic bases."

"Why?" Kincer asked, bewildered and sleepy.

"Because a hypercane is coming."

"A *what*?" Now Kincer was awake. He knew all about Ferrand's outlandish hypercane theory. He also knew that tropical cyclones were impossible in polar regions because the water temperature had to be at least—

"Oh my Lord," Kincer whispered. He had seen a report of the volcanic eruption on the news. Kincer's background was in geotechnical engineering—mostly rock-blasting dynamics—but he knew enough meteorology to realize that *something* was going to happen when the boiling lake was exposed to the atmosphere, although not exactly what.

"No time to pray now," Ferrand said. "We're running WeatherMod simulations on Athena. I'll let you know as soon as I have a quantitative prediction, something tangible to show the authorities. For now, just try to explain the science and tell everyone in Antarctica to prepare for evacuation."

Simulation output is not tangible evidence, Kincer thought. In fact, it's often completely wrong. "Lothair, what if we pull the alarm and nothing happens? We don't want to cause an unnecessary panic or make fools of ourselves. Until we know for sure that the storm is coming, I think we should—"

"We don't have time to publish a peer-reviewed paper, Mike. However this turns out, it will be a page in world history by next week."

"Fine, but I can't just call out of the blue and say—"

"Mike, *please*! It won't make any difference that we foresaw this cataclysm if we can't warn the world in time to prepare. I need your help because I don't have time to run around ringing alarms, and no one but you would trust me on this."

"What makes you think—?"

"Believe me, the storm is going to be *bad*," Ferrand continued. "I just don't know *how* bad yet. The only way we'll know for sure is to sit back and watch it happen, and we have a moral duty to not do that."

Kincer smacked the wall. "Okay, Lord have mercy, okay."

"Just try not to sound like a crackpot," Ferrand suggested. "You're a tenured professor and department head at the world's leading scientific institute, for God's sake. Just tell them that, and if they won't accept your credentials . . . ask if you can speak to someone with a clue."

Kincer heard a click followed by a dial tone. Try not to sound like a crackpot, he thought. It was a good thing Ferrand had not called FEMA himself—the excitable meteorologist had a tendency to wax poetic, especially when discussing his pet hypercane theory.

Kincer took a deep breath, smoothed down his goatee, and dialed 911.

The simulation results began trickling in at midnight. Meanwhile, Ferrand ordered two Super Supreme Pan Pizzas and several bottles of Mountain Dew for his students while they developed a new kind of model.

The Warner Basin model that was running with slight variations on most of MIT's computers had been constructed with the WeatherMod software, which Ferrand had developed to simulate hurricanes. The new model used a program called GSPT, developed at Cornell University specifically for simulating nuclear winter scenarios. GSPT stood for Global Stratospheric Particulate Transport. The new model simulated the Earth's entire atmosphere by dividing it into thousands of small cells that interacted via complex rules of meteorological dynamics. The program's primary purpose was to calculate the fraction of sunlight that would be blocked out under each of these cells by particles in the stratosphere. Ferrand gave the input file a particle source in a single cell positioned over the Warner Basin. The output from the WeatherMod simulations would yield the rate of that source, in metric tons of dust per second.

The GSPT run would also need other input parameters, such as the dust's grain size distribution and optical properties. Ferrand left John in charge and headed back to Building 54 to find the additional data he needed. When he reached his office, he opened a chat link between his computer and John's and forwarded the information as he found it. For an hour John sent nothing but confirmations that he had received the data. Then Ferrand heard the chat software chime and turned to his monitor. John's message was:

holly and chang went home. i live in somerville. the T stops running in 15 minutes. should i go too?

Ferrand hastily typed a reply:

NO! start GSPT run now. use particle source from weathermod run with no ice and 100 C h2o.

He clicked on the SEND button, cursing softly, then typed another quick message.

i'll give you a ride if we get done tonight.

Ferrand was digging through a pile of figures in the dustiest corner of his office, looking for a loose appendix from the original TTAPS computer modeling study that had resulted in the nuclear winter hypothesis, when his terminal chimed again and he crawled out from under a table to check it.

The message from John said:

i have results. i think you should come down and look. this is not for real, is it???

*   *   *

Dr. Kincer sped through the darkness in his old brown Mercedes, headed south from his home near the New Hampshire border. It was a Friday night, so the interstate was crowded even at one-thirty in the morning as he neared Cambridge, the last suburb before Boston. His destination was the MIT campus, where he would join Professor Ferrand at a videoconference with the world's disaster response authorities.

Kincer discovered that he could not leapfrog through traffic at more than ninety miles per hour with only his left hand on the wheel. His right hand was occupied with his cell phone. Since Ferrand had called him, he'd spoken with dozens of officials in Antarctica, Washington, even the United Nations in New York.

He dialed with his thumb while zooming around a Porsche, calling Ferrand to tell him the videoconference was already being convened in the other participating locations. After Kincer listed some of the more prominent people in attendance, Ferrand made a little strangled noise and said, "Jesus, Mike, you must have made some butt-scary phone calls."

"Indeed I did," Kincer said. "Do you have any scary figures and tables to back them up?"

"They're rolling off the printer as we speak."

"Good. You'd better pray to God you didn't screw up your input file, because you know where both our careers are going if we blow this much smoke and there's no fire."

Ferrand sighed, sounding exhausted. "Actually, Mike, you should wait until you see these simulated wind velocity maps and sunlight attenuation curves before you say that. It would be bad for us and the institute if I've screwed up, but frankly . . . I'm praying that I did."

Kincer hung up and glanced at his scribbled list of people to call.

A few minutes later he came upon a forest of red taillights, a bottleneck between two busy interchanges. He groaned and braked, scanning the blockade for a way through. "Hold on a sec," he said to the elderly woman on the phone. She was one of the directors of NOAA, the National Oceanic and Atmospheric Administration. His engine's smooth whine all but disappeared as he settled in behind a Buick Roadmaster with Maine plates cruising at sixty in the left lane. It felt like he was parked.

A space was available to the right of the Roadmaster. He honked and flashed his headlights. The Roadmaster cruised on, unperturbed.

Kincer activated his emergency flashers, pulled onto the shoulder, and gunned the engine. "Blind old geezer," he growled as he passed the Roadmaster, although he was arguably a geezer himself. In response to the gasp from his cell phone, he said, "Oh no, not you, ma'am."

He sped past the lights of the traffic jam, thinking: All these half-drunk kids out on dates and retirees off to spend the weekend with grandkids would pull aside and let me through if they only knew what's about to happen to their tiny world.

Because Dr. Kincer had something extremely vital to contribute to Ferrand's videoconference, something that might determine whether the world was still worth living in a year later, something that he could not risk failing to get across by not showing up in person. *He had to get there.*

He finished his call with the NOAA director and placed another one. A few seconds after he left the traffic behind, flashing blue lights suddenly reflected from all his mirrors.

Oh crap!

The lights were so bright and startling that Kincer swerved, nearly plowing into the concrete divider. It was not the first time he had wondered how many fatal accidents were caused on an average night in the United States because speeding motorists with legitimate emergencies—or those naive enough to make normal traffic speed when separated from the herd—were blinded and terrified by the lights and sirens of state troopers who had nothing better to do than generate paltry revenue by randomly handing out speeding tickets.

He glanced at his speedometer. He wasn't sure of the law, but at that many miles per hour over a hundred, he was probably headed for jail.

"Dr. Kincer? Dr. Kincer? Are you there?"

The police lights had interrupted his conversation with a general of the army at the Pentagon. "I'm here, General, but I've got a problem." He briefly described his predicament.

"Where are you?" the general asked.

"On my way to the conference."

"*Exactly* where?"

"Southbound on I-93, just past exit 34."

"What kind of vehicle are you driving?"

"An 'eighty-eight Mercedes 300E."

"You'll never outrun them."

"I figured that."

"Try to give me five minutes." The general hung up.

Five minutes for what? Maybe the general would contact the Massachusetts State Police and convince them to back off.

Looking in his rearview mirror, he saw two other police cruisers pull out from behind the one on his tail and speed ahead in the right lane. They were going to cut him off.

He jammed the accelerator to the floor, wishing—not for the first time—that his old Mercedes was a Corvette.

CHAPTER 19

Sounding the Alarm

Professor Ferrand collected a final page from the printer, dashed up one flight of stairs from the Athena cluster in Building 66, and ran across the street to the new extension of the Media Lab at the corner of Ames and Amherst. With its dark windows and slick white walls, the Media Lab was conspicuously different from the other buildings at MIT, most of which were made of huge gray sandstone blocks and looked far more ancient than they were.

Ferrand read his printout as he walked, trying to memorize a list of important points, looking up only to avoid walls as his short legs carried him around the lab for wearable computers and past the virtual reality studios. Finally he came to a facility so new that its memorial nameplate had not yet been installed in the clear plastic bracket above the door.

Trevor Richardson, director of the Media Lab, was waiting to let him in. Dr. Richardson unlocked the door, flicked on the lights, and led Ferrand into the world's most advanced videoconference room.

This was Ferrand's first time inside the tiny auditorium. It's like a one-tenth-scale replica of an IMAX theater, he thought. Steep stadium seating curved around one side. Behind the small stage at the base of the seats, the wall was covered with square flat video screens—one huge screen at least ten feet across, surrounded by a border of sixteen smaller screens.

Richardson walked over to a semicircular desk in one of the corners by the stage. Its top was a sloping black console covered with electronic controls, reminding Ferrand of a planetarium operator's station. The media professor flipped a switch, and the dead gray screens lit up with brilliant color. The images were so sharp and deep that Ferrand jumped back in surprise, half hiding behind a seat. "Can they see me?" he whispered.

Richardson shook his head. "Not yet. I haven't activated transmission. Pick a seat. The cameras will find you automatically from the direction of your voice."

Ferrand sat in the middle of the front row, staring up at the crisp high-definition images. Each of the smaller screens showed a close-up bust of one conferee. A blue banner across the bottom of the picture displayed the individual's name, title, and location. Ferrand felt his pulse accelerate a notch with each face he recognized. The night had been too hectic and too brief for him to realize at a gut level the full enormity of the historical events he was about to set in motion. Now the epiphany came all at once—jolting him with gut-rumbling adrenaline—as he saw the sheer collective eminence of the audience he was about to address.

The right column of screens showed the men in Antarctica: Marshall Dunn, Silong Lim, and Max Bloom. The commander of the military contingent at ICARE, Major Ronald Dawson, was also there, but to Ferrand's surprise Colonel Reed was not. Silong Lim had told him that Reed was leading the disaster response in the aftermath of Amery Station's collapse and was currently the highest-ranking American officer in Antarctica.

Two men and a woman from FEMA occupied the top row of screens. Ferrand knew none of them.

The director of the National Oceanic and Atmospheric Administration was in the upper right corner. The secretary-general of the United Nations was in the upper left.

All of the conferees in the left column were high federal officials. One was the secretary of defense, another the president's chief science advisor. The face in the bottom left corner was the most familiar of all—Gordon G. Davis, the president of the United States.

The big screen in the center showed an enormous round table covered by the white-on-blue globe insignia of the United Nations. All of the twenty or so seats around the table were occupied.

They all look cross and sleepy, Ferrand thought, every one of them. Which was no surprise, considering that Washington and New York were in the same time zone as Boston, and it was almost two o'clock on a Saturday morning.

Some of the conferees also looked skeptical, some scared. Ferrand swallowed with a dry throat, trying not to make a gagging noise. Richardson brought him a glass of water.

"This system is state-of-the-art," Richardson said. "The outgoing video signal occupies more bandwidth than all the phone calls in New York City. But it's simple to use. Just push the red button on your armrest if you want to stop transmission. Push the green button when you're ready to resume. Everything else is automatic. The software recognizes voices and displays the person who's speaking on the center screen. It also processes out background voices, so you won't be able to hear them. Are you ready?"

"Oh hell no," Ferrand gasped, clutching his broomlike hair and wiping sweat with his other sleeve. "Go ahead."

Richardson flipped another switch on the videoconference control console and left the room.

Ferrand saw his own ruddy complexion appear on one of the bottom screens, then squawked in surprise when an enormous computer-animated face—a blond young woman with witchy sky-blue eyes—flashed onto the huge screen in the center. Her common lineage with Japanese cartoons was obvious from her enormous eyes and button nose. In a sultry but booming voice, she said, "Welcome to the NetStar Millennium Cyberconference Center, Professor Ferrand. My name is Janine. I will be your session moderator. There are currently one hundred and twenty-one participants in four locations. The participants you see on the screens will be shown by default, but others will be shown when they speak. If at any time you would like to—"

Gesturing with his thumb, President Davis shouted over Janine, "Hit the green button, Professor."

Ferrand obeyed, trying hard to control his breathing. *This will definitely be a fiasco if I let myself get too intimidated to even talk,* he thought. *But where in the world is Kincer? He should be here by now.*

Janine disappeared when he mashed the button.

The president spoke first, his jowly face and bushy brown hair appearing on the huge center screen. "Major Dawson, where is Colonel Reed? I thought he was still in Antarctica."

"He is, sir," said Ronald Dawson, a bony freckled redhead. "I'm standing in for him during the conference so he can recuperate in the infirmary. He had a hard night—icequake, tractor crash, flood, turbulence . . . he should be patched up and around in a few hours, if he has no internal injuries."

This exchange threw Professor Ferrand so far off guard—he had expected to be the immediate center of attention—that he was startled when President Davis abruptly said, "Okay, Professor, what exactly is a hypercane? Is it something like a hurricane?"

"Yes . . . yes, Mr. President. The way a .44 Magnum is like a slingshot."

Davis scowled. "How much property damage and loss of life can we expect?"

Ferrand glanced at the printout clutched in his sweaty right hand. "The output of the most severe plausible scenario suggested that . . . that—"

"In general terms," Davis said, "how bad will it be?"

"Ap-apocalyptic, Mr. President. Along the same lines as global thermonuclear war, or one of the solar system's biggest asteroids striking the Earth."

The president's scowl deepened. "How many direct casualties?"

"Well . . . the winds probably won't hurt *anyone* directly, Mr. President, provided no one is near the Warner Basin."

Several conferees exchanged confused glances.

"Property damage?" Davis said.

"Tr-trivial," Ferrand stammered. "The ICARE base is designed to withstand katabatics up to two hundred miles per hour, and the wind speed at the base never exceeds one-eighty in our simulations. The central annulus of high-velocity winds will be confined to the Warner Basin and the surrounding mountains, plus some of the Ross Sea. Amery Station is the only significant structure within the severe wind radius, and it's already a total loss."

Now the conferees looked downright bewildered,

some openly angry. Several were murmuring to each other at the White House and the UN. Janine was editing out their voices, but Ferrand could guess what they were saying. Clenching his stubby fists, he concentrated on keeping his expression neutral for the camera. They're making me sound like a lunatic for calling a global alert, he thought. I have to take control of this exchange.

The secretary-general of the United Nations said, "Professor, even before you have explained your predictions, they have elicited an official response with unprecedented speed and cooperation. You should be aware that this is only the thirteenth Emergency Special Session of the General Assembly. Your colleague who arranged this conference assured us that the natural progression of events in Antarctica will have dire consequences for the entire world within a matter of days, or hours. Now you say there will be no deaths or fiscal losses, so would you mind explaining why—"

"If you'll give me a chance!" Ferrand blurted. "The hypercane's local impacts on Antarctica are not the issue. What we have to worry about is the change in global climate that will last for years after the storm is gone if we allow it to reach maturity and rage on until its energy is exhausted. In the most likely scenario I've simulated, the winds reached a maximum sustained speed over seven hundred miles per hour. That's fast enough to pick up boulders the size of cars and hurl them like bullets. As the cyclone spins up to full power, it will lift all the loose rocks around the basin and use them as an abrasive to scour the surrounding mountains. Billions of tons of bedrock will be ground into microscopic powder, then blown up into the stratosphere and dispersed by the jet streams.

"You have to stop thinking *storm* and start thinking *ice age,*" Ferrand continued. "Rock dust and water droplets will block out the sun, at least partially, over the entire planet. Crops will fail. Harbors will freeze. Species will go extinct, not including cockroaches and *Homo sapiens,* I'm sure, although we might kill each other off fighting over food, but . . . the environmental devastation from this event will be measured not in terms of slain organisms or even extinct species, but in the loss of whole ecosystems. And the ultimate toll on humanity won't be just the millions of casualties from famine and cold. It will be the destruction of nations."

Ferrand took a deep breath and a long drink, panting. He scanned the border screens. There was no murmuring now, and no one was replying, although they all looked profoundly alert.

Max Bloom spoke up from Antarctica. "Mr. President, if I may, I'd like to ask the professor a question."

Davis nodded.

Max faced the screen with a suspicious squint. He was pale, blond, and balding, with a round puffy face, a long neck, and a sparse cactuslike mustache. "Professor Ferrand, have you ever conducted research in Antarctica?"

"No."

Max nodded, his squint narrowing. "Do you have any kind of official connection with ICARE or any of the operations in Antarctica?"

"No, but—"

"That's what I thought," Max said. "I'm sure some of the government authorities present at this meeting have verified that you really are an expert on the atmosphere. But we have several atmospheric scientists working full-time in Antarctica, and hundreds more around the world have research projects going down here. Why have none of them said a word about this . . . this 'hypercane'?"

Ferrand wiped sweat, trying to decide how to explain. I should have anticipated this, he thought.

The secretary-general of the United Nations said, "It does seem strange that the person who brought this problem to our attention has no affiliation with an Antarctic program. Professor, how did you get the site-specific data you needed for input in your simulations?"

"I—I just made reasonable assumptions. That's always the first step in a modeling analysis."

Max Bloom gasped like a frog. "What about the *other* steps? You didn't even finish your analysis before calling us? How can you be a hundred percent certain that the world is about to end, based on unfinished computer models that didn't even use real measurements?"

Ferrand wrung his hands between his knees where the camera could not see them. "Predictive modeling is never a hundred percent certain about anything, Mr. Bloom. That's not the point."

"I'm sorry," Max said, rolling his eyes, "but it seems clear that we're simply jumping the gun here. The Antarctic economy is already in a shambles from the power outage. I can't imagine evacuating ICARE because of some computer model that doesn't even have real observations to back it up. Especially when the model is predicting something as ridiculous as winds blowing faster than a passenger jet flies."

Ferrand scanned the faces. They were murmuring again, and now *all* of them looked skeptical. He felt faint.

President Davis cleared his throat, lips pursed. "I'm inclined to agree with Mr. Bloom, Professor. Maybe you should have verified your computer results in some way before causing this much fuss."

"*We don't have time,*" Ferrand groaned, mopping his forehead with a sleeve.

"If your predictions are correct, that's true," Davis

said. "Just tell us what gave you the idea to run your simulations in the first place."

Ferrand described the phone call from Marshall Dunn and Silong Lim on the previous evening. Once he got started, he also found the words to explain the basis for his input assumptions—why he didn't need site data because the only variable parameter was the water temperature and that was controlled by the boiling point. His audience seemed to understand, but they still looked skeptical.

President Davis finally cut him off, excused himself, and hit his red button. Ferrand waited for six minutes, sweating profusely, while the president conferred in private with his advisors.

Finally the White House rejoined the videoconference. "Okay, Professor, you've given us enough justification to start preparing for the worst, but only after Dr. Kincer corroborates everything you've told us. Where is he?"

CHAPTER 20

Chase

One of the state police cars pursuing Kincer swerved into his lane in front of him. He looked to the left. Another cruiser was speeding along beside him, two feet away, filling his cabin with flashing blue light. The third car was on his rear bumper. After a four-minute chase, they had him boxed in.

The cruiser in front began to rapidly slow down. Kincer slammed on his brakes to avoid plowing into it. They herded him onto the right shoulder and stopped in the middle of the overpass between exchanges 30 and 31. He waited, listening to his pounding pulse, watching the cops get out and slam their doors and swagger toward him.

Kincer watched the headlights and taillights zooming past his car. All caught up in their mundane chores and petty passions, he thought. Assuming nothing that happens beyond the edge of town can significantly impact their lives.

An overweight trooper rapped on his window with callused knuckles, shining a painfully bright flashlight into his eyes. Dr. Kincer rolled down the window, keeping his hands where the troopers could see them. He hoped the smile he was straining to produce looked convincing.

"Please step out of your vehicle, sir."

Kincer got out. His long skinny legs felt weak. The traffic below the overpass was surprisingly loud. The young trooper with a crewcut marched him around to the passenger side, where they were safe from passing traffic. The cop had a long mustache and stank of cigarette smoke, even in the breeze blowing across the overpass.

"Turn around and place your hands on the roof."

Kincer obeyed, and the trooper patted him down for a weapon. "Are you going to arrest me for reckless driving?"

The cop silently grabbed his left arm and pulled it behind his back. Kincer felt a cold steel handcuff close around his wrist and heard it snap shut. The cop did the same with his other wrist, forcing him to lean over the car with his hands bound behind him.

What can I do to stall? "Listen," Kincer said. "There's an urgent international crisis that—"

"I need to ask you some questions, sir. Have you been drinking tonight?"

"No."

"Do you have a medical emergency?"

"No, but—"

"Why are you wearing a jacket and tie?"

That seemed like a strange question until Kincer remembered that it was two a.m. and the mismatching suit he had thrown on in thirty seconds was not something any sane man would wear on a date.

"I'm on my way to a meeting," Kincer said.

"With whom?"

"The president's chief science advisor, a bunch of

guys in Antarctica, and the prime minister of New Zealand, among others."

After a pause, the cop yelled to one of his comrades. "Hey! Get the Breathalyzer." Then he turned back to Kincer. "Sir, do you take any prescription medications?"

"I'm not schizophrenic!" Kincer shouted. "Just hit the redial button on the cell phone in my car. You'll get the operator at the White House. Ask her to—"

One of the other cops yelled, "Hey! What's that?"

Kincer heard it too, a dull thumping roar that seemed to come from below the overpass. Within a second, it increased to a tremendous onslaught of noise and was joined by a powerful wind that blew his thin black hair forward and turned up his coattail. He could feel his loose trouser cuffs flapping against his ankles. Tree tops that were level with the highway at both ends of the overpass swayed violently in the wind. Then a pure white light like a thousand full moons came on behind him, casting stark shadows across the car from him and the trooper still holding his bound arms.

The trooper let go and turned around. "What the . . . ?"

Kincer turned around too, half expecting to see an alien spacecraft. The trooper shielded his eyes from the blinding light with an arm. Kincer had to settle for turning his head sideways and glancing over the round guardrail from the corners of slitted eyes. He saw three intense floodlights hovering in the dark sky above a square building containing a Pizza Hut and a Dunkin' Donuts. One of the wobbling lights was just a few feet beyond the guardrail. The others were farther back. Kincer could make out a shimmering glass helicopter cabin and blurred rotor blades behind and above each light. He could also see what looked like tiny wings sprouting from the sides of each cabin. Slung under these winglets were dark cylindrical objects that looked like missile launchers.

An amplified voice boomed from one of the choppers. "Release your prisoner and return to your cruisers at once."

When they heard the amplified voice, all three of the state troopers darted behind the Mercedes—the closest cover they could find—and aimed their pistols at the helicopters. Kincer was left standing alone in the blinding floodlight beams. "Who are you?" one of the cops yelled at the top of his lungs.

"Holster your weapons," the amplified voice commanded. "We are fully armed and authorized to use deadly force. We are also videotaping your actions."

The cop yelled again, "Who are you?"

"This is a U.S. Army attack squadron. You are interfering with a military operation that is vital to national security. We will use whatever means necessary to prevent you from driving off this bridge with the professor."

Kincer heard electric motors on the helicopters and saw something moving beside each floodlight. Daring to look closer to the sunlike beams, he could make out the tips of several gun barrels aligned in a circle. He realized that each of the three attack helicopters had trained a rotary cannon on one of the police cruisers, two in front of his Mercedes and one behind.

Oh no, I'm going to be caught in a cross fire!

He knew that a half-second burst from those Gatling guns would make the Fords resemble giant cheese graters—and probably hit him with a few ricochets.

"Holster your weapons, *now!*" the voice shouted. The rotary cannons began spinning with an ominous electric whine.

Oh crap! Oh crap! Kincer knelt on the asphalt and squeezed his eyes shut.

The amplified voice said, "Okay, now unlock him."

Kincer opened one eye. The cannons were spinning to a halt. Rising up on his knees, he saw the cop with the mustache run around the Mercedes trunk, eyes wide with fear. The trembling cop unlocked the handcuffs and stood with his own hands in the air. The other two cops had also put away their guns and were holding up their hands.

Kincer saw two of the army attack helicopters tilt outward and zoom away from the formation. One of these hovered overhead. The other flew along the overpass, in the opposite direction from the traffic that was still speeding by. It stopped just beyond the overpass, hovering so low that traffic halted in the southbound lanes. The chopper that remained in position by the guardrail kept its rotary cannon trained on the front police cruiser.

Once traffic had cleared, the helicopter hovering overhead came down and alighted on the interstate. The pilot ran to Kincer and led him back to the chopper, pausing to let him get his cell phone from the Mercedes.

"This aircraft only seats two," the pilot yelled as they ran beneath the spinning rotor blades. "Normally I would have a copilot, but I flew in alone to leave room for you."

He buckled Kincer in with an elaborate seatbelt harness that went over both shoulders and between his legs. When they took off, the vertical acceleration made Kincer feel like he was being shot from a cannon. He had a full view of the city below. On his left were the white triangular towers and thick cablestays of the ten-lane Zakim Bridge, illuminated from below with ethereal blue light. On his right were the Prudential and John Hancock buildings, uptown Boston's two isolated skyscrapers. Straight ahead, the downtown night lights reflected in the broad glassy estuary of the Charles River.

"Where to?" the pilot yelled. "We scrambled so fast, they didn't tell us *anything*."

"That way," Kincer said, pointing toward the MIT campus. "Land by the tall concrete building with the thing on top that looks like a twenty-foot golf ball."

Ferrand pulled out his cell phone and called Dr. Kincer. A moment later he hung up with a weak smile. "He said he's just landing outside, Mr. President."

Max Bloom's puffy face was red when he spoke. "So you're going to evacuate ICARE?"

The president shrugged. "Professor Ferrand, you said the ICARE base should be safe from the wind. How certain are you of that?"

"Not certain at all," Ferrand said. "I tried to consider a worst-case scenario in the simulations, but a real hypercane has never been observed. It may behave in ways current theory can't predict."

"I think we should evacuate, just in case," said Marshall Dunn.

Max Bloom shot a murderous look to his left. Ferrand presumed that Marshall was sitting on that side of Max.

The president said, "What would you recommend, Professor?"

"Evacuation was my first thought too," Ferrand said. "But now I think it would be the worst mistake you could make."

Max nodded vigorously with a surprised smile.

"We don't know exactly how soon the storm will start," Ferrand explained. "Or how fast it will grow. Evacuation by air is obviously out of the question, since the storm could catch planes by surprise. Likewise, you wouldn't want to be on the nearby ocean when she really gets going. The Warner Basin is close enough to the Ross Sea for the winds to break up the winter pack ice and generate waves of unprecedented height, over a hundred feet, I'm sure. Even the largest vessels could be swamped."

"What should we do then?" the president asked with an exasperated shrug. "I assume there's no way to *stop* the storm."

"Remember," Ferrand said, "think ice age, not storm. I suggest you put together an emergency task force to start preparing for famine, energy shortages, transportation failures, sea level decline, political instability, mass religious—"

The door banged open and Michael Kincer bustled into the room. He took a seat beside Ferrand, who couldn't believe how calm the slender, dark-haired giant looked as he introduced himself to the distinguished audience in a brown blazer and a blue tie. The secretary-general asked him to confirm Ferrand's story, and he did. Then Kincer grinned and said, "You had a brilliant idea a minute ago, Mr. President, if I overheard you correctly in the hallway. There may actually be a way to prevent the hypercane, or to kill it before it reaches maturity. What I'm thinking of may not work. It will be dangerous and difficult even if it does. On the other hand, it may just save the world, if we act fast enough."

Michael Kincer continued smiling for the camera as the secretary-general of the United Nations said, "Surely you can't be serious about trying to stop the hypercane, Dr. Kincer. Controlling the weather is impossible. Isn't that right, Professor Ferrand?"

Ferrand nodded. "In general, no human technology is a match for the forces of nature. One ordinary hurricane can dissipate as much energy in twenty-four hours as the United States consumes in the form of electricity over a period of six months. We *have* had some limited success seeding clouds to increase precipitation or dampen cyclones before they hit land. In 1969 we seeded Hurricane Debbie with silver iodide particles. The storm's intensity decreased by thirty percent for a few hours, but that could have been a coincidence. And that was just a hurricane. Who knows how a hypercane would respond to seeding. I would not advise attempting to interfere in any way that might have unpredictable results."

The secretary-general said, "What do you say to that, Dr. Kincer? Is the outcome of your scheme predictable?"

"Absolutely," Kincer said. "It's true that modifying ordinary weather is impossible or at least unpredictable, but the unique geophysical situation that's going to make this storm so deadly will also make it uniquely vulnerable."

"Well, tell us!" said President Davis.

"First I'd like to hear if anyone else has any ideas," Kincer said. "Because your security advisors are going to *hate* this one, Mr. President."

Kincer paused. No one spoke. As if he were teaching a class, he said, "Okay then, why do hurricanes always dissipate when they move over land?"

"They need hot water to keep going," Davis said.

"Excellent!" Kincer said. "The hypercane will live only as long as it can feed on the heat stored in the Warner Basin lake, which is held back from the ocean by a narrow subglacial ridge across the basin's mouth. All we have to do is excavate a canal through that ridge so the hot lake can drain into the cold Ross Sea before the hypercane reaches maturity."

Kincer grinned at Ferrand.

His dwarfish colleague stared back in awe.

President Davis turned to someone beside him. "How long would it take to dig the canal?"

A new face flashed onto one of the screens. The blue banner at the bottom identified him as the Chief of Engineers and Commander, Army Corps of Engineers. "Weeks, at least," he said. "Maybe years, depending on how thick the ridge is, and how deep we have to go, and what kind of rock—"

The secretary-general said, "Dr. Kincer, it must have occurred to you that we wouldn't have time for the excavation."

"It did," Kincer said. "But all we need to do is punch a fast hole in that natural dam. It doesn't have to be a *neat* hole. Gentlemen, have you ever heard of Project Plowshare?"

CHAPTER 21

Operation Hypercane

Kincer proceeded to summarize Project Plowshare and some of the related government schemes of its time. "In 1956, the director of Livermore Laboratory in Berkeley, California, proposed using nuclear explosives to quickly dig a trench between the Gulf of Aqaba and the Mediterranean Sea to replace the Suez Canal, which had been closed by the Arab-Israeli War. Soon after that, the Atomic Energy Commission started promoting the use of underground nuclear bombs to excavate harbors, reservoirs, canals, and road cuts. They even did a test called Project Gnome, in which they detonated a 3.1-kiloton nuke that melted twenty-four hundred tons of rock. That was to see if the heat in the rock could be tapped to generate electricity—an idea similar to the design of Amery Station, in fact, except with man-made magma. Seven months later they carried out Project Sedan, which was a 200-kiloton detonation an eighth of a mile below land surface. It dug out a crater twelve hundred feet in diameter with a volume of 5.5 million cubic yards. The Australians actually got ready to use five of those 200-kiloton shots to enlarge a harbor near

Cape Keraudren on the northern coast so they could use bigger ships to haul iron ore to Japan. In 1968, President Johnson established the Canal Study Commission to design a new Panama Canal that would be excavated with nuclear explosives down to sea level. The new canal wouldn't have to use elevated locks like the existing canal and could accommodate the largest supertankers. The bottom line is this: Nuclear explosives can excavate large volumes of rock hundreds of times faster than conventional methods, and several civilian projects have already been designed to use them."

"Were any of those projects actually implemented?" Davis asked.

"No. None of them."

"Why not?"

"Primarily because civilian use of nuclear devices presented a strategic security risk. Also because the locals and site workers were in danger of being bombarded with radioactive fallout."

The president looked intrigued, Kincer thought. The secretary of defense looked absolutely horrified.

Surprisingly, the next response came from Antarctica. Marshall Dunn said, "Most of my crew survived the collapse of Amery Station, and most of our equipment is here at the ICARE base. We can drill the blast holes, Mr. President."

The secretary of defense spoke up, looking like he had a wasp in his trousers. "Gentlemen, this is absurd! Thermonuclear warheads are not sticks of dynamite. Aside from the obvious fact that they could be intercepted in transit by a terrorist group or a foreign enemy . . . they contain delicate electronics and complex detonation mechanisms. You can't just drop one in a hole, light a fuse, and walk away from it. The kind of operation you're proposing would require months of advance preparation to ensure security and a reasonable degree of confidence that it will succeed."

"I guess that means we'll have to do it without assurance of security and success," Kincer said.

The secretary-general said, "Mr. President, I must remind you that the Antarctic Treaty specifically forbids military weapons on or near the continent, especially nuclear—"

"We'll worry about that later," Davis snapped. He excused himself and blocked transmission from the White House for the next half hour.

Ferrand also logged off the conference and said, "The Pentagon will never go along with this, Mike. For all they know, we're a couple of spies who made the whole thing up to get our hands on the nukes."

Kincer shrugged. "What choice do they have?"

Ferrand thought about that. "They could choose to ignore us and then cover up the fact that we warned them when it turns out I was right."

Someone knocked on the door. Ferrand jumped up and answered it. It was John, one of his students from the Athena cluster in Building 66. He handed Ferrand a stack of laser-printed wind velocity maps. Before leaving, he also brought the professor up to date on the simulations that were still running. Just before the conference, Ferrand had received permission and instructions for downloading real-time images from a polar-orbiting visible-spectrum spy satellite. John was now tracking clouds on the time-lapse photos to calculate current wind velocities, which he used to calibrate a predictive WeatherMod simulation of the hypercane.

When the White House returned, President Davis said, "Operation Hypercane now has a green light, gentlemen. Mr. Dunn, Dr. Lim, I'll put you in touch with a team of defense engineers while you prepare to drill. You'll have to coordinate with them to figure out what kind of explosive devices you'll need. I also want you to wake Colonel Reed if he's at all able to fight—I'll need him to lead the operation once the nukes get to Antarctica. Meanwhile, I'll work on getting an airlift squadron ready to bring you the devices, along with someone who knows how to detonate them. Professors, will you stay in touch to advise us on the operation's technical aspects?"

"I'll be in my office," Kincer said. "You may need to sign a waiver or something so the bomb engineers can give me the true yields and blast pressures and so forth. I'll do some calculations to make sure the devices you send can do the job."

"Consider it done," Davis said. "Professors, a team of government scientists has just been dispatched to your campus to verify your claims. A special forces unit is also on the way to provide you with security for the duration of this crisis. Now that strategic weapons are involved, everything that's been said at this meeting is classified top secret. That also applies to your computer models, Professor Ferrand, so don't leave them lying around on some network server. Are we all finished for now?"

"No," Ferrand said, noisily shuffling through the printouts John had given him. "I just got word that the hypercane has already begun. Based on satellite data, enough heat appears to be escaping through holes in the ice sheet to establish a new cyclonic wind pattern in the Warner Basin. So far, the wind speeds are no greater than hurricane force, but the heat flux is rapidly increasing as the thin ice melts through. One of my students is now simulating the actual storm, not just hypothetical scenarios. He's recalibrating the model every half hour with real data. At this point we can project a realistic timeline of the storm's future progress."

"Good," Davis said. "How long do we have before we've got the end of the world on our hands?"

"Stratospheric debris and aerosol dispersal will begin in . . . let me see . . . eight hours. I'm sure Operation Hypercane cannot be completed within that time, so some degree of impact on world climate is inevitable at this point. If the hypercane is not stopped, it will continue to pump up dust for nineteen days, and half that length of time is enough to initiate a significant ice age."

"So we'll avoid the worst if we can drain the lake within a week?"

"No," Ferrand said. "I'm afraid that's not the limiting factor." He looked back and forth between two printouts. "Your deadline is actually thirty-two and a half hours from . . . from half an hour ago, which makes it . . . eleven a.m. tomorrow, Sunday. That's three a.m. on Sunday at ICARE."

"Why?" Davis said. "What happens then?"

"The gradually increasing wind will abruptly accelerate to several hundred miles per hour at ground level. Any structure or vehicle in the Warner Basin at that time will be totally obliterated, so you will have to complete all drilling and blasting—and get all personnel out of the basin—in less than a day and a half."

Davis looked ready to give up. Sweat was beaded on his long nose. "Mr. Dunn, is that even possible?"

Marshall spoke up from Antarctica. "It's conceivable, Mr. President."

"Then get started," Davis said.

"Professor," Marshall said, "if we will have to work within the storm, what should we be prepared to encounter?"

"Hell," Ferrand said.

"How big?"

"I said hell, but hail will probably be a part of it. You

should wear hard hats. There will also be other kinds of precipitation."

"What about lightning?" Dr. Lim asked.

"Oh yeah. Plenty," Ferrand replied.

"How high will the storm surge get?" Major Dawson asked.

"The current model predicts a peak of twenty-seven feet on the shore of the Ross Sea three days from now. That reminds me—the most dangerous thing might be the low pressure. It could cause altitude sickness—hypoxia, plus pulmonary and cerebral edema."

Major Dawson went pale. "How low will it get?"

"That depends on how close you get to the cyclone's eye. The region of superlow pressure will be confined to the very core of the storm."

"*How low?*" Dawson repeated.

"It bottoms at two hundred millibars on day two," Ferrand said. "For comparison, standard atmospheric pressure is about a thousand millibars, and the lowest pressure ever recorded in a hurricane is about eight hundred eighty. A person acclimatized to sea level can rapidly lose consciousness and die at three hundred forty millibars, so two hundred is definitely enough vacuum to suffocate you. It would basically be like exposure to outer space."

Ferrand waited a few seconds for other questions, then said, "Mr. President, I'd like to ask a favor. Could you have me flown to Antarctica immediately? I'll bring my field instruments to monitor the hypercane as it develops."

"Operation Hypercane is a military mission, Professor, not an academic expedition."

"I know it will be dangerous," Ferrand said, "but I would be honored to accept the risk. This will be a unique opportunity for science. We may never have another chance to observe a real hypercane."

"I sure hope not," Davis said.

"Besides, I could record live data for more accurate projections," Ferrand added. "It should give the work crews the clearest indicator of how much time they have."

"Very well," Davis said. "Pack your equipment and stand by. We'll get you down there."

CHAPTER 22

Infirmary

Half a kilometer inside a scenic mountain near Colorado Springs, behind 45-ton blast doors that could withstand a 1.5-megaton nuclear explosion, thirteen hundred federal employees watched the world's skies. Within the underground complex, fifteen buildings rested upon 1,319 thousand-pound springs to cushion the personnel and 240 mainframe computers in the event of nuclear attack. The primary mandate of this central hub of American and Canadian strategic defense was to provide the earliest possible warning of incoming missiles and bombers. Operated by the North American Aerospace Defense Command, the secure citadel in the belly of Cheyenne Mountain was commonly referred to as NORAD.

On a typical day, the NORAD staff monitored thousands of man-made objects moving through the atmosphere and low Earth orbit, including the eighty-three hundred stray bits of space junk that were larger than ten centimeters. Whenever an unidentified plane flew into U.S. airspace, or a missile was launched anywhere in the world, they knew about it.

A four-star general was visiting to observe the latest computer upgrades at the U.S. Space Command Missile Warning Center, so everyone was nervous on the evening Emma Cordon saw the smudge. Emma was a technician whose duty was to watch a single large monitor with her undivided attention for four hours each day, just in case she could spot anything unusual that had evaded NORAD's state-of-the-art artificial intelligence programs. The abstract pattern of green and blue squiggles on her monitor would have made no sense to a layman, but it was as familiar to Emma as a photograph of her three-year-old son. The image was produced by a satellite that orbited 830 kilometers over the Earth's poles with a period of 101 minutes.

In her two years at NORAD, Emma had never detected a bogey that the machines hadn't seen first.

The smudge began as a fuzzy blue cloud over Antarctica, near the western shore of the Ross Sea, with no other clouds nearby. In a matter of minutes it grew from a pinpoint to an opaque blob that obscured a hundred miles of coastline, like an amoeba devouring the continent. The smudge was probably some freak weather phenomenon or electronic artifact, Emma thought. Her shift was nearly over, so she also suspected that her tired eyes were playing tricks on her. Whatever the smudge was, it definitely wasn't a nuclear missile attack, so she hesitated before deciding to report it.

The alarms went off.

A cool female computer voice chanted, "Multiple bogey alert, Sector Eighty-one. Multiple bogey alert, Sector Eighty-one."

Eighty-one was Emma's sector. She zoomed in and

saw that the alarm had been triggered by a multitude of large objects flying around the center of her new smudge like buzzards circling a carcass. The largest objects were too small to be planes or ICBMs, but they were as big as automobiles. Emma's first thought was that she was seeing debris blown in the wind—she would have called the bizarre smudge a tornado if it hadn't been stationary and a hundred miles across—but how could windblown debris be so large? She selected one of the bright white points representing the orbiting objects and requested a velocity estimate.

Her screen said 360 miles per hour.

Emma blinked. Was a wind speed that high even possible? Maybe the circling objects were self-propelled after all. On the other hand, 360 miles per hour was only an approximate estimate, and the wind would be slower at lower altitudes due to friction with the ground. Still, Emma knew that the fastest ground-level winds ever recorded outside tornadoes were *much* slower than 360 miles per hour. The official record was 233 miles per hour from Mount Washington in New Hampshire, and then there was that fleeting report of a 235-mile-per-hour wind in a hurricane that hit Guam in 1997. Of course there had probably been even faster winds that were never recorded because they blew away the anemometers or there were no weather stations in the—

A heavy hand landed on Emma's shoulder, making her flinch, but she did not turn around. Her trained eyes never left the screen, not even for an instant.

"What's that big smudge?" the general asked. She recognized his voice from a brief motivational speech he had given earlier in the day.

"I have no idea!" Emma blurted.

"Huh," the general said, contemplatively.

Emma felt sweat trickle between her breasts.

A door banged, and Emma heard the familiar heavy steps of an overweight communications officer behind her. He approached the general. "I have a call for you, sir."

"Who is it? What does he want?" The general sounded annoyed.

"It's the White House, sir." Emma saw the communications officer's pudgy hand point past her ear at the monitor. "It's about that cloud over Antarctica. They know what it is."

Reed sat between the beds occupied by Angie and Lois in the trauma ward of the ICARE infirmary. The room smelled of latex and disinfectant. The harsh fluorescent lights made everything bluish white. A translucent curtain was drawn around the two beds, but Reed could see moving shapes and hear the hectic bustle of overcrowded patients outside it.

His big hands shook as he ladled chili into his mouth from the thirty-two-ounce can his nurse had brought him. He had learned in boot camp that a soldier had to eat, no matter what was on his mind.

Wind had made the flight across the Warner Basin a white-knuckle ride all the way, especially when the Super Stallion was leading the tractor convoy through the forest of mammoth geysers. For several minutes the bulky chopper had banked left and right like a jet dodging flak as the pilot threaded a course between the towering white cloud columns. They had almost crashed once while evading a new eruption of steam that blasted into the sky in front of them. Reed had felt like he was back over Baghdad. He wondered what would have happened if the pilot had made a mistake and the seventeen-ton aircraft had flown straight through one of the surging plumes of fog.

He had no recollection of the landing, which probably meant he had fallen asleep on the helicopter somewhere between the Warner Basin and the ICARE base. Since he had been awake and active most of the time for more than fifty hours, and was not aware of the hypercane, he had slept for nearly eighteen hours in the infirmary after his Friday-morning rescue. Then he had been subjected to hours of examination to make sure his many bruises were only superficial. While a doctor sutured his split forehead, Major Dawson and Dr. Kincer at MIT had briefed him about Operation Hypercane. Now it was ten a.m. on Saturday, and the mission to blast the subglacial ridge had begun. Marshall was directing the preconstruction of drill-rig components in the ICARE garage, and a team of excavators had already gone into the Warner Basin to locate and prepare the drilling site. Reed was so stiff and sore he could hardly move, but he planned to coordinate the overall effort from ICARE's radio room.

Maybe the storm won't get as bad as Professor Ferrand predicted, he thought. Maybe it will run out of energy before it can pump the stratosphere full of dust. But Reed knew better than to base tactical decisions on wishful thinking. And Ferrand's predictions had been precisely accurate so far, despite their apparent outrageousness.

As he wolfed down the cold chili, his imagination reeled with the implications of the hypercane. He could still hear Dr. Kincer's voice droning from the portable speakerphone, informing him that the world as he knew it would come to an end—that he might never see the sun again—unless they could blow away the natural dam across the mouth of the Warner Basin within the next seventeen hours.

His mind boggled at the scope and scale of the hypercane itself, and of the cultural and ecological holocaust that would follow. He knew that few people realized just how delicate the global web of political, economic, and industrial infrastructure really was. Most of the seven billion potential survivalists on the crowded planet had no idea how precariously their modern peace and prosperity were perched over a downward spiral of tribalism and anarchy, because they didn't know that organizations like his were busy every day and night responding to international crises with the potential to destroy it all if allowed to escalate out of control. But as commander of the Strategic Resource Development Center, Reed could picture in grizzly detail how modern civilization would crash and burn under the pressure of an instant ice age.

It would be like the nightmare world following a total global nuclear war, without the instant removal of a few hundred million mouths to feed. Reed's predecessors had worked out the basic scenario decades ago. First the stock market would crash. By the next day, inflation would skyrocket exponentially. Within a week the worldwide economy would have completely collapsed. Paychecks, savings, and insurance would be as worthless as investments. The value of cash would hang on for a while, but hoarding would remove it from circulation within a few months. Meanwhile, food and fuel would have to be rationed. Transportation, communication, and healthcare would break down. Crime would rise in proportion with unemployment. Epidemics carried by pests and polluted water would rage out of control. The United States had two years' worth of domestic food reserves, and no other nation would be in a position to take them, but mass starvation might still strike American cities during distribution delays. The eternal night would be filled with misery, confusion, and the many kinds of lawlessness and brutality that inevitably thrive on such chaos. By the time civilization began to recover, it would be set back at least two hundred years.

As long as he survived, Reed would probably end up commanding a peacekeeping force, and he knew what a grim duty that would be.

"The horsemen ride on the wind," he muttered.

Angie stirred. "I saw you and the doctor whispering." Her voice was hoarse and slurred from the codeine-analog analgesic they had given her. "Did he tell you anything about Lois?"

Reed shook his head, chewing. "It was about you." He set down the chili can and gently squeezed her elbow. He wanted to hold her bandaged hand, which was resting atop her white sheet, but he didn't dare touch it. He had watched, stifling his own groans of vicarious agony, while a nurse drained Angie's frostbite blisters to remove the toxic thromboxane that had accumulated in them. Afterward the nurse had slathered the wounds with aloe vera and given Angie a painkiller shot that helped her sleep.

Angie sighed. "How many fingers and toes will I lose?"

"Oh Lord, Pumpkin, it's not that bad . . . just minor frostbite. The doctor said it will take several weeks to know for certain, but he's pretty sure no tissue will have to be . . . removed. He said you might permanently lose some sensation in your fingertips, though. They'll also be hypersensitive to cold from now on, and more prone to frostbite."

"My feet?"

"They didn't freeze. You just wore them out. He said they're swollen but okay."

"They don't feel okay. How's Lois?"

"The same."

Angie raised herself on her elbows, and Reed leaned

aside so she could look past him at her critically injured mentor. Lois had remained comatose since her second head injury. She had started having trouble breathing during the rough flight back to ICARE. Now she lay on her back with her eyes closed in a special hospital bed equipped with extra-high guardrails in case she woke disoriented when no one else was around. A nutrient IV snaked into her right arm. A nurse had shaved off her long blond hair, but the doctor had not yet stitched up her scalp lacerations. Sixteen electroencephalograph wires were attached to her scalp with conductive paste. Her breathing was assisted by a ventilator with a flexible clear plastic tube inserted through her mouth.

Reed felt a pulse of grief and anxious dread with each *snick-chug-whoosh* of the electronic ventilator.

"Is my face bruised like that, too?" he asked.

Angie nodded.

Blue and purple bruises from the ride through the glacial moulin had fully blossomed on Lois's brows, cheeks, and chin. Elsewhere, her skin was deathly pale.

Reed pulled a package from under his chair and handed it to Angie. An orderly had fetched it from his quarters while she was asleep. It was wrapped in sky-blue paper with colorful toucans and puffins. "Happy birthday, Pumpkin. I'm sorry it had to be like this."

Angie smiled. "My birthday isn't until tomorrow, Dad."

"I know. I figured I'd better give this to you now, just in case."

She started to unwrap the present, but the paper hurt her fingers. As he opened the box of overpriced "technical" thermal underwear he had bought at an outfitter's— one of those stores catering to wilderness-worshiping yuppies with way more money than free time—he broached another subject. "Pumpkin, Lois and I did a lot of talking when we were floating in that pool. I . . . I think I really like her."

"I told you," Angie said. "But keep in mind that everything will feel different once we get back to the States, Dad . . . *if* we get back. And that Lois agrees with *me* about everything."

"I know," Reed said. "I don't care. It's not just compatibility. She and I went through a lot together when we were stranded in the water, clinging to each other for warmth. I could feel this incredible . . . compulsive . . .""

"Chemistry?" Angie said.

"I guess. I probably shouldn't talk to you about it."

"Who else can you talk to? I'm turning nineteen tomorrow, remember? I know how these things work. I promised Lois I wouldn't tell you this, but under the circumstances . . ."

"What?"

"Well, back at the rookery, I figured out that she kind of had a crush on you."

"Really? Why?" Reed said. "We had never met."

"Your voice, on the phone. She thought you were really . . . poised, when you were begging her to give me an internship as her assistant and explaining how I was depressed for a while, telling her about Mom and how much I hate what's happening to the world. I let her read the e-mails you sent me at the camp. They were all pretty basic—practical stuff—but she liked how you always reminded me that you love me at the top and bottom of each one."

Reed felt himself blush down to his shoulders. "You let her read the e-mails I sent to you?"

Angie grinned sheepishly. "All's well that ends well, Dad. There was nothing private in them. She also liked how you could spell and use correct grammar. She said

not many men are all that literate. It's a big peeve of
hers."

"Anyway, I want to see her again if we all survive,"
Reed said. "Who knows . . . that would be okay with
you, right?"

Angie grinned, leaned out of her bed, and hugged
him. "I love how you make things happen, Dad. You
never just fall when you can jump."

He stared at Lois's pale, inert form over his daughter's
bony shoulder and released a somber sigh. "I just wish
we could somehow know that she's going to make it,
and what kind of . . . condition she'll be in when she
wakes. That would make it a lot easier to concentrate on
what I have to do now."

"What's that?" Angie said, alarmed.

Reed grimaced. "Not much. I wanted to go on the
drilling mission, but I'm so beat up I would be more of a
liability than an asset."

Angie scowled. She had listened when he was briefed
about the hypercane, so she knew what he was talking
about. "You've done plenty already, Dad."

"So what? The mission is not complete. I don't mind
the pain, but I *can't stand* being a casualty. At least I can
still coordinate the operation from headquarters."

Finished with his meal, Reed kissed Angie's frost-
nipped forehead and jogged to the door, swabbing blood
from his crudely stitched brow with a sleeve. "Hang in
there, Pumpkin."

"Hey, Dad! If there's any way I can help . . ."

He looked back toward his daughter's hospital bed,
and tears came to his eyes. This is the young woman
who couldn't face living in a dormitory, he thought. Unbelievable. "The only thing I need you to do is rest and
get well."

Major Ronald Dawson, Reed's second in command,

came running along the corridor. Panting, he said, "I just spoke to the physical plant manager, sir. We'll only have heat and power for another twelve hours."

"The base is that low on fuel?"

"Afraid so, sir. The search for you and Dr. Burnham used up more than we expected, and then the drillers took all the fuel they could carry when they left a few hours ago."

The doctor had returned to check on Lois. He nodded toward her through the window in the door beside him. "I can't run this infirmary without heat and electricity, Colonel."

"The *Polar Star* is on her way with eight tank trailers of gasoline on her deck," Reed said. "ICARE has several snow tractors with standard commercial fifth-wheel hitches. We'll send them out on the sea ice to meet her as soon as she reaches the point where the ice is thick enough." Reed wished he had ordered a massive airlift of emergency fuel the minute he heard of Amery Station's collapse. He wanted to order a plane-load of fuel now, but the wind could soon be too strong for large, heavily loaded planes to land safely at the ICARE airstrip, which was the only landing field within hundreds of miles.

"By the way, the whole world—not just the ICARE base—could be in trouble if the *Polar Star* doesn't get here," he said. "The plane bringing the warheads is also hauling extra fuel that will be necessary to complete the drilling operation, but if it doesn't arrive in time, the only way to finish the drilling before the hypercane blows the rig away will be to truck a load of fuel from the *Polar Star* to the drilling site."

Reed was stepping down the hall as he spoke. Finally he broke into a backward trot. "Major, tighten up the restrictions for emergency fuel conservation and get your men to search the base for every can of gasoline. Empty any small motors you can find to help feed the main backup generator. I'll call right now to make sure the icebreaker isn't having any trouble from the storm."

CHAPTER 23

Squadron

Professor Ferrand loved flying.

Especially into hurricanes.

He nervously chatted with the pilots of the C-141B Starlifter as the heavy transport jet cruised thirty-five thousand feet above the sunny South Pacific. They mostly talked about the fine weather and the plane. The pilots told him that the first jet-powered plane to drop U.S. paratroops and the first air force transport jet to land in Antarctica had both been Starlifters.

Ferrand had been instructed not to discuss the mission itself, since all the personnel involved in Operation Hypercane had been briefed on a need-to-know basis. The pilots didn't even seem to know the special nature of their cargo, which included more than the ten-thousand-liter fuel tanks they had seen being loaded. The only thing Ferrand had let slip was that he was a hurricane researcher.

The Pentagon's primary concern was making sure the twelve W-80 nuclear warheads aboard the Starlifter were not intercepted by an enemy of the United States. To supplement its internal secrecy, the air force had assigned two small combat aircraft to escort the Starlifter. One was an F-16, the world's most versatile light jet fighter. The other was a Warthog, flown in at Tom Reed's personal request. Whereas the F-16 could defend the unarmed Starlifter from attack by air, the armored Warthog was optimally configured for battling threats from the ground or sea. Reed figured he could utilize the Warthog most efficiently since he knew *exactly* what it was capable of. Both planes were fully armed with a variety of weapons. Landing the fighters at ICARE would violate the Antarctic Treaty, but not as egregiously as the nuclear devices themselves, which were technically military weapons regardless of their intended use. A squadron of F/A-18 Hornets was also on its way from an aircraft carrier in Guam to reinforce the transport's defenses.

Ferrand stood in the middle of the cockpit, watching the camouflage Warthog cruising smoothly at the tip of the Starlifter's huge right wing. Like the F-16, most A-10s seated only one person. This plane was one of the few in which a bombardier seat had recently been added behind the cockpit, but Ferrand could see only one pilot. Below the high-mounted cockpits, the stubby nose was painted to look like a snarling snaggletoothed warthog, with huge tusks, devilish eyes, and hairy ears.

What a flying relic, Ferrand thought. With its rectangular tail fins and straight thirty-foot wings that met at the bottom of the fuselage and tilted upward toward the tips, the Warthog appeared to have more in common with the propeller-driven fighter-bombers of World War II than with the sleek gray F-16 on the Starlifter's other flank. The Hog's two enormous vertical tail fins were mounted at the ends of a straight flat plate that was so broad it looked almost like a second pair of wings. Just in front of this clunky double rudder, the backward-

tapering fuselage sported two enormously bulbous commercial jet engines, which might have made the Warthog
resemble a civilian aircraft if it weren't for the eleven
pylons of missiles and bombs slung beneath the fuselage
and wings, and the huge muzzle of the GAU-8 Avenger
rotary cannon jutting from the nose.

As Ferrand watched, the A-10 abruptly tilted away
and resumed flying beside the Starlifter at a distance of
several hundred yards. A few seconds later, a shadow
passed over the boxy camouflage airframe. Ferrand
looked up and saw an enormous jet swooping down
above the Warthog and pulling ahead. The new plane
looked even bigger than the Starlifter to him.

"Hey, look!" he shouted to the pilots. "Are we being
attacked?" He hadn't heard anything about another
transport jet joining the squadron.

The copilot laughed. "That's the KC-10A Extender
from Guam. The A-10 is out of gas. We'll need more
fuel before we get to Antarctica, too."

As he spoke, a rigid boom protruded down and backward from the rear of the Extender's fuselage. The
Warthog eased up toward the Extender's massive tail
section, and the in-flight refueling receptacle in its nose
mated smoothly with the boom. Five minutes later, the
two aircraft disengaged and the Extender disappeared
overhead—crossing over the Starlifter to fill up the F-16,
Ferrand surmised.

The Warthog resumed its position off the Starlifter's
wingtip. "Aren't the escort jets flying awfully close to
us?" Ferrand asked.

The copilot said, "At this altitude, a tight formation is
the usual—"

"*Holy Mother of God,*" the pilot said, as if he had just
seen Her in the thin upper atmosphere outside the cockpit. He was staring straight forward.

Ferrand clawed off his sunglasses and crowded between the pilots for a better view through the windshield.

Opposite the setting sun, the cloudless southern sky ranged from deep blue at the zenith through a hazy rainbow of colors at lower altitudes—azure, aquamarine, sea green, yellow, tangerine, and finally a pale coral where the sky met the gently curving edge of the ocean. Dead ahead, a dark mass loomed against the coral base of the sky like the dawn of a black sun. Antarctica was still over six hundred miles away—no land was in sight—but the brewing hypercane was already crawling over the horizon.

"That's no hurricane," the pilot said softly.

"What *is* it?" the copilot yelled.

The air force officers looked at each other, then at Ferrand. He saw fear and bewilderment in their eyes, and possibly reproach.

"Has there been a nuclear exchange?" the pilot asked.

"No," Ferrand said, still staring at the rising black dome.

The copilot said, "I don't think smoke from nuclear explosions would be that . . . *big*."

"Or that dark," the pilot added.

As they flew closer, the dark mass resolved into a wrinkled donut of low clouds about a hundred miles in diameter. The cloud bank rolled from top to bottom, creating and destroying pillowlike eddies that glowed a pale pink when they were born at the top but faded into gray shadows as they rolled back into the storm almost at sea level. The pooching and rolling eddies were separated by deep wrinkles that were as black as fresh asphalt.

A twisted pillar of opaque cloud at least ten miles thick sprouted from the center of the donut, rising through the fading sunset colors to an altitude much higher than the Starlifter. The top of the pillar flared like the mouth of a horn to form a flat pinwheel. Alternating streaks of brown dust and pink cloud spiraled outward, twisting around the pinwheel several times before blending and dispersing at its edges.

The sun had set behind the squadron, but it still shone on the upper half of the twisted cloud pillar and the pinwheel, which spread across the deep blue sky so high above the Earth that it gave Ferrand the impression of being in outer space.

The pinwheel was at least twice as wide as the fat donut of clouds at the pillar's base. It was also elliptical, stretching toward the upper left and lower right in Ferrand's view. The shape reminded him of a round spiral galaxy photographed at an oblique angle, although he knew from his simulations that the pinwheel in the sky was perfectly horizontal. It was also translucent, especially toward its wispy edges—Ferrand could see the pale ghost of the half-moon behind it.

It's real, he thought.

Ferrand had doubted his simulations all these years, even while staking his reputation on their results. What if the equations no longer applied at such hot water temperatures or high wind speeds? What if all his simulated hypercanes were an artifact of some glitch in the Weather-Mod code? Now he could finally lay those fears to rest as he beheld with awe and pride a phenomenon no human eyes had ever seen, knowing that he was the only person to whom the fantastic cloud formations were actually *familiar.*

Except why was the stratospheric pinwheel elliptical? That detail was unexpected, and it made him wonder what other surprises the hypercane might have in store.

"My God," Ferrand whispered. "Isn't that the most beautiful sight in the universe?"

"Just tell us one thing," the pilot said. "Are we going to fly *into* that?"

"*Yes!*" Ferrand said, ecstatically.

Seeing the horror on the pilots' faces, he added, "We'll at least have to skirt it on the east."

"Can you tell us what kind of conditions to expect?"

"The turbulence should be rough but manageable," Ferrand said. "Be prepared for sustained high winds, though."

"How high?"

"Extremely high. And possibly flying debris."

The pilot clinched his jaw. The copilot crossed himself.

If you think *that* storm is scary, Ferrand thought, just wait until it's fully mature. He could tell by looking that the hypercane was still in the first stage of infancy. "I'm going to set up my spectrograph at a window to analyze the chemical composition of cloud droplets. Let me know if you guys need any help. I've flown through lots of hurricanes."

"That's no hurricane," the pilot repeated as Ferrand jogged from the cockpit.

Macquarie Island was the ideal habitat for a hermit, especially a die-hard Australian hermit. Although it belonged to Australia, the narrow, thirty-kilometer, recently uplifted ridge of oceanic crust was located more than halfway between New Zealand and Antarctica's Commonwealth Bay, which was just around Cape Adare from the Warner Basin. For several years, the only inhabitants on Macquarie had been a team of archaeologists studying a derelict sealing station at Hasselborough Bay on the north end of the island and a lone Australian shepherd attempting to establish a flock at the south end on Meredith Point. As on all islands below thirty-nine degrees south latitude, cold westerlies blew year-round. The ocean winds were so constant and fierce that Macquarie was devoid of trees, but enough grass grew on its misty slopes and coastal peat moors to support a substantial sheep population, despite the damage done by feral rabbits released by sealers for food in the early 1800s. The temperature varied little from its average of five degrees Celsius, and rain fell more than three hundred days a year.

Roland MacGregor, the hermit shepherd of Macquarie Island, was retrieving a stray band of thirty-two merino sheep from the very tip of Meredith Point when a storm like none he had ever seen blew in. Macquarie Island was just north of the Antarctic Convergence, where warm temperate air normally locked horns with the frigid polar atmosphere, so Roland was accustomed to heavy weather. But sea ice never formed around the island and a berg from Antarctica drifted by only on rare occasions, so Roland knew something was wrong when he stood on a moist wind-polished boulder, shielded his eyes from the gale, and looked out to see a jumble of floating white slabs swirling in the current and washing up on the south side of the rocky point.

Within seconds after he spotted the ice floes, the sky grew darker than usual—*much* darker—and the fog that perpetually shrouded the island was blown away by the coldest wind Roland had ever felt. He did not have a thermometer in the pockets of his heavy wool clothing or on the motorbike he had ridden to the point, but the uncanny wind had to be at least ten degrees below freezing. Such frigid air was as unusual as the icebergs, considering that the lowest temperature ever recorded on Macquarie Island was only minus nine degrees.

The sheep grew restless in the wind, and Roland rushed to get them inland. As he herded them together, he noticed that the rocky beach had disappeared. Having never experienced the sea-level rise beneath a tropical cyclone, it did not occur to him that the beach had been submerged by a storm surge. Instead, despite the telltale pressure and popping in his ears, he wondered if his remote island was sinking into the sea. He had heard that the Macquarie ridge had been uplifted from the seafloor only a hundred thousand years ago, and at least once a year he'd experienced the frequent earthquakes that exceeded 6.2 on the Richter scale. Perhaps God had decided that all men should live in cities, he thought, and had noticed that expensive shipping and harsh weather were not enough to dissuade Roland from his reclusion.

With the heavy white sheep galloping in front of him, Roland crested a low rise on his motorbike and slammed on the brakes, skidding to a halt. The narrow isthmus connecting the knobby tip of Meredith Point to the rest of Macquarie Island was submerged beneath a swath of sea at least a hundred feet wide. It can't be very deep, Roland thought, trying to remember the exact topography of his bike trail, but he didn't dare try to ride or wade across the icy strait.

The sheep panicked when they found their retreat cut off. They began racing around the tiny point counterclockwise, just above the surf, searching for an escape. The fastest runners pulled ahead, leaving the lambs and pregnant ewes behind. By the time Roland had returned to the algae-slimed boulder at the peak to survey his situation, he was surrounded by a ring of bleating, galloping merinos.

As he watched, the surf rose and the ring of sheep constricted. The wind howled louder and grew even colder. Roland huddled between two boulders and shivered. The sky became so dark that he could not see the horizon to the south, and enormous dabs of snow began to pelt his tiny island.

The frantic sheep were eventually racing past so close to Roland's inadequate refuge that their feet splattered him with snow and mud. Then he heard splashing and a new kind of vocalization—more like the squeal of a pig than the baa of a sheep, he thought—and he stood up to see one of the rams swimming toward the mainland of Macquarie Island. The others lunged into the surf after their leader, even the lambs, maddened by the rising tide.

With their thick wool coats to insulate them, the swimmers made it halfway across the strait. Then their frantic paddling slowed and ceased as hypothermia overtook them. Their pale bodies went slack and floated in the waves, indistinguishable from the ice floes under the darkening sky.

The surf reached Roland's sanctuary, forcing him to climb back onto the slimy boulder. He squatted like a toad with both hands on the rock, fighting to keep his balance against the raging wind and his own frantic shivering.

He cried out in pain as the first wave of ice water sloshed into his boots.

He stood up to keep his bare hands out of the water, teetering and windmilling his arms. He knew he was facing the low ridge of Macquarie Island, but he could see nothing but dark waves, spray, and hurtling clouds. His head throbbed with the cold, but his feet had gone mercifully numb, now submerged almost to the knees. Though he could hear the wind shrieking across the main island with unnatural fury, the horrific sounds and sights of the growing tempest could not compete with the penetrating cold for his attention.

It had been ten years since Roland's wife died of asthma in Adelaide. The decade had been lonely and not prosperous, but at least he'd had the privilege of privacy, quiet, and solitude. All in all, he couldn't complain, since he thought it was better to die here than to live on in the stinking city.

A tall wave hit him from behind like a falling tree, knocking him off his slippery perch. He sank beneath the frigid surf, drifting away from the island, too paralyzed by the cold to swim.

CHAPTER 24

Into the Storm

In twenty-one years at sea, Captain José Hererra of the U.S. Coast Guard had never seen such waves. Countless times he had piloted the *Polar Star* through the tempestuous Southern Ocean surrounding Antarctica—the world's most treacherous waters—but never before had he genuinely feared for the safety of his modern and enormous vessel.

The Coast Guard cutter *Polar Star* and her sister ship, the *Polar Sea,* were the world's most powerful non-nuclear icebreakers. With three gas turbines delivering seventy-five thousand shaft horsepower to her three sixteen-foot propellers, the *Polar Star* could maintain a continuous speed of three knots through first-year ice up to six feet thick. By backing up and ramming into the ice at eight knots, she could crash through old pack ice up to twenty-one feet thick.

After a savage roll that nearly capsized his four-hundred-foot ship, Captain Hererra briefly took one hand off the helm to cross himself, thanking God that he was aboard one of the most durable vessels at sea. A freighter or passenger liner of the same size would have already broken up and sunk.

Ten-story waves were making the thirteen-thousand-ton *Polar Star* pitch and roll through the dark tempest like a one-man dinghy. Hail the size of baseballs battered the thick windows of the bridge cabin and thundered on the steel roof. Occasional flashes of lightning revealed whitecaps curling over the deck between the shadows of bottomless troughs.

Captain Hererra stood with his feet spread wide, hanging on to the helm to keep his balance. His XO had collapsed in a corner. Hererra could hear the man retching and moaning between the sheets of hail and the waves that crashed across the deck. Hererra had ordered the rest of the crew to go below and strap themselves in.

Until his seasickness became debilitating, the XO had argued that they should turn around and sail north out of the storm. Hererra had disagreed and held his course. According to the icebreaker's GPS receiver, which was beginning to fail on and off due to interference from the storm, they were only a few miles from the edge of the Antarctic pack ice. Hererra knew that these monstrous waves were whipped up by the friction of the wind against the sea's choppy surface, and that the hard smooth ice would prevent the sloshing feedback needed to create such waves. So he knew they would find calmer seas while cutting through the pack ice toward the continent, if they could just get to the ice without capsizing.

And then we'll all be heroes, Hererra thought. Provided the wind and waves lashing the foredeck didn't rip loose the moorings or rupture the tires of the eight silver gasoline-truck tanks with KIWI OIL stenciled on their sides. The tanks were considerably shorter than full-size commercial highway tank trailers, but they still weighed several tons each and presented large impact areas to striking waves.

Captain Hererra had cursed and marveled at the folly of transporting gasoline tanks on the *Polar Star,* rather than using the icebreaker to escort a tanker as usual. The *Polar Star* was a research and rescue vessel, and a tanker with the same displacement could have carried a hundred times more fuel. Now he understood, though. They had warned him that he might be sailing into a storm of unprecedented magnitude, and he had scoffed, and now the rigid reinforced hull of the *Polar Star* was ominously groaning and pinging with strain as she was tossed about by forces no tanker could have survived.

Hererra was looking down at his instrument panel when the ship ascended atop a particularly high wave, straining his legs with the effort of standing against the vertical acceleration. Lightning crashed, flashing a strobe on Herrerra's XO, who stopped in midretch to let out a piercing, warbling, childlike scream.

Hererra looked back and saw the XO pointing out the forward cabin windows. Lightning flashed again just as the force mashing him downward abated, and the icebreaker pitched forward to give him a full view of a wave trough that gaped wide enough to swallow his vessel whole. He guessed that the liquid chasm was at least three hundred feet deep, although he knew that no storm waves had been reliably reported in the open ocean with a trough-to-crest height much greater than a hundred feet.

The trough kept growing, opening like a yawning mouth. The *Polar Star* teetered on the crest of one side, and the crest on the opposite side of the canyonlike trough continued to ascend and sharpen, as if in slow motion because of its size.

Then the icebreaker pitched over at a vertical angle

and slid down the concave liquid slope like a surfboard. The friction of the water against her bright red hull offered so little resistance that Hererra's feet left the deck and he found himself dangling from the helm, disoriented by free fall. His XO continued to scream.

The *Polar Star* plunged into the sea at the base of the trough, submerging the cabin windows. Hererra was hurled painfully against the helm and the instrument panel. His XO flew across the room, banged his head against a window, and crumpled motionless on the floor.

Then the icebreaker bobbed backward and righted herself. Water streamed off the windows.

Hererra looked up, and lightning flashed just in time to show him the frothy wave on the far side of the trough leaning over them like a toppling skyscraper. He flung his arms over his head, huddling beneath the helm, as the three-hundred-foot wall of water rushed down at him. With the deafening crash came a spray of icy salt water across his cheek, and Hererra thought it was the end. When his lungs continued to take in air, he opened his eyes and saw that only one window had broken. He was sitting in six inches of water, but the *Polar Star* was still afloat.

Oh yes, he thought, marveling at the magnitude of what his ship had just survived. Then he felt the tug of upward acceleration, even stronger than before.

He had scrambled to his feet to look out the windows by the time the new wave beneath the icebreaker crested. As the ship tilted forward again, he expected to see another yawning trough in the next flash of lightning. Instead he saw a flat white plain. It was his turn to scream as the wave approached the ice pack, propelling the *Polar Star* on its crest.

The wave collapsed when the ice cut it off from the surging ocean below. The ship did not pitch all the way

over on its nose this time, and its descent was somewhat
slower than free fall as the liquid mountain supporting it
spread out across the ice. A shallow mound of water
surged ahead of the prow, digging up flakes of ice and
spilling down through cracks.

The 1.75-inch-thick steel hull crashed down through
the ice pack, smashing Captain Hererra against the floor.

Saturday, 12:34 P.M. ICARE Time

"Mayday! Mayday! Mayday!"

Despite the incredible turbulence slamming him
against his seat back, Professor Ferrand could not believe he was hearing those words from the Starlifter's
cockpit. He had been on enough dangerous flights to
know exactly what they meant. The *possibility* of disaster had always provided an exciting thrill on his hurricane research flights. Now that the disaster was actually
happening, the feeling was entirely different.

The fuselage had abruptly tilted up sideways and was
shaking so hard that Ferrand's eyes would not focus.
Nevertheless, he could see doors popping open and
equipment falling into the aisle. Some of it was his expensive scientific instruments. He heard breaking glass,
an engine cutting in and out, an alarm in the cockpit, and
close thunderclaps. He could smell ozone and raw jet
fuel. Farther back in the gloomy fuselage, where four defense technicians sent to detonate the warheads were
baby-sitting their cargo, someone was shrieking in terror
and pain.

"What happened?" Ferrand yelled at the top of his
lungs.

While the pilot shouted, "Mayday! Mayday! Mayday!" into the radio again, the copilot replied, "Something hit us."

"Debris?" Ferrand yelled.

"Wind," the copilot said.

"We've been in the storm for ten minutes!" Ferrand yelled. "What knocked us over sideways just now?"

"A wind *within* the wind," the copilot shouted.

That makes no sense, Ferrand thought. At this altitude, and this position within the storm, the wind should theoretically have been powerful but even. His models had never predicted sudden wind speed excursions, much less the kind of gust it would take to send one of the air force's largest planes out of control.

"Hold on," the pilot yelled. "It's got us again!"

The cabin spun over onto its other side, twisting so fast that it whiplashed Ferrand's neck. Before, it had been tilted so that his seat was at the top, suspending him against his seat belt. Now he was at the bottom, and things were falling on him. A heavy first-aid kit bloodied his nose. Then a fire extinguisher landed on his gut, knocking his breath out. He threw his arms up to protect his eyes from shards of glass.

"If anyone can hear us, we're going down!" the pilot yelled into the radio.

Lightning was flashing outside. Ferrand twisted around under a pile of debris to look out his rain-streaked window. Since the window now faced straight downward, he hoped to see how far below them the ground was.

A forking arc of lightning obliged him, and he saw the most terrifying vista imaginable. The Starlifter's right wing was broken off at the middle. Fuel spurted from the ragged stump. A range of jagged rocky mountain peaks alternating with crevasse-strewn glaciers was speeding by a few hundred feet below.

Ferrand wondered what would happen to the cargo of fuel tanks and nuclear warheads when the plane crashed.

He didn't even have time to start a prayer before the pilots completely lost control and the fuselage began tumbling chaotically. Despite his seat belt, he was tossed about so roughly that he couldn't breathe, and he lost all sense of spatial orientation. He noticed when the lights went out, and he caught another glimpse out his window, that the snow and rocks were much closer. Then the loose fire extinguisher paid another visit, this time to his left temple, and he lost consciousness.

The drilling crew began by excavating a round pit in the ice sheet near the center of the subglacial ridge damming the Warner Basin. They had brought nearly all of ICARE's earthmoving equipment, knowing that this was the only way they could protect themselves and their jury-rigged drilling apparatus from the growing wind.

"I've never worked at a site this dangerous," Marshall yelled to Lim as they dodged the edge of a bulldozer blade shaving up the ice. They were on their way from the command trailer to the flatbed where the framework drilling derrick was being welded together on its side. "I wish we could slow down enough to be safe."

But he knew they couldn't.

Lim pointed to a tracked vehicle towing a hopper up the gentle ramp that spiraled around the walls of the pit, which was approximately two hundred feet wide. The magenta hopper looked like the bed of a dump truck, and it was filled to capacity with a dome of white ice shavings. "It's starting to take too long to truck the ice up the ramp," Lim said. "We need a faster way to get it out of the pit."

"Are you sure we have to go down sixty feet?" Marshall said. At present, the pit was only half that deep.

"Absolutely," Lim replied, looking up at the zooming

streaks of charcoal cloud illuminated by the bright flood-lights in the pit. "If even the tip of the drilling derrick sticks up above the ice sheet, the wind will eventually tear it apart."

"Too bad we don't have a conveyor belt to lift the ice out," Marshall said.

Lim stopped, bouncing on the balls of his feet. "I know something else that may work just as well!" He frantically waved to the driver of a Bobcat 331 Mini-Excavator. When the little machine arrived, Lim shouted, "Get the welders to bring their gear and the fluid pump and meet me at the Super Dozer."

The flagship of ICARE's fleet of excavation equipment was the world's largest bulldozer, a D575A Super Dozer acquired from a Komatsu Mining Systems distributor in Sherwood, Queensland, Australia. This 157-ton, road-stripe-yellow behemoth had a blade twenty-four feet wide and eleven feet tall in the center. Exerting a ground pressure of 21.5 pounds per square inch, the Super Dozer could not safely be used on sea ice, but its sheer momentum and 1,150-horsepower engine made it indispensable for quickly carving roads through both glacial ice and soil.

It had turned out that the heavy Super Dozer blade, which had a nominal capacity of ninety cubic yards of earth, could scrape up a full truckload of ice shavings in one trip around the circular pit. When the dig began, the Super Dozer and a Caterpillar D11R dozer both stayed busy, pausing their clockwise revolutions around the pit only long enough for endloaders to scoop up the shavings they had collected. But now the spiraling ramp carved into the pit's wall was so long that the Super Dozer was standing idle most of the time, waiting for the tractor-hopper combos that served as dump trucks to return from the surface.

Marshall walked with Lim toward the mammoth yellow Super Dozer. "You want to *pump* out the ice spoil?" He knew that pulverized coal was sometimes recovered from mines by mixing it with water and pumping it through pipes.

"Exactly," Lim said. "Now all we need is water."

After removing the small dozer blade from the Bobcat, they welded it beneath the left end of the Super Dozer blade. The Super Dozer then took the outside track during the rest of the excavation, leaving the center of the pit to the Cat D11R. As the Super Dozer blade scraped around the pit clockwise, the welded-on Bobcat blade cut out a trench six feet wide and two feet deep at the base of the walls. Marshall's men poured a tank of thick surplus oil into the trench and ignited it. Hedgerows of smoky flame shot up the walls. With sooty meltwater draining down the walls in sheets, all the liquid water they could possibly need soon pooled in the trench beneath the burning oil.

They hoisted the large impeller pump that would later circulate drilling fluid through the borehole, and mounted it on the Super Dozer's hood between the vertical exhaust pipe and the safety railing. Then they chained the large-diameter flexible hose on the sucking end of the pump to the slots atop the dozer blade so that the metal nozzle at the end of the hose was positioned a few inches above the bottom of the burning trench. With the twenty-four-foot blade angled forward on the right and backward on the left, the ice shavings were continuously rolled across the blade into the trench, where they mixed with the liquid water and were eventually sucked up by the pump.

The flexible hose from the outlet end of the pump was mounted to a smaller bulldozer that circled atop the rim of the pit, staying above the Super Dozer and spraying the slurry of water and ice away from the pit. The solid ice shavings settled out of the slurry as it fell, freezing in place and slowly building up a ridge that curved around the pit and provided additional protection from the wind. The water from the ejected slurry drained away on both sides of the growing dike, and the half that drained inward flowed back down the pit's wall, helping to replenish the supply of water in the trench.

When the dozer-pump-hose system was assembled and started up, Lim stood back and appraised it with satisfaction, looking up and down the silver hose between the big yellow machines. Marshall stepped up beside him, shaking his head. "You know, it'll be a miracle if that contraption doesn't come apart and kill somebody, or spray us with ice water, which would be just as bad."

"The hoses are secure," Lim said. "But I'm worried about the pump. I don't know how long the impeller can keep grinding up ice cubes."

They stepped into the command trailer to try the radio again. They had been attempting to hail the ICARE base at regular intervals, but their reception was jammed by the hypercane.

"How far can the drilling engine go with the gas we have?" Marshall asked.

Lim shook his head. "We wasted a lot of fuel hauling the ice out of the pit and waiting for the trucks to finish. . . . Unless another shipment gets here, we won't even make it down to the bedrock."

In the dim electronics-packed radio room, Reed could hear the wind roaring over the sheet-steel roof and whistling through the guylines anchoring the ICARE base to the Earth. Instead of wondering whether the storm would really get as bad as Professor Ferrand had

predicted, he was now wondering if it might get *worse,*
maybe even bad enough to blow away the base.

He was trying to reestablish radio contact with the
Polar Star. According to the last transmission from the
icebreaker, she was being mauled by dangerously high
seas. As he glanced at the clock—eleven hours to go
until the base ran out of gas—he got a call from an aviator who identified himself as Captain Jerry Calendri,
pilot of the F-16 that had been escorting the C-141B
Starlifter.

"Sir, the Starlifter is down! I repeat, the Starlifter has
gone down!"

"Where?"

"I'm not sure."

"You didn't see her go down?"

"No, sir. We lost visual contact after she veered off
course."

"Why didn't you follow?"

"We tried, sir. We couldn't catch her."

"In an F-16?"

"She was caught in some kind of freak gust, sir."

"Did you maintain radio contact?"

"Only for a few seconds."

"How do you know she isn't still in the air?"

"She was missing half a wing, sir."

"Couldn't have gone far, then."

"Actually, I think the wind blew her a long way," said
Captain Calendri. "We conducted a visual search until
the storm got too rough and we had to pull out. The Starlifter was last sighted flying across the Warner Basin, but
we saw no signs of a crash on the ice sheet, so the wind
must have swept her into the mountains on the other
side."

"When was she hit?"

"About twenty minutes ago."

"Damn it, we need every second, Captain. If you can't fly in the storm, we'll have to get a search party going on the ground."

"We've been trying to reach you constantly, sir. The storm has a lot of electrical activity. It must have been jamming our radios."

"What's your position now?"

"I'm about to land at the airstrip on the Ross Ice Shelf."

"What about the Warthog?"

"He's back there somewhere, sir. I left him behind when chunks of ice started hitting us."

"Double back, Captain. Pronto. Let the Warthog set the pace, and stay just within visual range behind him. If he runs into whatever hit the Starlifter, you'll have enough warning to evade it, and you can report where he crashed."

"It was his idea to separate, sir. My Viper was taking a real beating. Tommy knew what he was getting into when he started flying that slowpoking hunk of—"

"Don't knock the Warthogs, son. They can survive ten times the structural damage it would take to kill that delicate show-plane of yours."

"I know, sir. That's why I hightailed it."

Reed thought for a moment. The aviators knew their flying conditions better than he did. If they judged that the storm was too rough for the F-16 to linger with the slower but sturdier Warthog, he should trust them.

"Okay, Captain. Proceed to the airstrip. Good luck landing on the ice. Call me when both planes are safely down."

CHAPTER 25

Icebreaker

José Hererra, captain of the *Polar Star,* was astonished when he woke. He had not expected to survive the ship's fall from the crest of a thirty-story wave onto the hard ice pack.

The bridge cabin was cold, wet, and lit only by the dim orange emergency lights. And the floor appeared to be tilted sideways. But all of the instrument panels were still glowing, and he could feel the familiar jerky vibration of the icebreaker plowing at full throttle through thick sea ice. Another sailor had taken over the helm, and two paramedics were bandaging Hererra's bleeding head.

"Are we sinking?" he asked.

"No, sir, and we're still on course."

"Taking on water?"

"Only a little from the deck. No holes in the hull."

"Why are we listing, then? Is the heeling system malfunctioning?"

Since the heeling system from her original design had been reinstalled, the *Polar Star* was capable of rocking back and forth to avoid becoming icebound. The rocking was generated by pumps that transferred thirty-five thousand gallons of water between tanks on opposite sides of the ship within fifty seconds, applying twenty-four thousand foot-tons of torque to the hull.

"No, it's the wind, Captain. It's hitting the starboard side hard enough to keel us over several degrees."

"The gasoline tanks! Are they . . . ?"

"Two fell overboard. The other six are still secured to the deck."

Hererra grinned, reeling with pain, and affectionately patted the wet floor. "I knew she could do it."

"There is one problem, sir." The sailor handed him a headset with a spiral cord stretched from the bridge's main radio. Hererra fit it on over his bandage and yelled, "This is WAGB-10, the captain speaking."

A frightened male voice shouted, "The ice pier . . . waves on the turning basin . . . broken up . . . tractors can't reach . . ."

"Say again?" Hererra shouted. He could barely hear the radio over the wind roaring past the bridge cabin. "You're with the trucks coming to meet us?"

The next reply was just as garbled by whistling storm static, but Hererra pieced together its gist. The *Polar Star* was presently breaking in through the thin first-year sea ice that had formed over the channel used by ships every summer to come and go from ICARE. Ships normally exchanged their cargo at a pier carved out of thick solid fast-ice that was attached to the continental shore near the western corner of the Ross Ice Shelf. The *Polar Star* or her sister ship, the *Polar Sea,* broke up the ice every year across a broad area next to the pier to provide the ships room to turn. Apparently, the wind had whipped up waves on the turning basin that were strong enough to destroy the pier, and now Hererra was going to have to deviate from the usual channel, cutting into the thicker and harder multiyear ice until he reached a point where the sea ice itself was sturdy enough to support the heavy tractors and tanks.

After five minutes of shouting on the radio, they had settled on a new rendezvous point, and Hererra ordered the port breakout from the ICARE shipping channel.

Reed called Major Dawson and Max Bloom to the radio room so they could plan a search for the downed Starlifter. Dawson had been the chief officer at ICARE before Reed's arrival, and Max was responsible for supervising all corporate operations, so Reed assumed that together they could help him draw on resources among both the military and civilian personnel.

The three men stood around a light-table on which a map of the Warner Basin and the surrounding areas had been unrolled. In the dim room, the backlit paper illuminated their faces from below with greenish light and vague shadows of the features on the map. They leaned close so they could hear each other over the roar of the wind outside.

"Who do you think we should send to retrieve the warheads?" Reed asked.

"The helicopter could look for them," Max suggested.

"No," Reed said. "The wind is way too rough by now."

"I think the important thing is to get a team under way before the storm gets any worse," said Dawson. "That matters more than who goes."

"I doubt that, sir," said a young man strolling swiftly into the room in a combat aviator's anti-G suit. Captain Jerry Calendri, Reed presumed, pilot of the F-16. Calendri was a handsome Italian-looking young man with dark, baby-smooth skin. He must have been well into his twenties, but he looked like a teenager to Reed, and his eyes held a sly, self-confident squint. Typical fighter jock, Reed thought.

The black plastic-and-nylon anti-G suit brought back thrilling memories for Reed. Its purpose was to squeeze a fighter pilot's lower extremities with bladders of compressed air to help keep blood circulating to his brain during high-G maneuvers that could cause him to black out.

Reed noticed a large white *J* painted on the suit's breast as he returned Captain Calendri's salute. "Glad you made it, son. Who do *you* think we should send?"

"Someone who knows those mountains," Calendri said. "Especially if that's the best map you have—looks like it has only one topographic contour every . . . one hundred meters. I've done quite a bit of trekking in the Andes, sir, and I have to tell you that I've never seen terrain as treacherous and confusing as the area where the Starlifter must have gone down. All those rocky peaks sticking up through the ice cap don't seem to make any sense, because the ridges joining them are hidden beneath the ice. If you send in a search party without an experienced guide, they'll end up at the bottom of a crevasse, or buried by an avalanche, or . . . or just plain lost."

"Could you lead the search?" Reed asked.

Captain Calendri shook his head. "I'll volunteer to go, sir. I could help the team get through any technical mountaineering we have to do. I'd even be willing to tackle those mountains with that crappy map instead of an experienced guide if portable GPS receivers would work in the storm, in Antarctic temperatures, but—trust me—they won't. And you can't rely on a compass this close to the magnetic pole. That leaves us without any navigational aids, at night, in literally the worst weather ever. Like I said, the only way to search for the Starlifter without chasing our tails—missing some areas and crossing others more than once—is to take along someone who can recognize each individual peak from any viewpoint."

Dizzying apprehension hit Reed as he realized one possible implication of what Calendri was telling him. He handed the aviator a pen and motioned him to the map. "Show us the area where the Starlifter might have gone down."

Calendri drew a circle on the map.

"That's a mighty big circle," Dawson said.

As Reed had feared, the circle was in the heart of the Ellis Mountains, the range of nunataks Lois and Angie had just spent the winter exploring. He looked at Dawson and Bloom. "Well?"

"What?" Max said.

"Who do you have that knows the Ellis Mountains?"

They both shrugged.

Reed quickly stepped around the table to the console of ICARE's public-address system. He knew PA speakers were embedded in the ceiling of every room, even the restrooms.

He cranked the volume to maximum and repeated his request five times, begging anyone who had traveled in the Ellis Mountains to call the radio room. Then he and the other three men stood in silence, watching the phone.

A caterer from the mess hall handed out sixteen-ounce cups of steaming coffee. Reed examined the black fluid, swirling it in a vain hope for a glimpse of translucence against the white Styrofoam. Used motor oil, he thought—then he sniffed it—at least fifty thousand miles overdue for a change. He blew steam away from the surface and took a scorching gulp. "Ah, just the way I like it."

He sat down, straddling the chair backward, resting his chin on the chair's back and staring at the phone. A war was raging in his guts between the painkillers for his lacerated forehead, the canned food he'd been sustaining himself with, and the mess-hall coffee. He couldn't remember feeling this worn out since the first week after he'd sent Angie away to college.

"How long do you think we should wait?" Max asked.

"A little longer," Reed said, irritably. He guzzled the rest of the scalding drain cleaner, then crumpled the cup and tossed it across the room into the waste can. He tried massaging his face to help wake himself up, but every tug pulled painfully on the stitches in his forehead.

"What about Dr. Burnham?" Dawson said. "Her research camp was close to those mountains. Did she ever go into them?"

"She did, but she's still unconscious," Reed said.

After another few seconds, Reed hung his head with a heavy sigh. "We can't wait any longer. Major, take Captain Calendri and start putting a team together. I will personally lead the expedition."

Major Dawson looked shocked by the change in plans. "Colonel, are you sure that's a good idea? You've been through hell already, and that gash on your head . . ."

Reed gently prodded the bloody bandage above his eyes. "I'll be fine."

"If you leave the base, who's going to coordinate Operation Hypercane?" Dawson asked. "Three missions will be going at once—the drilling team, the search for the crash site, and the tractors hauling gasoline back from the icebreaker."

Captain Calendri said, "Sir, pardon me, but I think the major is right. You'll be risking your life for nothing if we don't have a guide who knows—"

"At this point, we don't need to coordinate," Reed said. "We just need to complete our separate missions as fast as possible. And we *will* have a guide." He hung his head with a groan. "Dr. Burnham is not the only one who spent the winter skiing around in the Ellis Mountains."

CHAPTER 26

Search Party

Reed found Angie's doctor. "Can she walk?"

"She shouldn't," the doctor said.

"*Can* she?"

"Yes, but it will hurt. Severely."

He jogged into the trauma ward and gently shook his daughter awake. "Pumpkin, you're not going to believe this. There's something we need you to do after all. It's going to be extremely dangerous, so you don't have to do it if you don't want to. You need to think about that before making a commitment, because you can't back out once we start."

Angie sat up in her hospital bed, groaning, and looked at her hands. Most of the swelling had subsided, thanks to an advanced antiinflammatory drug she had received. "What is it, Dad?"

He told her about the Starlifter's crash, and how Jerry Calendri had convinced him that they could not find the warheads and get back out of the mountains alive without a guide who knew the terrain. "And we didn't hear from a single volunteer who has ever navigated in the Ellis Mountains," he added.

"Oh boy," Angie said.

He unrolled the map and showed her the circle Captain Calendri had drawn. "Did you spend enough time in this area to know your way around it?"

She nodded. "I know those glaciers and nunataks like I know our house in Virginia."

Reed took a deep breath, clenched his jaws. "Will you join our search party to navigate for us? I'll be with you every step of the way."

"Dad, I don't think I could keep up. I'm definitely not able to ski."

Reed jumped up and paced in a circle, blinking and clearing his throat. I hate this, he thought. Angie's frostbite was only superficial, and unlike other kinds of life-threatening trauma, hypothermia left few lingering symptoms once a victim was warm, provided she'd kept breathing as Angie had. Reed knew that although hypothermia was the leading killer of outdoor enthusiasts, it could actually be beneficial to victims of other injuries. It had prevented several battle casualties in the Falklands by reducing their oxygen demand, and children had been known to recover after forty-five minutes under water because cooling had preserved their brain cells. Deep hypothermia was even induced deliberately during some kinds of heart surgery. But he also knew that his daughter was dangerously exhausted and suffering terrible pain, in no shape to climb the world's coldest mountains in the world's worst weather. "If you don't want to go, just tell me and you won't have to. But we really need you, Pumpkin, so don't worry about keeping up. I'll carry you if it comes to that."

She threw off her sheet. "Of course I'll go. Get everyone else together. We'll have to outfit them with climbing gear and decide on a route. Is that crappy map the best you've got?"

Reed nodded. "I guess nobody foresaw a need for a good map of that area."

He tucked an arm around Angie's frail waist to help support her as she stepped down from the bed. She winced and sucked in her breath when her weight shifted to her swollen feet.

When Reed and Angie got to the radio room, Major Dawson had already assembled a search team of ten able-bodied young men, all of them military. As Reed passed by Captain Calendri, he did a double take at the white *T* painted on the breast of his black plastic anti-G suit. I could have sworn that letter was a *J,* he thought.

Calendri saw him staring and saluted. "I just got here, sir, but the others brought me up to speed."

"Huh?" Reed said.

Another young man wearing sweaty blue long johns turned to face him. As he saluted, Reed saw that a large *J* was monogrammed under his sweat-soaked collar, and that he looked like a clone of the aviator still wearing an anti-G suit. The man pointed to his doppelganger. "Sir, this is Thomas Calendri, the Warthog driver. He's my little brother."

"Cut out the 'little' crap," Thomas said. "It just confuses people."

"You *are* ten minutes younger," said his twin.

Thomas rolled his eyes.

"You wear letters to help people tell you apart?" Reed said.

"Yes, sir," Jerry said. "Even our mom has trouble."

"Clever. Make sure you find parkas of different colors to wear on this mission." He turned away, then looked back at the twins. "Tom and Jerry? You've got to be kidding."

"Our parents had just immigrated to the States and didn't want to give us Italian names," Jerry said.

"They have a sense of humor but no conscience," his brother added.

Reed introduced Angie and announced that she would be their navigator. Several of the men looked at her askance, and he knew what they were thinking. "My daughter is tougher than she looks," he said. "She nearly died of hypothermia a few hours ago, and she has some frostbite injuries, but she's the only person who knows how to get us through those mountains. So you'd better look out for her, and I'll tell you this once—if any of you give her a hard time out there because she's a civilian and a woman, you'll never know what hit you."

They all looked away.

"Now, communications," he said. "It turns out that ICARE has lots of portable headset radios, so each person will have his own. We may need them to hear each other over the wind once we step out of the vehicles." As he talked, he handed out microphone headsets that would fit under a tight hood. A thin wire attached each headset to a receiver unit that could be zipped into a parka pocket.

"We are going to be transporting nuclear weapons in nonsecure territory," he added. "Assuming the world hangs on past tomorrow, theoretically, armed terrorists could be listening in, prepared to steal them. I don't know about the rest of you, but I'm not trying to save the world just so some asshole can come along and nuke it. Therefore, maintaining secrecy is still a priority. Do not use civilian radios to discuss the warheads. Only use the encrypting military radios in the snow tractors. When your headset is on, do not refer to the weapons directly. Instead, reference them as 'survivors,' as if this were only a rescue mission. Is that clear?"

They nodded.

"We'll need helmets, wind goggles, and supergaiters," Angie said, shouting over the wind outside. "Also one-piece expedition suits and mouthless ski masks, not just balaclavas. We can't afford to expose any skin at all. At polar temperatures, that kind of wind will frostbite bare flesh instantly, especially moist eyeballs. If we have to do any serious climbing, we'll also need rope, full-body harnesses, helmets, webbing, pitons, ice axes, rigid crampons, and plastic boots."

The twins simultaneously raised their hands. Reed pointed to them. "Where's the supply room?" Jerry said. "We can gather equipment while you guys pick an approach route and a search pattern."

"You know what all we'll need?" Angie asked.

Thomas winked at her. "We're technical rock climbers."

"And ice," Jerry said.

"Extreme," Thomas added.

Dawson gave them directions to the supply room while the others gathered around the map on the light-table.

"Our best bet is to climb Shackleton Peak," Angie said. "It's taller than the surrounding nunataks, so it will give us a view over most of the search area. If we can't see the crash from there, we'll have to descend and trek through the hidden valleys, one by one. How much time do we have?"

Reed glanced at the wall clock, briefly calculating that the base had less than ten hours of fuel left. If the *Polar Star* or the tractors meeting her failed to arrive in time, he and Angie would be away when ICARE's furnaces and emergency generators shut down. Most of the healthy personnel at the base would probably survive the cold and dark—they all had polar clothing—but Lois would die in seconds without her electronic ventilator.

"The drilling team has decided they only have time to drill one hole," Reed said. "So we have to hope that placing all of the explosives up and down in a vertical line will be enough to blast through the subglacial ridge. If we can retrieve the fuel tanks on the Starlifter or at least one tank truck gets from the icebreaker to the blast site before the drilling rig runs out of gas, and nothing goes wrong with the drill, they'll have the hole ready by midnight. In order for our mission to be successful, we'll need to arrive no later, along with the 'survivors.' The computer models at MIT estimate the zero hour to be sometime around three in the morning, and the crew will still need to lower the 'survivors' into place and clear the area for detonation. After that, the wind will grow strong enough to rip apart the drill rig and scatter the equipment."

Angie glanced at the clock. "Eleven hours. That means we're screwed unless we can see the crash site from Shackleton Peak. Let's go. We'll plan the ascent on the way."

Reed turned to Major Dawson. "Take your men and help the aviators get our gear. We'll meet you in the garage."

After the soldiers of assorted ranks had cleared the radio room, Reed tucked the map under his belt, picked his waifish daughter up in his arms, and jogged down the hallway with her.

"I can walk, Dad. It just hurts."

"I know, Pumpkin. But I want you to save your strength for the mountains."

After listening to radio static for an hour, Captain Her-erra finally managed to reestablish contact with the tractor convoy. "Are you still on course for the rendez-vous?" he shouted into his handset.

"No!" the driver replied. "We already got there, but we . . . wind breaking up the sea ice now . . . tractors might sink or drift away if we cross the cracks . . . have to drive your ship closer to shore."

Hererra jumped up, steadying himself on the shoulder of a medic, and limped to the nearest windows. "Port floodlights!" he commanded. "I want to see the ice."

A row of yellow beams lanced through the dark storm from the left side of the ship. Hererra could see nothing but blurred streaks of white and shadow zooming away from the window, converging in the distance with in-credible speed. He realized the streaks were horizontal missiles of snow whipping around the cabin, carried on the wind from the starboard side. The white streaks were snow dabs within the floodlight beams. The dark streaks were closer dabs that were not illuminated. He had never seen such huge blobs of snow in the air. Polar snow-flakes were normally small, dry, and hard.

The tractor drivers will never find us in this whiteout, he thought. With the wind howling like this, they may not even hear us crashing through the ice as we steam past them.

He hoped the convoy included a superb navigator. They had apparently been relying on dead reckoning since leaving the land behind. The *Polar Star*'s heavy-duty GPS receiver was now completely useless due to the storm, so the lighter units the tractors might be carry-ing were bound to be on the blink as well.

Peering through the blizzard, Hererra finally managed to focus on the ice below him. Indeed, it was cracked into interlocking polygons of all sizes. He had never seen sea ice this thick broken up by anything other than the hull of his own ship. As he watched, a broad low wave passed by beneath the ice, briefly lifting the floes and grinding them together. He also felt it rock the *Polar Star.*

"Where are you?" Hererra shouted into the headset microphone.

"On your bearing, thirty-one kilometers from land," the tractor driver said. "The cracks are still advancing. We'll have to keep pulling back until you reach us."

"How fast?"

"About fifty meters every five minutes, but—"

"That's fine," Hererra said. "We can outrun the cracks and catch up to you. Spread your tractors into a line parallel to the coast to make sure someone sees us coming."

"—but I think the cracks are advancing faster than they were a while ago," the driver continued. "And you'll have to slow down as the ice gets thicker, right?"

"That's correct," Hererra said, "but I still think we can make it, unless . . ." He limped back to the electronic chart table, which displayed a map of the local Antarctic coast. Contours running parallel to the shore represented the expected thickness of the sea ice at this time of year. At the location of the tractors, the ice was twenty-five feet thick, four feet thicker than the maximum thickness the *Polar Star*'s hull was designed to penetrate.

"Oh no," Hererra whispered.

His legs suddenly felt so weak that he wanted to sit back down on the cold wet floor.

The sailor at the helm said, "What's wrong, Captain?"

"Nothing," Hererra said. "Maintain your course, turbines at full power."

Saturday, 3:26 P.M. ICARE Time

Two tracked polar vehicles—one a red Hägglunds, the other a yellow Snocat—pulled into the lee of a rock formation that Reed found difficult to believe even as he peered up at it. The black natural wall was at least four hundred feet high, less than a hundred feet thick, and over two thousand feet long, jutting out into the Warner Basin ice sheet from the Ellis Mountains near the emperor rookery. The brooding monolith towered so high in the darkness that Reed could see its top only when it was silhouetted by lightning in the storm clouds rolling violently across the sky.

"Lois said this is a giant volcanic dike," Angie explained, "formed from magma that intruded a vertical crack and crystallized slowly. Now it's exposed because the softer rock around the crack has eroded away."

The vehicles drew close to the vertical rock face, where they would have maximum protection from the hypercane wind, and Reed saw in the headlights that the stone was composed of coarse greenish black crystals, many of which were stained by an orange tarnish from chemical weathering.

"Will we need tethers?" he asked.

"The wind is loud," Angie said, "but I don't feel it hitting the tractor here." She bounced on her seat, testing the amount of force needed to shake the Hägglunds. "No, it's calm this close to the cliff."

"Stay here," Reed said. He slid open the door and stepped out, carefully hanging on. Angie was right—the air was eerily calm. It also wasn't nearly as cold as he had expected, although it was still below freezing. The roar of the hurricane-force wind raging around the end of the dike and over its top pummeled his ears at all frequencies.

He stuck his head into the yellow Snocat. "Let's go! Come over to the Hägglunds so Angie can explain our route."

Jerry and Thomas Calendri were the first to step out.

Instead of following Reed, they approached the vertical wall of dark crystalline rock. They walked slowly, reverently, arms upheld in identical fashion, as if approaching a sacred idol. "My God, it's magnificent!" one said. "I can't believe we've never heard of this face," said the other.

Reed pointed. "In the tractor, men."

"There should be twilight out here at this time of day," Dawson said as his troops climbed into the crowded Hägglunds. It was only 3:30 P.M.

Reed looked up. He could see nothing but pitch darkness between flashes of lightning. "I guess the clouds are too thick."

Thomas Calendri squatted beside Angie's seat. "Why did we stop here?"

"This is where we begin the ascent," she said.

There were several gasps of surprise. Dawson pointed to the map Reed had opened on a seat. "Why don't we just drive up this valley? It's right in front of us."

"That 'valley' is an alpine glacier," Angie said. "It's full of hidden crevasses big enough to swallow these tractors whole. Even if we don't fall through a thin snow bridge, the ice is too mangled to traverse."

"Could we cross it on foot?" Dawson asked.

Angie shrugged dismissively. "Yes, given time."

"The warheads weigh almost three hundred pounds apiece," Reed added. "We can drag them short distances by hand, but not all the way back from the mountains."

"So you plan to *drive* to Shackleton Peak?"

"Exactly," Angie said. "Look here. This dike forms the tip of a ridge that remains above the glaciers all the way to the summit." With her red and swollen right forefinger, she traced a crooked line to the nunatak from the spike of converging topographic contours representing the vertical dike. After cresting the nose of the dike, the contours were sparse but maintained the downhill-pointing V shape characteristic of a continuous ridge.

Dawson frowned. "Colonel, even if we could some-how get a tractor *up* there, the ridge is bound to be too rough to drive along—cliffs, boulders, crevices."

"No," Angie said. "I walked out to the tip of this dike to take aerial photographs of the rookery. Eons of wind have smoothed the top."

"What do you think the wind is doing *now*?" Dawson said, looking desperate. "We'd be exposed to the worst of it on a high ridge. Wouldn't it blow a boxy tractor off like a leaf?"

"It might," Angie admitted. "The wind will be our biggest problem."

Thomas Calendri said, "Maybe we could drive just below the ridge, on the lee side."

Angie shook her head. "This dike is flat on top. Far-ther up, the sides of the ridge are covered with snow. If we tried to drive on it, we'd just start an avalanche that would sweep us down to the glacier."

Dawson sat back, looking jaded. "This is nuts, but it doesn't matter. There's no way to get a tractor up onto this wall of rock."

"We'll see," Reed said. "A heavy bulldozer is on its way from the drilling site. It's bringing two thousand feet of cable rated for a tensile strength of twenty tons. We'll attach one end to this Hägglunds—it can cross rougher ground than the Snocat—and the other end to the dozer. The dozer can hoist the Hägglunds up the dike by driving away on the other side with the cable crossing over the top."

Dawson had gone pale. "Are you serious? How do you plan to get the cable up there? Throw it?"

"Of course not," Reed said. "The wall's at least a hun-dred yards high. Someone will have to climb it."

"No way!" said both of the Calendri brothers.

"I know it's cold out there," Reed said, "and it won't be easy to grip the rock with gloves, but at least we're on the side with no wind."

"The cable will be too heavy to carry," Jerry said. "You want us to take a rope up?"

Reed nodded. "First some thin cord. We'll use that to pull a thicker rope across the dike, then the cable."

"You're just going to *drag* the Hägglunds to the top?" Dawson said. "What if the cable gets hung and snaps?"

Reed shrugged. "Then the Hägglunds will fall. Are there any volunteers for the climb?"

All but two of the men froze like rabbits in the headlights of a semi, looking at their feet.

"Yo!" said Jerry Calendri. "Right here," said his twin. Both of the handsome youths were holding up their right hands.

"I can't believe you guys actually *want* to do this," Reed said.

Jerry said, "We don't, sir. We're both tired from the flight, and we've never climbed in air this cold. And our clothing is going to get in the way, big time."

"But whoever climbs won't have to ride up in the suspended tractor," Thomas added. "*That* will be scary as hell."

CHAPTER 27

Free Solo

On Reed's command, they all disembarked from the Hägglunds.

The Calendri twins paced back and forth at the base of the vast rock wall. Its coarse greenish crystals gleamed in the light from their headlamps as they peered upward. They paused to confer every few seconds, pointing up at some ledge, bump, or indentation. He caught some of their conversation.

". . . at least a 5.12."

"No way, 5.11 at the most."

". . . holds all over it, sure, but every one is a crimper or manky and we have to wear gloves."

The twins were arguing over the difficulty of the climb. In the American rating system, a 5.12 was a moderately difficult vertical rock climb that could not be completed safely without a rope and should only be attempted by experts. Crimpers were tiny fingertip holds, and mankies were holds that were unstable. Reed didn't know the jargon, but he knew it didn't sound very safe, and he could feel the tense concentration behind the twins' identical expressions of simultaneous excitement and dread.

They finally turned and walked toward him, grim-faced, fiercely debating something else.

"I'm first," Thomas said.

"No way," Jerry said. "I'm stronger."

"By two pounds on a two-fifty pull-up," his brother scoffed. "Sorry, bro. I outrank you."

"So what? I'm a better climber, too."

"Hey, just 'cause you beat me up El Cap by thirty seconds—"

"What's the matter?" Reed said. "You can't do it?"

"We'll find out, sir. Do you have a quarter?"

Reed reached into his pockets. "I think so."

Jerry flipped the quarter. It tumbled above his face, glinting in his headlamp beam. "Call it."

"Tails," Thomas said.

The quarter landed on the ice, spun, and came up heads.

Without a word Thomas turned to his brother and hugged him. "Be careful, aye?"

Jerry ran back to the wall and picked up the coil of thin white cord one of the men had brought from the Snocat.

Thomas hastily dug something from an inner pocket of his parka and yelled, "Hey!" He threw the object when Jerry looked up, and Reed saw that it was a gold-plated locking carabiner, a D-shaped ring used to connect items of climbing gear.

Jerry caught the carabiner. "I'll never understand how you turned out superstitious," he yelled, but he pocketed the lucky charm.

"What was that all about?" Reed asked.

"We had to decide which one of us would make the ascent," Thomas explained, watching his twin climb.

"What? I thought serious rock rats never climbed alone."

"Normally we wouldn't, because normally safety is number one. But all that matters now is getting the cable up there."

"Won't you still need to belay each other?" Reed asked.

Thomas impatiently shook his head. "We don't have time for protection. Besides, this face has lots of holds but no crevices—there's nowhere to wedge a cam even if we wanted to."

"Still, if you were roped together—"

"Sir, if we were roped together, and one of us slipped, we would both fall, and the mission would be over—no one here but us could scale that face. Trying it one at a time, the probability of at least one of us dying is greater, but so is the probability of at least one of us making it."

"I'll take your word for it," Reed said, watching Thomas. The Warthog pilot began pacing back and forth at the base of the wall. His brother was ascending rapidly, despite his bulky clothing, contorting into monkey-like positions that struck Reed as agonizing if not impossible.

"So you'll try the climb if he falls?" Reed said.

"Yes, sir, that's the plan, but . . . um . . ."

"What?"

"I'm sorry, sir, but if Jerry falls, I'm not a hundred percent sure I'll be fit to climb a wheelchair ramp."

Forty feet above them, Jerry turned his head from the black igneous rock and shouted, "I can feel it vibrating from the wind on the other side."

Reed yelled to Dawson's men. "Move the tractors back and turn them toward the cliff to give him light."

Soon the Hägglunds was shining its headlights on the black dike from a hundred feet away, and the Snocat was positioned three times as far back. The vast black wall shimmered with rusty orange highlights from surface weathering. As Jerry neared the top, he left even the dim upper edge of the illuminated area, and all Reed could see of him was his weak headlamp fitfully creeping upward.

Thomas paced back and forth beneath his brother like a caged bear.

Reed walked back to the Hägglunds to get a better view of the upper wall. He lurched and spun around when someone behind him tapped his shoulder.

The rear end of a house-sized yellow bulldozer was parked just ten feet behind him. It was the biggest self-propelled machine he had ever seen that did not fly or float. Yet he had failed to hear its approaching engine over the hypercane's roar.

"You drove backward all the way here?" Reed shouted as the driver climbed down from the high cab.

"Yes, sir," said the overweight driver, although he was a civilian from Marshall's crew. He shoved his bearded chin to one side, popping his neck. "She's faster in reverse, nearly nine miles per hour."

After explaining the plan to the dozer's driver, Reed called over some of Dawson's men to help remove the truckload of fat steel cable coiled around the hot vertical exhaust chugging out burnt diesel fumes above the machine's hood. As they finished, he heard a cheer from the group at the base of the dike and looked up at the looming black monolith.

Reed sprinted toward the group. "Where's Jerry?" he shouted.

Thomas pointed to a thick orange rope slithering up the wall from a coil on the ice. "He's over. He already started pulling up the big rope."

They had two cables. Both were long enough to reach over the dike, so they connected one to each front corner of the Hägglunds. When Angie and all of the men were securely strapped into their seats, Reed gave the order by radio for the bulldozer to start pulling.

They had to wait an agonizing two minutes for the cables to pull taut. When the Hägglunds's front end finally lifted off the ice with an abrupt jerk, Reed felt a surge of adrenaline and said, "Here we go!"

Thomas Calendri crossed himself and muttered a prayer.

Angie was looking out a side window.

Major Dawson shot a reproachful glare back at Reed as the Hägglunds tilted all the way back and began its gradual and silent ascent. All of his men sat rigidly, white-knuckled and grim-faced, reclined on their backs like astronauts in a rocket during the countdown.

Reed twisted around and watched the lights of the Snocat receding in the distance below him. Except for the spot they illuminated, the ice sheet and the crumbling glaciers a mile to the left were hidden in darkness between flashes of lightning. He wasn't sure which was more terrifying, swaying in the suspended tractor in a black and dimensionless void, or seeing how far away the ground was when lightning raced through the clouds.

Two-thirds of the way up the dike, Dawson shouted, "Hey, I think we're going to make it." Color had returned to his face, and he was smiling.

The Hägglunds abruptly jerked and tilted sideways. The men were held in place by their seat belts, but all of them yelled in surprise and fright. The machine swayed back and forth for a moment, slowly and silently. No one breathed. Then Reed heard a brief whistle followed by a deafening *slam* as the broken cable whipped against the Hägglunds's roof, caving in a linear dent from one end to the other. The windshield shattered, and Reed closed his eyes just in time as shards of glass rained down over the passengers.

As he cleared glass from his face and chest, he realized the tractor had stopped climbing. Oh no, the other cable is hung too, he thought.

His portable radio crackled. "Are you guys okay back there?" It was the bulldozer's driver.

"Yes, keep going," Reed said, relieved that the dozer had just stopped.

As the ascent resumed, he cinched his hood against the cold air pouring in through the broken windshield. Then he heard several bangs on the hood and felt something sharp strike his bandaged forehead. "Goggles!" he yelled, realizing that rocks dislodged by the cable were falling on the tractor.

When he put on his own goggles, they squeezed his sutured laceration, shooting intense stinging pain back between his eyes.

He looked over at Angie, wondering why he had not heard a sound from her. She was still staring out her window as if she had not even noticed the cable snapping. He brushed broken glass from her curly brown hair. "What's wrong, Pumpkin?"

She didn't turn around. "They're gone," she sobbed. "They're just . . . gone." Looking past her, he saw in the next flash of lightning the broad expanse of ice where the emperor rookery had been. The location of each huddle was clearly marked by a disk of pink and yellow guano stains, but not a bird was in sight. The nascent hypercane had swept them all away.

For the first time, Reed felt genuine sadness over the loss of nonhuman lives. It was not just sympathy for his daughter, he realized, although his grief was surely trivial compared to hers. It was as if he could actually feel the life force of the planet ebb by a significant increment with the extinction of the emperors.

"Will you tell Lois about the rookery when we get back?" Angie asked, still weeping as she put on her goggles. "I don't want to do that."

"Yes, if she ever wakes up," Reed said. "And if we ever get back."

He tried to contact the ICARE base, but his portable radio could not penetrate the storm. For all he knew, the *Polar Star* had sunk, and the backup generator powering Lois's electronic ventilator would run out of gas in—he glanced at his watch—six hours and twenty minutes.

Saturday, 4:17 P.M. ICARE Time

It had been an hour since the *Polar Star* had reached sea ice so thick that she could no longer continuously cut through it. Since then, she had been repeatedly backing up and accelerating through the open water to ram the ice in front of her. Captain Hererra was back at the helm, hanging on with both hands whenever the thirteen-thousand-ton vessel slammed into the ice. After the initial jolt of impact, the prow slid up onto the ice, tilting the bridge backward. Then the heavy hull crushed the ice and the bridge dropped back to a horizontal position, sometimes with a series of jarring thuds, sometimes with a single stomach-thrilling drop.

Hererra nervously eyed the electronic chart. It said the ice was now thicker than the maximum his ship could penetrate, but the tractor drivers on the radio had still not sighted her. He wondered what would be the first sign that she had reached her true limit. Will she bounce off the ice instead of riding up over it? Will she slide back off instead of crashing down through?

The next collision came, and this time it felt different.

Before, there had always been a solid thud followed by a knee-straining upward boost. This time the thud was more of a *crunch,* and Hererra was thrown forward against the helm instead of being lifted upward. He got his balance and looked around. The bridge was not tilted as it should have been.

"Captain! Captain!"

The voice on the intercom was too distorted with panic for Hererra to recognize it. "Go ahead," he said.

"The port hull is breached amidships. She's flooding fast!"

I should have known the reinforced bow wouldn't be where she fails, he thought. I should have realized how hard the wind is shoving us against the ice to port.

"Have you shut the bulkhead doors?" he shouted into the intercom.

"We can't. They must have been damaged in the storm."

Hererra knew what that meant. He glanced at a panel of orange lights on the wall. The front two were lit, indicating that automatic bilge pumps had kicked in. As he watched, a third one flickered for a second and then remained on.

He activated the *Polar Star*'s public-address system. "All hands! All hands! This is the captain speaking. Emergency masters, lower your lifeboats to the ice and prepare to abandon ship. All others to the bridge."

He hung up the microphone and flipped a red switch on the ceiling that activated a loud alarm.

"Johnson!" he shouted to a sailor behind him. "Get the crew manifest and count heads when everyone gets here."

He dialed the storeroom in the bow of the ship. There was no answer. That meant the room was already flooded and abandoned. He dialed the crew's quarters just aft of the storeroom and asked the sailor who answered for an estimate of the flooding rate. What he heard made him groan with dismay, but it could have been worse. His ship was doomed, but the 139 crew members—over a quarter of whom were women—would have time to get off.

"Rafferty!" he shouted to a man who had just entered the room. "Can you launch a helicopter in this wind to go look for the tractors?"

"Sorry, Cap. Both of the Dolphins blew off the pads about a minute ago."

Hererra called the tractors. "You will have to drive across the cracked floes after all. This is as far as we go. . . . Why? Because we're *sinking,* that's why! We'll try to off-load the gas tanks onto the ice, but we may not be able to. I suggest you hurry."

Hererra let off the TALK button. "Morgan, go to the foredeck crane."

"Aye, aye, Captain."

"Stanley, Gonzales, rope yourselves to the deck and make your way to the tanks. Don't unlash them until you've attached the crane cable. Work fast, men."

Hererra watched from the bridge as his sailors fought their way out into the storm far below him. Stanley and Gonzales had to crawl on their bellies across the snow-plastered deck. At least the deck's tilt helped them slither along—the ship was already listing a little low in the bow. The wind whipped at their parkas so violently that Hererra feared the garments would rip and blow away. If that happened, the men would freeze before they could drag themselves back inside.

Morgan got to the new heavy-cargo deck crane and swung it around toward the long silver truck tanks. As he lowered the cable from the end of the horizontal boom, its hundred-pound hook began swinging in the wind.

"Look out!" Hererra shouted as the hook whipped past Stanley's head. Then he forced himself to be quiet except for a low groan, knowing that the men on the deck far below could not hear him.

Thank God we had the foresight to wrap each tank in a harness of chains, Hererra thought. They couldn't possibly have improvised a way to lift the tanks at this point.

He had picked Stanley and Gonzales for this job because of their legendary strength. For years they had alternated the title as the *Polar Star*'s arm-wrestling champion. As Morgan positioned the crane boom over the nearest tank, they climbed up the fat steel cylinder's side by standing on its tires and then hanging on to the chains.

Gonzales reached the top first and bent down to give Stanley a hand. As he did so, a gust flung the heavy cable hook against his back. He fell behind the tank trailer. Looking under the long silver cylinder, Hererra saw him hit the deck, facedown. Still hanging on to the chains, Stanley indecisively looked back and forth between the swinging hook and his fallen partner. Gonzales was trying in vain to get up—Hererra saw him moving his arms, dragging himself.

Stanley decided to go for the hook instead of helping Gonzales. He squatted on his knees atop the tank, leaning into the wind, and hooked his ankles beneath two tight chains. Then he warily watched the hook, waiting for it to swing within range. When it finally zoomed past his chest, he lunged forward and wrapped both arms around it. The tire-sized hook's momentum tried to drag him off the tank, but the chains held his ankles. He lifted the thick steel ring that connected all the chains, dropped it over the hook, and gave a thumbs-up toward the Plexiglas crane operator's cabin.

To prevent the linkage from coming unhitched, Morgan applied tension to the cable and chains with a swift jerk of the crane boom. Then he waited for Stanley to untangle himself, climb down, and unscrew the bolts that anchored the tank to the deck. All the while, Gonzales slowly dragged himself away from the tank, leaving a trail of blood in the snow.

When Stanley waved his hands, signaling all clear, Morgan swiftly lifted the tank and swung it over the side of the ship. The long heavy cylinder began swaying, pitching, and twisting in the wind. As Morgan began to let out the cable, lowering the tank, Hererra grabbed the intercom and called him. "Stop! Morgan, the tank is going to bang into the hull if you don't extend the boom farther."

"I can't, Captain. It's too heavy."

"You have to try. Even if the tank doesn't rupture against the hull, you have to set it down beyond the brash ice around the ship."

"I'm telling you, she won't hold," Morgan pleaded, "especially swinging around like that." He began lowering the tank, ignoring Hererra's order.

A front corner of the long silver tank smashed against the bright red hull. Even on the distant bridge, Hererra could feel a faint impact. The ship's thick hull was undamaged, but he could see the wrinkled metal where the corner of the gasoline tank was caved in. At least it didn't appear to be leaking.

Morgan extended the crane boom.

The tank moved away from the hull.

Now free to roam, the tank began swinging wildly back and forth. Hererra could feel it rocking the whole ship slightly. Then he saw the crane operator's cabin begin to move. At the bottom of each swing, when the tank's downward force on the boom was greatest, the

thick bolts securing the base of the crane pulled an inch
or two out of the ship's deck. Hererra pressed against the
bridge windows and yelled, "Morgan, get out of there!"

The sound of Morgan screaming came over the intercom in response.

The crane base tore loose from the deck. The tank disappeared over the ship's side, followed by the boom, the
Plexiglas operator's box, the broken base, a trail of
twisted wires, and a shower of sparks. A fountain of hydraulic fluid spurted from the hole in the deck like blood
from an artery, ejected by the central hydraulic system
that powered the ship's cranes, hoists, and anchor.

Hererra could not hear or see the tank's impact, but he
saw the flood of iridescent gasoline surge outward
across the ice, below the sparking wires. A moment later,
a fan of orange flames erupted all around the starboard
side of the bow. The leaping flames and smoke stretched
into black and orange streaks carried back across the
deck by the wind. Hererra stared in horror as the five full
truck tanks of gasoline remaining on the deck were
bathed in fire.

Stanley lunged behind a floodlight mount, hunkering
down where the flames could not touch him. But Gonzales was caught on the open deck, still dragging himself
toward safety with his arms. His body briefly flared in
the stream of fire as his hair and clothing ignited and
burned away.

The orange flames and streaks of black smoke were
gone a second later, blown away by the wind. The ashes
of Gonzales had also disappeared, leaving only an oval
of charred paint on the deck. Flames flickered for another second from the tires at the rear ends of the tank
trailers, then even the burning rubber was extinguished.

Hererra dared to breathe. The tanks had not been exposed to the fire long enough to explode. A few of the

outer tires on the dual wheels had blown out, but all of the inner ones still looked serviceable.

The leader of the tractor convoy called on the radio. "Hey, I'm glad you guys lit a fire so we could see your ship. We were passing right by you, way off to the side."

A sailor on the bridge said, "What are we going to do now, Captain? We can't off-load the other tanks without the crane."

Hererra paced around the helm, limping.

He snatched up the radio mike. "Do any of your tractors have attachments for excavation work?"

"Yes," the driver said. "Mine is a snowplow, and one of the others has a backhoe arm."

"Perfect," Hererra said. "I'll tell you what to do when you get here."

He turned to his assembled crew. "Go help Stanley unfasten the other tanks, and drain at least a fourth of the gas in each of them over the side."

CHAPTER 28

Minicane

Saturday, 6:11 P.M. ICARE Time

Reed watched, second in line on the climbing rope, as Angie crouched in the lee of a boulder and peered down through binoculars from the snowy north face of Shackleton Peak. The wind had prevented them from reaching the rocky summit, but they had managed to circumnavigate it at an elevation higher than the surrounding mountains. After finding the ice and snow disturbed by nothing but wind on the two sides of the triangular peak that offered the broadest views, Reed had nearly given up hope of finding the crashed Starlifter. Now he just prayed he could get Angie and Major Dawson's men back out of the mountains alive. The wind had nearly blown the Hägglunds off the ridge several times on the way up, and he knew it would be a lot worse on the way back down.

It was a good thing the storm was producing lightning over the Ellis Mountains. They had brought portable floodlights, but the batteries had turned out to be too heavy to carry once they left the Hägglunds. I just hope

we don't get electrocuted up here at such a high elevation, Reed thought. He had already seen lightning bolts
strike several of the surrounding peaks.

Angie patiently huddled like a roosting falcon, waiting for the next flash of lightning to reveal the landscape
below her. If only her mother could see her now, Reed
thought. Whatever problems had held her down in the
past, and whatever was going to befall the world if they
failed to stop the hypercane, he felt confident in the re-
silience of anyone with the grit to push her endurance
and courage as far as Angie was pushing herself now. If
he and Lois could both make it out of Antarctica with
her, Angie would be as prepared to face an uncertain future as any young person could be.

He felt her tugging on the rope to get his attention.
When he crept up beside her, he saw through her frosty
goggles that her eyes were squinched up with a smile.
He yelled over the wind whipping around the boulder.
"You found the plane?"

"No."

"Then what did you see?"

"Wait for the lightning," she yelled. "This isolated
cirque is inaccessible from the valleys, so Lois and I
never looked here, but I should have known what they
were doing all along."

"What *who* was doing?"

Lightning flashed, and Reed saw a high valley shaped
like a triangular bowl. The north face of Shackleton
Peak formed one of its three sides. The other two sides
were faces of adjoining nunataks. The ice that had accumulated in the bowl over eons was escaping through one
corner of the triangle, where a steep, narrow, jumbled
glacier spilled into the valley below. The high peaks
sheltered the bowl from wind on all sides.

In the center of the bowl, thousands of emperor penguins were milling around in tight huddles.

"This is fantastic!" he exclaimed. "They'll be protected down there, no matter how fast the wind blows. Did these penguins come from your rookery?"

Angie nodded. "They were not dying after all, except those who failed to make the journey. They were just establishing a new rookery, as if they knew something was going to happen to the old one. Now the mystery is why they moved. They couldn't have actually known a hypercane was coming."

Reed returned her grin. "Can I tell Lois this part too?"

A voice behind him yelled, "Can you see the Starlifter?"

Reed's brief elation evaporated. The flickering lightning had clearly illuminated every cranny of the glacial cirque, and there was no sign of a crashed plane.

Lightning flashed and Angie yelled, "Look!"

He missed it, but she kept pointing, and the next flash showed him a trail of penguins wandering up one side of the cirque from the new rookery, like ants on a foray from their nest to a garbage can. The line of squat, black-and-white pilgrims was climbing to another glacial landform that was mostly hidden by a rocky ridge but appeared to be a one-tenth-scale replica of the cirque. Beside the queue of waddling climbers, other emperors were swiftly sliding back down to the rookery on their bellies, one at a time. Reed remembered Angie describing the strange mode of locomotion in an e-mail. It was called tobogganing, and it was unique to penguins.

"Are they moving the rookery again?" Reed yelled.

"No. They're just coming and going," Angie said. "Besides, that's not the easiest way in and out of the cirque. Penguins don't get much excitement when they're on land—I'll bet they're going to look at something interesting."

"Like what?" Reed asked.

"We might as well go see."

They descended from Shackleton Peak along the ridge leading to the corner of the cirque the penguins were visiting. Halfway there, Angie yelled, "Stop! I see a light," and raised her binoculars.

"What is it?" someone asked. "What do you see?" said another.

"It's the Starlifter," said Jerry Calendri, who was looking through his own binoculars. "I see a bent tail fin sticking up."

"Hey, someone's alive!" Angie shouted. "Beside the light. I see him waving."

"Which side?" Jerry asked. "What does he look like?"

"He looks like . . . like a little kid with stiff blond hair and a sunburn."

"Something hit me on the head before the crash," said Professor Ferrand, "and I'm sure my right foot is broken. Other than that I'm fine, unless there's a radiation leak."

In which case we might all be dead already, his eyes told Reed.

The Calendri brothers were exploring inside the torn and dented fuselage with headlamps and a radiation counter they had found on board. So far, they had not come across any indication of dangerous levels.

"Are any other passengers still alive?" Reed asked.

"I don't think so," Ferrand said. "The cockpit is jammed full of snow. I gave up trying to dig out the pilots. One of the defense engineers lived for a long time with his leg cut off. He drew this, and said it was for your eyes only."

Reed took the crumpled and blood-smeared notebook page Ferrand was holding out in a trembling glove. The crude pencil drawing looked like an electrical diagram.

"It shows how to rewire the warheads for simultaneous manual detonation," Ferrand said.

Reed examined the page. A heading across the top read, "These have a Category F Permissive Action Link so two people are required for firing, but they gave us both codes. Just enter the codes in the twelve-digit switches on the firing control transmitters." A table of codes followed. Below the table was a crude schematic of a disassembled warhead with the title "Yield adjustment procedure." The schematic included parts with labels that looked only vaguely familiar to Reed: the deuterium-tritium reservoir, the pulse neutron initiator tube, the depleted uranium radiation case, the uranium oralloy fusion pusher/tamper, the bonded beryllium/plutonium double spherical shell surrounding the supergrade plutonium levitated core of the fission primary, the concentric cylinders of uranium, lithium-6 deuteride, and the fusion secondary made of plutonium, and the digital encrypted firing signal receiver. An ironic note was scrawled at the bottom of the page:

Handle the warheads gently. Electrical or mechanical trauma could trip the Weak Link safety switches that kill the detonators in case their Strong Link mechanical shields have been breached.

Wonderful, Reed thought. After the Starlifter's crash, the warheads were probably all duds.

He glanced around and shoved the page into his parka, keenly aware that the information on it was probably as secret as American military technology could get, and priceless to several fanatical terrorists.

One of the Calendri twins emerged from the dark hulk of the fuselage and sprinted toward them through the deep snow.

Jerry stopped running and pointed up the hill behind the warped aluminum wing panel Ferrand was sitting on. "Hey, Tommy, here they are!"

Reed looked where he was pointing, relieved that he was not reporting a leak. Twelve white plastic cases were lined up in a neat row in the trampled snow. The heavy-duty cases were the size and shape of children's coffins. Each bore the colorful official seal of the U.S. Department of Defense, a bald eagle with a red-and-white-striped shield on his breast, gripping three arrows in front of a blue background.

Some of the crates were covered with black smudges and glove prints.

"Oh man, I thought we'd lost a dozen thermonuclear warheads for sure," said Jerry Calendri, gasping for breath. "Why are they all out here?"

Ferrand held up the sleeves of his parka. Reed saw that the fabric was charred, even melted through to the insulation in places. "There was a fire on the plane. I managed to drag out the nukes—I'm strong for my size—but all of my instruments got burned up."

"What about the tanks of fuel you brought for the drillers?" Reed asked.

"They never caught fire," Ferrand said. "But you couldn't carry them even if you could get them out of the plane."

Reed grimaced. "The drillers will have to rely on the *Polar Star*, then. Do you have any idea what caused the crash?"

Ferrand glumly shook his head. "But I do know that it

means something is missing from my simulations. They never predicted freak bursts of wind lurking inside the hypercane. We'd better watch out for more—they may touch down on the ground, too."

Deep in the bowels of Cheyenne Mountain in Colorado, three NORAD generals and assorted staff stood before a wall that displayed a Mercator projection of the globe. Behind the translucent glass map, a composite of 114 computer screens was used to show all sorts of critical information, from the locations of bogeys in the atmosphere to the sinusoidal paths of spy satellites. The locations of enemy targets and friendly assets could also be displayed, along with ocean and weather data or satellite images of the ground.

Diane Mitchell gaped in awe as she joined the generals, not just at the sheer density of military and geophysical information displayed on the vibrantly colored wall, but also at the incredibly sharp resolution of the images. "This makes me dizzy!" she said. "It's like looking at the Earth from space."

"High-definition monitors," said General Liang. "Thank you for joining us, Dr. Mitchell."

"You mean I had a choice?" It was 12:30 A.M. on a Saturday night. Diane had woken, heart thumping, to a loud roar and bright lights in the street outside, followed by vigorous knocks on her front door. When she opened it, armed soldiers whisked her aboard a helicopter and on to the NORAD citadel. All they told her was that a strategically vital mission was in danger from some kind of terrible storm, and that they needed her expert advice. She was a meteorologist specializing in tornadoes at the National Center for Atmospheric Research in Boulder, so she agreed to join them.

Her shock and fear had turned to excitement on the way.

"What are all the little green lights for?" she asked. The sparkling wall displayed hundreds of bright green dots. Some were on the oceans in the Southern Hemisphere. Others were within the continents, also primarily in the Southern Hemisphere. But most were tucked into bays along the coastlines of North America, Europe, Brazil, South Africa, Australia, and New Zealand.

"Those are installations gearing up to help with the mission," said General Liang. "Or with the . . . aftermath, if we fail—the mission is supposed to be completed eight hours from now, sooner than ships from any of those harbors could get there."

"Those can't all be military bases," Diane said.

Liang nodded. "Most are airports or industrial facilities."

As if that weren't confusing enough, many of the green lights were in nations that were not traditional allies of the United States. Several were on the border of Russia. Diane said, "What kind of military mission would require such an international— Hey, what's that thing on the coast of Antarctica? It's the size of Texas!"

"That's the storm," Liang said.

"Is this a video feed from a satellite?"

"No. It's a computer animation based on infrared snapshots."

Fascinated, Diane stooped to look closer. "Why is there a military mission in Antarctica? I thought the treaty wouldn't allow—"

"The objective of the mission is to stop the storm, Dr. Mitchell. That's classified information, by the way."

She stared at him. Now this experience had gone beyond weird. Before she could think of anything to say, he pointed to one of several tiny round clouds just beyond the edge of the white galaxy-like cyclone centered over the Pacific coast of Antarctica. "These little monsters are the reason we need your help."

Diane knelt on her knees so she could scrutinize the high-definition image from just inches away, tucking down her skirt as she bent over in front of the throng of male officers. The little clouds looked like scale replicas of the big cyclone but were less than a hundredth its size. The rotation of the main storm was barely perceptible at this scale, but the tiny replicas were obviously spinning clockwise.

"What are they?" she asked.

"That's what we were hoping you could tell us," said General Liang. "The mother storm started flinging these things out about an hour ago, as if the bitch was *reproducing*. Hey, Jarvis, show her the wind-speed data!"

A second later, the computer-animated storms were replaced by garishly multicolored blobs. Instead of spiraling clouds, the cyclone and its tiny offspring were now bull's-eyes. The mother storm ranged from cool blue at the periphery to a ring of bright red around the black eye at its center. The smaller cyclones appeared to have no eye, and their centers increased beyond red to orange, yellow, and white. Diane could now see that several of the tiny storms were also circulating *within* the big one, starting as white pinpoints near the eye and growing through embryonic stages as they moved outward.

She glanced at a legend of wind speeds that appeared over the South Pacific. Red represented two to three hundred miles per hour. White was five to six hundred miles per hour. "These units must be wrong," she said.

General Liang grimly shook his head. "The units are right. Now you see why we need all the help we can get."

Diane stood, wobbling. "Are the little ones dissipating as they move away from the mother storm?"

"Yes, rapidly, but they pose a major threat to our forces in the area, especially within the bigger storm where it would be nearly impossible to see or hear them coming. We believe one of the vicious little monsters has already caused the crash of a very important plane."

"Can you predict their course with the computer extrapolation you were showing me a minute ago?"

"Roughly," Liang said. "But the weirdest thing about them is how they zigzag back and forth as they travel. Each one ends up clearing a path much wider than itself."

Diane shuddered. "I'm sorry, General. I've never heard of such bizarre behavior, and I have no idea what could be causing it. But I can tell you who might be able to help."

General Liang stepped close, eyes wide. "Who?"

"Lothair Ferrand at MIT."

Liang groaned and shook his fist at the ceiling.

"What's wrong?" Diane asked.

"Remember that crashed plane I told you about?"

"Yes."

"Ferrand was on it. His students in Cambridge are running computer simulations of the storm for us, recalibrating them with new observed data every half hour. The simulations were doing a good job of predicting the storm's behavior at first, but they gave us no warning at all of these little devils popping out."

Diane was tracing where the microcyclones appeared to be going with her finger. "Hey, why is there a green light on the shore of the Ross Sea?"

General Liang stepped closer, concentrating on the image. Diane saw his eyes narrow. She said, "Whatever that installation is, one of these little white killers is headed straight for it."

The general turned and barked out orders. "Demming, get ICARE on the horn! Now! They have a minicane coming in."

CHAPTER 29

Icefall

Saturday, 9:08 P.M. ICARE Time

"Stop!" Reed said, looking out through the broken windshield of the red Hägglunds. They had dragged the heavy warheads to the vehicle and driven back down the ridge from Shackleton Peak to the black dike jutting into the Warner Basin. Now they faced the prospect of driving out on the slender four-hundred-foot wall of rock and using the remaining cable to descend to the ice sheet.

The tractor rocked and vibrated in the wind as if the mountains were having a magnitude-eight earthquake. Reed could see streaks of ice and rock debris shooting up from crevices on the windward face of the dike. "The ridge wind is a lot stronger now than it was when we came up," he yelled.

"I could barely control the tractor *then*," the driver replied. "What do you want to do?"

"I don't know. It will obviously blow us away if we drive out there."

"Look here," Angie shouted. She held up the map. It

fluttered in the icy wind swirling in through the windshield frame. "Off to the right, there's a huge crevice
that reaches at least fifty meters back into the rock face.
It's on the windward side, but it may offer enough protection for us to climb down on foot."

The Calendri twins studied the map and shook their
heads, looking worried. "The wind will actually be
stronger in there," Thomas said. "The crevice is open at
the top and on the windward side. The mouth is wide,
but the walls narrow together and the bottom curves upward in the back. That means the wind entering the
mouth will be compressed, blowing faster and faster all
the way back, then shooting upward."

"Exactly," Angie said. "All we have to do is pick a
point near the back of the crevice where the wind is
blowing upward hard enough to counteract gravity. The
descent will be a piece of cake."

Thomas still looked worried. "Gravity is predictable.
Wind is not."

"Yeah, but we don't have any better ideas," said his
brother. "Let's go for it. Time's wasting."

They parked the Hägglunds close to the long black
crevice, then tethered themselves to the vehicle before
stepping out. Reed did not like the looks of the roaring
plume of debris shooting up into the dark sky from the
crevice's tight end. Wherever they descended, it would
have to be far enough from the back of the crevice that
they wouldn't get pummeled to death on the way down.

"We'll have to lower the warheads first," he yelled.
They attached the Hägglunds's winch cable to the carry
handles on all twelve of the white coffinlike crates, then
lowered them into the crevice.

The Calendri twins approached the crevice on tethers
to look down with a portable floodlight and select a
route. "Bad news," Jerry said when they staggered back

to the Hägglunds. "The walls are covered with icicles, layers and layers of them. Apparently the top of this rock gets warm enough to drip in the summer."

"It's the highest icefall we've ever seen," Thomas said. "A WI-7 for sure. With novice climbers, I'd say we don't stand a chance of all getting down it alive."

"Did you bring ice climbing gear?" Angie asked.

Jerry nodded. "But ice anchors are never as secure as rock protection. And this is hard waterfall ice, not alpine ice, so driving in screws won't be easy. It's going to be a slow descent, and each of us will have to use perfect form."

Reed volunteered to take the lead. There were no objections, although the Calendri twins started bickering over which of them would bring up the rear. When Jerry pulled out Reed's quarter, Thomas said, "No way, bro. You got to climb the wall. I'm taking the top of the rope on the descent."

The twins made sure everyone was properly outfitted with a helmet and a body harness and secured to the rope with a quickdraw and a brake. Reed was followed by Angie, then Dawson and his troops. They placed Professor Ferrand in the middle where others could help him along, since he was unable to climb on his own with a broken foot.

When they were ready to leave the partial shelter of the crowded Hägglunds, Thomas made an announcement, shaking the end of the soft orange rope in front of him. "Okay, listen up! This is a standard eleven-millimeter dynamic climbing rope. Its length is fifty meters. That's not long enough to reach the bottom of the crevice, and we may need the rope again before we get down to the ice sheet, so we can't just secure the rope up here and leave it behind. That means our lives will depend entirely on the security of the ice anchors we screw into the wall.

We'll descend one at a time, from the top of the rope to the bottom, then repeat the process. Except when you're the person moving down the rope, *keep yourself anchored to the wall at all times.*"

"Why can't we use the winch cable to climb down?" Angie asked. "It's already in the crevice and reaches the bottom."

"Our harness gear will only work with a kernmantle rope," Thomas said. "It won't latch on to a hard steel cable."

"Won't this take too long?" said Dawson.

"We'll move as fast as we safely can," Reed said.

Angie said, "Try to keep all your skin covered. That wind will frostbite you to the quick faster than you can blink."

"Wait," Thomas shouted as Reed reached for the door. "I haven't told you the best part. The updraft will be stronger than gravity at first. We'll have to climb upside down to fight it."

Dawson went pale again. "You expect us to climb down a wall of icicles *headfirst?*"

"Don't worry. The wind will hold you up," Thomas said.

"Actually, it will blow you up and away if you don't hang on," Jerry added.

"Farther down, the wind will be blowing slower and more from the side," Thomas said. "When gravity takes over, we'll turn around and rappel the rest of the way."

Reed swung open the door. "Okay, let's go!"

They staggered through the ridge-top wind to the crevice.

Reed stooped on his knees at the edge. Hanging on to his headlamp, he thrust his head into the surging updraft and looked down. The vast wall below him looked like wax that had dripped down the side of a white candle.

The icicles came in all lengths, from inches to tens of feet. Some had once hung free from ledges, but their tips had broken off in the wind. Others had coalesced into wavy curtains clinging to the cliff. Reed could barely see the sharp rocks jumbled at the bottom of the crevice, at least a hundred yards down. The white warhead crates looked like grains of rice, haphazardly piled among the dark boulders.

The crust of ice was thicker in some places than others, forming long fluted protrusions that looked like Corinthian columns sliced in half vertically. The Calendri twins had selected one of these as the descent route.

Reed told the others to stand back from the crevice and belay him, allowing enough slack in the rope to reach several yards down the wall. They took up secure positions, leaning into the wind and digging their crampons into the ridge-top regolith of rock and ice.

At Jerry's suggestion, he returned to the Hägglunds and traded in his mountaineering ice axe for two matching Black Diamond ice tools that had shorter handles. The tools had identical picks that were more steeply canted, reverse curved, and serrated with teeth on the handle side to grip the ice like a harpoon. One tool's head had a hammer opposite the pick. The other had an adz for chopping footholds. Both tools had a hefty loop of nylon webbing at the end of the handle for the climber's wrist.

Reed practiced gripping the handles, one in each hand, then sprinted toward the dark crevice, pumping his legs at full throttle. He launched himself headfirst over the precipice with both ice tools upraised, timing the leap so that he was falling back down when his body entered the updraft. His momentum carried him downward until the rope pulled taut, slamming him against the icicle column upside down. Before the wind could drag him back up, he plunged the pick of each tool into the column.

The picks held.

But Reed could barely hang on. In addition to pulling him upward, the wind was hitting him from the side, trying to shove him toward the rear of the crevice. It whipped at his parka so hard that the soft fabric beat painfully against his sides. Icy air forced its way in around his tightly cinched hood and blew down his back. It's hard to even breathe in this, he thought. At least he had goggles, so he could keep his eyes open.

Whenever he tilted his head back, his gaze focused on the sharp rocks far below.

Hanging on to one ice tool, he holstered the other and reached into the bag on his chest for an ice screw. Then he felt the inserted pick slipping out and frantically fumbled for the tool he had just put away. He managed to lodge it in time to hang on.

"The wind is too strong here," he yelled. "I'll have to go lower to screw in." Looking between his knees, he saw Angie leaning over the top, a glove to one ear. Obviously no one could hear him, and he couldn't let go of the axes to gesture. He decided to just start climbing downward and hope that Angie could read his mind.

They gave him enough slack to keep moving. He alternately jiggled each pick loose and reseated it a few inches farther down the ice column. He tried to propel himself by jamming the two forward-projecting teeth of each crampon into the ice, a technique Jerry had called front-pointing, but he could not coordinate all of his limbs in the wind. He ended up pulling himself downward with his strong but tired arms, allowing the wind and the rope to hold the rest of his body against the wall.

As he descended, the upward component of the wind gradually diminished.

When he passed an arm-sized icicle stump, he used the flat broken surface as a temporary foothold against the updraft, standing upside down. Now daring to free one hand, he pulled out an ice screw and drove it into the column as the Calendri twins had shown him. The screw was a fine-threaded steel tube about eight inches long with a flange on the head for attaching a rope or harness. He started it at an angle by tapping the flange with his hammer, then cranked the screw around with the ice tool's handle. The displaced ice did not shatter because it could slide up inside the thin hollow tube. After cranking in a second screw, he waved back to Angie and yelled, "Go!"

Watching between his legs, he saw her pull herself downward along the rope, scrabbling at the wall with her crampons. She hung on to one of his legs while anchoring herself.

"How are you doing?" he yelled.

"Okay," she shouted.

He could not see her face—she was holding it out of the wind—but he could see her frail shoulders trembling with effort. He wondered how much her frostbite blisters and overused feet were hurting. It was hard to believe she was enduring it all without even complaining. Reed had seen strong men her age emotionally disintegrate under milder stress.

Soon everyone was anchored to the ice column in a vertical line, upside down, bowing their heads against the wind whipping at their clothing. Each climber's crampons were scant inches from the next climber's head. When the highest climber, Thomas Calendri, had anchored the top of the rope to the wall, Reed resumed his descent, dragging the bottom of the rope down with him. The others fed the orange rope through their harnesses to give him slack. Pulling himself downward became easy—the challenge was clinging to the wall and resisting the increasingly strong sidewind. He was just beginning to wonder if he should turn around when he felt himself falling headfirst. In a moment of heart-stopping terror, he realized that he had gone too far—his weight was now greater than the drag of the updraft, and it would only get worse as he fell. He looked down at the sharp rocks accelerating toward him, too scared to yell.

Reed's climbing harness bit into his shoulders, flipping him upright. He could see nothing but spinning ice and rocks as he slammed against the wall, but he realized that the rope must have jerked taut. Thank God the ice screws at the top of the rope held!

He looked up. The others were still fastened to the wall at the top of the rope. He screwed himself in, right side up, and beckoned to Angie. Everyone but the Calendri twins had soon joined him at the bottom of the rope, executing an about-face along the way.

Reed was less than halfway down the icefall, but he could not safely resume his descent until Thomas Calendri had brought down the top of the rope. Then they could repeat the maneuver they had just completed. After the top of the rope was reanchored as close as possible to the present position of its bottom, Reed would climb farther down with the bottom end until he ran out of slack, hopefully without falling again.

Thomas Calendri felt his harness jerking, and his heart began pounding like an unbalanced wheel. He was upside down, just below the top of the crevice, watching his brother descend the rope headfirst. He looked at the ice screws in front of his chest. The jerking had felt like an anchor pulling loose, but both of his screws were still securely embedded in the half column of ice.

He felt the jerking again, and this time he saw a white

crack propagating through the translucent ice between
two of the many coalesced icicles that made up the
bulging column. The crack did not open. It was just an
infinitesimally thin but opaque plane that was perpendicular to the crevice wall. It began on the right side of the
column and spread at least six feet straight up and down
before it stopped growing.

Thomas yelled as hard as he could, tearing his vocal
cords. "Jerry! Screw in! The ice is breaking up!"

His brother continued down the rope, headfirst, unable
to hear him over the wind.

This can't be happening, Thomas thought. Ten more
minutes and we would have been at the bottom. The vibrations transmitted to his harness through his screws
were increasing. He looked at the ice in front of him
again. As he watched, another vertical crack formed on
the left side of the half column and propagated fitfully
up and down the wall. The segment of the half column
that supported Thomas and the top of the rope was still
in place, but it was no longer fused to the ice on either
side of it.

A new whistling sound began. That could only mean
the cracks were beginning to open. Someone down there
must be hanging from the rope instead of his own anchors, Thomas thought. The force was ripping the ice
near his screws away from the surrounding ice and the
underlying rock face.

He had a spare ice screw in his pouch. Trembling with
panic, he yanked it out, leaned past the crack on his
right, and cranked the screw in as fast as he could. He
tied the end of the rope to it, then untied the rope from
the two failing anchors. Once the rope was no longer attached to the cracking column, he breathed a sigh of relief, then remembered that his body harness was attached
to both the old anchors and the rope.

He had started desperately trying to unhook himself from the failing screws when he heard a sucking sound. He saw the back of the translucent half column go white as air invaded between ice and rock. Knowing he was out of time, he drew his survival knife from his right boot and slashed the main strap of his climbing harness. At the same time, he lunged sideways and grabbed the new ice screw with his free hand. The severed harness was yanked from his torso as a three-by-twelve-foot segment of the half column containing the two doomed anchors fell away from the wall.

"Ice!" he screamed, just in case they might hear him.

Thomas was hanging upside down by the grip of one gloved hand. Fortunately, the force of the wind dragging him upward was almost counterbalanced by his weight. He pulled himself down far enough to latch the belt in his pants to the end of the climbing rope with his lucky gold-plated carabiner, which Jerry had returned after climbing the dike.

He watched the airborne ice slab. It must weigh at least a ton, he thought. At first it levitated about a yard from the wall as if by magic, tilted horizontally like a tabletop. Then it began to rise on the updraft, and Thomas hoped it would be blown out of the crevice. Looks like we're going to make it after all!

The ice slab abruptly flipped up on its edge. With its broad side no longer facing the updraft, its weight took over and it shot down the crevice like a cannonball. Jerry was executing his about-face, halfway down the rope. He looked up and saw the slab coming at him, but he had no time to react. Thomas watched the slab recede below him, rotating as it fell edgefirst, silhouetted above his brother's vertical headlamp beam.

When the slab struck his brother, Thomas felt the rope jerk him away from the wall. He wondered how badly

Jerry was hurt as he drifted toward midcrevice, suspended facedown by the updraft with all of his limbs sticking out. An impact hard enough to pull out the screw holding the top of the rope must have injured his brother severely.

Thomas drifted upward until the rope stopped his ascent. He saw Jerry hanging in his harness—faceup, back arched, still attached to the rope but several feet from the wall. At first he thought Jerry was thrashing his arms and legs. Then he realized that his brother's body was limp but so close to the point where gravity and wind drag were equal that his limbs were being flung up and down by the turbulent wind. He looked like a marionette on the strings of a hysterical puppeteer. All of the other climbers were still at the bottom of the rope, anchored to the wall and looking upward at the disaster in progress above them.

Thomas's first impulse was to jackknife and try to dive down to his stricken brother by reducing his windward surface area. But when he saw that Jerry was slowly sliding down the rope, he decided to remain aloft to hold the rope taut and vertical. The force of the rope pulling on his belt was excruciating to his lower back, but making a kite of himself was the only way to keep Jerry sliding down to where the others could anchor him to the wall.

The ice slab continued falling down to the jumble of sharp rocks at the base of the crevice, where it shattered into thousands of shards. Some of the broken pieces bounced high enough to be swept back up in the wind, their ratio of drag to weight much higher than that of the huge parent slab.

Thomas noticed that he was drifting toward the rear of the crevice, and that his wind drag was growing stronger as the walls closed in on him. He saw Jerry fall into the arms of Dawson's men. When they grabbed him and started inserting his screws, Jerry lifted his head and began to jerk his limbs like a newborn.

Yes! He's alive!

Thomas tried to dive. It didn't work. The updraft was too strong so far back in the crevice. Next he tried to pull himself down the taut rope with his hands, but he was not strong enough to do that either. He saw that Dawson's men were trying to reel him in, but they were having no luck.

A chunk of the shattered ice slab came up at Thomas like a missile, a blurry streak out of the shadows below. It hit his left shin. He felt the bone break and come apart. One end of the offset bone jabbed the inside of his calf muscle. The other end stretched his skin. He was surprised by the volume of his scream—he had drifted back to where the crevice walls were so close together that they held in the sound in spite of the wind.

The blow to his leg knocked him sideways. He slammed into the wall opposite the one they were descending. After bouncing off, he swung back across and slammed into the other wall. The oscillation continued as he was swept farther toward the rear of the crevice. The tension on the rope—and on his back—steadily increased, and more flying debris began to batter him.

He looked down along the rigid rope. Jerry was leaning sideways, trying to reel in the orange lifeline. His face was unnaturally red with strain and bloody on one side. The others were wildly gesticulating and shouting at each other, their headlamp beams waving all around the ice-coated fissure. Thomas could not make out their words over the wind, but he could guess what they were arguing about. A white patch was fitfully expanding beneath the dark ice around Jerry's new anchors. That meant the rope was pulling hard enough to detach the ice

from the underlying rock face again, only this time it
was not the weight of other climbers pulling the top of
the rope loose; it was the updraft exerting so much drag
on Thomas that he was pulling the bottom end loose.

I'm going to drag them all off the wall, he realized.
And no one but us even knows where the warheads are.
If we all die here, the hypercane will become unstop-
pable.

He pulled his knife from his boot again.

As he reached to cut the rope, his back slammed into a
wall. Excruciating pain shot up his spine from a point
beneath his belt. He dropped the knife. It whipped away
into the darkness above him, disappearing among the
other windblown debris.

Thomas drifted for a few seconds, dazed by the blow.
When his eyes focused again, he saw that Colonel Reed
had climbed up over Dawson's men and taken hold of
the rope alongside Jerry. A slack loop of orange rope
hung between the colonel's straining arms—the broad-
backed officer was actually beginning to reel the rope
down. Thomas couldn't believe it. The rope tension felt
like at least five hundred pounds to him.

Thomas was so dazed by the unbearable pain in his
back that he could hardly think. He noticed that the pain
in his broken shin had completely disappeared. In fact,
he could not seem to feel anything below the viselike
belt. He tried to bend his knees, looking back at his
boots. His legs continued flopping limply in the wind,
not responding at all to his motor commands.

My back is broken, he realized. Next it will be my
neck, and I'll just be hanging here totally helpless.

The force pulling down on his belt abruptly released,
then resumed with a jerk that folded him backwards.
Now he was even farther back in the crevice and several
feet above its top. He could see the red Hägglunds off to

one side and the long top of the black dike stretching into the darkness on the other. The wind drag and flak-like debris were even worse than before.

Looking down the rope, he saw what had caused the brief release of tension. Jerry had been pulled loose from the wall. He was now dangling from the taut rope in the middle of the crevice again. So was Colonel Reed. A slab of fused icicles even bigger than the one Thomas's anchors had pulled loose was just breaking up on the rocks at the bottom. The other climbers were still anchored, but the back of the thick half column of ice was turning white all up and down behind their embedded screws.

Weak and trembling from his injuries, he reached down and pulled the end of his belt free from the loops in his pants. He grasped the belt in both hands, groaning with effort, and tugged with all the strength he had left.

He saw his brother's anguish when their eyes briefly met.

The buckle prong finally pulled out of his belt, and Thomas was launched backward into the dark sky. The freed orange rope whipped in the wind as if still reaching up for him. As he gained altitude, the other climbers' headlamps receded to a tight constellation of stars in the depths of the dark crevice. A second later, the crevice was nothing but a wan sliver of light on the black ridge far below, and Thomas was finally consumed by the hypercane.

CHAPTER 30

Drilling Pit

Captain Hererra sat in one of the ICARE tractors while he watched the upraised stern of his beloved *Polar Star* slip beneath the churning waves. Once the ship was completely submerged, the track-equipped vehicles approached her narrow channel from the upwind side. The drivers had wanted to approach from downwind, to make sure the tractors were not blown into the water, but the wind was freezing the tops of the waves into airborne chunks of all sizes, hurling thousands of frozen projectiles across the ice sheet like cannonballs.

The tractor with a backhoe arm dug a crude ice ramp down to the water, and they towed out the five remaining gasoline tanks. Unlashing the tanks from the deck and replacing part of their contents with air had allowed them to remain afloat when the *Polar Star* sunk.

Retrieving the tanks wasted almost four hours.

With the loss of the ship he had served on for so many years, Hererra began to feel the pain of his injuries as the convoy headed back toward land. Fifty-three million dollars down the drain, he thought. Literally. I just hope it was worth it.

The driver beside him continuously tried to contact the ICARE base on his radio, until they finally came within range. "Hurry! Please hurry!" said the nearly hysterical ICARE operator.

"Why?" the driver asked. "We still have time before the generators run out of gas."

"It's not that," the operator said. "A piece of the storm has broken off and is headed this way. It may destroy the base after all."

A piece of the storm? What's that supposed to mean?

The drivers climbed the bluff beneath the ICARE base as fast as they could with the heavy tanks in tow. Hererra wished they would slow down. The steep road and tight switchbacks would have been scary enough in daylight, without a wind battering the mountainside so hard that the drivers had to constantly fight for control.

Hererra kept telling himself that the wind was not as bad as it seemed, until he saw the tank ahead of him begin tilting back and forth so far that the wheels on opposite sides alternately lifted off the graveled road. "Stop!" he shouted as the tank's rear end began bouncing up and down.

The wheels of the tank on the outside of the narrow road-cut slipped over the edge. The tank tilted and swung out into the dark void. Hererra could now see the tractor that was towing the tank. It was sliding backward and sideways, despite its steel tracks digging deep ruts across the road. A man on the passenger side opened his door and leaped out, but he never hit the ground. The wind flung him backward away from the mountain until his thrashing body disappeared in the black sky. Then the tank dragged the tractor off the road. The two machines came unhitched in midair, and both plummeted toward the ice shelf hidden in the darkness below.

"One down, three to go," the driver shouted, hugging the cliff as closely as he could. "I'll bet we're next."

Saturday, 10:48 P.M. ICARE Time

Angie pointed out through the Snocat's windshield. "There!"

Reed gazed through the blizzard of wet apple-sized snow dabs streaking across their path. In the darkness ahead, he could see a white glow emanating from the ice sheet, lighting up the blowing snow and the low racing clouds. The driver turned toward the glow, and soon Reed could see the foreshortened round opening of the drilling pit. In addition to the soft white glow from floodlights, he saw the tips of orange flames and their flickering reflections on the pit's glistening-wet far wall. The wind was also stretching a plume of thin black smoke across the ice from the pit.

"Something's on fire!" Reed shouted.

He grabbed the radio handset and hailed the drilling crew. For the first time since his search party had passed the pit on their way to the Ellis Mountains, they were within the short radio range imposed by the hypercane. Marshall Dunn soon reassured him that the tall orange flames were only from the moat of oil they were burning to provide slurry water and heat for the workers.

Reed was awestruck by the scale of the excavation as the Snocat's driver cautiously descended the spiraling ramp into the pit. His view was no longer obscured by the blizzard—the wind carried the snow so swiftly that the few dabs falling into the pit impacted the downwind wall within a yard of the top. Marshall's crew had erected a steel framework derrick in the center of the pit, resembling the slender wooden towers that had been built over the earliest American oil wells. Four floodlights were mounted at the tapering derrick's tip, which was precisely level with the surrounding ice sheet. The light beams were directed down the derrick's four sides, supplementing the orange flickers from the fire moat with harsh white radiance.

Looking down, Reed saw at least thirty vehicles of all types parked randomly around the flat white floor of the excavation, which was crisscrossed by bulldozer ruts. An iridescent yellow-green fluid was pooled in several of the ruts, especially close to the drilling derrick.

"Look!" He nudged Angie, pointing to a tractor hitched to a silver tank trailer with KIWI OIL stenciled on its side. "That tank is from the *Polar Star.* They made it."

Angie didn't look very thrilled. "Yeah, but it doesn't necessarily mean any tanks made it to the ICARE base."

Reed understood her point. If Lois still needed her electronic ventilator, and none of the gasoline tanks reached the ICARE base before its backup generator ran dry, she was still going to die.

He returned his attention to the pit. A rectangular vertical drilling stem was swiftly rotating at the center of the derrick, driven by a long sprocket chain stretched between a gear housing at the top of the stem and an exhaust-belching motor on a flatbed trailer. The gear housing at the top of the stem was about halfway up the derrick. Above it, a flexible black hose stretched the rest of the way up through the framework, then back down the outside of the derrick to a vibrating pump on the ice. A second hose, attached to the other end of the pump, snaked into a pit that was full of the iridescent yellow-green liquid. Reed could see a whirlpool in the slimy-looking fluid where it was being sucked into the hose. The flow into the hose was compensated by fluid dripping into the pit from a sieve that was straining out ice shavings. Four workers with snow shovels were scraping the shavings off the sieve as they accumulated. The slurry of green fluid and ice shavings was being decanted from a spout on one side of a steel cylinder embedded in the ice around the rotating drill stem. The dented cylinder was at least ten feet across and four feet high and full to the brim with the ice-laden fluid welling up from the borehole.

Reed inferred that the pump was continuously recirculating the drilling fluid to clear ice shavings from the bit, forcing the fluid down through the hollow drill stem and back up the borehole outside the stem.

Marshall and Lim were standing near a barrel of burning oil, gesticulating with their hands, giving orders to the rig workers frantically swarming around the site. Two of the workers were standing on a circular platform near the top of the derrick. Reed watched as the stem stopped rotating and two thick chains hoisted the gear housing at its top up to the platform where the workers could reach it. When they hastily decoupled the fluid hose from the top of the stem, the greasy yellow-green liquid gushed all over them and dribbled down through the framework. They laid the hose aside so that the fluid spewing out of it mostly landed in the cylindrical basin at the bottom of the drill stem. Then they lowered the gear housing again, added another twenty-foot length of hollow rectangular stem, and reconnected the hose to its top.

The drilling resumed as the yellow Snocat reached the bottom of the ramp. Reed jumped out when the vehicle stopped and shook hands with Marshall and Lim. "I believe you ordered one dozen thermonuclear warheads. Here they are, on time with . . . fifty minutes to spare. I just hope they're still intact enough to detonate."

Lim was already rattling the locked rear doors of the

Snocat, trying to pull them open. "Where are they? Let me see them!" He stepped aside, bouncing on the balls of his feet, while Reed unlocked the doors and climbed in.

Reed unfolded the bloody notebook page one of the dying defense technicians had given to Ferrand after the plane crash. "You know, I always half expected to wake up one day at the end of the world," he said. "But I figured nukes would be what *caused* the end. I never imagined we'd be using them to stop it." After locating the combination, he opened the triple lock on one of the crates and lifted its heavy lid.

Lim lunged into the cramped compartment, looked into the padded coffinlike box, and slammed the heel of his right hand against the Snocat's metal roof. "No!"

"What?" Reed said, startled by the clang.

Lim stared into the crate, aghast. Nestled within the padding was a plain aluminum cylinder three feet long and a foot thick. "The warheads are at least an inch too wide for the borehole," he said.

"Did you use the biggest drill bit?"

"Of course," Lim said. "We have bigger rock bits, but we could not get them down through the ice hole. I was afraid this would happen. I did not know the size of our largest ice bit at the time the nukes took off."

They climbed out of the Snocat and spread the grim news while Dawson's men disembarked and unloaded the warheads. What the drillers had already accomplished was amazing, Reed thought. He couldn't believe how fast they had excavated the huge pit and erected their rig. Could such an effort really have come to naught for lack of a single tool? He could see Jerry Calendri glumly looking out a window at the moat of burning oil, resting his bandaged forehead on the glass. Had the young aviator's twin brother sacrificed himself for nothing?

Reed gave the bloody notebook page to Lim. "Here. You'll need this if we figure out how to drill the hole. It shows how to rig the detonators and adjust the warheads for maximum yield."

Lim's eyes widened and his chapped lips puckered. "Colonel, I'm only a *civil* engineer."

"Not anymore," Reed said. "That's top-secret defense technology you're looking at."

"What can you tell me about the warheads?"

"Not much. This is the first time I've seen one. These are W-80 tactical nukes, meant for cruise missiles launched from planes and submarines. We still have about two thousand of them in service, I think. They aren't as powerful as the warheads used on strategic platforms like ICBMs and the B-2, but the housings on those would definitely have been too big. These W-80s are adjustable from five to one hundred fifty kilotons. I'm sure you'll want to crank the yield all the way up."

Reed turned to Marshall and asked if the drilling team had received any radio broadcasts from the ICARE base. Marshall informed him that they had not.

"There has to be something you can do to enlarge the borehole in the ice," Angie said. She was squatting beside the barrel of burning oil, lifting her goggles to rub her tired eyes. "Why can't you just use one of the rock bits to drill a bigger hole in the ice? Even glacial ice is softer than rock, right?"

"Ice is softer," Marshall said, "but it's also a lot less brittle. Rock bits don't *cut* through the rock, they just rotate heavy knobs against it to bust it into tiny fragments that can be washed out of the borehole in the drilling fluid. If we tried that with ice—I've seen this—the bit would just sit there and spin. The ice wouldn't break up.

An industrial glacier bit uses a whole different strategy—it has radial blades to slice away the ice like an electric shaver head."

Reed walked up and pulled Angie aside. "Pumpkin, I got Jerry to agree to drive on to the ICARE base. I think he has a busted rib. I want you to go with him."

She nodded, swaying with exhaustion. "I hope Lois is awake when we get there."

"Me too," Reed said.

"What are you going to do, Dad?"

"The rest of us should stay here in case we can help the drilling crew."

Angie hesitated as if trying to think of something, then hugged him. "Will I ever see you again?"

"I hope so, Pumpkin."

Angie lurched, and he thought she was letting go. Then he realized that she was still squeezing his chest and had begun sobbing. He held her for several seconds. Her shoulders sagged, and the force from her arms tilted downward. Afraid she was going to collapse, he gently parted her embrace and held her up with one arm while he walked her back to the Snocat.

Professor Ferrand was leaning against a fender on one foot. "Aren't you going back to the base with Jerry?" Reed asked him.

Ferrand shook his head. "I may be able to help solve your borehole problem."

Reed abruptly stooped so he could see eye to eye with the extremely short meteorologist. "You have an idea?"

"No," Ferrand said. "But I'm working on it."

Even that made Reed feel hopeful. Ferrand was the only scientist in the pit.

Reed helped Angie board the Snocat. Jerry Calendri was in the driver's seat, watching the drillers. The flames reflected in fresh tear streaks on his cheeks. Reed gripped his shoulder and leaned close to whisper. "Are you sure you're okay to drive, son?"

Jerry nodded, flashing Angie a half smile. "I'll get her safely back to the base, sir. I promise."

Reed made sure Angie's seat belts were tightly buckled and her headset radio still had good batteries. "It won't take you long to get beyond radio range, but try to call me if anything goes wrong," he said.

"Dad, please come back with us. They don't need you here anymore."

"They might," he said, hugging her one last time.

Reed got off and stood watching the Snocat as it pulled away up the ramp. He could see Angie through a window. She was weeping and waving at him. He waved back.

"Mr. Dunn! We punched through!"

Reed turned to see everyone running toward the derrick. Even Professor Ferrand was hopping in that direction to see what the commotion was about. Reed gave him a hand.

"How does it feel?" Reed asked.

"My foot? It hurts something awful."

"I mean seeing this." Reed nodded up at the dark clouds and snow blobs streaking over the pit in the howling wind. "You must be proud that you accurately predicted something so . . . unprecedented."

"Oh, that," Ferrand said. "I'll be proud later, if I'm still alive."

Everyone gathered beneath the derrick, around the cylindrical basin of yellow-green drilling fluid. The fluid level was rapidly subsiding, the swirling iridescent surface rotating clockwise around the drill stem. When it reached the bottom, the borehole began sucking in air with a rasping, whistling gurgle. A minute later the suck-

ing sound ended, and all was quiet except for the hypercane raging overhead.

All of the men standing around the drill gazed at Lim
with expressions of fear and exhaustion. Lim grimly
stared down the dark borehole and grunted a Chinese
curse. Reed glanced at Ferrand, whose expression belied
only physical pain, no brewing ideas. Marshall shouted
orders. "Pull the stem. Then drop the float and the
plumb." His voice conveyed authority but no enthusiasm.

Reed noticed that the floor of the ice pit was frozen
solid, yet the greasy green drilling fluid that had pooled
in vehicle ruts remained liquid. He pointed to one of the
puddles. "What *is* this stuff?"

"Mostly propylene glycol antifreeze," Lim said. "Plus
a cocktail of corrosion inhibitors including triethanol-
amine, sodium dodecanedioate, and benzotriazole."

"Why did it drain out of the borehole so fast?"

"We'll know in a minute," Lim said.

Reed paced around the derrick as the workers pulled
out the drill stem. The sound of the drilling fluid draining down the hole had reminded him of something, but
he could not remember what. He tried to put the incipi-
ent flashback aside so he could concentrate, but the
memory was something so terrifying that it would neither go away nor reveal itself.

One of the men shouted, "The float stopped at sea
level, Mr. Dunn."

Lim said, "That explains where the fluid went,
Colonel. The Ross Sea has many fjords that reach back
into the subglacial ridge. We obviously drilled into one
of them."

Reed's flashback suddenly came forth—the brutal ride
down the glacial moulin with Lois. He grabbed Lim's
shoulder. "We can *melt* the sides of the borehole!" He

pointed to the moat of burning oil. "Just pour hot water down it!"

Lim and Marshall glanced at each other, then shook their heads. "That water is not actually hot," Lim said, looking up at Reed as if explaining to a child why he couldn't drive to the moon and back. "Even if it were, there would not be enough. If we dump cold water down the hole, it will freeze to the sides and make the hole even smaller."

Reed slumped against the empty fluid basin.

"Hey!" Ferrand shouted, grinning. "I know where you can get all kinds of boiling-hot water, if you dare."

Reed, Ferrand, Marshall, and Lim looked at each other, then burst into conversation.

"How much pipe do you have?" Reed asked.

"Truckloads," Lim said. "Literally. We brought all the pipe ICARE had, in case we needed to pump water out of the borehole."

Reed looked where Lim was pointing. Three flatbed trailers with risers like logging trucks were stacked to overflowing with silver metal pipe at least eight inches in diameter. "Will it reach the subglacial lake from here?"

Marshall was already unfolding a map of the Warner Basin. Lim checked the scale and measured with a stubby forefinger. "Easily," he said.

"Can your pump drag water that far?" Ferrand asked.

Lim nodded. "The pump won't move the water fast enough, but that doesn't matter. The hydrostatic head level in the Warner Basin is much higher than sea level, so once we get a flow going into the borehole, the pipe will siphon water from the lake so fast . . . so fast it may tear the pipe apart."

"There's just one problem," Ferrand said. They all glanced at him. Reed thought he looked ready to give up again. "The floating ice sheet is still intact several kilometers into the Warner Basin," Ferrand continued. "It will be too thick at the end of your pipe for you to break through to the water."

"How do you know that?" Marshall said.

"In my simulations, a wind speed this slow would indicate that less than a quarter of the ice sheet is open, so its thickness near the edge is probably still close to the original thirty-seven meters."

Reed glanced up at the menacing clouds rolling overhead so fast that they blurred in his vision. Slow?

Lim kicked the metal fluid basin with a resounding clang, cursing in Chinese again. "We don't have the time or equipment to set up another drill, and there's no other way to cut through that much ice."

"Actually, there may be," Reed shouted, running to the nearest tracked vehicle.

He climbed behind the wheel and slammed the door. When most of the hypercane's roar was shut out, he heard whimpering. He looked behind him, wondering what it was. It sounded like a lost puppy whining, but that was impossible.

Finding nothing on the backseat, he looked at the floor in front of it. There he saw Maximillian Bloom, CEO of the American corporate conglomerate at ICARE. Max was hiding in the shadows, clutching the back of the front passenger seat in a trembling embrace. His puffy round face was covered with red blotches and tear streaks. His sparse blond mustache was caked with mucus from his nose. At first the tall executive was hiding his eyes, but when he realized Reed was staring at him, he glared back and wailed, "What do you *want*?"

"Get out," Reed said.

"No!" Max barked.

Reed looked away from Max's face, shuddering from

vicarious humiliation. The last person he had seen make an expression like that was his secretary's colicky newborn. "Suit yourself," he said. "But—trust me—you don't want to go where this tractor is going."

"I don't care!" Max howled.

Reed revved the engine and pulled up beside the men at the drill. "Get in, Professor. Marshall, is anyone else here wounded?"

Marshall shook his head.

"I'll be ready to punch a hole in that damned ice sheet in about an hour," Reed said. "Wire the warheads, lay your pipe, and stay on the radio. I'll tell you how to prepare."

CHAPTER 31

Rocks

"I can't believe he cut himself loose like that," said Jerry Calendri. "I should have been able to pull him in."

"Huh?" Angie opened her eyes and tried to focus on Jerry, who was driving the yellow Snocat toward the ICARE base. The injured young aviator kept both hands on the vibrating wheel, fighting the wind, except when he swiped at his tears.

"Maybe I shouldn't have insisted that we descend through the crevice," she said.

"It worked," Jerry said. "We got the warheads down in time."

A minute later he said, "People always asked us what it was like to have a twin. I don't think I ever told anybody what a special gift it is . . . having someone who thinks like you do, who really understands you. People look for that their whole lives and never find it. You know?"

"Yeah," Angie said. "I know *exactly* what you mean."

"We both wanted to be pilots since we could walk. I guess we went for such different planes so we wouldn't be alike in *every* way. They're both cool, you know. Just different. The Warthog is like a monster truck. The F-16 is like a Ferrari. We used to tease each other all the time. He'd call me an arcade ace, because all the controls in an F-16 are electronic, and I'd call him a bus driver."

Angie was startled, then excited, when her father's voice came over the radio. "Hold up, you two. I'm headed your way. We can travel together."

"All right! Slow down!" she said to Jerry.

"I'll try," he said. The wind was behind them, contributing more propulsion than the engine.

"Jerry, can you fly your brother's plane?" Reed asked.

"The Warthog? No, sir. Not a chance. I'm strictly a fly-by-wire pilot. A Hog driver has to manually steer, brake, and look out the windshield to see where he's going. Besides, I'm in no shape for pulling Gs with a busted rib."

"Okay, that's what I thought," Reed said.

After a minute of braking they saw the lights of another vehicle approaching the Snocat from behind through the horizontal blizzard. Angie spoke into the radio hand-mike. "Thanks for deciding to come back with us, Dad."

"Have you contacted the base yet?" Reed asked.

They had been out of touch with ICARE since leaving to look for the warheads. The storm had doubled its fury in that time, so they had no way of knowing whether the base was even still standing, much less whether Lois had woken from her coma or passed away.

"We've been trying," Angie said. "Still nothing. I sure hope—"

Clang! The Snocat lurched forward, whipping Angie's head back against her headrest.

"Dad, did you run into us?"

"What was *that*?" Reed asked simultaneously.

"I think something in the wind hit us," Jerry said.

Slam! The Snocat jerked again as if hit by a wrecking ball.

"It came from above that time," Jerry shouted.

Angie twisted around and looked along the bare steel roof. She saw a deep dent protruding downward near the back, as if a two-ton fist had smashed the Snocat.

Slam! Clang! Slam!

"Calendri, report!" Reed bellowed. "What's happening up there?"

"I think we're being bombarded by airborne debris, sir. Are you catching any?"

"Negative. We—"

Angie heard a loud *clang* over the radio.

"*Now* we are," Reed shouted.

In a nasal voice that was pitched high with panic, someone in her father's vehicle yelled, "Stop! Take me back! I changed my mind!"

"It can't be just ice," Jerry said.

"There are no rocks anywhere around here," Angie yelled, but she knew Jerry must be right. It's like being caught in a meteor shower, she thought. But these can't be real meteors. They would blow the Snocat apart. "I don't get it. How can the wind lift such big rocks?"

"*This* wind didn't," Jerry said. "It must be blowing harder somewhere over land."

Slam!

This time the noise and jerk were followed by a swirl of cold air in the Snocat's cabin, and Angie could suddenly hear the unmuffled fury of the wind outside. She looked behind her again. There were several dents in the roof, plus one large hole with sharp silver teeth of torn metal bent downward around its edges. A brown rock the size of a soccer ball was bouncing around on the floor.

Angie pulled her goggles up into place and reached

for her helmet. "Jerry! Step on it! We have to get out of here!"

"I *am*," Jerry said. "With the wind, we're doing at least ninety. We're going to blow the crankshaft or slip a track."

Crash! The Snocat's windshield imploded, spraying safety glass against Angie's face. Despite the goggles, she instinctively shut her eyes and kept them closed as wind whipped broken glass around the cabin.

She felt the Snocat turn sharply to the right. "Jerry! I think we should keep going straight. That will get us away from the rocks faster than going in—hey!"

The Snocat careened to the left, then swung right again. "Jerry! What are you doing? Can't you see?" She remembered that he had not been wearing his goggles when the windshield broke.

Jerry did not answer.

"Hey, what's wrong?" she yelled.

Reed was shouting over the radio. "Calendri! Report! What just happened?"

Broken glass was still stinging Angie's face like a swarm of bees, but she could no longer stand the terror of not being able to see. Holding her goggles tightly against her cheeks, she opened her eyes and looked at Jerry.

And screamed until she was breathless.

Jerry was slumped with a flat boulder on his lap. His arms hung down limply at his sides. Blood was streaming down them and dripping on the floor from his fingers. Where his face had once been, there was only a concave pulp of mangled flesh with a few protruding shards of bone.

Reed shouted, "Angela! Jerry! Anybody! Pumpkin, are you all right?"

Angie weakly grabbed the radio mike. "Dad! Help! Jerry's dead."

There was no reply.

She leaned over and grasped the Snocat's vibrating steering wheel, which was warped and bent downward. Her sore hand slipped off—the wheel was lubricated with Jerry's blood. She wiped her glove on her parka, then grabbed the wheel with both hands and gave it an experimental tug. It refused to budge.

"Dad, the steering wheel is bent and I can't turn it."

"Kill the engine."

She removed the ignition key. The Snocat slowed a little. "We're still moving, Dad. The wind is pushing us. I'll try the brake."

She unbuckled her seat harness and lunged across Jerry's bloody lap. Fighting the wind coming through the broken windshield, she attempted to heave the flat rock off him. It was too heavy. Turning sideways, she stood on one leg and tried to stick the other one down past his knees toward the foot pedals. Her calf jammed between the rock and the dashboard.

"I can't reach it!"

"Angie, you have to."

She squatted and tried to reach around Jerry's legs with her right arm. She could feel the brake pedal with her fingertips. Grunting and digging her crampons into the Snocat's rubber floor, she pushed herself forward, trying to squeeze her shoulder past Jerry's knee. An edge of the rock raked across her collarbone. Still she pushed, but she could barely move the brake pedal.

"It's no use!" she shouted into the radio. "I can't reach. What are you going to do, Dad?"

"Angie . . . there's nothing I can do."

"What do you mean?"

"We got separated in the rock storm. I can't see you anymore."

"We must be headed the way the wind is blowing," Angie said.

"Angela sweetheart, you have to gain control of that tractor. I . . . I can't look for you right now. I still have to do something for the drillers, and we're out of time."

Angie had never heard her father's voice so strained, not even in the days of torment following the wreck that had killed her mother. I'm going to die out here after all, she thought. She sat in the bloody bouncing aisle, wondering what to say.

"Dad, are you still there?"

"Right here, sweetheart."

"I just . . . it's all right, Dad. I trust you. I hope . . . I hope you make it back home. You and Lois, both."

"I'll come back for you later, Angela. And I'll find you. I promise."

Reed had been so sure that his life had already shown him the deepest inner misery a man could ever feel. He had also thought he was too tough to cry on the job. Now he knew he'd been wrong on both counts.

He held his course, both hands steady on the wheel and the accelerator pedal flush on the floor, as tears streamed down his cheeks. He was glad Ferrand looked away and kept quiet. In the backseat, Max was also weeping, and muttering so incomprehensibly that Reed could not tell whether he was cursing or praying.

Reed had stated the truth when he'd said they were out of time. It was now 11:50 P.M., and according to the latest runs of Ferrand's hypercane simulator that he knew about, the deadline for human activity in the Warner Basin was still 3:00 A.M. He had also meant what he said about returning for Angie after penetrating the

ice sheet for the drillers, but he knew that his chances of
ever seeing his only child again were essentially zero.

Just before he'd lost sight of the Snocat's taillights, it
had veered into the Warner Basin, directly toward the
open boiling lake at the core of the hypercane.

CHAPTER 32

Twister

Sunday, 12:22 A.M.

José Hererra had never been so happy to reach a destination as he was when the crawling convoy of tractors towed the three remaining gasoline tanks into the outskirts of the ICARE base. Then the operator on the radio said, "Stop! Don't go to the above-ground tanks. That tornado thing blew them away."

"It already hit?" the driver said.

"It zoomed by about a minute ago and took out the west end of the base."

"You want us to park by the furnace?"

"Okay . . . wait."

Hererra could hear a moment of panicky background chatter.

"Don't park!" the operator shouted. "Go to the new below-ground tank we haven't used yet. Hurry! The bloody thing is coming back. You have to unload the gas before your tanks are blown away."

The driver swung right, running over the toes of a huge gravel pile. They drove past a long glass greenhouse, a tall radio tower, and an array of satellite dishes vibrating in the wind.

This must have been the west end, Hererra thought as they passed by a scored concrete slab surrounded by ground augers and the frayed guylines still attached to them. There was no sign of the building's walls, roof, or contents.

The ride got bumpier, but the driver didn't slow down. Hererra looked out at the ground. The glacially compacted rocky soil had been plowed up as if by a tiller. Jesus! Wind did that? The steady gale that was now strumming the base's intact guylines and howling around its walls was faster than the few hurricanes Hererra had sailed through, but it certainly couldn't claw up the Earth itself.

The drivers parked the long cylindrical tanks in a triangle around a capped pipe sticking up a few inches from the torn-up ground. By placing a front fender of each tractor against a rear corner of another's tank, they created a partial barrier to shelter the inside of the triangle.

"Here she comes!" the driver shouted as he flung open his door and swung down from the cab.

Hererra heard a guttural roar screaming in the distance. He looked out through the driver's open door. The ground sloped down from the tractor to the edge of the bluff surrounding the base on three sides. The pale blend of ice, dirt, and rock was weakly lit by the floodlights of the base behind him, but Hererra could see nothing except darkness beyond the bluff, which he knew stood hundreds of yards above the Ross Ice Shelf.

Within the vast expanse of blackness beyond the bluff, he could hear one of the unpredicted phenomena that the generals at NORAD had taken to calling minicanes. It shrieked like a chorus of damned souls and growled like a pack of hungry predators, and it was coming closer.

"Go! Go! Go!" the driver shouted as he rounded the front of the tractor, grasping the high bumper tubes to pull himself along through the wind.

Cringing against the passenger door, Hererra dared to take his eyes off the growling black void and look behind him into the triangle. Several men were dragging deflated hoses from the three silver tanks toward the pipe in the ground.

Hererra saw flashes reflected in the window and turned back toward the driver's open door. He could see the minicane now. Despite the utter darkness beneath the hypercane clouds, the broad funnel of spinning cloud and ice debris was visible because small forks of lightning crackled all over its blurry surface like scurrying white spiders.

The funnel was fatter and more diffuse than a tornado. It was also spinning a lot faster and—strangest of all—seemed to have an elliptical rather than circular cross section. The long axis of the ellipse was rotating clockwise, slower than the wind itself, so that the funnel turned a broad side to Hererra every two or three seconds. This alternating orientation made it appear to expand and contract. The thing looks like it's *breathing,* he thought.

He was glad that the funnel was still farther from the base than he had assumed when he could only hear it. It was twisting, tilting, and meandering all over the flat white ice shelf. But it was also accelerating toward him.

Hererra lunged across the seat, slammed the driver's door shut, and huddled on the floor, peeking out the windshield. The men dragging the hoses were almost to the inlet pipe of the buried tank when they bolted back toward the tractors. The growling and shrieking abruptly grew so loud that Hererra pressed his palms over his ears. It's like being inside a jet engine, he thought. The tractor began to lurch and sway. Clangs, bangs, slams, and crashes were added to the roar, and he knew that the rest of the ICARE base was being ripped apart.

He peeked out the window again. The triangle between tractors was deserted. The abandoned hoses were writhing in the wind like angry snakes.

This is only the outer edge of the whirlwind, he thought. Any second now, the faster core will get here and drag these tankers off the bluff. Then the *Polar Star* will have sunk for nothing. The base won't get any fuel after all, and they'll still need it if anyone survives.

There was no time to waste. He unlatched the passenger door and let the wind drag it open, throwing him onto the bumpy ground. The wind rolled him over again and again like a log rolling down a hill. His hips slammed against something hard, and he curled around it, realizing that it was the pipe sticking up from the buried tank.

Lightning was flashing almost constantly, like a mob of wrathful paparazzi. Forcing his eyes open against the wind, which seemed strangely warm, he saw the drivers from ICARE and his crew from the *Polar Star* huddled beneath the tractors and tanks. They beckoned for him to join them. The strobing lightning reflected in their eyes and made their gestures appear choppy.

Over the hood of a tractor, Hererra saw ICARE's tapering framework radio tower twist left, then right, then launch straight upward like a rocket, spinning clockwise. The satellite dishes were next. Some were blown apart as if by explosives, ejecting panels of parabolically curved fiberglass and wire mesh into the wind. The spindly steel frames that were left behind bent and flattened windward like bushes stripped of their leaves.

Some of the dishes broke loose from their moorings intact. One flew horizontally over the triangle of tankers, spinning like a UFO, trailing a sparking wire. A distant explosion behind one of the tanks briefly lit up a jumble of corrugated steel panels, fiberglass insulation, and furniture swirling overhead.

Hererra saw that the men beneath the tank upwind of him were holding one of the hoses. "Throw me the nozzle!" he yelled, still hanging around the vertical pipe by his hips.

They could not hear him, but they understood his gestures and flung the hose into the wind. Hererra caught the hose as it whipped over him and reeled in the brass nozzle at its end.

As he unscrewed the cap of the buried tank's inlet pipe, he saw that ICARE's house-sized pile of coarse road gravel was rapidly shrinking. A plume of airborne gravel was whipping upward from the tip of the pile like smoke. Within a few strobes of lightning, the minicane had devoured the entire pile.

Bang! Screech! A steel I-beam at least six inches wide impaled one of the tanks, penetrating both sides. It lodged in place, protruding from the exit hole. Aromatic gas dribbled into the wind and spattered Hererra's face.

He plunged the hose nozzle down into the open pipe and made a cranking gesture to the men beneath the truck tank. One of them twisted a valve, and Hererra saw the hose inflate with flowing gasoline. His body was now flopping up and down against the ground downwind of the buried pipe, but he held the nozzle in place, smelling the vapors and feeling the gasoline surge through the hose.

He watched the long cloud of gravel swoop up and around the base, then back toward the tankers. It impacted the greenhouse just upwind, instantly shattering every panel into thousands of razorlike shards. Hererra knew that if he just let go, he would be swept up into the storm ahead of the airborne gravel and glass, and that wherever he eventually landed, his death would be relatively painless. But he chose to hang on and drain as much gasoline into ICARE's tank as he could.

He saw the wind-driven gravel and glass shards rip through the tractors and the men cringing beneath them a millisecond before he too was cut to shreds.

CHAPTER 33

Waves

Ferrand heaved a sigh of relief when he saw a fork in the road with a tilted neon-yellow sign. Despite the sign dancing in the wind, he could read ICARE BASE beside an arrow pointing right, and ROSS SHELF AIRSTRIP beside an arrow pointing left.

Thank God we're almost there, he thought. They'll have morphine at the base. My foot is killing me.

A bewildered moan escaped his lips when Reed took the left fork.

It was accompanied by a string of curses from Max Bloom, who was now sitting up in the backseat, wishing he had stayed at the ICARE base to begin with. That had been his original plan, but almost everyone else had volunteered to help with the drilling mission, and Max had been unable to stand the thought of being left alone at the base with the wind howling so viciously outside.

"I have to go to the airstrip," Reed explained. "You guys can drive back to the base from there."

The road ran along the base of a steep bluff on Ferrand's side. Groaning, he pressed against his frigid window and looked up the looming dark slope at the tight switchbacks of the other road. "The ICARE base is on top of that high bluff?"

"Yes," Reed said.

Ferrand could see the prominent rim of the bluff silhouetted against the swirling hypercane clouds by frequent flashes. "It looks like a lot of lightning is concentrated up there for some reason."

Reed tried to radio the base again, for at least the twentieth time since they had left the drilling pit. He looked gravely concerned when there was still no answer. "This close, we should be able to raise them no matter what the storm is doing," he said.

The road abruptly turned away from the bluff and headed straight across the Ross Ice Shelf, another flat white plain indistinguishable from the ice sheet in the Warner Basin to Ferrand, except that he could see the shelf's jagged edge off to the left. "How far is it down to the water over there?" he asked.

"Two or three hundred feet."

"Straight down?"

"Straight down."

"Let's not get too close."

"I'm just following the marker flags."

Ferrand still wondered how Reed planned to cut through the Warner Basin ice sheet at the end of the siphon pipe. Instead of conversing, the colonel had spent the trip concentrating on driving at top speed. He had also talked over the radio with the drilling crew and the Snocat, but except during the hail of rocks, all his words had been spoken into his headset microphone too softly for Ferrand to hear over the wind. "I assume you're going to get on a plane here," Ferrand said. "But I don't see how that can possibly help you to—*whaugh!*"

Ferrand gripped the dashboard and Reed slammed on the brakes as a long silver tank trailer plummeted from the sky in front of them. Ferrand had just a split second to read KIWI OIL on the side of the tank as it shot down into the headlight beams. The tank fell on its rear end. Its eight rubber tires broke off and bounced across the ice in all directions. The thick steel walls of the tank folded upward from the impact like an accordion. Then two pieces of grinding metal struck a spark, and the gasoline bursting radially from the crushed base of the tank ignited.

Reed swerved left to dodge the expanding fireball, but it overtook them. Ferrand was temporarily blinded by bright yellow light and felt searing radiant heat on his face. Then the wind blew the flames away from the tractor. All he could see at first was a silhouette of the windshield frame stenciled onto his retinas by the green afterimage of the fireball. But he could feel the tractor spinning around, slinging him against his door, and he could hear Max repeatedly screaming.

We're going to slide off into the ocean!

Sure enough, when his vision began to clear, he saw that the jagged horizon separating the ice shelf from the dark void beyond was getting closer with each revolution of the tractor. Suddenly the ice beneath them was somehow wet despite the subfreezing air. The tractor continued spinning out of control, its headlight beams swinging around like a berserk lighthouse beacon.

Ferrand closed his eyes and waited for free fall.

The tractor stopped.

He opened his eyes and looked out. Seeing nothing but blackness, he looked down. The ice shelf ended a few inches beyond his door. Hundreds of feet below, he saw the churning sea in the wan light of the elongated horizontal fireball stretched across it by the wind. The thin pack ice that should have covered the ocean at the end of winter had apparently broken up and completely disintegrated under the grinding force of the hypercane.

The dark sea surface seemed to be rapidly receding. Ferrand wondered if it was an optical illusion caused by his vertical perspective, or by his dizziness from the spin. Then a long horizontal flicker caught his attention, approaching out of the darkness far out to sea.

He suddenly realized why the ice shelf was wet near the edge—the line of reflection was a monster wave. "Get away from the cliff!" he yelled to Reed.

The tractor's engine had died during the spinout. Reed was cranking the starter, but it wouldn't turn over. The wind was buffeting the tractor from the landward side, scooting it inch by inch closer to the edge.

"Hurry!" Ferrand said.

The wind suddenly got louder. Cold air swirled through the cabin. Ferrand turned and saw that Max had opened the back door on the landward side.

"Stop!" Reed bellowed. "Stay in the tractor. The wind will take you."

"Shut the door!" Ferrand added.

With Max's door standing open, the wind was shoving the tractor even harder, jolting it toward the precipice. Ferrand looked down from his window again. This time he could not see the ice—it had disappeared back beneath the vehicle's steel track shoes. There was no way to tell how far the track was jutting out over the edge.

The great wave had begun to break and had closed the distance by half.

Max appeared oblivious to their shouts. He was stumbling away from the tractor, one slow step at a time, planting his crampons in the ice and leaning into the wind at a forty-five-degree angle.

Ferrand lunged into the backseat and shut the door.

The engine started. Reed yanked the gearshift into first. "Come on, come on!" he said. The tracks spun on the wet ice, then caught.

They pulled away from the edge and headed toward
Max. At the same moment, Ferrand saw Max stumble.
The panicked executive was dragging his upraised right
foot forward against the wind, and one of its front crampon points caught in the flapping fabric of his other
pants leg. He pitched forward, hands flailing.

The wind was already propelling him back toward the
tractor before he landed. He clawed in vain at the ice.
Then the wind flipped him onto his back, and he
thrashed madly against the air. He began to spin as he
slid across the wet ice, accelerating as if in free fall.

"He's going to hit us," Ferrand yelled.

"I know," Reed said. "I'll try to catch him." He
stopped the tractor, unlatched his door, and held it open
against the wind with a foot. Leaving his seat harness
buckled, he stuck his head and one arm out.

Max zoomed toward the tractor with a piercing shriek
that Ferrand could hear even over the wind. He slammed
into the front bumper tubes with a jarring thud, spun up
over the hood, and smacked into the windshield headfirst. Ferrand reflexively recoiled from Max's bloody
nose and bulging eyes when the executive's face
smashed against the glass. For a fraction of a second
Ferrand could see Max's teeth and his tongue between
them, all pressed against the glass by the wind. Then
Max slid off the side of the hood opposite Reed, leaving
behind a bloody streak. Ferrand watched the limp body
skid and tumble off the ice shelf as Reed shut his door
and put the tractor in gear again.

As they accelerated, Ferrand felt a jarring tremor and
concluded that the mammoth wave had finally struck the
high ice cliff behind them. Looking back, he saw white
froth shoot upward into the dark sky like an inverted
waterfall. A second later the spray splashed down all
around them. Reed turned on the windshield wipers,

which had brushes for dry snow and dust instead of rubber blades. The thick brushes smeared the freezing seawater into translucent streaks of white ice that covered the windshield.

"Can you see?" Ferrand shouted.

"No."

"Then slow down!"

"No time," Reed yelled, ducking to peer through a gap in the windshield ice. The swinging brushes gradually rubbed the white crust away.

As they left the wet area, they began to pass assorted debris strewn across the ice. In addition to rocks and ice chunks and pieces of the gasoline tank, there were sheets of red corrugated steel and items of heavy furniture. Ferrand saw a toilet sitting upright, undamaged except for a crack in the base. Its lid was flapping in the wind.

A steel hospital bed was blowing across the ice on its side. It caromed off Reed's door and kept going. Ferrand could see nothing especially interesting about the bed, except that it had extra-high guardrails on all four sides, but he noticed that Reed twisted around to stare at the bed as if in disbelief.

When they arrived at the airstrip, Reed headed straight for a plane that was staked down to the ice with cables over its wings. As they got closer, Ferrand saw the plane's camouflage paint, straight wings, riveted armor plates, and the huge dual rectangular tail fins mounted at the ends of a flat span a third as wide as the wings. He recognized the plane as the A-10 Warthog that had helped escort the crashed Starlifter.

Ferrand glanced at the tons of missiles and bombs suspended beneath the Warthog's wings, and comprehension dawned. He stared at Reed in awe. "You're going to *bomb* the ice sheet!"

Reed gravely nodded.

"Why didn't you just call in an air strike from New Zealand?" Ferrand asked.

"They'd take too long to get here, and they don't have the right tools for the job," Reed said. "If any plane can survive flying rocks and whatever tore the wing off the Starlifter, it's this baby here. Fast fighters also don't pack the kind of firepower that this ugly duckling does."

"Why don't you let the pilot who flew the Warthog down here do this?"

"The 'cane already got him—it was Thomas Calendri."

"Do you know how to fly one of these planes?"

"I hope so," Reed said. "I used to."

CHAPTER 34

Eye

The Snocat continued rolling deeper into the Warner Basin, propelled by the hypercane. Angie tried and tried to reach around Jerry's legs to the brake pedal, always failing. Even if she could reach the brake, she realized, the Snocat would just take off again as soon as she let the pedal go. There was no way to lock the brake on, as far as she knew. And the wind might even be powerful enough to scoot the heavy vehicle across the ice with the tracks locked in place.

She could feel the air pressure dropping. Pain in her ears forced her to continuously gulp and yawn. Her sinuses also hurt. After a while, aches began in her teeth and joints, and she felt weak, light-headed, and short of breath.

The ice became wet, glaring in the headlights. The air wafting in through the broken windshield steadily grew warmer and more humid, forcing Angie to remove layers until she was wearing nothing but her boots and the baggy red thermal underwear she had received for her birthday. We must be getting close to the open water, she thought, wondering if the Snocat would plunge into the boiling lake without warning.

She stuffed all the outer clothing into her waterproof climbing gear bag in case of rain, knowing she might need dry insulation again later. She also stuck in her radio headset, burying it beneath the clothes where it was bound to stay dry.

She couldn't see how fast the Snocat was going in the darkness, but judging by the wind swirling in through the open windshield frame and the clanking hum of the tracks, it was hurtling even faster than it had before the attack of the wind-driven meteors.

Lightning raced across the sky. Wiping sweat—an unfamiliar sensation—Angie looked up at the opaque gray clouds. They puckered and undulated like dense smoke clinging beneath a ceiling in a burning house, appearing so low that she could reach up and touch them.

The thunderclap brought drenching rain that pounded the Snocat's hood and blew in on Angie, soaking her curly brown hair and thick underwear. Cringing on the floor, she gasped and sputtered and blinked, wondering if she would drown *before* reaching the open water. The thinness of the air made the feeling of suffocation even worse. This deep inside the storm, the pressure was so low that her heart raced and her lungs labored, trying to provide enough oxygen.

The next flash of lightning was a ground strike. It hit the ice less than a hundred yards in front of the Snocat. Both the blinding white arc and its reflection on the wet ice temporarily branded blue streaks onto Angie's retinas, and the thunderclap felt like a punch in the chest. The strike bored a shallow crater in the ice, and steam exploded upward from a disk around the impact where radiating current had vaporized the standing water. As the Snocat sped on, she saw that the crater was actually a long trench. The wind must have moved the lightning bolt that far while it was cutting into the ice, she thought.

Lightning struck the ice again, and this time Angie felt a mild shock course through her wet body. The jolt reminded her that the metal-tracked Snocat was the only object protruding above the perfectly flat plain. Angie was not accustomed to worrying about being struck when she was on the open ice sheet, because lightning was so rare in the usually arid atmosphere over Antarctica. Nevertheless, she knew she was now in immediate peril from the lethal force of electricity.

While wondering if she would feel the electrocution or never know what hit her, she became aware of a dim glowing band stretching across the darkness ahead. Soon the diffuse low light was all around her. The rain and lightning stopped. The light was coming from ahead, not through the clouds, but the opaque cloud ceiling began to climb, giving her the ironic feeling that she was emerging from the storm.

Angie heard a hissing, sizzling sound over the wind. Then she saw a curtain of spray and steam shooting up from a crack in the ice ahead. She ducked just in time as the Snocat rolled across the crack and hot spray sprinkled the back of her neck through the open windshield frame. Peeking out again, she saw that the ice was crisscrossed by a random web of steaming cracks.

The pink and gray surface of the clouds curved upward at an ever-steeper angle until it formed a vertical wall. Angie gazed up in wonder, supporting the back of her head with a hand. She gasped for breath in the rarified air, noticing that it smelled of sulfur.

The Snocat was now in the open beneath a vertical cylinder of cloud that was many miles wide and so tall that it appeared to taper to a point at the zenith. Pale moonlight was diffusing into the cylinder through what seemed to be roughly its upper half. Its rotation was visi-

bly faster at higher altitudes, stretching streaks of alternating pink, brown, and gray into long climbing spirals.

It's like the inside of a cosmic candy cane, Angie
thought. This must be the hypercane's eye.

A flood of steaming water surged against the right
track of the Snocat, flowing around the machine and
away on the left. Angie looked to see where the flood
had come from. The jagged edge of the floating ice sheet
was about a quarter mile to the right, running nearly parallel to the Snocat's bearing, curving away fore and aft.
Beyond the edge was dark open water, mostly hidden by
swirling mist. A high wave rose up out of the mist and
broke onto the ice sheet, surging toward the Snocat like
a tidal bore, steaming and crackling with boiling bubbles. This time the flood was even deeper than before.

The Snocat gradually angled closer to the open water.
Each wave breaking onto the ice hit the vehicle harder
than the previous one, until the surges of boiling water
were violently shoving it to the left and threatening to
pour in through the windshield frame. Angie gripped the
dashboard and stared toward the lake in terror, squatting
on her seat in case a boiling torrent spilled in and pooled
on the floor. She saw a flickering orange light through
the mist over the water, and a cone-shaped shadow beneath it. As the Snocat blew even closer to the shore, the
shadow resolved into a steep mound of black basalt protruding from the center of the lake. A fountain of bright
orange lava was spurting from its peak, raining back
down on the cone and the nearby water.

The Snocat slammed to the right, toward the lake,
throwing Angie onto the floor.

More rocks?

The impact had been too solid for a wave, and it had
come from the side opposite the lake. Looking back, she
saw a flat slab of ice at least ten feet thick and thirty feet

wide sitting on the ice sheet. The Snocat's left fender was mangled. It had obviously collided with the slab and glanced off.

Angie knew for sure that the wind could not lift a slab of ice the size of a house, especially here in the eye where the wind was milder. So how had a broken chunk of the ice sheet that must have weighed a hundred tons gotten up here onto the intact part?

She looked ahead, bracing for another collision. As she had feared, the ice in front of the Snocat was strewn with more flat-topped, vertical-sided slabs. Several were directly in her path. I'm about to be shot into a gigantic pinball machine, she thought, trying to guess which slab the Snocat would crash into first.

A monster wave hit from the right, scooting the Snocat to the left. Angie looked out through the left windows. Beyond the onslaught of water swirling around her vehicle, she saw a vertical fault scarp at least two feet high where the thinner ice close to the volcano had dropped down relative to the surrounding sheet.

"Oh crap!"

She hugged her seat back and closed her eyes, knowing what was going to happen when the swiftly skidding Snocat slammed into the scarp broadside. Sure enough, when the left track caught on the scarp, the Snocat flipped over onto its left side and kept skidding on the far side of the fault. Boiling water swirled in through the windshield, filling the left half of the cabin. Angie felt hot steam on the small of her back where her shirt had ridden up. Looking down, she saw the water subside, carrying Jerry's body out through the windshield. The huge rock that had been on his lap was lying on the left wall.

The Snocat's roof slammed into one of the stationary

ice slabs. The impact tore loose Angie's grip, and she fell into a foot of scalding water.

"*Eeeyow!*" She lunged upward and grabbed her seat again. Dangling from her arms, she got her feet out of the hot water by bracing her crampons on the now-vertical dashboard.

The Snocat creaked and gurgled. It also wobbled back and forth in the howling wind, but it no longer seemed to be skidding across the ice. Angie clung beneath the horizontal seat back. "Ow, ow, ow," she whimpered, trembling from the scalding pain. The wave had cooled enough by the time it reached the Snocat to not give her any serious burns, but the scalding still stung like acid on the frostbite blisters and her raw wrist where the cold steel door handle of Lois's shelter had claimed a patch of skin.

The pain finally subsided and she got enough breath back to move again. She swung one leg up, kicked open the heavy passenger door above her head, and climbed up to look out.

The Snocat's roof was precariously pinned by the wind against the side of a rounded ice slab about fifteen feet thick and sixty feet across. If the rocking vehicle slipped an inch in either direction, the wind would shove it on around the slab and across the wet ice to the next one.

Angie felt a growing vibration and turned to look at the lake. The hot wet wind blew her drenched hair back. Another wave was just breaking on the shore. It was twice the size of the one that had overturned the heavy Snocat, and its frothy crest bore several floating ice slabs. So *that's* how they got up here, she thought. In the distance, the pieces broken off from the edge of the ice sheet looked tiny, but she knew they weren't.

And she knew the wave would hit the Snocat in a few seconds, dislodging it.

The wave bore down on her, leaving behind a planar contrail of steam in the dim moonlight. She looked down into the dark cabin to make sure the flood from the last wave had completely drained, then dropped onto the broken left windows. Where was her bag of climbing gear and outerwear? She frantically looked around. When she finally found the waterproof sack beneath the driver's chair, she grabbed it and clambered back up to the open passenger door.

The wave hit the front of the Snocat just as she stuck her head out. It shoved the vehicle backward along the convex wall of ice, perpendicular to the wind. Angie pulled her legs up through the door and squatted on the vehicle's slippery side. She could feel hot steam as the flood rose, eventually submerging all of the Snocat but the side panel she was clinging to. Hanging on to the open passenger door, swaying for balance, she rode the capsized tractor as it twisted around the ice slab and accelerated downwind.

On the lee side of the huge stationary slab, she saw another slab that was much smaller, only about as high as the overturned Snocat. Its flat surface was just above the steaming water. She also saw that the Snocat was skidding toward a steam-belching fissure in the ice sheet that was at least twenty feet wide.

Gripping her bag of gear and clothing, she let go of the door and leaped.

CHAPTER 35

Warthog

Sunday, 12:49 A.M.

Reed glanced at the location coordinates in his Head Up
Display, a transparent computer screen in front of the
cockpit's windshield that superimposed targeting and
systems status information on his external field of view.
"I'm in position to begin the sortie," he said into his helmet microphone. He was banking the Warthog in a steep
turn over the crashing moonlit waves of the Ross Sea.
The hypercane had completely disintegrated the thin
winter ice that had cloaked the ocean just a day before.

"Good luck, Tom," said Marshall Dunn from the
drilling pit.

"We're with you, Colonel," Professor Ferrand added
from the airstrip on the Ross Ice Shelf.

Reed had decided to report his progress to them during his bombing mission so they would know if and
where he went down.

He pushed up on the throttle as he leveled his camouflage flying battle tank, aiming straight into the gloomy
horizontal slit between the reaching waves and the disk

of dark, rolling, lightning-streaked clouds. He had worried all through the harrowing drive from the drilling pit to the airstrip that he would not remember how to get the Warthog off the ground. But even after all these years, the plane felt as natural as his old Chrysler. The familiarity of the tight cockpit comforted him as he nodded with exhaustion and clinched his aching fists with the certainty that his probability of success—and survival—was less than fifty percent.

Regardless of the likely outcome—of its price to him and his loved ones—he had to try. If this sortie failed, the hypercane would become unstoppable.

He hailed Marshall again while accelerating in a straight trajectory toward land. "Once I get under those clouds, I'll be flying mostly blind. This jet has no visual aids except a crude radar. Are you sure all the men on the ground have pulled back?"

"Yes," Marshall said. "They're all in the drilling pit. Try not to hit the pipeline or the tractors, but there are no personnel on the ice."

"And there's nothing else out there that might resemble my target?"

"I hope not, Tom. If there is, it's history, right?"

Reed planned to hit the ice with everything he had, and the Warthog was armed to the teeth. The eleven pylons beneath the fuselage and wings held six unguided Mark 82 general-purpose bombs and six AGM-65G missiles with IIR seeker heads. The thirty-millimeter GAU-8 rotary cannon was also fully loaded.

The 565-pound Mark 82 general-purpose/low-drag bombs allowed a Warthog to function as an old-fashioned dive bomber, plummeting from the sky to deliver a heavy dose of explosives directly onto a stationary target from just a few hundred feet above the ground. Each bomb contained Tritonal 80/20 explosive inside an inch-thick cast-steel shell that accounted for about half the bomb's weight and would provide a source of shrapnel when it fragmented upon detonation.

The A-10 also carried Mavericks, deadly-accurate air-to-ground missiles that could punch through any tank or naval vessel and most underground bunkers. Reed recalled that he and the other Warthog drivers had expended Mavericks like bullets in the Gulf War, and that eighty-five percent of the missiles had supposedly detonated on target. He was also more optimistic because the Mavericks aboard the Warthog were the G version, which carried a large three-hundred-pound blast fragmentation/penetrator warhead and could transmit video back to the cockpit from their IIR seeker heads.

IIR stood for Imaging Infrared, which meant the missiles could track a target based on the shape it presented to a crude infrared videocamera. The older guidance systems based on black-and-white television probably couldn't have seen a target through a dark and debris-laden hypercane, Reed thought. And the new MMW seeker head—a millimeter-wavelength active radar scanner that identified a target by its three-dimensional shape—would not be able to distinguish one patch of the flat ice sheet from another. Marshall had assured Reed that he could make the target literally red-hot, so Reed was confident that infrared video was the ideal seeking technology for the task at hand.

Unfortunately, the oblique firing angle between his fuselage and the horizontal ice sheet meant he probably would not get much benefit out of the Warthog's distinguishing weapon, the General Electric GAU-8 Avenger rotary cannon. The Warthog's fuselage had been designed around this most devastating of all rapid-fire guns, which stretched twenty-one feet up and down inside the plane. The Avenger cannon was a space-age weapon based on the Gatling gun design dating from the American Civil War. Fully loaded with 1,350 rounds, it had the size and weight of a small car. Redundant seventy-seven-horsepower hydraulic motors drove its linkless ammunition feed and rotated its seven two-meter barrels around a single firing mechanism, delivering up to seventy rounds per second. Combined with a Mach-3 muzzle velocity and projectiles with the mass of a hammer head, this rapid rate of fire made the Avenger the most potent gun ever carried by an aircraft.

The cannon's magazine was loaded with ammunition made of depleted uranium, the low-radioactivity metal left over after most of the fissionable U-235 had been removed from natural uranium to make nuclear weapons or reactor fuel. It was the densest metal known, with a specific gravity 1.7 times that of ordinary bullet lead. When one of the cigar-sized 4,650-grain slugs hit an enemy main battle tank at Mach 3, the impact instantly deposited enough energy onto an area the size of a penny to lift thirty tons by one foot, penetrating up to four inches of the world's toughest armor. In addition to being the densest metal and highly toxic when inhaled, depleted uranium was also extremely reactive with oxygen at high temperatures. A slug would disintegrate after penetrating a tank's armor, and the impact energy would ignite the resulting dust, causing it to burn hotter than a blast furnace inside the tank.

If a hole could be punched in armor—or in an ice sheet—Reed knew he was in the right machine for the job.

But he was taking a beating. His ACES II ejection seat shook and vibrated as if he were riding a motorcycle up a flight of stairs. He wondered if Marshall could understand his transmissions with his helmet microphone bouncing back and forth so frantically.

"I just penetrated the clouds. Turbulence is raunchy. Heavy snow is bombarding my canopy. Estimated time to target is two minutes."

As long as he didn't encounter large hail, Reed had no fear of the snow cracking the narrow, bullet-resistant front panel of the Warthog's windscreen, but he was afraid it might choke his engines and cause them to stall. He had come up with his plan to bomb the ice sheet after remembering that the Fifty-third Weather Reconnaissance Squadron, better known as the Hurricane Hunters, flew directly into fully mature hurricanes. But the Lockheed WC-130s flown by the Hurricane Hunters had turboprop engines, which were safe to fly through a heavy downpour because the external propellers deflected rain from the turbines. The large volume of air sucked in by the huge General Electric TF34 high-pass turbofans on the Warthog made them more efficient than pure jet engines at the Hog's low operational speeds, but they were exactly the wrong kind of engines to fly through dense precipitation. He knew that the titanium compressor blades had held up well against sandstorms and bird strikes, but he wasn't sure what heavy snow and pouring rain would do to them.

At least he would have a chance to put her down with the remaining engine if one of them choked, since the Warthog was designed to keep flying with either engine shot off.

At first he flew within the opaque clouds to maintain a safe altitude against possible downbursts, fighting the hypercane by flying at an upwind angle to his intended course. As he got closer, he descended until the ice sheet came into view and the Warthog skimmed along the undulating base of the clouds.

"I see the pipeline!"

This close to the seaward edge of the cloud cover, he

had just enough moonlight to make out the colorless shapes of objects on the ice as the boxy Warthog swooped down to a low altitude of eighty meters. To the right, he could see the thin dark line of the water pipe stretching in front of him until it disappeared in the blizzard. It was marked at regular intervals with the brilliant white point and pink halo of a ground flare.

"Slowing to minimum loiter speed."

Reed edged to the right until his bearing was parallel to the pipeline but still a hundred yards left of it. He could see eight or nine flares ahead of him at a time. Twice per second a new flare emerged from the blue-gray gloom at the end of the pipe, and the flare that was closest shot back beneath his bomb-laden right wing, blurring into a streak like a highway reflector.

He saw a snow tractor loom out of the blizzard. It was parked on the left of the pipeline, facing away from it, attached to the pipe by a thick coiled chain. Reed knew that if he succeeded in penetrating the ice sheet, this tractor and three others already in position would be used to drag the end of the pipeline sideways until it dipped into the water.

The second tractor came into view as the first one flashed backward beneath the Warthog's right wing.

"I just passed the first vehicle," Reed reported. "Twenty seconds to target. I'm powering up the AGMs."

He reached above his head and flipped a bank of six switches, then activated a small square monitor in the upper right corner of the black, gauge-packed instrument panel in front of him. The monitor showed the crude infrared image picked up by the head of one of the AGM-65G missiles. The picture was a seemingly random patchwork of smudges in various shades of dark green against a black background. The smudges were spreading outward, moving slowly at the center of the screen but zooming into blurred streaks as they passed beyond the field of view on all sides.

Reed counted the tractors as the Warthog zoomed over them. As the fourth and last tractor came into view, he made out three distant points of brilliant light in the darkness—the red-hot targets Marshall had promised him. They were huge piles of flares, all burning together, arranged in an equilateral triangle with one point aimed toward the approaching Warthog. A perfect target designation, Reed thought, even better than a simulator. All he had to do was drop his ordnance in the center of the triangle, which was rapidly becoming brighter and less foreshortened as he passed over the last tractor.

"Target is acquired."

He glanced rapidly back and forth between his windscreen and the seeker head display, which had recalibrated itself to the high infrared intensity of the flare piles. The three points of light on the display stood out like white suns with green coronas against the black background. A faint green streak extended from each sun to the left edge of the monitor. Reed wondered for a moment if the streaks were some artifact of the imaging software, then realized they were thermal plumes from the burning flares blown horizontally by the wind.

He pressed a yellow button beside the screen, and a set of flashing red crosshairs appeared in the center of the growing triangle of lights. "Infrared image is locked on."

Reed flipped the red plastic covers up from two toggle switches above the monitor screen, glancing above them to verify that he had already set the two other missile fire control switches to the position marked with a big three. These upper switches controlled the number of missiles simultaneously launched at his fire command from the three-rail mounts under each wing.

"Five, four, three, two, one. Missiles away!"

He flipped both of the fire switches up and pulled back on the stick. White exhaust plumes from the Mavericks briefly extended in front of him as the Warthog leaped upward, relieved of six missiles that each weighed 670 pounds.

Although climbing at a steeper angle, the plane continued approaching closer to its target as the missiles curved downward in front of it. Reed ignored the cloud layers streaking by his cockpit and watched the Constantly Computed Impact Point of his unguided bombs on the Head Up Display. When it reached the center of the target triangle where the missiles would strike, he pressed the pickle button with his thumb so all his ordnance would land on the same spot. The Warthog's climb steepened even more when 3,390 pounds of unguided low-drag bombs dropped away from its pylons.

Reed directed all of his attention to the infrared seeker head monitor to make sure the six AGMs stayed locked on to their clearly designated target. At more than fifty thousand dollars apiece, they'd better be smart enough not to get blown off target by the wind, he thought.

The triangle of green suns expanded faster on the monitor as the missiles accelerated and their trajectory curved in a downward arc. All three hot spots simultaneously zoomed off the screen, and the display went blank for a second. Then flashing red letters appeared across the screen: DETONATION ON TARGET.

An instant later he felt and heard the concussion from the missiles. It was followed by a rapid sequence of even louder booms as the unpropelled bombs exploded.

Reed exhaled and returned his attention to flying the plane. "I scored a direct hit!"

He paused while the cheers in the drilling pit died down.

"I still have to circle back and verify that I punched through the ice."

The Warthog was angled upward at its maximum climb rate. The orange fireball reflecting on his canopy quickly faded. Turbulence got worse with increasing altitude. Before Reed could bank the plane and begin his descent, he felt a series of sharp knocks accompanied by loud clangs that could not have been caused by mere turbulence.

"I'm catching flak up here!"

Better dive fast to get out of the line of fire. He twisted the highly maneuverable Warthog to the left until it was flying with the wind behind it and its left wingtip pointed straight downward.

"How big is the debris?" Marshall asked.

"No spinning farmhouses . . . so far."

If there was a response, Reed did not hear it. In fact, all he could hear for the next several seconds was ringing in his ears from the sharp *gong* of some invisible but very tangible projectile striking the tail section. He jerked his head back and watched over his shoulder as half of the Warthog's symmetric double rudder flapped away in the wind like an epileptic bat. The steady whine of the two fuselage-mounted engines disappeared beneath a warbling whistle from the mutilated tail.

Marshall yelled, "What happened, Tom? What's that noise?"

"I just lost a tail fin!"

After a pause, Marshall said, "Start calling out your coordinates so we'll know where you go down."

Even with his tight insulated helmet, Reed was having trouble hearing the radio over the noise from the Warthog's asymmetric slipstream. When he finally figured out what Marshall had said, he replied, "I'm not going down, unless I lose the other tail fin. Hogs are designed to fly back to base with half the tail, one engine, and up to sixteen feet of a wing shot off. I'll be back to the kill zone in a few minutes."

Assuming my fuel lasts that long.

The second time he glanced back to see how much of his tail was gone, he saw liquid dribbling away from a cat-sized hole in one of the Warthog's integral fuselage fuel tanks. This didn't really worry him—he knew that the honeycomb-like reticulated foam inside the tank would retain most of the fuel even with such a huge puncture.

The suspense made Reed nauseous as the Warthog crept up on the broad crater its ordnance had left, skimming just above the ice. Because he was now flying into a wind that was much faster than his stall speed, he was able to slow to a few miles per hour relative to the ground. As he crawled over the crater he got a clear view of its bottom, and his queasiness turned into a pounding headache.

"The bombs didn't go through," he said, aghast. "There's a crater the size of the Great Pyramid, but it's as dry as a bone."

In spite of his headache and fatigue and the wrenching vibrations from the mutilated rudder, Reed could think clearly enough to realize that he had only one option left.

CHAPTER 36

Kamikaze

Angie lunged across the steaming, swirling flood, one leg outstretched and the other behind her. When her forward crampons crunched into the small ice slab, she windmilled her arms, trying not to fall backward.

She spread-eagled forward onto the slab and lay there for a moment in the spectral moonlight, like a sacrifice staked out on an altar, trying to catch her breath despite the painfully low air pressure. The huge slab adjacent to the small one she'd jumped onto sheltered her from the wind. The flood from the wave subsided. The toppled Snocat caromed off two more of the stationary ice slabs before disappearing into the steam-belching fissure that cut across the ice sheet a few hundred yards downwind.

The air in the hypercane's eye was balmy, hot in fact, but lying on the ice in her soaked thermal underwear quickly made her shiver. She crawled to the juncture of the two slabs and squatted on her crampons at the base of the cliff formed by the larger one. There was nearly no wind so close to the wall. She pulled the compact field radio from her gear bag, donned the headset, and tried to call for help. "Dad? Marshall? ICARE? Anybody?" She had to stop, heaving for breath, feeling her lips tingle with hypoxia.

There was no response.

After all she had been through in the last three days, Angie wondered if her fate was to die of simple asphyxiation in the choking half vacuum of the cyclone's core.

Movement caught her eye, and she looked up to see an ice block smoothly skidding across the wet ice sheet, spinning as it went, driven by the wind. Only then did it occur to her to wonder why the slabs she was using for shelter, and the others around them, were immobile. Thinking about it, she realized that they must have frozen into place at a time when the wind was slower. It would not have taken long for the ninety-below-zero interiors of the slabs and the ice sheet to refreeze a thin film of water between them.

She wondered what would happen if a sliding mass of ice crashed into the one she was cringing against.

No sooner had that thought struck her than the block she was watching impacted a stationary slab a hundred yards away. With an audible pop, the stationary slab detached from the ice sheet and slowly began to slide downwind. The steaming fissure devoured both of the free slabs, which were slightly larger than the one she was perched on.

She saw another slab whiz past on the other side of her sanctuary, then another, and another. A second later, dozens of slabs were zooming across the ice on both sides of her, all on parallel downwind trajectories. She tensely watched the moonlit stampede, realizing that one of them was bound to knock hers loose sooner or—

Thud!

The huge formation behind her thumped against her back, throwing her down on her knees. Holding her breath, she waited for her small slab to start sliding toward the fissure.

It remained in place.

The thump had just been the shock wave from an impact. The fifteen-foot-by-sixty-foot slab behind her was still holding fast to the ice sheet. She saw the smaller piece that had hit it roll around its side, gradually accelerating again.

Next time I won't be so lucky, she thought.

She frantically dug into the bag of climbing gear, glad she had salvaged it from the Snocat in case it might help her hang on against the wind. After stepping into a body harness, she began twisting an ice screw into the wall of the large slab. If an impact from upwind knocked the large formation loose, the dinky slab she was standing on would certainly break free as well, and then plunge her to a scalding death in the downwind fissure. But the large slab was broad enough to glide across the fissure and keep going.

As Angie reached to attach her harness to the inserted ice screw, a terrific jolt threw her against the wall. She bounced off and fell, her legs swinging off the side of the small slab. She clawed at the ice and managed to grab the gear bag, but then she slipped backward and fell down to the wet ice sheet six feet below.

She tried to sit up, dazed and dizzy, groaning from pain in her back.

Something cold nudged her left shoulder, shoving her back down. Then it pressed against her hip, pushing her across the ice. She looked up and saw a fifteen-foot wall of ice towering over her. The last impact had obviously dislodged the larger slab, and now it was accelerating ever so slowly as the wind surged around it from the opposite side.

Angie tried to get up again, but the thousand-ton formation was pushing her faster now. Looking downwind, she wondered whether the slab would collide with another one, smashing her between them, or glide across the steam-belching fissure and shove her into it.

Even through the bottomless thunder of the hypercane, Marshall could hear the damaged Warthog returning along the pipeline. In addition to the distinctive whine of its engines—more like a power saw cutting paneling than a jet—the half-amputated rudder made a warbling whistle.

Along with Silong Lim and hundreds of idle workers, Marshall gazed up at their round window of sky. Above the flickering orange fire moat and the glistening wet walls of the pit, he could see nothing but parallel gray and white streaks of snow and debris zooming across the ice sheet. Even the low clouds were now obscured behind the blurred maelstrom of wind-driven detritus, which was illuminated from below by the pit's flames and floodlights.

Marshall looked around at his men. They had all heard and felt the rapid sequence of concussions when the Warthog had dropped its ordnance at the end of the pipeline. Now they stood around barrels of burning oil, awaiting orders.

The Warthog's pale gray underside finally zoomed across the pit, glowing in the reflected white radiance from the drilling derrick's floodlights. The airframe cast a sharp shadow on the maelstrom above it. The shadow blinked on and off as the anticollision beacon atop the fuselage rotated and flashed. Horizontal vortices swirled into the pit from the downward-cambered Hoerner wingtips, disrupting the black smoke rolling up the walls from the fire moat.

As the noise of the low-flying jet receded back into

the continuous thunder of the hypercane, Marshall removed his radio headset and stared glumly at the idle
drill.

The Warthog sped out from under the rotating clouds,
cruising a hundred yards above the raging sea. Reed
banked the plane into a sharp turn, swooping sideways
with his right wingtip pointing straight up. Since it had
seemed to bring him good luck in the Gulf War, he pre-
ferred banking left to execute an about-face. After the
abrupt turn, the Warthog swooped down lower over the
water and accelerated again. He had returned to the precise start point of his initial run-in to optimize the align-
ment of his final approach.

The men in the drilling pit listened as the Warthog returned, heading into the hypercane again. This time the
plane zoomed over the pit much faster than before.

"What's he doing now?" Lim asked.

Marshall shrugged. "The last time we talked, all he
said was that it was probably his last transmission."

Reed followed the precise trajectory of his first run-in,
but this time he took it at the highest speed he could control with the damaged tail, close to the jet's theoretical
maximum of 420 miles per hour. The flares along the
pipeline zoomed by so swiftly that they blended into a
streak across the right corner of his view.

The piles of flares designating his target had been
blown away by his first attack, so he kept a close watch
on the pipeline and tractors until the dark shadow of the
crater loomed from the blizzard. Then he pulled the stick
back all the way, and the Warthog shot upward. The sudden centrifugal force ground him into his seat.

He had to gain altitude to maximize the length of the

nosedive that would be his final desperate maneuver. He knew that more large debris like the rock that had mutilated his tail section might be waiting to rip off a wing or smash his canopy once he ascended into the hypercane's upper layers again. Nevertheless, he hung on to the stick and ignored the vibrations trying to rip him apart as the Warthog climbed through the low disk of clouds.

Visibility inside the clouds was zero. He might as well have been in a cave, or submerged in murky water. Lightning strobed all around him, but all he could see was white flashes in the milky media outside his unnervingly small canopy. Vibrations from turbulence rattled his teeth, juggled his internal organs, and made his skin itch.

Stark white moonlight flooded the canopy when the jet shot upward out of the clouds at forty thousand feet, near the Warthog's operational ceiling. Reed squinted and blinked. The roar and beating from turbulence also ceased, leaving him with a sensory afterimage of eerie stillness and silence, like floating in space. He could even hear his own rapid breathing, and his skin tingled all over.

The thin atmosphere outside the Warthog's fragile canopy was utterly tranquil and transparent. The high moon was sharper than he had ever seen it. The largest craters and maria were precisely defined.

Once his eyes adjusted from the darkness inside the storm, he looked to the south and saw the colossal tower of cloud rising from the core of the hypercane. The pillar was twisted like a rope, its random bumps and wrinkles stretched into spirals of pale pink, gray, and brown. The rotating cylinder also appeared as solid as a rope, stretched taut all the way into space like a tether between the Earth and the Moon.

He wondered where Angie was, and if she was still

alive. He had no way of knowing that she was directly beneath the central stalk of the hypercane, that the twisted cylinder of cloud and dust was hollow and translucent, bathing her nightmare world of ice, wind, and steam in wan moonlight. He tried yet again to raise her on the radio, thinking his altitude might help, but the only voice on the air was the hypercane's crackling and whistling static.

The quickest way to turn around for his nosedive was to execute a tight vertical loop. Unlike some fighter jets built for speed, the heavy Warthog's engines were not capable of thrusting it straight upward. Nevertheless, the highly maneuverable subsonic aircraft could do a vertical loop by simply trading its forward momentum for lift during the climb.

As the cockpit tilted back so that he was facing straight upward, he could see the top of the cloud pillar flaring out like the mouth of a horn, spreading across the sky to form a thin elliptical pinwheel of dust and cloud that stretched nearly from horizon to horizon. At the ends of the ellipse, the wisps of cloud dissipated and the spirals of dust coalesced into dark curving tails that arched out over the ocean as far as he could see, which was hundreds of miles at his altitude.

Reed surmised that the tails were the stratospheric jet streams that would eventually spread the dust into a cloak over the entire Earth if he failed. He was acutely aware that the cloak would eventually become either invisibly thin or as black as tar, and that the difference would depend entirely on his skill and determination over the next sixty seconds.

And on the Warthog's construction.

And on luck.

As the Warthog's stubby snaggletoothed nose leaned back over its damaged tail, Reed listened to the maneuvering tone in his headset, keeping the jet on a controllable course by avoiding the sound that meant his attitude was unstable.

When the fuselage was upside down at the apex of the loop, he looked "up" at the rotating cyclone beneath him. In the cool moonlight, the solid disk of clouds looked deceptively tranquil and firm, like a soft place to land. Their spiraling puffy surface was tinted a light blue like cotton candy. What a beautiful panorama, Reed thought. After all those years of crowded airports and choking neckties, at least he had been granted one last glimpse of stunning scenery.

Yelling a defiant war cry, he accelerated straight downward at full throttle toward the undulating opalescent surface. The Stability Augmentation System began shaking the stick to warn him of an excessive attack angle. When the Warthog punched down into the hypercane, darkness returned and the strobing lightning resumed. So did the quaking turbulence, even worse than before because of his unprecedented speed.

Since he could not see the ice sheet through the clouds, he was fortunate that this Warthog was one of those that had finally been retrofitted for N/AW (Night/Adverse Weather) attack capability a few years after NATO forces had been grounded by foul weather in the war over Serbia. He activated the pod beneath his left wing that contained a Westinghouse Terrain Avoidance and Attack Radar. As he had hoped, the bomb crater appeared as a round shadow on the radar's monitor. The crater was not directly below him, but his efforts to compensate for the hypercane wind had prevented him from being blown too far to the side.

The Warthog's asymmetrical tail began wobbling like an unbalanced centrifuge, revolving in a circle, causing the fuselage to precess around a point between the

wings. The wobble also caused the double cockpit to re-
volve counterclockwise, swinging Reed to the right, then
upward, then to the left, then down. The stomach-
wrenching cycle repeated again and again, faster and
faster.

He hung on to the cable-and-hydraulic controls with
all his might, determined to maintain control to the end.
The APN-194 radar altimeter indicated that the ground
was coming up fast. After setting a new A-10 speed
record somewhere in the clouds, he continued to hold
the throttle at full thrust and his bearing locked on the
center of the Earth, wondering if the damaged subsonic
airframe would remain intact for the few seconds necessary to complete his mission.

The opaque clouds abruptly disappeared as the diving
jet sped into the blizzard below them. At first Reed could
distinguish nothing but the snow blobs racing up at him.
Then the deep bomb crater he had blasted in the ice
sheet materialized out of the gloom directly below.

The Warthog's position and bearing were perfect.

CHAPTER 37

Riding the Wind

The thousand-ton ice slab behind Angie continued to accelerate in the wind, shoving her across the wet ice sheet toward the steaming twenty-foot fissure that had devoured the Snocat. She instinctively tried to resist the implacable force by digging her crampons into the ice and shoving against the cold wet wall with her back, to no avail. She also looked around for a way to escape. The smaller slab she had been perched on before her fall had already slid beyond her reach.

I could just get up and run, she thought. But where could she go? Maybe she could make it out of the huge slab's path before it pushed her into the fissure, but then what? She would probably lose her balance in the wind, then slide into the fissure anyway. Or another wind-driven slab would zoom across the ice like the devil's own hockey puck, clobbering her before she could dodge. And if that didn't happen, another boiling wave from the lake would cook and drown her before washing her into the fissure. Come to think of it, the next wave was already overdue.

She glanced up at the ice screw she had lodged securely in the great slab's vertical side. It was too high to reach, but there were more screws in the bag of climbing gear she was clutching. If she could just climb on top of the slab and anchor herself down, all of her problems would be solved for the moment. She would be well above the scalding wave floods. Collisions might give her whiplash, but they wouldn't squash her like a bug. And the big slab was broad enough to slide over the downwind fissure without even getting stuck against its far wall.

She lunged ahead of the wall and struggled to her feet before it could catch up with her, slipping on the wet ice until she managed to balance on her crampons. Then she frantically rummaged in the bag, found an ice screw, and began inserting it in the wall. The slab had begun to rotate counterclockwise as it slid toward the fissure, so she had to jog backward and sideways to keep up with the screw. The wind began to tug at her wet hair, although she had fallen in the middle of the slab's lee side. She looked up and saw that she was nearing the frenetic spray and ripples where the wet ice sheet was exposed to the full force of the wind.

Angie frantically fumbled to attach her body harness to the screw before the slab could rotate it into the wind. Just in time, she latched a carabiner between her chest strap and the hole in the screw's head flange. The wind hit her right side and slammed her left side against the wall as the slab's rotation dragged her windward.

She looked back just as the steaming fissure disappeared behind her around the slab's rotating wall. Now she would not be able to tell how close the fissure was until she rotated around to the opposite side. And she knew that whatever side she was on, the steam belching from the fissure would cook her like a lobster unless she was on the slab's top by the time it got there.

She reached as high as she could and screwed in another anchor, then grabbed hold of it and stepped up onto the first one. Now clinging to the side, she no longer had to run to keep up with it—a good thing, since the slab's glide and rotation were both accelerating.

The broad fissure came into view again when she was about halfway up the fifteen-foot wall. It was still getting closer, but Angie realized that she was sliding on a trajectory almost parallel to the fissure. That was both good and bad. It meant she would have more time before the slab's walls were bathed in steam, but it also meant the steam bath would last longer.

Centrifugal force began pulling her away from the wall as the slab's rotation accelerated. As she fought the force to insert another screw, the thousand-ton natural merry-go-round swung her around to where she could not see the fissure again. "Aaaaa!" Angie yelled as the toe points of her crampons slipped out of the ice and her legs swung out behind her, away from the wall, painfully arching the small of her back.

Reed watched the altitude tape on his Head Up Display as he fought the cockpit's revolving wobble. At sixteen thousand feet, he rotated the function knob on the Head Up Display control panel to Weapons Delivery Mode 1, put the master switch on ARM, and set the gun rate to high.

The Warthog had no more bombs or missiles attached to its external pylons, but within the narrow fuselage was the GAU-8 Avenger rotary cannon, by far the most powerful rapid-fire weapon ever installed in an aircraft.

Reed realized he was going too fast to fire all of the rounds in the Avenger cannon's magazine before he reached the ice. The gun's thirty-millimeter cartridges were each the size of a hammer handle, so the full magazine carried only 1,350 rounds, enough to last for twenty seconds of continuous fire. The cannon was designed to shoot in bursts of at most two seconds, so Reed had to just hope that the frigid air would prevent the barrels from melting down.

He would have started shooting sooner, but the plane's unexpected wobble would have wildly dispersed his shots—the two-meter gun barrels could only fire in the direction the fuselage was pointing. The Avenger's high muzzle velocity made it a deadly accurate weapon under ideal conditions. It was designed to shoot tanks anywhere within four thousand feet because eighty percent of its shots would strike within a forty-foot circle at that distance. Reed was still higher than four thousand feet, but the bomb crater he was targeting with his N/AW radar was also larger than a tank.

Squeezing the cannon trigger in both hands, he simultaneously opened the Warthog's decelerons, ailerons that split above and below the wing to slow the aircraft and stabilize it during a dive attack. The sudden drag mashed him painfully forward against his seat harness. A cloud of sparks and chips boiled up from the ice as the depleted-uranium slugs drilled in at seventy rounds per second. The rotary cannon's continuous fire slowed the diving plane with even more deceleration than the open speedbrakes on its wings, recoiling with a force of nine thousand pounds, as much thrust as one of the jet's engines.

Even after the armor-piercing momentum of Reed's shots had been absorbed deep inside the ice sheet, the depleted-uranium slugs became dense blobs of molten metal that burned at more than two thousand degrees Fahrenheit, vaporizing the ice around them so fast that they continued to descend as if falling through a vacuum. A tiny fireball erupted from each bullet hole, winking out in the wind when the burning slug was quenched by the water below.

Reed watched for liquid water in the crater as the ice closed in and the area he was strafing shrank. After firing for a few seconds, he saw that the wobble-induced revolutions of the gun pipper in the center of his target reticle were confined to an area inside the crater. That meant the rest of his shots would trace out a neat inward spiral, perforating a broad disk of ice that was already thinned by his bombs. If the disk did not disintegrate under the fusillade, at least it would be weakened before the Warthog's thirteen-ton airframe crashed into it, which was exactly what he planned if he did not see water in time to pull up.

If it came to that, he wondered if the 1,365-pound titanium-beryllium "bathtub" surrounding the cockpit to protect the pilot from direct antiaircraft hits would pass through the ice sheet intact, and whether it would release his body into the dark water below in one piece.

A voice blared from the LASTE Ground Collision Avoidance System, warning him of the imminent crash.

Reed estimated that he was two seconds from impact when he saw the shredded disk of ice dissolve into a splashing fountain of water. He leaned back on the stick with all his strength and waited for the crash, certain that he was too late.

The Warthog's blunt nose finally began to tilt upward.

At the bottom of the turn, he could see the debris-scoured ice whizzing by beneath his cockpit, so close that he could have safely jumped from the plane if it had been stationary. Then he felt a jolt as the retracted main landing gear bumped the ice. The Warthog was designed so that its large wheels protruded halfway from their wing fairings even when fully retracted, making a belly landing possible with minimal damage to the aircraft once all ordnance had been dropped.

"Marshall, the hole is open!" he shouted into his headset mike. "Repeat, the ice sheet is open! Get your men to the tractors!"

Not a very poetic announcement, Reed thought, especially considering that he had just won the last near-impossible battle in his mission to stop the first ice age in over ten thousand years. Oh well, he was lucky for a chance to say anything—another projectile could rip the UHF blade antenna off his fuselage at any moment.

In the radio background, Reed heard whoops and cheers echoing in the drilling pit over the hypercane's roar. He had succeeded—the fate of the world was now in the hands of the drilling crew—but he did not share their feelings of triumph and celebration.

He had already climbed and banked toward the core of the hypercane, where he thought Angie's Snocat was most likely to be. He was not sure what he would do in the unlikely event that he found his daughter alive. The Warthog had a double cockpit, one seat in front of the other. It was one of several that had recently been retrofitted following a previously scrapped design so a copilot could help with the increasingly complex Night/Adverse Weather targeting systems. When Reed had seen the extra seat, he had immediately started planning how he might use the plane to rescue Angie after his mission was complete. But no matter how optimistic he wanted to be, he knew there was absolutely no chance that he could land inside the hypercane without spinning out and crashing.

That had zero impact on his determination to find her.

CHAPTER 38

Countdown

Angie could feel the centrifugal force of the spinning ice slab flinging back her hair, deforming her face, and straining the anchor her harness was attached to. It wasn't so bad when she was swinging around the windward side, because the wind against her back helped compensate for the force. But on the lee side it felt like either her harness or her back was bound to break.

As she screwed in the first anchor on the slab's top, she felt hot steam on her legs and looked down. The broad fissure was just disappearing behind her. She knew she would get a full blast of steam on the next revolution.

Now that the slab was rotating so fast, she couldn't just pile onto its top and rest. She would have to anchor in, even on the flat surface, to keep from being flung off. Grasping the head of the screw she had inserted on top, she dragged herself onto the slab and curled around the inside of the screw just as a fountain of steam surged up the wall.

There she remained until the spinning slab had left the fissure behind. A side stitch burned like a stab wound between her ribs, and her breath came in desperate gasps, as if she had just summited Mount Everest.

When the dizziness of hypoxia began to let up, she made her way to the center of the slab's rotation, tied herself to a fully inserted ice screw with a double figure-eight knot, and tried to radio her father as the slab sped increasingly faster across the melting ice sheet.

"Come on, Dad, answer!"

She gasped and panted, barely able to breathe now, much less shout into the radio.

As she had expected, the only response was static from the hypercane.

She rolled onto her back and watched the twisting cylinder of clouds and dust that climbed to infinity above her, glowing with diffused moonlight. She wondered whether the great ice slab she was riding across the Warner Basin would eventually crash through into the lake, or slide out of the eye and be struck by lightning, or simply collide with another object and shatter.

2:32 A.M.

Reed flew in a crude search spiral, starting in the area where he had last seen Angie's Snocat and expanding the search outward. In addition to squinting down through the snow and rain and airborne debris he encountered, he continuously attempted to hail his daughter on the radio. His voice grew hoarser each time he shouted into his headset mike, begging her to answer.

He watched in growing dismay as his fuel gauge declined. The Warthog was still losing a slow but steady dribble through the hole a wind-driven rock had punched in the tanks, making it impossible for him to judge exactly how much flight time he had left. When more than an hour had passed since his successful sortie, and he

guessed that about thirty minutes of fuel remained, he
got the call from Marshall that he had been dreading.

"We're ready, Tom."

"That fast?"

"It only took the siphon a minute to enlarge the ice
hole. Then the subglacial ridge turned out to be soft, so
the rock drilling was a breeze. Lim wired the warheads
for manual detonation using the hand-drawn diagram
you gave him. The zero hour is here, so let's pray it
works."

Reed paused as long as he thought was acceptable,
then said, "Okay. Set the timer and get out of there."

"Go!" he heard Marshall shout to his men.

The warheads could be detonated by an encrypted
radio signal, but Reed and the others had decided not to
trust the radio transmission over the distance of the minimum safe standoff for the drilling crew. Therefore, they
had planned to leave the transmitter behind in the
drilling pit with a timer that would activate it fifteen
minutes after they left.

"Tom, you'd better clear out too. The nukes are underground, but the hole is shallow and not filled in. There's
bound to be some kind of blast at the surface, maybe radioactive fallout."

"Negative," Reed said. "I'm going to keep looking for
Angie." He signed off so he could start trying to call her
again.

Angie woke on her back with warm rain hitting her
closed eyelids. She blinked and coughed, trying to sit up
against the wind. Lightning was strobing almost continuously, but between flashes the air was as dark as the inside of a closed coffin. She glanced at her luminous
wristwatch, which was somehow miraculously still
working, and saw that nearly an hour and a half had

passed since she'd crawled onto the skidding ice slab. She could feel the vibration and rotation that meant she was still moving. The vibration seemed far more intense and high-pitched than it had the last time she could remember.

Despite the hot wind, she was shivering from lying prone on the ice in wet clothing. Her feet and hands throbbed with pain, not the burning agony that had afflicted their skin during rewarming but a deeper ache caused by her new hypersensitivity to cold.

How could I sleep at a time like this?

She knew the answer. No one could sleep with such pain and terror. She had literally passed out from exhaustion once she was securely anchored down to the slab's flat top.

She ran her sore fingers over the controls of her radio in the darkness. It's bound to have shorted out in the rain, she thought. To her surprise, the radio worked, but still no one answered when she croaked out a hoarse plea for help.

The wind was the strongest she had ever felt, tearing at her hair, lips, and eyelids. She could only breathe with her back turned to it, and she had no doubt that it would blow her away into the sky if she were not firmly fastened down. After more than an hour, the huge round slab had surely speeded up to its maximum wind-driven velocity, so she wondered how the wind could still be whipping over its surface so fast. She looked across the ice sheet when lightning flashed again and saw that she had been blown around to the edge of the Warner Basin on the side opposite ICARE—she recognized the sharp crags penetrating the low clouds a ways to her left. The glimpse of land also confirmed what she sensed from the vibration. The slab was moving at unbelievable speed— several hundred miles per hour, she guessed. The distant nunataks were sliding past her as if they were just hundreds of yards away instead of several miles. No wonder the wind was so strong even relative to the slab—the slab itself was zipping across the dark ice sheet at jet speed.

She tried the radio again. "Dad . . . if you can hear me . . . this is probably my last call. I can barely . . . breathe, and I think . . . I'm about to get struck by lightning."

The radio crackled, whistled, and buzzed.

Lightning flashed, and she saw an unexpected glint of gold behind her. What could it be? Was it him? Somehow trying to rescue her? She forced her face into the wind, clamping her lips shut. When the next flash came, she briefly opened her eyes, shielding them from the driving rain with a hand.

The thing bearing down on her was not a rescue. It was a rolling nightmare—one of the turbines from Amery Station, denuded of its cylindrical housing. It was rolling across the ice on its side, like the cutting head of an old push-powered lawn mower. Along the hundred-foot shaft were six sets of twenty radial gold-plated blades, blurring as they spun and gleaming in the lightning like freshly sharpened machetes.

Angie turned away and shielded her eyes as the gold-plated turbine swiftly caught up. She heard the blades crunch into the edge of her ice slab, break away from their shaft, and whistle through the air. She saw flickers of gold spinning into the sky downwind, then felt a breathtakingly sharp pain in her upraised right hip.

Fighting the wind, she reached a hand down in the darkness to feel the wound. The side of her soggy thermal underwear was gashed from the point of her right buttock to the front of her thigh. Straining her neck to look down, she saw in the next flash that a stream of blood was blowing away from her hip in the wind.

She wondered if she was already hallucinating from shock when she heard a hoarse and gravelly voice on her radio. *"Pumpkin! Are you there? Please, please respond this time!"*

2:40 A.M.

"Marshall!" Reed yelled into his headset mike. "You have to stop the timer. I found her."

"Tom, I can't," Marshall said. "We're already miles from the drilling pit. The nukes are going to blow in five minutes."

"No!" Reed bellowed. "That's not long enough. I need at least twice that long to pick her up."

"Pick her up? What are you . . . are you serious?"

"Yes," Reed said. "I'm going to try, regardless."

"I'll do what I can," Marshall said after a pause. "We headed downwind to make time. Even if I can drive upwind, I may not make it back to the pit before detonation."

"But you'll try?"

"I'm . . . already . . . trying," Marshall grunted.

"God bless you," Reed said.

Marshall swung the Komatsu Super Dozer broadside to the wind, holding down the throttle. Even the 157-ton behemoth began to slide sideways, and he could hear and feel chunks of debris slamming against the door of the high cab. Then the yellow-orange dreadnought began to grind its way upwind, the high ridges on its track shoes grappling the ice like claws. Twenty-four feet wide and eleven feet high, the flat dozer blade caught a

blast of wind that was almost too forceful for the engine
to resist, but it also deflected debris from the windshield.

Four minutes later, Marshall careened down the spiraling ramp into the deserted drilling pit, letting the left
track bounce against the wall and tying a rope tether
around his waist as he drove. When the dozer skidded to
a halt by the framework derrick, he ran to the small
trailer containing the detonation transmitter and stopped
the timer with several seconds to spare.

Back in the dozer cab, he tried to call Reed with the
good news, but he couldn't get through.

Marshall started to reset the timer, and only then did
he realize what he was going to have to do. The wind
was now so strong that powerful eddies were swirling
inside the pit. The warheads in the borehole were supported by a cable hanging from the spindly derrick,
which was rattling and clanking in the wind, even swaying a little. Since he couldn't reach Reed, Marshall had
no way to find out when the colonel had rescued his
daughter or given up. It might actually take an hour or
more, he thought. But he could not set the timer that far
in advance and drive away, because the derrick might
not hold up that long.

Now that he saw how the derrick was shimmying,
straining at the ice augers holding its legs down with
guylines, he realized the timer had been a bad idea in the
first place. The only sure way to guarantee that the warheads were detonated was for someone to stand here in
the pit and send the signal before the derrick and the radio-
transmitter were blown away.

Sitting in the idling dozer, Marshall looked down at
the head of the round silver key sticking out of the black
box on his lap. His big right hand moved to the box. His
long thumb and forefinger gripped the key. The surest

way of all would be to turn the key right now, he thought.

On the other hand, he knew that Reed couldn't possibly have had enough time yet, and he was pretty sure he could turn the key before the warheads dropped out of position if he saw the derrick falling apart.

He hesitantly moved his hand away from the key, then gripped it again, uncertain.

He decided to wait as long as possible. He doubted that Reed could rescue Angie, but perhaps the colonel himself could survive if he gave up and flew away from the blast zone in time.

Marshall positioned the Super Dozer at the side of the pit where he had a good view of the trembling derrick, then tensely sat on the springy driver's seat with a firm grip on the detonation key, determined to give Reed and Angie every second he could.

CHAPTER 39

Detonator

2:48 A.M.

Angie lay on her side, still anchored securely to the ice slab. When lightning flashed, she could see a thin crimson streak stretching downwind into the darkness among the blur of horizontal rain whipping past her. The streak was blood oozing from the aching gash in her hip.

While watching for any sign of her father's plane, she saw a straight silver line on the ice ahead, crossing perpendicular to the slab's path. The long thin object extended far enough to disappear into the haze of rain in both directions. In the next instant, the slab blasted through the long object, knocking several segments of it apart, and Angie realized that it was a metal pipeline.

She radioed Reed to tell him about the pipe, thinking it might help him locate her.

"That must have been the siphon!" he said. "You're smack in the nuclear blast zone. I'm on my way."

In just a few minutes, the slab had been blown a quarter of the way around the basin. That meant it must have made several revolutions while she was unconscious. No wonder he'd had a hard time finding her.

Angie heard a whine like a power saw, accompanied by a warbling whistle. She looked toward the sound and saw a distant silhouette shaped like a double cross racing toward her beneath the clouds. It was a shape she recognized easily from the photographs on the walls of her father's office, except that one of the cross's two shorter arms was missing.

She attempted to wave, feeling her sluggish heart pound with hope, but the wind pinned her hands at her sides. "Dad, I see you!" she shouted into the radio.

"I have a visual on you, too," he replied. "I'm going to circle and approach from downwind."

"What are you going to do?" she asked.

"I don't know," he said. "We'll make it up as we go."

In the next strobe of lightning, she saw the Warthog's gray belly roll away from her as the plane tilted into a tight left turn. The camouflage top of the airframe faced her for a moment, flying perpendicular to her heading, the anticollision beacon blinking and rotating atop the narrow fuselage. Then the plane angled back into the wind and swooped down low as if to land, coming at her head-on.

"Dad! Watch out!"

She hid her face in her hands and curled into a ball. It looked like the heavy armored plane was going to plow right into her hurtling ice slab.

When nothing happened, she peeked through her fingers. The Warthog was still approaching, but with unnatural slowness, as if in a dream. She noticed that the landing gear was down. The plane gradually drew so close that she could see her father's dark head and shoulders. He was wearing a crash helmet with a dark glass visor that reflected the lightning. A black breathing mask covered his face. A thick oxygen hose snaked down into the cockpit from his chin.

"Hey, it's working!" he shouted over her radio.

"*What's* working?"

The Warthog was so close that its thick upward-tilted wings stretched from side to side of the ice slab. Bright formation lights glowed at their tips, and they rolled slightly back and forth like a boat on a wavy sea. Then the armored subsonic airframe edged forward over the slab *and stopped in midair.*

He's hovering like a helicopter, Angie thought, staring up at the gray belly of the fuselage and wings a few feet above her head. Actually, she realized, he was flying *backward* relative to the ground. The wind was moving so much faster than she was that the Warthog could fly into it at that differential speed without stalling. "Now what?" she yelled.

The Warthog seemed to be rotating clockwise, but she knew that was an illusion caused by her slab rotating counterclockwise.

"I'm going to try to touch down," Reed said. "See if you can jump into the second cockpit behind me."

The plane eased backward until only the nose was over the slab. As it gradually descended, the cockpit seal running crosswise above his head parted, and the backward-opening bubble canopy began to rise like the top of a convertible car. When its front edge had lifted a few inches above the narrow vertical windscreen, the wind tore it off. The canopy zoomed back along the fuselage and shattered against the tail. The shards were instantly gone in the wind.

A second later, the lid of the rear cockpit met the same fate.

Angie yelled into her radio. "I can't do it! If I let go of the ice, the wind will knock me off the slab."

The ring of gun barrels jutting beneath the Warthog's nose bumped against the top of the slab. The brief contact jerked the nose sideways in the direction the slab was rotating. For a terrifying moment, Angie thought her father had lost control. The plane leaped up and backward, yawing and pitching like a seesaw. It rolled so far that she thought the downward-cambered left wingtip would scrape the ice sheet.

"You were right," Reed yelled as he stabilized the airframe. "That's not going to work. Can you think of another way?"

Angie vigorously shook her head.

"Try," Reed said. "I'm almost out of fuel, and they're going to set off the nukes any second now."

2:59 A.M.

Marshall sat in the Super Dozer cab, gripping the detonation key, his eyes glued to the quaking derrick. The wind had increased only a little in the few minutes since he had decided to sacrifice himself to make certain the detonation signal was sent while the warheads were still in position. Nevertheless, *something* was rapidly changing in the maelstrom of air, snow, and debris above him. The frequency of lightning had abruptly increased, and a new noise was emerging from the storm's continuous roar. It sounded more like an animal than a wind, Marshall thought—a gigantic predator growling and snarling.

He wanted to look up at the sky but did not dare take his eyes off the derrick. Then the lightning and growling increased even more, and he could no longer resist. He glanced up through the windshield. An opaque surface formed by gray and white streaks of debris was still all he could see above the drilling pit.

He was about to resume watching the derrick when a spinning vortex of dark debris reached down into the pit, writhing like the arm of a gargantuan octopus. Small forks of lightning skittered up and down its blurry surface. After probing the other side of the pit, the giant rotating tentacle briefly retracted and then shot down straight at him.

"No!" Marshall yelled.

He started to turn the key.

Before the nerve impulse could travel down his arm, the tip of the writhing twister grasped the Super Dozer like the hand of God, lifting the 157-ton machine by its blade. The dozer wobbled and spun around its long axis in midair, throwing Marshall from his seat. As he fell, his right forefinger yanked the detonation key out of its slot by its chain. He heard the lost key clanking against sheet metal somewhere in the cab. Through a side window, he caught a glimpse of the spindly derrick twisting back and forth like a tortured prisoner. Its guylines were beginning to pull the ice augers out of the pit's floor.

Marshall slammed headfirst into the back wall of the cab. His neck folded forward, mashing his stubbly chin against his chest. The rest of his long body crumpled into a twisted pile, and the detonation transmitter slipped from his limp hands.

Angie knew there was a rope in her gear bag, but she also knew the wind would whip it away if she took it out. She reached in and pulled out just one end of the orange rope, then tied it to the ice screw anchoring her to the slab. She tied the other end to the chest strap of her body harness.

Without hesitation, fearing that she'd lose her nerve, she jumped up and ran, ignoring the ache in her slashed hip and expending her last scant reserve of oxygen. At first she managed to dig in her crampons and sprint downwind toward the hovering Warthog, angling sideways to compensate for the slab's rotation. Then the wind flung her off her feet.

She expected to land on the slab, or on the ice sheet fifteen feet below it. Instead she just tumbled and spun through the air, as if falling but without the sensation of weightlessness. She felt the wind tear off her radio headset, along with a handful of hair. Her gashed hip slammed into something hard, and the Warthog's gray belly filled her view, upside down and foreshortened by her perspective. The headlight on the landing gear lowered from the nose briefly blinded her. Then she spun around and saw the rotating ice slab, also upside down.

The rope was stretched taut. She realized that the wind was suspending her in midair several yards ahead of the skidding slab, far enough that her father could lower the plane to the slab's level without risking another collision.

She flailed with her arms, trying to grasp the plane's blunt nose. Her left hand hit the muzzle of the Avenger cannon, and she thrust her first two fingers into one of its seven barrels. That stopped her from floundering and allowed her to turn right-side up, but she still could not pull herself toward the cockpit. Above the painted row of interlocking warthog teeth and the soaring tusk, the beast's fiendish left eye seemed to be glaring straight down at her.

Fabric slapped her face. She grabbed it with her other hand.

"Hang on!" Reed yelled. This time she heard his real voice. She let go of the cannon barrel and grabbed the parka he was reaching down to her. With one arm on the Warthog's vibrating controls, he used the other to swing her up toward the open rear cockpit. She grabbed the side and piled in headfirst.

He reached out with a knife and cut her rope, then allowed the plane to climb until they were hovering at a safe altitude.

"Stay down," he said, struggling back into the parka he had used to haul her in. "What happened to your clothes? We'll be out of the rain in a minute, but you'll freeze once we leave the hot core of the storm."

Angie pointed to her waterproof gear bag, which was tied around her waist. She had righted herself in the seat and was putting on the flight harness. "Hurry . . . can't breathe," she gasped. Then she hunkered down and dug out her parka as the Warthog's acceleration squashed her against her seat and the wind tore at her wet hair even harder than before.

Marshall slowly became aware of the agony in his neck. Then other parts of his body lit up with pain, one by one. His vision began to focus, fading in and out. He saw red splotches all over the interior of the Super Dozer's cab and wondered what they were. Then he realized they were blood. Apparently the twister had flung him around the cab while he was unconscious.

He had been so proud of himself until now. Despite the hectic and dangerous working conditions in the pit, he had led his crew through the operation without anyone even getting hurt. Success had been literally at his fingertips.

The detonator!

He frantically groped around the floor. No, it was a wall, he realized. The dozer was lying on its side. The massive machine was also vibrating and rocking, but at least it seemed to be back on the ground, no longer tumbling in midair.

He found the little black box, but the key was still missing.

His gaze fell on his watch, which was cracked but still operating. The time was 3:03 A.M., just past the time when the hypercane wind was supposed to accelerate to speeds that no human, snow tractor, or drilling derrick could withstand. Marshall wondered how accurate that simulation-based deadline was.

He could not see the derrick. In fact, his view of the whole pit was blocked by the floor—the roof of the driver's cab was leaning against a wall. He tried to move, intending to climb across the seat and open the upper side door. His left arm was obviously broken in several places, but his right arm still worked.

Grasping the steering wheel, he realized his legs were stuck, somehow jammed beneath the seat. There was no way for him to climb up to where he could see the derrick.

He could feel his strength fading fast and knew that he had probably regained consciousness only for a fleeting moment.

What happened to the key?

He groaned and slammed his one good limb against the back of the seat in frustration.

The key fell onto his chest from the upper side of the seat.

Lying on his back, he dragged the detonation transmitter against his bloody side, inserted the key, and turned it.

CHAPTER 40

Fire and Water

Twelve identical electrical impulses simultaneously sped down the borehole through wires strung from the detonation signal receiver in the trailer beside the wind-racked derrick. The minuscule impulses entered each of the twelve armed nuclear warheads within nanoseconds of each other, close enough in time that the shock wave from the first explosion would not reach the last warhead before its own fission primary could implode its tritium core with enough force to give birth to a miniature star.

Just as stars of sufficient mass end their long lives with a supernova, each of the twelve palm-sized stars aligned up and down the borehole expanded into a swelling ball of heat and light, converting a few grams of matter into unfathomable quantities of energy. The primary radiation from the nuclear reactions of fission and fusion was absorbed by the surrounding rock and ice before the shock waves had even left the bomb casings, but then the expanding spheres of heat and pressure vaporized the borehole walls indiscriminately, splitting the glacier and the bedrock ridge at many times the speed of sound.

*   *   *

A thin sliver of moonlight stretched across the darkness in front of the Warthog. Reed flew toward it as fast as he could stand to in the open cockpit, knowing that the moonlight marked the edge of the hypercane. Despite the windscreen in front of his face, the wind tore at his shirt and held his head firmly back against his seat. At least he had a helmet with a visor to protect his eyes, and an oxygen mask to help him breathe.

He hoped Angie was okay, but there was no way to find out. Blood that could only have been hers had spattered against his windscreen while he was hovering downwind of the runaway ice block.

They were above the heaving ocean when the dark waves and clouds abruptly lit up with blinding white light that cast long shadows ahead of them.

"Don't look back!" Reed yelled, knowing that Angie couldn't hear him.

The light pulse immediately began to fade and turned from white to yellow to orange. He saw the Warthog's stark elongated shadow racing across the clouds ahead of them. Then the shock wave hit, thrusting the plane forward with a moment of heart-crushing acceleration. Reed fought for control as the sturdy airframe bucked and shuddered. He could see the shock wave expanding ahead of them, compressing the air enough to warp the moonlight passing through it and shattering wave crests into explosions of spray.

Holding his breath, he watched his instruments for any signs of disturbance. He knew that the electromagnetic pulse produced by high-altitude nuclear explosions could make delicate electronics shut down or go haywire for hundreds of miles. Fortunately for him, the EMP was sent out not by the nuclear reaction itself but by the scattering of electrons from atmospheric molecules ionized by primary gamma rays the reaction emitted. That meant an underground blast should not produce an atmospheric EMP—the primary gammas would be shielded by the ground cover even if it was blown away a nanosecond later.

His gaze settled on the fuel gauge.

The tanks were dead empty.

He banked back toward the continent, heading for the Ross Ice Shelf. The course would bring them even closer to the fallout zone than they already were, but they would freeze or drown in seconds if the Warthog's engines died and he had to ditch it in the ocean.

A flaming meteor the size of a bus zoomed diagonally across the Warthog's path and splashed into the churning sea. Reed could smell acrid smoke as he flew through its trail. He wondered if the smoke was radioactive. Then a swarm of red-hot rocks began plunging on all sides, whistling and leaving trails of smoke that arched through the moonlit sky from a point to his right.

Looking right, he saw a city-sized crater above the glaciers descending from the Warner Basin to the Ross Sea. A mile-high column of billowing fire rose from the center of the crater, illuminating its walls. Above the level of the ice sheet, the fire column bent downwind. The curling ball of incandescent plasma atop the mushroom cloud's stalk had already been stretched by the wind into the shape of a closed umbrella, bending around the basin with the curvature of the cyclone.

Did it work?

He scrutinized the crater in the light of the nuclear fire. He could clearly see the division between the white layer of ice around its rim and the darker bedrock strata below. A misty torrent was surging across the center of the crater, from the Warner Basin to the Ross Sea. At first he could not be sure what he was seeing. The titanic deluge was too distant for individual waves and cascades to be discernable. It was just a streaking white band that undulated across the crater and down a glacier to the sea. Then he saw the ring of floating ice that remained in the Warner Basin begin to break up and spill down the new channel through the subglacial ridge. The jostling floes looked like grains of sugar, but he knew they were the size of airports.

"We did it!" he yelled. His whole battered body buzzed with elation.

Angie yelled something too. Reed couldn't understand her, but he noticed that the shout did not sound elated. He craned his head sideways, and the next time she yelled he understood: "Pull up! Pull up!"

He yanked the Warthog into a steep climb, looking down. After turning toward the airstrip, he had slowed and descended to the minimum safe altitude so they could go as far as possible on the fumes left in the fuel tanks.

A sequence of perfectly semicircular waves was expanding radially across the tempestuous ocean from the place where the deluge was plunging down from the continent. At first he could see no apparent reason for Angie's panic. Then the first wave swept beneath the climbing Warthog, nearly touching its damaged tail. For a moment Reed could see the individual streaks of moonlit foam on the mountain range of water just a few yards beneath his aircraft.

Approaching the tall white cliffs of the Ross Ice Shelf, he hailed the airstrip and asked to speak to Professor Ferrand. "Try to get hold of the Tsunami Warning Center in Hawaii," he shouted. "Tell them the Pacific Rim is in for it."

With its energy source taken away, the updraft in the eye of the hypercane began to stall like a failing heart that merely quivers instead of pumping. And just as the cells in the peripheral tissues of a dying animal live on for hours after its death, the cyclonic winds continued to spin around the mighty storm's dead core, scouring the nunataks ringing the Warner Basin with levitated debris hurled at twice the speed of the fastest hurricanes. But eventually the momentum of the spinning air mass bled away, its kinetic energy absorbed by the collisions between air, ice, and rock. The plume of dust seeping into the stratosphere pinched out and ceased. The suspended boulders plummeted to the ground. And the clouds parted, exposing a sterile landscape of scored bedrock to the light from the aurora and the moon.

There was also one other source of light in the middle of the Warner Basin, a dim orange glow. The new volcano growing in the center of the old caldera continued to spew pahoehoe lava at exactly the same rate as before the hypercane, unfazed by the wind, the blast, or even the unprecedented flood from the draining lake. As potent and implacable as the elements of wind and water may be in comparison with the pitiful efforts of human technology, the Earth's slowly writhing molten interior is equally indifferent to the brief disturbances called storms in the planet's rarified veneer of atmosphere and oceans.

The hypercane wind had mostly subsided by the time Reed, Angie, and Professor Ferrand crested the bluff and drove their tractor across the scoured ground where the ICARE base had once stood. It was half past five in the morning and still dark. Nothing remained of the base but cracked foundations. They saw no signs of survivors.

Until they got to the once-indoor swimming pool.

When Reed curiously looked over the lip of the open pool, he was stunned to see a crowd of wet, cold, miserable individuals staring back at him. They were huddled together in a foot of standing water, shivering. Many were injured. In addition to familiar faces from ICARE, he saw Silong Lim and several other men from Amery Station. He learned later that the pool was the closest thing ICARE had to a bomb shelter, so they had pumped out as much water as they could after NORAD had warned them of the approaching minicane.

He spotted Lois. She was prone on a gurney. He felt suddenly ill and disabled when he saw that all of her life support and monitoring equipment was gone—no ventilator, IV, EEG, or heart monitor. She was utterly motionless, despite the babbling voices all around her and people bumping her gurney. Her skin was a shade paler than he had ever seen it. Deathly pale. Reed wondered why they had not even bothered to cover her face.

CHAPTER 41

Sunrise

"Where's the doctor?" Reed yelled.

Someone in the pool pointed.

He saw the doctor rigging a splint on a man's arm. "I have a casualty losing blood up here," Reed shouted. "Can you at least stitch her up until the medevac arrives?" He had already called for an air force medical evacuation unit. Their planes would be landing on the Ross Ice Shelf in a few hours.

The doctor worked his way to the edge of the crowded pool, toting a case of supplies. Reed whisked him up onto the concrete slab, then pointed to the tractor where Angie was waiting. "I saw Dr. Burnham. Is she . . . ?"

The doctor nodded. "Yes, she started breathing on her own about two hours ago. She came out of the coma a little later."

Reed clasped the doctor's arm. "Are you serious? She's awake? I saw her on that gurney and thought—"

"She's sleeping," the doctor said.

"Brain damage?" Reed asked.

The doctor shook his head. "She could move all of her limbs, and she answered all the basic questions—speaking plainly—so I doubt there will be any serious memory loss. It may take months, but I would bet on a full recovery at this point."

Reed ran ahead to tell Angie. Then he ran back to the pool's edge, jumped down, and splashed his way to Lois. She was covered by an electric blanket with insulated wires draping above the water to a chugging generator. The gasoline must have arrived after all, he thought.

Later he learned that the fuel delivery had indeed spared her life. He also learned that Dr. Pavros Corcoros had been unable to recover from the damage that inhaling a few cups of boiling water had wrought in his lungs. He had passed away sometime before the minicane hit the ICARE base.

Reed gently brushed Lois's long bangs back from her eyes and kissed her bruised cheek, then held one of her hands. Her eyes fluttered open and she spoke in a hoarse whisper, straining with the effort. "Where's Angie?"

"She's in the tractor. She's going to be fine."

While waiting to board a plane at noon, Reed was mobbed by a small gang of reporters. He faced away from the sliver of sun on the flat marine horizon to the north, forcing them all to squint and shield their cameras from the glare. A young man wearing a tie and a point-collared shirt beneath his red expedition suit thrust a frost-coated microphone in front of Reed's chin. "Tell us how it feels to save the world, Colonel."

"It hurts all over," Reed replied, glancing around at the camera lenses gleaming in the horizontal rays of ICARE's first sunrise in half a year.

A young woman who had cut a hole in her balaclava for her ponytail stepped in front of her colleague and proffered her own microphone. "But aren't you the man who stopped the hypercane?"

Reed shook his head. "His name was Marshall Dunn."

Two hours later Reed was headed home over the sunny South Pacific on another U.S. Air Force C-141B Starlifter. This plane was equipped to carry 103 litter patients plus several ambulatory passengers during emergency medical evacuations. It was his first opportunity to sit still and think since leaving home the morning of the Amery Station collapse. He would rather have been sleeping than thinking—he had never been so far behind on sleep—but he was still too uptight.

He was also nauseous from exhaustion and sad for the many lives that had been lost, but at the same time he felt a deep satisfaction. It was more than the usual pride from accomplishing a difficult mission. There really *isn't* anything more gratifying than saving the world, he thought.

"I guess we will have to rebuild both Amery Station and the ICARE base," said Silong Lim, who sat beside Reed with a patchwork of adhesive bandages covering cuts on his face from flying bits of broken glass. The engineer was looking out his window at the calm, glittering sea. "I'm going to miss Marshall," he added.

"So will I," Reed said. "There will never be another one like him." Then he said, "ICARE is not going to rebuild."

"*What?* Why not?"

"Because I don't think the conquest of Antarctica is working out. And we've already done enough damage. The ecosystems of the coast and the Southern Ocean will have a hard enough time recovering from the storm and the radioactive fallout."

Lim glanced suspiciously at the bandage on Reed's head. "So?"

"So, as soon as I can get to my desk, the SRDC is going to withdraw its support for ICARE. Without us, the companies will pull out as fast as they can cut their losses. That goes for the foreign quadrants as well."

"Hey, Dad!"

Reed looked back along the Starlifter's aisle. Angie was beckoning to him. He got up and made his way back to her, grabbing a ceiling rail to steady himself against the dizziness of battle fatigue.

Angie nodded toward Lois, who was in the litter next to hers. "She woke up and wanted to talk to you."

The drums in Reed's chest turned into a salute of 155-millimeter howitzers.

Lois weakly smiled up at him and held his arm. Her voice was still feeble and hoarse. She whispered in his ear. "I've invited Angie to spend her fall break with me. I plan to be back in shape by then. I'd love it if you would come with her."

"I'll be there," he said.

Lois tried to smile. "Tom, are you sure this is what you want? With what you and Angie have gone through and all the craziness here . . . it might not be as easy as it was when we were clinging to each other just to stay warm. Now would be the time for you to consider that."

"I did," he said. "You must have blinked and missed it. Besides, who says we need to stop?"

Lois's weak smile grew stronger. Then her expression turned apprehensive. "Maybe I shouldn't bring this up now, but . . . Angie said you're going to disband ICARE. Does that mean no more research money?"

"No. Even without rebuilding or new development, we have a lot of cleaning up to do before we can decommission the existing facilities. I may even manage to make your budget for spying on the penguins double again, on one small condition."

"What's that?" Lois whispered.

"You promise not to encourage Angie to go anywhere near Antarctica, ever again." He glanced up at his daughter to check her reaction. She had already dozed off.

Lois weakly pulled Reed to her, kissed him, and solemnly said, "I promise."

JAMES FRANCIS

DANGER'S HOUR

The submarine USS Tulsa is silently tracking a Russian nuclear sub when another sub collides with the Tulsa—sending her to the ocean floor. Now, Captain Geoff Richter must struggle to maintain order inside the crippled ship—as the oxygen is slowly depleted, power systems begin to fail, and time runs out.

0-451-41041-6

To order call: 1-800-788-6262